IN BIG TROUBLE

Books by Laura Lippman

LAURA LIPPMAN

IN BIG TROUBLE

A TESS MONAGHAN NOVEL

wm

WILLIAM MORROW
An Imprint of HarperCollinsPublishers

P.S.™ is a trademark of HarperCollins Publishers.

FIRST WILLIAM MORROW PAPERBACK PRINTING: JUNE 2015

FIRST HARPER PREMIUM PRINTING: MARCH 2012

FIRST WILLIAM MORROW HARDCOVER PRINTING: DECEMBER 2009

FIRST AVON BOOKS MASS MARKET PRINTING: JANUARY 2001

Library of Congress Cataloging-in-Publication Data has been applied for.

ISBN 978-0-06-240064-2

15 16 17 18 19   OV/RRD   10 9 8 7 6 5 4 3 2 1

Despite the San Antonio map at my side, helpful friends, and my own impeccable memory, chances are I got some things wrong about the place I consider my second hometown—out of plain carelessness, or because I exercised a novelist's prerogative to make stuff up. *Don't* blame: John Roll, or any of my Texas in-laws, particularly Carolyn Fryar, who are all awfully good sports about the crazy woman their son married; Rick Casey of the *San Antonio Express-News*, who stopped to answer my questions even as he was fending off (unrelated) death threats; Bob Kolarik, also of the *Express-News*, who has been reading my novels longer than anyone; or Caitlin Francke of the *Baltimore Sun*, who didn't once laugh at my pathetic Spanish. I am also indebted to Joan Jacobson, Lisa Respers, Peter Hermann, the Gosnell-Branch clan, the denizens of DorothyL and La Luzers everywhere, particularly those girls and boys who liked to dance at Los Padrinos and the Bonham Exchange, drink at Mel's and the Liberty, then eat at Earl Abel's and Taco Cabana. (And no, Jeannie, I haven't forgotten Rolando's Super Tacos, but I'm still mad about them closing on Sundays.)

A note about music: While the band described within these pages is wholly a product of my imagination—I have yet to hear a Stephen Sondheim tune set to salsa rhythms, although I would certainly like to—dozens of musicians contributed a private soundtrack that created an instant cantina in my Baltimore office. They include Hal Ketchum, Brave

Combo, the Mavericks, Alison Krauss, Emmy Lou Harris, the Dixie Chicks, Johnny Reno and the Sax Maniacs, Willie Nelson, Flaco Jimenez, Ruben Blades, the Texas Tornados, the Fabulous Thunderbirds, the Perpetrators, and as always, Nancy LaMott and Elvis Costello.

PROLOGUE

A sign hangs next to the cradle of Texas liberty, reminding visitors that concealed firearms are not permitted on the grounds.

She stops and examines this as if it were new to her, although the sign has been posted for several years now. "Don't bring your gun to the Alamo," she intones, to see how it sounds out loud, then laughs, startling a little boy. ("Mama, that lady is talking to herself. Mama—") *Don't bring your gun to the Alamo.* A nice phrase, but it doesn't make the cut. She won't record it in one of her little notebooks, the ones where she keeps her lists of first lines, fragments of poems, names for everything. Names for bands, names for songs. Names for the children she'll never have and titles for the memoir she'll never write, although her story packs some shock value, even in these jaded times. Oprah would need a whole week to get it all in.

Within the walls, it's like being in a shallow dish—azure sky above, the taller buildings crowded around, dwarfing the Spanish mission, which isn't very big to begin with. She walks through the gardens, noting the placement of each plant, each bench, each sign. Change is not to be tolerated. She picks up a cup with a little electric blue raspa juice inside and drops it in the trash, as fastidious in her own way as the Alamo's keepers, the Daughters of the Republic of Texas. It is a shrine, and not only to Texas liberty. A shrine to her, to them. She even brings the same breakfast every time—two barbacoa tacos, coffee, an elephant ear, and the Sunday paper. She gets the pastry, while the tacos are for him, her own holy ghost.

He had been the first to bring her here, although she later learned she had not been the first he had brought here. Important distinction. Nor would she be the last, as it turned out. "Ever had breakfast at the Alamo?" he had asked her that first morning when they finally pulled away from each other, eyes bright, bodies limp, the cheap pearls of her broken necklace rolling beneath them, pressing into their flesh, so her skin was beaded like the white gown she had worn earlier. When everything was over, when she was banished from his life and had nothing left, she still had those words. "Breakfast at the Alamo." She knew others would be charmed by them as she had once been charmed.

And she began to see how a former lover's tricks could be appropriated and turned against him.

It was only a matter of time before the two of them showed up one Sunday with different, unwitting partners. She caught his glance across the courtyard, held it tight. The young woman with him had tried to see where his gaze had strayed, but he grabbed her hand and retreated. He had a horror of scenes, of anything ugly and public.

She didn't. That was her power. He had never shown up again, hadn't dared, and Breakfast at the Alamo became her exclusive property. Her signature, her trick of the trade, her trade for the trick. Rolling toward the warm body next to her on a Sunday morning, eyes still closed, mouth closed, too, so as not to inhale too much of the sour smell that strangers brought to one's bed. "Hey, darlin', ever had breakfast at the Alamo?"

Breakfast at the Alamo. Now that was a great name for anything—a band, a memoir, a betrayal. It was on all her lists. The world was full of poetry. Pick up a menu, for example, and there was "Shaved Meats, Piled High." That was going to be volume one of her unwritten memoir. She also liked the sign that had hung next to the Tunnel of Love at the old Funland amusement park: "C'mon Scaredy Cat, Let's Go Through." Of course, you had to be "this tall" to ride that ride, according to the grinning elf who stood next to the entrance with his measuring stick. By the time she was tall enough, Funland was long gone, its fixtures sold at public auction. Goodbye Scaredy Cat. And goodbye elf, you smug little S.O.B., with your measuring stick and your smirk for all those under five feet.

So she found her inspiration in the headlines and the rack cards, from the days when a sleazy tabloid king had owned one of the local papers. SEWER BOY STILL MISSING. GUNNED DOWN PREGNANT CAT FIGHTS FOR LIFE. GLUE DOG ON THE MEND. LITTLE GIRL IN BIG TROUBLE. TRUANT SAYS, "LET'S RAPE CHRISTY'S

MAMA." 10,000 TOENAILS AID IN CANCER FIGHT. These, too, went into her little notebooks.

The lists had been something else they had done together, her gift to him. Sudden thought: Had he stolen those, as she had stolen Breakfast at the Alamo? Did he carry a notebook like hers, impress his new girls with the music of everyday life? No, he wouldn't make a list with anyone else, she was sure of that. Because he was better than she was. That's why she loved him still. That's why she hated him.

She works slowly through the paper and her elephant ear, savoring both. As always, she saves the society pages for last. It's skimpy this week, not much going on. Pretty soon the fall parties will start and that will change. Everyone who's anyone is on the circuit from Halloween on, especially now, with this stupid All Soul Festival. She used to be an anyone.

She closes her eyes, enjoying the sun, which has finally begun to relinquish its summer-tight grip on the city. It feels good. It feels good just to be alone. A few days ago, the flaws of the latest man had surfaced all at once, the details swimming into focus, the way a photo's image takes shape in a pan of developer. His pores were too large, his eyes the wrong color, his ties the wrong width. He wasn't tall enough. They were never tall enough, no one was tall enough. He didn't have the guts to go through with it. Another list to keep and maintain, a catalog of defects that always began and ended the same way: *Not him*.

But you don't have to be with someone to have breakfast at the Alamo. Actually, it's better alone. As long as she stays in the gardens. She doesn't like the buildings—the Long Barracks, the high-ceilinged souvenir shop where she once coveted the blue and white Alamo dinnerware. The buildings are cold as crypts, chilled by the horrible memories they hold. Places can remember, too. But here, in the garden, beneath the hot, healing sun, the soil has forgotten all the blood it has known. She wishes she could forget. She wishes she could remember. *Wake up, Mommy. Wake up, Mommy.*

"Tienes sueños, pobrecita?"

The voice makes her start, and the barbacoa tacos tumble to the ground from her lap. Tienes sueños— *Are you sleepy?* He uses the Spanish reluctantly, at her insistence. But it's so much better in Spanish: *Do you have dreams?* Nothing but.

She squints into the sunlight.

"Why are you here?"

"I couldn't find you this morning. I worried."

"We broke up. Remember, I broke up with you?" Not cruel, just stating the facts.

"I know. And I know why. But I can't turn my back on you."

"You're going to help me?" Incredulous, not quite trusting him, although she wants to so badly. She needs an ally.

"I promise," he says. "I'll help you, and you'll help me."

She wonders if he thinks this means he'll get to crawl on top of her again. As much as she could use his assistance, she isn't sure she could stomach *that*. Once she's done with a man, she's done. It's like trying to reheat a cup of coffee. Dark, bitter stuff. But she doesn't think he's trying to find a way back into her bed. Truth is, he had seemed even less interested than she, if such a thing were possible.

But he's going to help her. Her mood takes off, like a rocket. In her joy, she pleats the grease-stained bag from her breakfast into a tiny accordion and pretends to play it. "A little conjunto music, ladies and gentlemen. Please welcome la señorita con la concertina, la señorita mas bonita, la señorita de las carnitas, la señorita de Suenos Malos." She sings, one of her favorite old folk songs. "Ay te dejo en San Antonio." *I've already left you in San Antonio.*

A few tourists look up, smiling hopefully, as if her song might redeem their wasted morning. The Alamo can be the ultimate anticlimax, the guaranteed disappointment to end all disappointments, at least for those who dream of wind-swept plains and a Davy Crockett who looked like John Wayne. "It's so small," outsiders always complain. "And there's a Burger King across the street." Personally, she likes the way the mission is plopped down in the middle of real life. Home of the Whopper meets the fort of the whopper, with all its little lies, all those stories told to make it cleaner, better, nicer. Davy Crockett swinging old Betsy, Jim Bowie groaning on his cot with a broken leg, William Barrett Travis drawing the line that separated the men from the boys. Death made people so pure. Did it matter if none of it was true? Did it matter if all of it was true?

"Maybe I should sing a few bars of the 'Yellow Rose of Texas.' Bet I'd make some money before the Daughters kicked me out."

He isn't amused.

"If I help you, then you have to listen to me, do things my way. You have to stop doing shit like this. Nice and normal, remember? That's how you fly under the radar. Nice and normal."

"Who wants to be nice? Or normal?" She drops her makeshift accordion, begins breaking apart a scab on her calf. It reminds her of bacon, the way it crunches in her fingers. She scratches her shin, drawing fresh blood. Normal is giving up. Normal is everybody else, going on with their lives. Normal is the real sickness, the pretense that lets your body live while your soul shrivels inside. Besides, she wants him to know she's back in town, wants him to be aware of her. She wants him to sit up in bed at night, wondering if he just felt her hot breath on his neck. *Tienes sueños, pobrecita?*

Blood dribbles down her leg, warm as a teardrop. He grabs her hands, holding her fingers tight so she can't pick at herself anymore. "Everything you want, you'll have," he says, his voice almost pleading. "But you have to trust me."

She shakes her head up and down, pretending to agree, trusting no one and hoping no one trusts her. *Everything you want.* Men made such promises so easily. Alamo dinnerware, a new pearl necklace, a car upon high school graduation, a safe place in the world, love everlasting. It's her lot in life to have nothing she wants, she knows that now. She sees herself as she wants to be, sleeping peacefully, just like the photograph. Sees him as she wants him to be, screaming, screaming, screaming, his mouth as round and wide as the entrance to a carnival ride

that never ends. *C'mon scaredy cat, let's go through.*
She's ready. She's tall enough now—and old enough,
and sad enough, and desperate enough.

She's ready.

1

Tess Monaghan hated surveillance work, something of a problem for someone who made her living as a private investigator. Do what you love and you'll love what you do, they told her. Well, she loved everything else about her job. Loved being her own boss, loved being her only employee. She was even starting to love her gun, which she knew was kind of creepy. Unfortunately, surveillance work was a private investigator's bread-and-butter, and she loathed every minute of it, especially in the cause of romantic disputes. Besides, it was just so passive. All her life, she had hated waiting for things to happen. She yearned to be an instigator. Yet here she was again, slouched down in the front seat of her car, camera ready to document someone else's bad behavior.

She stared at the faded plaster king who welcomed guests to the Enchanted Castle Motor Court on Route 40. Time had not been kind to him—his purple coat had whitish spots that made it appear as if it were moth-eaten, his face was pitted, and one eye had faded away, so his once-genial smile was now more of a leer. Still, he made her feel nostalgic, for Maryland's past and for her own. There was a time, almost in her memory, when Route 40 was the major east-west highway across the state of Maryland and these kinds of campy stucco cottages had beckoned to travelers with neon promises of air-cooled rooms and fresh pies in the diner.

As for Tess, she had lost her own virginity in this particular motor court, at the allegedly sweet age of sixteen. The wine had been sweet at least. Mogen David, hijacked from her Gramma Weinstein's Seder almost two months earlier, because teenage Tess had been methodical about her bad behavior. The younger version was always plotting, looking ahead to the night when she could just get it over with—first drunk, first dope, first sex—mark another milestone on her path to adulthood. Why had she been in such a hurry? She couldn't even remember now. Anyway, it hadn't been bad, it hadn't been good. In fact, it wasn't unlike her early rowing practices. Sore muscles you didn't even know you had on the day after. But it got better, and she got better at it. Just like rowing.

This was the part she remembered the best: The motor court's diner had still been open then and afterwards she had blueberry pie, hot, with vanilla ice cream, the chubby king smiling benignly at her through the glass. That had been just perfect. To this day, blueberry pie made her blush. Now the diner was just a rusting aluminum shell. Despite the reputation fostered by the film *Diner*, Baltimore had a severe diner deficit, if you didn't count the modern, ersatz ones, and Tess sure didn't. "Where have you gone, Barry Levinson?" she sang softly to herself. "Charm City lifts its hungry eyes to you." No more diners, no more tin men. No Johnny U's Golden Arm, no Gino's, no Hot Shoppes Jr.'s, no Little Taverns.

Great, her litany of fast-food ghosts had made her hungry. And her right leg was cramping up. She eased the driver's seat back, tried to massage her hamstring, but a twelve-year-old Toyota Corolla just didn't afford much room when you were five-foot-nine and most of it was inseam. Damn, she hated surveillance work. She tried to make it a rule not to take such assignments, but principles had to be suspended sometimes in light of certain economic realities. Or, in this case, when a certain friend had promised her services without asking first.

At least the client was a woman. She was a sexist about this, no other word. But in her experience, cuckolded men tended toward violence against others, and she didn't want that on her conscience. Women were masochists, dangers to themselves. Usually. Tess looked at this it way: Four thousand years after the Greeks, Medea would still be front-page news, while feckless Jason wouldn't even rate a question in *Cosmo*'s Agony column.

Not that women's cases weren't lose-lose propositions in their own way. If you didn't get the goods on hubby, some women didn't want to pay for the time put in, they didn't get that a job had been done, even if it had yielded no results. These were the kind of women who tipped poorly in restaurants, on the theory that they provided food service all the time without compensation.

But if you *did* turn over a discreet set of photographs of hubby leaving, say, a motor court on Route 40, a redhead giantess in tow, the kill-the-messenger syndrome kicked in—literally. One cheated-on wife had aimed her neat little Papagallo pump at Tess's shin. Tess had counted to ten, left the suburban palace that was about to loom large in the divorce case, and discreetly let all the air out of the tires on the woman's Jeep Cherokee.

So she charged more now. She told would-be clients it was because surveillance work was a bore, which was true, but it was really the aftermath she hated, the moment of truth, which was anything but boring. "Excuse me, ma'am, while you're weeping and thinking about the implications of this information for your twenty-year marriage and your two children, could I trouble you to write me a check?" Tess had started taking much bigger retainers and sending refunds. Easier on everyone.

Unfortunately, this particular wastrel-husband had eaten through the retainer in the first week, without actually doing anything. A nervous type, he cruised the city's best-known prostitution strips, window-shopping, beginning negotiations, then breaking them off at the last minute. Tess had taken a few photographs of women bent toward his car on long, skinny legs, but such photos paid no premiums in divorce court. He could always claim to be asking for directions.

Today, however, he had finally settled on a tall

redhead with a towering beehive and the knotted calf muscles that come from years of wearing spike heels. A real Amazon, even alongside Tess's Amazonian proportions. He probably thought a hooker with some meat on her bones was less likely to be a junkie. Or maybe he went in for kinkier stuff, which required a woman with those cut biceps and triceps.

They had gone in about five minutes ago. Because she had followed Mr. Nervous at a particularly careful distance, Tess hadn't been able to take a photo of the happy couple on their way into the honeymoon suite, and she didn't do in flagrante—that was just too gross. But she'd get them on the way out. Which would be—she checked her watch—ten, fifteen minutes at the most? He didn't look like the kind who would set any records for stamina. He had been saving up for this too long to draw it out.

Still, Tess was unprepared when the door was flung open at what her datebook notes would later establish was the seven-minute mark. As she fumbled for her camera, she saw a flash of red—the hooker's hair—followed by a gray blur, Mr. Nervous, who threw himself on top of the fake hair as if it were a fumbled football in the end zone.

The hooker stalked out, still fully attired, in a tight red leather-look dress and matching shoes. The real hair was short and wispy, a dark brown color only a shade deeper than Tess's. It wasn't a bad cut, but something about it struck Tess as not quite right. No, it probably just looked funny because it was matted down with sweat.

"You better give that back to me," the hooker told Mr. Nervous.

"When you give me my money back, you freak," he said, scrambling to his feet and running toward his car, trying to hold onto the wig even as he dug for his keys.

The hooker was fast. With a few quick strides, she had crossed the patch of gravel parking lot and leaped on the man's back, teeth sinking into his ear as if it were a pastry. He screamed, falling to the ground, where the two began rolling back and forth like two kids scuffling on the playground. Tess felt as if she had seen this before. She had. It was the great ladies room fight from *The Valley of the Dolls*, only this time hairless Helen Lawson was kicking Neely O'Hara's big, flabby butt.

"You'll pay for my wig, too, see if you don't," the hooker said, still perched on his back, frisking the john's pockets as he twisted beneath her. One of her high heels fell off and became an impromptu weapon, perfect for jabbing into the small of his back. Moaning, Mr. Nervous clutched the wig to his chest with both hands and curled up in a tight ball. In his gray suit, rolling back and forth, he reminded Tess of the potato bugs she had tortured in her youth.

"That wig cost more than the trick," the hooker screamed. She must have been telling the truth, for she seemed reluctant to grab it and end up in a tug-of-war with the man. Instead she just kept swinging her red high heel at his back and head.

"Fuckin' freak," Mr. Nervous rasped out. "Give me back my forty dollars and I'll give you your wig."

"Hey, I *earned* that forty dollars," the hooker replied. She had crawled away from him and seemed to be looking for an opportunity to land a quick kick in his crotch but the man stayed curled up in his potato bug position.

"Don't remind me! Don't remind me!" He was hysterical, his voice a high-pitched scream.

Just as Tess was beginning to wonder if she was obligated to intervene—she was still a little fuzzy on the ethics of private investigation, if any—the manager of the motor court ran out and threw a small bucket of ice at the two, as if they were dogs in heat. The man gasped and relaxed his grip just long enough for the hooker to grab the wig.

"This is a respectable place," the manager said. "You got the wrong end of Route 40, you wanna be carrying on like this."

"I wanted a woman," her client's husband moaned, facedown in the leaves, covering his head, although the blows had stopped. "All I wanted was a woman. Is that so much to ask?"

The prostitute stood, extending one leg and then the other to check the fishnet stockings for runs, assuming a flamingo posture to slip the literal stiletto heel back on, then pulling the wig over her—no, his—wispy brown hair.

"In that case, honey, you should've picked someone without an Adam's apple," the rechristened redhead said, pulling up his dress to show off black lace panties, the sleek line disturbed by a kind of asymmetry never seen in a Victoria's Secret catalog.

Another Kodak moment. Tess clicked away, hoping her body wasn't shaking so hard from suppressed laughter that the photos would end up out of focus. *The Valley of the Dolls* meets *The Crying Game* in the parking lot of the Enchanted Castle Motor Court.

She put her car into gear and headed back into the city, still thinking about blueberry pie. A little farther up Route 40, she considered stopping at the Double-T Diner, but she realized the pie she wanted was somewhere else. Back at the motor court, almost fourteen years in the past, and forever out of reach.

"No more adultery patrol," she said, sitting across from Tyner Gray, the lawyer who had pushed and prodded her into this line of work, then took credit for every good thing that had happened to her as a result. Time for him to start shouldering a little blame as well. "It's too demeaning. I'd rather go through someone's garbage."

"Don't be hyperbolic, Tess," Tyner said, writing out a check in his large, fancy script. Technically, all of Tess's clients worked through Tyner, assuring them confidentiality. But this particular wronged spouse had been the daughter of his college roommate, so Tyner was going to break the news, play show-and-tell with the photos. There was some small comfort in that.

"You forget I've really gone through garbage, looking for those telltale credit card receipts. I was Dumpster diving just last weekend, on a fraud case. Remember, the pierogi dispute in Highlandtown? A little spoiled food, some coffee grounds, but it's not so bad if you wear good rubber gloves. It's better than watching some stupid john wrestling with a transvestite hooker."

Tyner pushed away from his desk and rolled his wheelchair across the office, storing the ledger on a low shelf by the door. Everything was low here—

shelves, file cabinets, tables—and so streamlined that it appeared as if Tyner hadn't finished moving in. Visitors mistook the look for minimalism. They didn't stop to think that rugs caught beneath one's wheels or that antique furniture was little more than an obstacle course of sharp, unforgiving corners. Which was the intended effect: Tyner didn't want people to stop to think about his wheelchair. Now in his sixties, he had been a paraplegic for more than two-thirds of his life, struck by a car not long after winning an Olympic medal for rowing.

"At least you don't have to tell Myra's father that his son-in-law not only tried to cheat on his daughter, but proved to be exceptionally bad at it. All too characteristic. Richard's a fuck-up, even when it comes to fucking up. I was there when Myra brought him home twenty years ago and I never liked him. But you can't give friends advice about love."

"Really? You butt into my love life all the time."

Tyner grinned wickedly. "You, my dear, have a sex life. There's a difference. Not that you've had even that as of late. Speaking of which—" He rolled back to his desk. "This came for you yesterday. Postmarked Texas."

The envelope Tyner held toward her could not have been plainer. White, the kind with a blue-plaid lining that hid its contents. Suitable for sending checks or other things of value.

Or things you just don't want anyone else to see.

"Aren't there something like twelve million people in Texas?" she said, hoping she sounded nonchalant, even as she held her hands behind her back, staring warily at the envelope.

"Closer to nineteen million. You know exactly one of them, however. Right?"

"That I know of."

She took the envelope from him. The address had been typed, the stamp was generic, a waving flag. She would have expected something more whimsical. The series with the old bluesmen, or perhaps a cartoon character. She turned it over, held it up to the light. Whatever was inside was feather-light. The postal system suddenly seemed miraculous to her. Imagine moving something so delicate across thousands of miles, for less than the cost of a candy bar.

"Why did it come here, instead of my office?" she asked, in no hurry to open it, although she wasn't sure why.

"You've been in Butchers Hill less than six months," Tyner said. "You weren't there before . . . well, before."

Before you kicked him in the teeth and kicked him out, only to have him return the favor when you changed your mind.

"Bo-erne, Texas," she said, looking at the postmark. "Never heard of it."

"It's pronounced Burn-e," Tyner corrected. "Don't you read newspapers since you stopped working for them? It was all over the papers a few years ago. The Catholic church and the Boerne government went all the way to the U.S. Supreme Court in a battle over zoning laws. The church claimed that separation of church and state meant it was exempt from zoning."

"Gee, I don't know how I ever missed a fascinating story like that," Tess said. "You know how I love a good zoning yarn." She still hadn't opened the envelope. It was fun, torturing Tyner. He bossed her so about everything—work, rowing, life. If he was insistent on playing Daddy, he deserved a little teenage petulance in return.

"I guess you want to read it in private," Tyner said, even as he held his letter opener out to her.

"No!" The harshness in her voice surprised her. She hadn't thought about Crow for days, weeks, months. She had her share of exes, enough to field a football team if she went all the way back to junior high, and was allowed to resurrect the one dead one in the bunch. It didn't seem a particularly scarlet past to her, not for someone who had just turned thirty. More like coral, or a faded salmon color.

"I mean, this is no big deal," she added. "For all we know, he's probably just writing about some CD or book he had left in my apartment." But the only thing he had left behind was a ratty sweater the color of sauteed mushrooms. Her greyhound, Esskay, had unearthed it from beneath the bed and used it as part of her nest.

"Just open it."

She ignored Tyner's letter opener and unsealed the flap with her index finger, cutting herself on the cheap envelope. Her finger in her mouth, she upended the envelope. A newspaper clipping that had been glued to an index card slid out onto Tyner's desk, and nothing more. The clipping was a photograph, or a part of one, with a head-and-shoulders shot cut from a larger photograph, the fragment of a headline still attached over the head, like a halo.

The hair was different. Shorter, neater. The face was unmistakably Crow's, although it looked a little different, too. Surely she was imagining that—how much could a face change in six months? There was a gauntness she didn't remember, a sharpness to his cheekbones that made him look a little cruel. And his mouth was tight, lips pressed together as if he had never smiled in his life. Yet when she thought of Crow—which was really almost never, well maybe once a month—he was always smiling. Happy-go-lucky, blithe as a puppy. "The perfect postmodern boyfriend," one of her friends had called him. A compliment, yet also a dig.

In the end, it was the gap in temperament, not the six-year age difference so much, that had split them up. Or so her current theory held; she had revised their history several times over the past six months. He had been so endearingly boyish. Tess had been in the market for a man. Now here was a man, frowning at her. A man In Big Trouble.

That was his problem.

"There's no sign which newspaper it came from," Tyner said, picking up the card and holding it to the light, trying to read the type on the side that had been glued down. "The back looks like a Midas Muffler ad, and that could be anywhere in the country. Didn't Crow head off to Austin last spring?"

"Uh-huh."

"So what are you going to do about it?"

"Do about what?"

"Crow, and this trouble he's in."

"I'm not going to do anything. He's a big boy, too big to be playing cut-and-paste. In fact, I bet his mommy lets him use the real scissors now, instead of the little ones with the rounded-off blades."

Tyner rolled his wheelchair a few feet and grabbed the wastebasket. "So throw it away," he dared her. "Three-pointer."

Tess tucked the photo and envelope into her notebook-sized datebook, the closest thing she had to a constant companion these days. "My Aunt Kitty will want to see his photo, just for old time's sake, take in the spectacle of Crow without his purple dreadlocks. She was his friend, too, you know."

Tyner smiled knowingly. But then Tyner always smiled knowingly at Tess. He was one smug, insufferable prick, and proud of it.

"Sometimes," she said, "I think it's your personality that qualifies you for the Americans with Disabilities Act."

"*Everyone* qualifies for the Americans with Disabilities Act," he replied. "But a select few of us have to put it on our license plates. I keep trying to decide what little symbol should be riding on your bumper, but I haven't figured it out yet."

Tess left Tyner's office, intending to head straight to the bank, then back to her office, where Esskay waited, probably snoozing through the gray October day. She reminded herself that she was a businesswoman, a grown-up, with checks to write, calls to return, and a dog to walk. She didn't have time for little-boy-rock-star-gonnabes and their games.

As she crossed Charles Street, the open door of the Washington Monument caught her eye. Like many things in Baltimore, it needed a compound modifier to achieve true distinction: first permanent monument to the first President to be built by a city or government jurisidiction. A tiny George was plopped on top, his profile as familiar to Tess as her own. More so, really, for how often do you see your own profile? She saw George almost every day, staring moodily down Charles Street. Soon enough, he'd be dressed up with strings of lights for the Christmas season. Spring would come, and the parks around him would fill with daffodils and tulips. Summer, and he would seem to droop a bit, like all of Baltimore did in the July humidity. Fall, the current season, was Baltimore's best, its one unqualified success. George must have a fine view from where he stood. Yet here Tess was at his feet, a Baltimore native, and she couldn't remember ever climbing his tower and seeing the world as he saw it.

Suddenly, it seemed urgent to do so. She walked inside, stuffed a dollar into the wooden donations box, and skipping the historical plaques and displays at the base, began to make the climb, counting each step as she went.

The circular staircase was cooler than the world outside, its air thick with some recently applied disinfectant or cleanser. As Tess began sucking wind about a third of the way up—even someone who exercised as much as she did was ill-prepared to climb so many steps so quickly—she felt a little woozy from the fumes. Still, she climbed, her knapsack and long braid bouncing on her back. Up, up and up—220, 221, 222, 223—until she saw the ceiling flattening out above her head, a sign that she had come to the end, step 228.

Plexiglass shields and metal gates kept one from venturing out on the tiny parapet that circled Washington's feet, but the view was still extraordinary. Funny, she had never realized what a squat city Baltimore was, how it hugged the ground. The effect was of a low, paranoid place, peering anxiously over one shoulder. She looked east, to where she lived and worked. Then to the north, a scarlet and gold haze of trees at this time of year. Closer in, she could pick out the roof of the Brass Elephant, her home away from home. She turned to the west, to that ruined part of the city between downtown and Ten Hills, the neighborhood where she had grown up, where her parents still lived.

She saved Washington's view, the south, for last, then swiveled her head a hair to the right so she was actually facing southwest. Was there really some place called Texas past the Inner Harbor and its slick, shiny buildings? It seemed unfathomable. She felt like one of Columbus's contemporaries, trying to grasp the idea the world was round, like an orange. Assuming such a comparison had ever been made. If history had taught her anything, it was to distrust the history lessons of her childhood, with their neat little aphorisms that all seemed to be about stick-to-itiveness and moral fiber.

Still, the world looked pretty flat from here. It was all too easy to imagine falling over the edge if you strayed too far.

2

Crow's photo from the newspaper stayed hidden in Tess's datebook for several days, slipped between two weeks in March. There was no significance to those dates, they just happened to be the place where his likeness remained, almost forgotten. Almost, but not quite. And because everywhere that Tess went, her datebook was sure to follow, Crow was always tucked into the crook of her arm, or riding papoose-style in her knapsack.

He was there when she found a man wanted for a paternity test in Baltimore. (She found him in paternity court in another county, giving a blood sample there. Everyone had his ruts and routines, it seemed, habits he just couldn't break.) He rested in her knapsack as she took photos of an intersection that figured in a complicated insurance claim. Crow went to her office, bounced on the backseat of her car, spent the nights on the old mission table where they had once eaten dinner together. Tess would wake in the mornings with a vague sense of anxiety and go to bed the same way, trying to isolate the thing that was bothering her. Then she would remember, and become angry all over again. It was unfair of him to try and manipulate her, to trick her into calling when he had left her. *In Big Trouble*. And so it went, around and around in her head, until Friday came and it was Girls' Night Out.

The only "out" in Girls' Night Out was take-out. After all, Laylah was far from restaurant-ready and Kitty proved so distracting to waiters and bus boys. They hovered close, their service so constant that it was impossible to maintain a conversation. This, in turn, infuriated Laylah's mother, Jackie—not because her own drop-dead gorgeous looks were slighted, but because she liked to speak without others eavesdropping. So the girls stayed in, with Tess bringing pizza from Al Pacino's and Kitty relying on Chinese or Japanese carryout. Jackie was the experimental one, arriving with Styrofoam boxes from whatever Baltimore restaurant struck her fancy. Tonight it was Charleston's, which had meant cornbread, she-crab soup, oysters fried in cornmeal, a rare steak for fish-averse Tess, and pureed vegetables for Laylah. At least everyone could share the dessert, a pecan pie that Kitty was now slicing.

Tess watched the knife sinking into the sweet pie and suddenly thought of Crow. The connection was probably worth analyzing—was it the nuts that reminded her of Crow, or was she still on that pie-sex jag? She could think about that later. Or, better yet, not think about it ever again.

"I forgot to show you this," she said to Kitty, pulling the clip from her datebook.

"Crow! One of the best employees I've ever had here at Women and Children First," Kitty said, focusing on Crow and ignoring the headline. "For one thing, he actually liked to read, which seems to be less valued among bookstore clerks than the ability to make espresso. The haircut works. Don't you think he looks handsome, Tesser, now that he's gotten his face?"

"I suppose so," she said, leaning over her aunt's shoulder, which smelled of apricots. Kitty's scent was always changing, and her fragrances were often sweet, overbearing things that would have been cloying on another woman, yet they always worked on her. Tess wondered if that was the secret to her eternal appeal. Although in her forties Kitty had her pick of men barely half her age. With her red hair and perfect skin, she reminded Tess of a line from John Irving. Something about a woman who not only had taken care of herself, but looked as if she had good reason to do so.

"'In Big Trouble.' Aren't you the least bit curious?"

"Not really. It's some cut-and-paste job. He probably did it with a computer."

"Then how did he get it on newsprint with a muffler ad on the back?" Kitty asked, holding it to the light, just as Tyner had.

"I don't know. I don't care."

"She's lying. I can always tell when she's lying," Jackie said from the kitchen floor, where she was crawling after Laylah, who was in dogged pursuit of Esskay around the big oak table. The baby squealed and grabbed her mid-section, as if to mount her for a quick race. Esskay galloped away, rolling her brown eyes at Tess. *What have I done to deserve this?*

"What does the dog say?" Jackie prompted. "What does the doggie say?"

"Mooooooo," Laylah replied, all dimples and eyes as she grabbed for Esskay's collar. Tess was sure that Laylah knew what the doggie said, but she was already carving out her own identity, preparing her perfect mother for life with someone determined not to be so careful and circumscribed.

"I get confused about your recent romantic history," Jackie drawled. It was as if she had caught Tess taking Laylah's side in her mind. "Is Crow the one who came after the one who was hit by the car but before the one who's now in prison?"

"Crow was a dream, the sort of good guy that women always claim they want," Kitty answered for her. "If Tess hadn't been so preoccupied with Jonathan, she might have seen that. But deep down, she was too busy mooning over him to see what a gem Crow was."

Mourning, not mooning. "How's life on Shakespeare Street?" Tess asked, hoping to change the subject. "I mean, other than the free babysitting that you get by living a half-block from here, how do you like city life after the 'burbs?"

"Lot of folks keep asking me if I'm lost," Jackie said, pulling Laylah into her lap. "What they mean is, they *wish* I was lost."

"Fells Point is still pretty white," Kitty said sympathetically. "But it could be worse. I heard a black woman over in Canton had her mailbox blown up the week she moved in."

Jackie tried to wipe Laylah's face clean. Since arriving less than an hour ago, the baby had managed to shuck the pink shoes that matched her jumper and lose one sock. She was a mess, she was gorgeous, her face so full of joy that it was contagious. It made Tess smile just to see her.

"At least my Lexus is the right color," Jackie muttered, but her features softened when Laylah patted her cheeks with baby hands, as if imitating her mother's futile motions with the washcloth.

"Who wants whipped cream on their pie?" Kitty asked. At last, something everyone could agree on.

"So what do you think?" Kitty asked Jackie as soon as Tess's mouth was full. "Is Tess really interested in Crow, and pretending not to be? Or do you think she's in love with him, and being stubborn out of some misplaced pride?"

"I don't know if she was ever in love with him. I wasn't around then. But she's definitely not *finished* with him, you know what I mean? Sometimes a man is like, well, like this piece of pie when you're supposed to be on a diet. You stick your fork in it, you break it up, you move it around on your plate, you put all this work into *not* eating it. You're still obsessed with it."

"Really?" Kitty was so taken by this analogy that she stopped in midbite. "I've never felt that way about a man. Or a pie, for that matter."

"Well, Aunt Kitty, you've never left so much as a crumb behind." Tess had tired of being discussed in the third person. "Although it's been what—almost an entire month since you've 'dated' anyone?"

Kitty shrugged. "Just not interested, I guess. As long as we're using food analogies, you could say I've got a bad case of Jordan almonds."

"Huh?"

"I used to love Jordan almonds," she said matter-of-factly, as if Tess should know this. "I ate them every day. Then one day, I never wanted another one."

"Are you saying you never want to be with another man, or that you've finally gotten tired of the himbo parade that's been marching through your life?"

Kitty held out her plate to Esskay and let the dog lap up the traces of whipped cream. When she spoke again, her voice was slow and careful, as if she were making a confession.

"A new UPS man took over the route today. He came in with a shipment of books, wearing his shorts, although it's a bit late in the season for that. He had the nicest legs. You know how I like men's calves. Single, he made a point of letting me know, and very keen to see the Fritz Lang double bill at the Orpheum. I was two sentences away from having a date with him, if I wanted one. But I didn't, and I don't know why."

"I swore off men, even before I had Laylah to worry about," Jackie said. "When I was trying to build my business, I felt as if I were a battery and they drained all the energy out of me. Now I'm a single mother and all the energy *is* drained out of me. Even with help—and all the support I'm getting from you guys—I'm exhausted most of the time. What would I do with a man, even if I could find one? And what would a man do with me? Watch me fall asleep in front of the television at nine o'clock?"

Tess said nothing. Her recent abstinence from men—from love, from passion, from all entanglements, however wrongheaded—had felt like a twelve-step program. One day at a time, and she was always aware in her mind of just how many days that had been. She liked men. They used to like her.

"I don't seem to meet guys anymore," she said. "Is that because I turned thirty?"

"You're healthier," Kitty said. "Mentally, I mean. You don't give off that damaged vibe you used to have. There's a large class of men with a homing instinct for women who are vulnerable, and that's why there was always someone lurking, ready to take advantage of you."

"You're not damaged, and you've always had your pick of men," Tess pointed out.

"I'm at the other end of the spectrum—true indifference. They start off thinking I'm the perfect woman because I want them only for their bodies, then end up saying I'm heartless. If you only knew how many men had accused me of objectifying them, or using them for sex."

Kitty laughed, pleased with herself for being such a cadette. Laylah clapped her baby hands and laughed with her, while Jackie just shook her head and snorted: "White girl craziness."

It was one of Jackie's favorite expressions, but Tess thought it didn't apply here. Different pathologies for black and white women, but pathologies all the same. Valuing the men who didn't value you. Settling for vicarious power, instead of grabbing your own chunk of it. Worrying about the size of your butt. She had a sudden yearning to sweep Laylah up in her arms and tell her that they'd have it all worked out by the time she was a grown-up.

Jackie picked up the clipping that Kitty had left on the table. "He is kind of cute. I hope you're going to call him, make sure he's okay."

"I am *not*. Let him call me if he wants to talk. My home number hasn't changed, even if it's unlisted now."

"You know for a fact he sent this?" Jackie had switched to her professional persona, the steely-eyed Grand Inquisitor who had built her fund-raising business into such a hot property that clients ended up auditioning for her.

"Well, no, but he's the only person I know in Texas."

"The only person you *know* you know in Texas. Besides, what if he really is in a bind? I know you, girl, you'll never forgive yourself if something happens to that boy."

Kitty nudged the portable phone toward Tess with her elbow. Tess ignored it, pouring herself another glass of wine. "If I were to call—*if*—do you think I would do it here, within your hearing?"

Jackie and Kitty smiled smugly at each other, while Laylah made another pass at Esskay, squealing in delight when the dog ran away and slunk under the table, whimpering piteously.

"What does the doggie say, Laylah?" Jackie asked automatically.

"Meow," Laylah said. "Meeeee-ow."

* * * *

Not even an hour later, Tess sat on her bed in the third-floor apartment above the store, Esskay nestled beside her, yet another glass of wine on her bedside table. Almost eleven o'clock. An hour earlier in Texas, and a Friday night. He'd be out, of course, performing with his band, lots of Texas girls staring at him hungrily. Texas women were reputed to be better-looking than women from elsewhere. She imagined a super-gender with hard bodies, harder hair, tanning-bed tans, and those taut neck cords that come from years of expert bulimia. Barfing sorority girls with credit cards, convertibles, and eager, grasping mouths. Girls who kept a man out late, assuming he got home at all.

So if she called now, she'd get his machine. A machine would be a nice compromise, actually. Ideal, even, the equivalent of a drive-by shooting in the gender wars. *Tag, you're it.*

"What city?" asked the mechanical voice attached to the 512 area code.

"Austin," she said into the alloted portion of silence.

"What listing?"

"Cr—Edgar Ransome." She had to grope for his real name. Crow had always been Crow to her.

The voice provided ten digits and she punched them in from memory, only to hear another mechanical voice: "I'm sorry the number you have called is not in service . . ."

She stared at the phone, puzzled. The phone must have been cut off pretty recently if he was still listed. Oh well, Crow wouldn't be the first musician to miss too many phone bills. Although his doting parents, the ones who had been so tolerant of his six-year plan at the Maryland Institute, College of Art, had always been good-natured about subsidizing him.

And if he were really in trouble, he'd go to them. Why hadn't she thought of this before? An only child like her, Crow had been brought up in a much more stereotypically worshipful home. In fact, his ego was so intact, his self-esteem so genuine, that it was as if it had been baked in his mother's kiln and coated with layers of shiny glaze. At least, she thought his mother had a kiln. She hadn't really paid close attention when he spoke of his parents, but she remembered something about his mother's ceramics, his father's economics classes, which had sounded vaguely Marxist to her. A pair of gentle, retrograde hippies, raising their son simply to be.

She flipped open her datebook. It still surprised her to see how busy her life had become. The fall was full of meetings and appointments. It wasn't just work and workouts, either, but dinners with old and new friends, even "dates" with her mom. It had been nice, being sought-after, but suddenly all those names and numbers and addresses just made her weary.

Under R, she found the information Crow had inked in long ago, when these pages were emptier. There was his number, in the little Bolton Hill studio apartment he had all but vacated while they were together. His birthday, 8-23 ("Two Virgos!" he had written in his ecstatic, spiky handwriting, and she liked him for not making a crude joke at their expense). His clothing sizes, his Social Security number, the number of his favorite Chinese takeout place, and just in case she ever needed him during his infrequent trips home, a number and address for his parents in Charlottesville.

"Much too late to call strangers," she told Esskay. "After eleven, all phone calls are bad news."

Esskay, still disgruntled at her undignified treatment at Laylah's baby hands, gave Tess a skeptical look, snorted, and rolled over, turning her bony spine toward her. Tess dialed the phone, rehearsing her opening lines. *You don't know me but . . . We've never met but . . . Did your son ever mention we were sleeping together until I broke his heart, then came crawling back and he broke my heart, so now we're really even-steven, and I don't owe him a thing, right?*

"Hello?" A woman's voice, low and husky. Not a Southern accent, for the Ransomes were New England transplants. But the clipped Bostonian edges seemed to have been smoothed down by the years in Virginia.

"Is this the Ransome residence?"

"Yes. Who's calling?" There was something tentative in the voice, something fearful. Tess realized that bad news must often begin this way: Is this so-and-so's residence?

"We've never met but I'm Tess Monaghan—"

"Oh, Tess!" Mrs. Ransome's relief was so intense it seemed to flow through the phone. "I feel as if I know you. How's your aunt, Kitty? And the greyhound, I want to say its name is Jimmy Dean, but that's not quite right, is it?"

"Right section of your supermarket. It's Esskay, as in the Schluderberg-Kurdle Company of Baltimore, finest pork products ever made."

"Of course, Esskay." She laughed, but shakily.

"Tess Monaghan. I feel as if I conjured you up in a way. Because I've been sitting here, thinking I should call you."

Some organ—heart, stomach, intestines—lurched inside Tess. "Has something happened—I mean, do you have news of Crow? I tried to call him tonight—"

"But his phone is disconnected. I know, I know. It was turned off six weeks ago. A week later, our last check came back from Texas, marked return to sender. I was hoping you might have heard from him, or know something more."

"Not really." The clipping didn't count, for it only deepened the mystery. Besides, it surely would cause this kind woman more concern, and that couldn't have been Crow's intent. "So you haven't heard anything for more than a month?"

"Three weeks ago he called and left a message on our machine, at a time when he knew we'd be out. 'Don't worry,' he said, and we've been out of our minds with worry ever since. Are you sure he hasn't tried to get in touch with you?"

Tess studied the clipping. Less than a week in her possession and it already had a worn look, as if it had been handled many, many times. "I had something in the mail recently, a photo of him, nothing more . . . He's cut his hair." An idiotic segue, but it was all she could think of.

"I knew he would reach out to you. You were such a good influence."

"I was?" As Tess recalled, Crow had committed at least one felony under her tutelage. Then again, that was before they started dating, and it had not been her idea.

"He finished school at last. Even the breakup had its positive aspects. He went to Texas, decided to get serious about his music."

The conversation seemed increasingly surreal, and Tess found herself conscious of the wine she had been drinking all evening. But perhaps Mrs. Ransome had been sitting by her phone, dialing the same number that no longer rang in Texas, sipping her own drink?

"Well, it was nice to talk to you at last," she offered lamely. Mrs. Ransome seemed to know so much about her, while Tess couldn't remember anything more about Crow's parents other than a few scraps of details. Had she not been paying attention? Sometimes she had tuned out Crow's happy prattling. It hadn't seemed to require close attention.

"I'm sure you'll hear from him soon," she said. "Crow's always been responsible."

"That's my point," Mrs. Ransome said. "He's too responsible to do this to us, unless something is horribly wrong. We were thinking of hiring someone—"

"I'd be glad to help you," Tess interrupted. "Make some inquiries, hook you up with someone in Texas."

"—but your call seems providential, I realize now. Not to sound too Celestine Prophecy–ish, because I'm not that kind of person. Usually. But things do happen for a reason, don't you think? I need a private investigator and here's one calling me, one I know to be a fine, trustworthy person."

"I'm really not—" Tess stopped. It wasn't that she didn't consider herself fine and trustworthy, it was just that Mrs. Ransome's exalted opinion sounded suspiciously like one shoe dropping.

Mrs. Ransome wasn't listening. It was possible that she had never really listened. From the moment she heard Tess's voice on the line, she had been working toward just this, focusing on a single goal in her own gracious way, intent on throwing down this second shoe.

"Tess Monaghan, would you find my son?"

3

Thirty-six hours later, Tess was en route to Charlottesville. She owed Crow's parents the courtesy of a face-to-face rejection, or so she had rationalized, only then could she make them see the sense of finding an investigator who knew the territory. There were worse ways to spend a crisp Sunday in October than driving along the edge of the Shenandoahs.

Strangely, Tyner had wanted to come along, claiming she was too nice, that she was just a girl who couldn't say no. But it seemed to Tess that he was desperate for a distraction. He was restless lately, bored with his job and his routines, which surprised her. She had thought such feelings belonged exclusively to the young.

"Don't worry, I'm not going to take the work," she had assured him. "I just want to make sure they hire someone reputable, someone who won't run up a huge bill and never do anything more than place a classified ad."

"Your Toyota can't make Charlottesville," Tyner had said. "We'll have to take my van."

"As Tonto said to the Lone Ranger, what's this 'we' shit, Kemo Sabe? Besides, a car with 130,000 miles on it can easily go 400 miles more."

"But maybe not all in one day. And if you should decide to take the case—"

"It would be a disservice to them to take their money. The only thing I know about Texas is 'Remember the Maine.'"

"'Remember the *Alamo.*' 'Remember the Maine' was the Spanish-American War."

"See? That's how little I know."

Tyner gave her a sour look. "I remember when the public school education in Baltimore was something to brag about."

"It still is. I only got beaten up once in four years. It was a school record."

So it was that Tess's Toyota headed out of Baltimore on Route 40 on Sunday morning, bound for Charlottesville, with Esskay the only passenger on board. Although it was slightly out of their way, she went west, then south along the Shenandoah Parkway. That kept them out of Washington traffic and gave Esskay a chance to see the fall leaves.

Tess knew the first part of the route well enough, from the dozens of school trips to Skyline Drive and Luray Caverns, where she always had to relearn the difference between stalactites and stalagmites. "C for ceiling, stalactites hang down." Another brain cell wasted.

But once south of the Natural Bridge, it was all new to her. She wasn't much of a traveler. There had been the road trips for crew in college, a few trips to New York, a wedding in Chicago, one spring break on the Outer Banks. When there had been time, there had been no money, and now that there was money, at least a little of it, there was no time. Or maybe she just wasn't inclined to make the time.

The truth was, she had never really understood the lure of travel. Strange faces, strange sheets, upset routines. And for what? To look at some scenery, as she was doing now. Pretty enough, but nothing to leave home for. Tess remembered Kitty making a present of her childhood Viewfinder. Tess would have been around six or seven at the time, so Kitty was the glamorous young-old aunt, not even out of college yet. Tess had dutifully held the Viewfinder to her face and depressed the switch, taking in the Golden Gate and Hoover Dam, Mesa Verde and the Four Corners, the Astrodome and the Alamo. (Of course she knew the Alamo.)

The only places that touched her were close to home. Poe's grave, for example—she swore she had felt an icy breeze on her cheek, as if he had just passed by. Green Mount Cemetery, home to John Wilkes Booth.

Maybe it wasn't local places after all, but a perverse fondness for graveyards.

Once in Charlottesville, Mrs. Ransome's careful directions led her past the university and into the heart of an old residential neighborhood with mature trees and substantial houses. Tess had expected something a little more ramshackle, a run-down bungalow with a "Property Is Theft" sign on the unlocked front door. But the Ransomes' house sat far back on a well-kept lawn, an Arts and Crafts bungalow at odds with its more traditional neighbors, but undeniably pretty and charming.

A small woman in baggy print pants and bright purple sweatshirt, her dark hair an uncontrollable mass of curls, opened the front door. She looked just as Tess had imagined her—a casual refugee from the sixties, indifferent to fashion and appearance.

"I'll show you how to come through the back way," she said, using a hillbilly accent, perhaps for comic effect. "A little easier to get in through the kitchen. Besides, I just mopped the front hall."

"It's good to meet you, Mrs. Ransome." Tess held out her hand, to forestall the hug she feared was coming. Bostonians were supposed to be reserved, but you never knew.

"Miz Ransome?" The woman squinted at her, confused. "Oh, you mean Miz Kendall. She's in her studio, finishing up. But she'll be in directly to see you. I told her on the walkie-talkie box that you was here."

The garden behind the house, screened from the front by a privet hedge, came as something of a surprise, a hidden art gallery, much bigger than one would guess from the street. Here, large bronze sculptures in a variety of styles sat among weaving paths.

"I don't think the sculpture garden at the Baltimore Museum of Art has as much stuff," Tess said to Esskay, who was inspecting one of the more abstract works.

"No, but it's of better quality," said a tall woman who was coming along the path, from a cottage at the rear of the garden. She wore a dusty green smock over her clothes and there was a streak of something on her right cheek, but she was otherwise impeccably groomed. Her dark hair was worn up and held in place by tortoiseshell combs. Tess had tried the same style herself, but her hair always slipped from whatever moorings she used, and she had gone back to her serviceable, dependable braid.

"Tess," the woman said, studying her. "You look just as I imagined you. Well—not imagined, really. Crow had so many pictures of you."

He did? That was news to Tess. She had bought her first camera when she started working as a private detective.

"Mrs.—Ms. Kendall?" She held out her hand.

The woman ignored her hand and embraced her. "Call me Felicia."

"Felicia Kendall? But I've heard of you."

Felicia Kendall blushed, as if embarrassed by her fame. "I hope Crow wasn't boasting."

"Quite the opposite. He made it sound as if his mother dabbled in ceramics as a hobby. But you're Felicia Kendall. Your work is famous enough so that even a philistine like myself knows who you are. I remember when you received the commission for the new H. L. Mencken sculpture. Crow never said a word."

Felicia smiled warily. "Children see their parents differently than others do. I was always Mommy first. Which is as it should be."

"Does that mean that you put Crow's needs ahead

of yours?" That would explain much, Tess thought. His happiness, his trust in the world.

"No, not at all. In fact, we always believed Crow would be happier if we were happy. We left Boston and came to Charlottesville for that reason, even though Chris's career probably would have . . . traveled at a sharper trajectory if he had remained at Harvard."

Again, Felicia blushed for no reason Tess could detect. Happy parents make happy children. Tess wondered if her own parents had ever considered anything so radical. Not that her parents had been unhappy, but they had been more focused on their relationship with each other than their relationship with her. She had often felt like an outsider in their house, the sole disruption to what otherwise would have been an uninterrupted idyll of passionate fights and more passionate rapprochements.

"Are you tired after your drive?" Felicia asked. "I've made up Crow's room for you. Or perhaps you'd like a drink, a cup of tea or coffee? It's still warm enough to sit out here, at least before the sun goes down."

Before Tess could answer, there were footsteps on the path, the scrape of the latch on the garden gate. Tess saw something catch light in Felicia's face, and she wondered what it would be like to be that happy about another person's comings and goings, even after twenty-five years.

Then she saw Chris Ransome, breathing heavily, his face glowing after what must have been a long, glorious run. He was tall, like his son, with short black hair, the same pale, sharp face, and the same long legs.

And he was at least ten years younger than Felicia Kendall. Possibly fifteen.

"Tess Monaghan," he said, holding out his hand. "It's a pleasure."

She did not take his hand, but stood looking at the couple standing together—the man so much like his son, the tall, handsome woman with her upswept dark hair and broad shoulders. She had seen this couple before. She had seen them reflected in the glass of her own terrace doors, in the windows of the shops in Fells Point. A younger version of this man, and a younger version of this woman, but still so much the same that she felt a convulsive shiver. Déjà vu was, she knew, simply a matter of the brain getting things in the wrong order. But she really had seen this couple, many, many times. "Imagine us just like this, on our Christmas card," Crow had said the first time they had slept together, catching her by the hip as she rose naked from the bed, making her face the mirror over her bureau. It had been the most appalling thing anyone had ever said to her after sex. It had also been the most appealing.

So now she knew: Crow had wanted a girl just like the girl who married dear young dad.

That night, Tess was lying on top of the bedspread, staring at Crow's Dave Matthews Band poster. She felt as if she had said nothing but no all evening. *No, she didn't want the job. No, she didn't want another help-ing of potatoes, although they were delicious, thank you. No, she didn't know if she could work in Texas, didn't even know if she was licensed to carry there, wasn't even sure she was allowed to have her gun here with her in Virginia.*

No, please don't give Esskay any more ham, it had too much sodium. No, she didn't know anything, hadn't heard from Crow until the letter had arrived. No, no, no.

Yet Felicia and Chris still hadn't given up. They probably thought it a master stroke, putting her in this boyhood room, full of Crow artifacts. But it had only strengthened her resolve to get away from them and Charlottesville. Felicia and Chris, who had given their son everything he ever wanted, seemed determined to give her back to him.

What they didn't understand was that he didn't want her, and she didn't want him.

A knock at the door, and Chris Ransome poked his head in.

"May I come in?"

"It's your house."

He took the desk chair, a scarred wooden one that looked as if it had caught the overflow of several experiments with an old-fashioned chemistry set, the dangerous kind.

"You were so quiet at dinner." A slight smile. "Except when it came to a particular monosyllable, you hardly said anything."

"I have your best interests at heart. You're right to be concerned, you just need to hire someone who knows Texas."

"But you know Crow."

"Do I?"

Chris Ransome's hands beat an unconscious tattoo on Crow's desk, which was covered with a boy's various collections—bird nests, rocks, arrowheads. The whole room had a museum quality to it, preserved not so much as if Crow might return, but as if future generations might wish to see it exactly as it was. *And here's where the famous composer-artist-future President played with model airplanes and studied the night sky with this Nature Store telescope.* Tess's parents had turned her room into a sewing room the moment she graduated from college.

"I'm not sure what you mean, Tess."

"I mean—" It seemed petulant to continue lying on the bed, so she swung her feet to the side of the bed and sat up. "I mean I knew your son for more than a year, worked alongside him in my aunt's bookstore, dated him for almost six months. But I didn't know anything about him. Either I wasn't listening or he wasn't talking. A little of both, I think."

"What didn't you know?"

"I didn't know his mother was Felicia Kendall, for one thing. And that you were some hotshot at Harvard."

"Not particularly vital information, if you ask me. Besides, we moved to Charlottesville so Crow could be someone other than the son of the famous sculptress and the 'Harvard hotshot,' to use your terminology. A parent's fame can crush a child."

"Felicia said you came here because you couldn't be happy in Boston."

"Did she?" Chris fiddled with the placement of the bird nests, lining them up, although they looked perfectly aligned to Tess, then moving them around as if they were cups in an ornithological version of three-card monte.

"Were you famous?" she asked on a hunch, a vague memory stirring. "Or notorious?"

Chris smiled. His resemblance to Crow was still disorienting for Tess. In many ways, he was what she had thought she wanted when she was unhappy with Crow—a grown-up version of same.

"Now see, that's why Felicia and I want to hire you. You're intuitive."

"Don't flatter me, please. Just answer."

Chris looked like a child forced to recite for company. "It's hard to imagine now, but twenty-five years ago Felicia and I were the scandal du jour, at least in our hometown of Boston. I hasten to add that the threshold for notoriety was much lower back then."

"What did you do?"

"We had an affair." He smiled at Tess's is-that-all-there-is expression. "Shocking, isn't it? Shocking to think it was once shocking. Felicia's husband was my thesis adviser at Harvard. I was his star student, I was going to bring home all the big prizes one day. I had theories that were going to change the world. Instead, I turned my own world upside down. I fell in love."

He rearranged the bird nests yet again, but his voice now had a warm, dreamy quality. He liked this part of the story.

"I fell in love and Felicia became pregnant. Wait—that construction makes it sound as if it were something *she* did. When it was really something I wanted. I got her pregnant, because I was desperate for her. I didn't think she'd leave her husband just for me, but I knew she would leave for a child. It's not that she didn't love me, but Felicia was a careful, deliberate woman. She didn't have much experience in doing what she wanted, as opposed to doing what was expected."

"But you changed that."

"Eventually. Crow arrived before her divorce was final, and we never did get around to marrying officially. Yet it was the age difference that really scandalized people. Our ages, and the things I supposedly 'gave up' for her. I was twenty-two she was thirty-three. Silly, isn't it, how age trips people up?"

Tess, who had agonized at times over the six-year difference between her and his son, did not answer Chris's question. "Does Crow know all this?"

"Oh yes." Chris frowned. "Actually, he may not know we never married. Little boys don't care much about such things, do they? They don't ask to see wedding pictures. If he had asked, we would have told him, but I don't remember it coming up. We celebrate our anniversary every year, only it's the anniversary of the night we met. May 30. A Memorial Day weekend party. Felicia was wearing pale green."

Tess ransacked her memory, trying to find some little piece of the story. Crow must have told her at least part of it. Yet nothing was there.

"I didn't know *any* of this," she said, intending to sound plaintive, but achieving only a low-grade whininess. "Yet Crow knew how my parents met, what they did for a living. He knew which bars fell into my father's territory as a Baltimore city liquor inspector. He even knew what my mother does at the National Security Agency and that's technically classified."

"She's a supervisor, right? A tall woman, like you,

given to matching her shoes to her outfits as exactly as possible."

Tess stalked over to Crow's bureau, where his childhood collection of *Star Wars* figures had been laid out on a rough woven cloth. "See? You even know how my mom *dresses*. That's more than I knew about Felicia. How can you say I knew Crow at all?"

"Crow is one of the world's listeners."

"He chatters all the time," Tess objected.

"Yes, he does. But he never really gives out any information about himself, does he? He talks about the latest thing he's read, the song he's working on, something strange and wonderful he saw on the street. But he doesn't talk about himself. He's un-usual that way. He fools a lot of people into think-ing they're close to him, but few really are. All the words, all that chatter, is a way of keeping people at a distance."

"So I'm right—I never really knew him. I'm even less suited to finding him than I thought."

Chris stood up. "I need to show you something. Down in Felicia's studio. Do you mind?"

The night was cold and crisp, one of the first true autumn nights this season. Their breath was visible as they walked through the garden, to the cottage from which Felicia had materialized that afternoon. Chris Ransome unlocked the door and flicked on a light.

"Crow had his own studio here." Chris grinned with a rueful self-awareness. "We've always been a little indulgent, I suppose."

"Would I understand your theories?" Tess asked suddenly, stalling for time. She felt uneasy, almost frightened of seeing whatever Chris Ransome found so urgent. "Your ones about economics, I mean. Could you make them so simple that a bonehead like myself could get it?"

"If I can't, then it's my failure, not yours. The basic premise is plenitude."

"Plenitude?"

"Simply, there really is enough."

Tess's mind balked at this. "Everything I see says we live in a time of scarcity, that there are too many people and not enough resources."

"Well, the theory of plenitude begins with changing one's definition of what 'enough' is. Look, I brought you here to show you Crow's studio. To convince you that you did know him, and he knew you."

He opened a door on the far end of the large room where Felicia worked. Moonlight poured through the windows, and before Chris flicked on the light, Tess had a sense of hundreds of canvases, from large to small, surrounding her. When the light did come on, she saw there were no more than a dozen, and they were all quite small.

But every face looking back at her was hers.

There she was, in pastels, in pen and ink, in oil, in crayon. She was clothed; she was nude, her hair was braided, her hair was undone. Even Esskay, who had arrived so close to the end of what would be her time with Crow, had managed to creep into a few of the pictures. There was one of the two of them sleeping, their bodies mirroring each other. It made Tess blush to look at it, to think of Crow standing over her and the dog, studying them, remembering all the details, including the dirty white socks she wore to bed. The only thing she wore to bed.

"We didn't know they were here until a week ago. We've always respected his privacy, but after he stopped calling and writing . . . well, we thought he might have left some sort of clue behind."

"You know I did try to make amends," Tess said, feeling a little defensive. The etiquette of the situation overwhelmed her. She was standing in a room with an ex-boyfriend's father, looking at naked pictures of herself. She had never read Emily Post, but she was pretty sure this situation had not been covered. "He didn't want to try again. He said it was too late for us, and he was probably right."

"These things happen. Felicia and I are the last people to be judgmental about the ways of the human heart. What did Faulkner say in his Nobel speech? 'The heart wants what the heart wants.'"

"Actually, I think that was Woody Allen, at the press conference about Soon-Yi. Faulkner said the conflicts of the human heart are the only thing worth writing about." Every now and then, it helped, being an English major. Not often, but sometimes.

"I know they're the only thing worth living for." Chris Ransome picked up one of the smaller studies, a nude that had been exceptionally kind to Tess's rounded figure, narrowing the waist just a shade, deepening the almost-dimple in her chin, removing any dimples farther south. But the leg muscles were hers, Tess thought, and that little dent by her tricep. She had worked hard to get her arms cut like that.

Ransome studied the picture, then looked at Tess thoughtfully. In another man, the look might have been salacious, offensive. But Chris Ransome looked at Tess as if she were merely another in the series of beloved objects his son had toted home over the years. The arrowheads, the rock collection, the *Star Wars* figures, the Nature Store telescope. A swallow's nest.

"Felicia and I know we could hire someone else, Tess. We probably should. But there is something unfinished between you and Crow. I won't put a name to it, but whatever it is, it's like a divining rod. You'll find your way to him. Or he'll find his way to you. No other private detective can offer us that."

He pulled something from his pocket. "This is the last postcard Crow sent to us, before he disappeared."

The card wasn't a photograph, but a hand-tinted drawing of blue flowers dotting a green field. "Texas blue-bonnets," said the legend on the front.

On the back, Crow had written: "I feel as if I'm starting over. Things here are not as expected, but that doesn't make it bad, right? As Dad said, I am following in an outlaw tradition by coming here. GTT, Crow."

"GTT?" Tess asked Chris.

"Gone to Texas. It's what outlaws wrote on their doors when they headed out to the frontier. 'I've gone to Texas. Don't bother to look because you won't find me.'"

"Is that so?" Tess said, lifting her chin. And they had her.

Tess called Kitty the next day from Abingdon, Virginia, just before crossing the line into Tennessee.

She called the private line, knowing Kitty would be in the store and the machine would pick up. She didn't want to explain why she was going, she just wanted to go.

"It's Tess," she said. "If Tyner calls, tell him I'm headed for Texas. I'll call him tonight, when I've crossed the Mississippi." She figured that was just far enough to be safe from Tyner's wrath, that the Mississippi was wide enough to keep the volume of his voice from reaching out and lassoing her home.

She had a generous per diem and a sizable advance. She had her Toyota and her overnight bag. She had a week's worth of clothing purchased in less than thirty minutes at an outlet mall with a Gap and an Old Navy. She had the sweats she always carried in her trunk, along with a jump rope and a basketball. She had her dog, her datebook, and her copy of *Don Quixote*, because she had gotten in the habit of carrying it around, thinking she still might finish it one day, if only by osmosis. She had seven pairs of heavy-duty white cotton underwear, which had cost only a dollar at some off-brand store, possibly because "Wednesday" was spelled "Wenesday."

It was enough. Or at least plenty. Chris Ransome was right: You just had to change your definitions.

4

Tess, who never paid close attention in seventh grade social studies, had expected Texas cities to spring out of vast, dusty prairies, then disappear quickly in the rearview mirror. But Austin seemed to begin in fits and starts as a series of strip centers along Interstate 35. Where were the green fields with little blue flowers? What had ever happened to Lady Bird Johnson's Highway Beautification program? Her eye was drawn to the strange names of local groceries and convenience stores. HEB, Circle K, Stop 'n' Go.

Traffic was heavy, too, worse than any rush hour she had ever experienced back home. Even when the Toyota crested a hill on I-35 and she saw the Texas Capitol building ahead, the glimmer of a river or a lake beyond it, she was still unmoved. She also was overwhelmed and exhausted. What had she been thinking?

"You shouldn't be in Texas by yourself," Kitty had scolded when Tess called her earlier that day. "Tyner will have a fit when he hears. He's already called here twice, looking for you."

"I'll call him pretty soon," Tess said. She was at a roadside restaurant in Waco, the Health Camp, which seemed to specialize in spectacularly un-healthy food. A gas station attendant had given her the tip when she filled up her car outside Dallas that morning. She sucked up the dregs of her coffee milkshake, gave Esskay the last bite of burger and bun. More bun than burger, but Esskay was still grateful.

"Where are you going to stay?"

"Some fleabag motel that takes fleabags, I guess."

"That won't do. You should be in a place where you have access to a fax machine, or even a computer if you need one. I know a bookstore owner down there. He might put you up, as a favor to me, and help you find your way around." There was a strange, awkward pause, and Kitty laughed a coy, most un-Kittyish laugh. "We . . . were together, at that convention for independent booksellers a few years back. The one in San Antonio."

" 'Together?' Aren't you shy all of a sudden. Why haven't I heard about this adventure before?"

"Keith was different." Kitty sighed. "He runs Quadling Country."

"Come again?"

"Keith's store. It's like mine, a store for children and adults, only with an emphasis on fantasy, with a comics department on the side. Quadling Country. From the Oz books."

"Oh, where Glinda lived. Right. But comic books and *fantasy*?" Tess made a face, even though Esskay was the only one there to see it. "You mean sci fi and outer space and little green men and images of the future that almost always include some kind of monorail system?"

"Don't be a snob," Kitty admonished. "Besides, I can't remember the last time I saw a book of any stripe in your hands."

"Hey, I'm almost finished *Don Quixote*," Tess pointed out. Just five hundred pages to go. She had actually read a little bit here at the Health Camp. It was surprising how much of the famous stuff—the windmills, the muleteers, the barber—came at the beginning of the book. Or maybe not so surprising. Probably a lot of people lied about reading the damn thing.

"I'll call Keith as soon as I hang up," Kitty said. "But let me give you the directions to his store first."

"You've been there?"

"Oh, yes. My last vacation."

"You said you went to Atlanta for a bookseller's convention."

"Did I?"

Tess left the highway and drove west along Sixth Street, which appeared to be home to a good portion of Austin's club scene. Wouldn't it be nice, Tess thought, if she could just see Crow striding along here, guitar case in hand? So easy and simple. But things had never worked that way for her. The long way around was the route she always ended up traveling.

About two miles west of the downtown district, Quadling Country sat on a small hill above Sixth Street. The two-story purple house didn't have the spick-and-span quality of Kitty's Women and Children First, but it was large and enticing, Tess supposed. As was the young man bounding down the crumbling concrete steps.

He was young, of course. Tess had expected that much, although this one was something of a record, even for Kitty. He looked to be nineteen, a strapping but very dewy nineteen. He must have needed instruction in all aspects of life, from bed to bath and beyond. But he didn't seem as hangdog as most of Kitty's castoff lovers. Maybe the distance, the whole gestalt of the convention fling, had inoculated him against the inevitable disappointment.

"Are you Tess? And this must be Esskay. Cool dog." Esskay, ever the sucker for a compliment, promptly attached her face to his leg and began whimpering for attention. "Kitty called to say you'd be here this afternoon. But you must drive kinda slow. That was almost two hours ago. I can make it from Waco to here in less than ninety minutes."

"Well, I drive pretty fast, too, when I know a place," Tess said, and instantly felt as if she were all of two years old. "But the traffic was horrible, and I was worried about speed traps."

"Speed traps? Like, only if you're going above a hundred. Let me get that for you." He tried to lift the duffel bag of new clothes from Tess's shoulder.

"I can carry it," she said, wrestling it back from him.

"Of course you *can*. But you're a guest here. You're just gonna have to take our courtesy even if it kills you." He grinned at Tess, a little wickedly, and she sensed that his idea of Southern hospitality might include late-night visits to lady guests, if they were so inclined. Of all Kitty's young louts, this one was the youngest and most loutish by far.

"How did you come to have your own bookstore, anyway?"

"Well, I only run the comics section, but it's the best one in the city. I won the readers' poll in the *Chronicle*, even."

"And you are . . ."

"I don't know," he said. "What am I?"

Tess blushed. "I mean, how old are you?"

"I'll be eighteen in April."

Jesus. This one wasn't even legal.

"And you met Kitty . . ."

He put his hands on his hips and stared her down. "So, do you like ever ask a direct question, or do you just play this fill-in-the-blanks game? 'Cause I gotta tell you, it's annoying."

"Look, Keith, I'm just trying to figure out how my aunt ended up in what is probably an illegal relationship even under the statutes of this backwards state."

"Keith? I'm not Keith, I'm Maury, his son. And who are you calling backward? As I recall, Maryland was all over the news not long ago because a thirteen-year-old married her twenty-nine-year-old boyfriend." He stopped, then allowed himself a sly smile. "So you thought I was getting it on with Kitty? Crazy. Not that I would mind scrounging my dad's leftovers. He's got pretty good taste."

"Keith is your dad?"

"Right. He's at Whole Foods, picking up some stuff for vegetarian lasagne." Maury suddenly looked the way Esskay did when some off-limits food was simmering on the stove. "We're death on red meat around here."

"Texas vegetarians? Isn't that an oxymoron?" Great, she had come all this distance to a place famous for barbecue and fajitas, only to end up in a household where meat was banned.

A sputtering bright yellow Triumph pulled up on the side street.

"There's my dad now. Guess I'll go help him with the groceries." He was back to smiling, bouncy Maury now. "He's not threatened a bit, if I lend him a hand."

The man who got out of the car was short and stocky, pot-bellied in truth, with thinning hair. *Maybe he had fallen apart after Kitty had thrown him over.* The Kitty that Tess knew took up with young men like Maury, not pudgy guys of her own age, and ran through them as quickly as Esskay devoured rawhide bones. Keith's face was round, pleasant but ordinary. Maury's genes obviously came from some long-legged, long-ago stunner of a leftover, to use his parlance.

"Tesser," Keith said, balancing his canvas grocery sack in one arm, pulling her to him with the other and kissing her on the cheek. "Not to be overly familiar, but I was almost your uncle, you know."

"Oh, sure." She had never heard of him and he knew her family nickname. That seemed fair.

"A magnificent woman, your aunt. I just couldn't see moving to Baltimore, leaving my life here. And she felt the same way about Texas."

"Uh-huh."

"I'm glad we could finally be friends, although it

wasn't always easy. When she called today and asked me to put you up, I couldn't have been happier. I look forward to us getting to know each other."

"Absolutely."

Tess grabbed Esskay's leash and followed Keith and Maury into Quadling Country, wondering if anyone ever really knew anyone.

Texas was hot in October, with no promise of the autumn weather that had settled over the mid-Atlantic. Tess—traveling with Maury at Keith's insistence—drove to Crow's old neighborhood on the city's north side, a place called Hyde Park, beyond the University of Texas. She tried not to complain, but the Toyota's air conditioner had given up just last month. Back in Baltimore, this had not seemed particularly urgent.

"I don't see how you stand it," she said for the fifth or sixth time, shrugging out of her leather jacket, then the denim shirt she had worn over her T-shirt.

"Stand what?" Maury asked. "Wait, turn here, this is the block you're looking for."

The address to which Crow's parents had sent checks through the month of August was an old Victorian, cut up into at least six apartments by the count of the mailboxes. Names had been affixed randomly—one with an old-fashioned label-maker, others with scraps of paper held in place by layers and layers of Scotch tape. Groves, Perelman, Lane, Gundell, Linthicum. None of the names meant anything to Tess. She rang the bell for number 5, which had been Crow's apartment.

"No answer," she told Maury.

"Would you answer if you were an illegal sublettor? Like Dad told you over dinner last night, there's no way an apartment is sitting vacant in this market. The question is whether the landlord kicked Crow out to up the rates, or if he found someone to take his place. Let's try the door." He started up the steps ahead of Tess, but she passed him on the landing and reached the door marked No. 5 before he did.

"I'm looking for Crow Ransome," she called through the door, after knocking and getting no reply. She heard footsteps creeping toward the door and away again, as if someone had peered through the fisheye and decided not to answer. "Look, this door is so thin I can practically hear you breathing through it."

"You got the wrong place," a voice called from the inside. "Never heard of anyone by that name."

"No, it's the right place. And I know whose name is on the lease here, and it sure isn't yours," Tess said, her voice louder now. "I'd hate to track down the landlord and tell him you're not the one on the lease."

Her bluff brought results. A marijuana-laden breeze drifted into the hall as a skinny man in baggy plaid shorts opened the door. He had red hair pulled back in a scraggly pony tail and pink, blotchy skin. His hairline was as high as it could be and still be considered a hairline at all.

"You with someone official?" he asked.

"I'm a private detective looking for the man who used to live here. Crow Ransome. You know him?"

"Never heard of any Crow."

"Maybe you knew him as Ed or Edgar."

"Eddie?" *Eddie?* "Okay, sure, a little. I mean, I

met him when I took over the place. I gave him cash up front for the next six months, he pays the landlady. He makes an extra 25 dollars a month on the deal. Everybody's happy, you know?"

"Twenty-five dollars isn't that much. Why didn't he just break the lease and have his mail forwarded to wherever he was living?"

The man was beginning to relax, or maybe he was just too stoned to stay anxious. He yawned, leaned against the doorjamb, scratched the gingery hair under one freckled arm. "I don't know. He had moved in with this chick, and he needed every peso he could get. Maybe he wasn't sure it was going to last. We kind of left it open. I knew if he showed up here before his lease was up, I had to let him have it back. Those are the breaks."

Moved in with some chick. Tess was having a little problem getting past that one piece of information. When she didn't say anything right away, Maury jumped in.

"So when was the last time you saw him?"

He needed to think about this. "September? Anyway, a while ago. He came by, picked up his mail, not that there was much, a letter from Virginia, which he told me to mark 'Return to sender.' Although he always looked real carefully, as if he thought something else might be in there, too. He told me he was going to be out of pocket for a while, but promised he'd keep paying the rent. I hope so. I'd hate to lose this place."

From what Tess could see through the open door, it wouldn't be much of a loss. The remodeling of the old house had been done as cheaply as possible. The walls looked like painted cardboard, the kitchen wedged into one corner was nothing more than a two-burner stove and a half-sized refrigerator.

"Did you have a number for Crow? For Ed, I mean."

"A number? Oh, you mean like for the phone." He wandered back into the apartment, scratching himself at intervals, until he found a scrap of paper on the floor, near his own phone. "I think this is it."

Tess glanced at it, then checked it against her date book. "This is the number he had here, before it was disconnected."

"Oh, yeah, that makes sense. It was disconnected for a while, but I got it turned back on." He crumpled it into a ball and tossed it on the floor.

"What about the girl, the one he had moved in with?" This was Maury again. Tess would have to tell him later that they were not partners in this enterprise, that he was to stop asking questions. "Did you know her? Do you know where they lived?"

Another yawn, another scratch. "Naw. I saw her once, when Eddie stopped by. She was pretty, like a little doll. Real blond hair, big blue eyes, and cheeks that looked like she had little pink circles painted on them, but natural, you know? I noticed her because she looked like one of the sorority girls around here, except kind of sad-looking, too. Like she was tuned into some frequency only she could hear. He called her lady. At first, I thought it was generic, like 'my old lady.' But it might have been her name."

"Blond hair, blue eyes, pink cheeks, sad-looking. Anything more, uh, specific?"

He shook his head. "Naw. Beautiful girls are everywhere in Austin. You get kind of numb to them after a while. Not numb, exactly, but you stop making those real fine distinctions. It's like eating too much Mexican food. Just burns out your taste buds."

Maury nodded in commiseration. Tess was mystified—she hadn't noticed that Austin was so burdened with pulchritude, although she had observed that bodies here ran to a taut, lean look quite unlike the mesomorphs back home.

"Here's the number where I'm staying, please have him call if he should stop by again." She handed over one of her business cards, skeptical of how it would fare in this apartment's filing system. "One last thing, do you know where he played?"

"Played what?"

"With his band. Where did they perform?"

"I didn't even know he was in a band, but I guess everyone in Austin is. Everyone who's not a movie star or in software," he amended. "Man, what you damn Yankees have wrought."

"Yankee? Crow was from Virginia and I live in Baltimore. Check a map sometime, Maryland lies below the Mason-Dixon line."

"You telling me you're a Southerner?"

It was an astute question, one no Baltimorean could answer. The map said one thing, the city's architecture said something else, its race relations something else again. It was both, it was neither. "Just giving you a little geography lesson."

"What's this about, anyway? Eddie in trouble? He seemed like a good guy, but you never know."

Tess avoided his questions by asking one of her own. "What do you do, anyway?"

"Me? I'm a student."

"You look like you're almost thirty."

"Try thirty-five. But I'll have my master's by the time I'm forty if I don't get distracted again, wander off to Mexico for a while. I worked a couple years down in San Miguel de Allende, but that's almost too American now. I'm thinking Merida, maybe farther down the coast in the Yucatan. Tulum. Or I could just keep going, all the way to Belize. I don't know. Whatever comes next."

"Whatever comes next," she repeated to Maury, once they were back in the car.

"What does come next?" he asked. "Where do you want to go now?"

"I was just quoting Crow's tenant. Seems like an enviable way to live. Except that when I lived that way, I didn't realize how free I was. I just thought I was unemployed."

Maury held his forefinger and thumb out toward her. "You are about this close to singing a Joni Mitchell song and you don't even know it."

"No, what I'm saying is that things are different here. In warm climates, people are more relaxed about being down on their luck, because spending a night outside isn't a matter of life and death."

"So, you don't have any homeless guys up in Baltimore?" he asked.

"Okay, my theory needs a little refining." Still, there was something in the weather here, or the water, that changed one's perceptions of time and possibilities. If Crow had caught this local fever, he could be anywhere.

With anyone.

5

They took a break, heading back to Quadling Country to wile away the hours until the clubs started opening. A late-afternoon run along the paths near Town Lake gave Tess a glimpse into Austin's charms. Here was a city that worshipped fitness, that accommodated those who exercised. Quite unlike Baltimore, where chain-smoking drivers liked to force runners off the roads for the sheer sport of it. It should have been a perfect fit for her. If only Tess believed in perfect fits. Thanks to Kitty, she had been raised on the real Brothers Grimm, where Cinderella's sisters sliced off their toes and heels to cram their feet into that stupid glass slipper.

A few scullers and sweep rowers were working out, and she found she missed her own unpretentious little Alden. The rowing season was almost over in Baltimore, she would lose some of the best days if she stayed here too long. But she would be home soon, she reminded herself. Things were simpler than she or Crow's parents had realized. He had moved out to be with a woman. She'd probably find him—and her—on Sixth Street tonight. All she had to do was walk him to a pay phone, and she was out of here.

So why had he stopped calling his parents? she asked herself, as she ran along Town Lake. How to explain the postcard? Crow might still be angry enough to play such a prank on her, but why would he want to worry his parents?

Her best guess was that carelessness was the prerogative of sons and daughters everywhere, at every age. After all, she hadn't called her parents since she arrived in Texas, and she waited to phone Tyner's office until last night, when she was sure of getting the machine. There were times when one was in too much of a hurry—or too much in love—to stop and talk to anyone.

It was after ten and they were walking north along the street that bordered the west side of the UT campus when Maury said: "You want to stop and get something to eat? I'm dragging. There's a good place not too far."

"Vegetarian?" Tess asked skeptically. She was dragging, too, although not from hunger. It had been depressing, going from music club to music club, showing photos of Crow—one as Tess had known him, with his dyed dreadlocks, and the one in the newspaper clipping. *Have you seen him? Have you seen him?* No one had.

"Barbecue."

"Barbecue? I thought you had given up red meat."

"Sure, at home. But I can eat what I want when I'm out—as long as I brush my teeth before I come home. I can come home smelling of marijuana, but if Dad catches a whiff of burger on me, I'm grounded."

The thing was, no one here knew Crow or Edgar or Ed or Eddie. They had started with the better places, along Sixth Street, where the local headliners played. And, as Maury kept telling her, a local headliner in Austin was a pretty big deal in the city that was home to Willie Nelson, Shawn Colvin and a lot of other people that Tess had never heard of. Then they had worked their way out and out and out, in ever-widening circles, until they were checking depressed little bars where some kid might be allowed to play in the silences between televised sporting events. Still, no one remembered a guy named Ransome, with or without a doll-like girl.

Now she and Maury were walking through the university section, just in case Crow and his band had been reduced to playing for handouts.

"Or we could go to Sonic," Maury offered. "Get a chili dog."

Tess could accept that no one had hired Crow, although she had always thought Poe White Trash as good as any punk band she had heard. It was harder to believe that no one remembered him. Crow had been so vivid, so alive. He had always made an impression on people.

"Can't you even remember if he ever came in here looking for work?" Tess had asked one club manager.

The manager was the kind of person who never made eye contact, keeping his gaze riveted over one's shoulder, in case someone more interesting might appear on the horizon.

"You know how many kids I see in a typical week? Everyone who gets off the Greyhound thinks he's going to be Austin's next whatever. The place is like Hollywood in the forties. Everyone wants to live here."

"Really?" Tess had said. "I don't."

He met her eyes then, in order to scoff properly. "As if you *could*."

"So what do you say?" Maury demanded.

"To what?"

"Barbecue or chili dogs. Ruby's is right up here at the top of the Drag, if you don't mind walking a little ways."

"The Drag?"

"Guadalupe Street, the very concrete beneath your feet. Hey, is there anything you want to see on campus? We could cut through there, if you like. Maybe you could post WANTED signs or something on the community bulletin boards."

Tess looked at the utility poles of Guadalupe Street, so covered with fliers that they might be made of papier-mâché. "I don't think so."

"Don't you want to see the campus, anyway? See the Tower?"

"The Tower?"

"Charles Whitman, baby." Maury's eyes lighted up. "Did you know that there was, like, this whole family that was shot inside the Tower that day and they lay there—lie there? *lay* there—throughout the whole thing and one of them was *alive*."

"How interesting," Tess said. Still, she understood why Maury would find such a tale fascinating, as long as it was in the abstract. Paradoxical as it might sound, it was often the very lack of experience that made people calloused. She considered telling him some of the things she had seen in the past year. A couple gunned down in their bed. A body in a ditch. A cab coming out of the fog to dispatch a young man in the prime of his life. All the "reality" shows on television couldn't make you understand what it was like to be there at the exact moment when life ended, when someone's soul, for want of a better word, ebbed from the body. But Maury was a boy, a handsome, happy boy who sold comic books for a living. He wasn't remotely interested in reality, which made him a strangely agreeable companion.

As she and Maury walked, she continued to scan the faces of the buskers and hustlers along the Drag. A young woman played her violin, a lovely classical air soaring over the street, but she didn't even look up when coins dropped into her open case. They passed a little open-air market with glass and beaded jewelry, a textbook store crammed with burnt orange and white accessories. A young man sat on top of a trash can, whaling away on a set of bongos.

A young man she knew. Well, she was overdue for one brilliant moment of plain, unadulterated good luck.

"Gary!"

It took him a second to register that someone was calling his name, and there seemed to be far too much subtext in the changes his expression went through on its way to recognition. Confusion, the momentary joy of spotting a familiar face in a land of strangers. Finally, he settled for something petulant and sulky.

"Tess Monaghan. Fancy meeting you here."

"Ditto."

"So, what's up?"

"Maybe you can tell me. I'm looking for Crow."

"Good luck." He unfold his legs, crawled down from the top of the trash can. "I haven't talked to that fucker in weeks."

"What about Poe White Trash?"

"Deader than its namesake. The name never did go over down here. The few times we got a gig, usually at some freebie festival, someone would call the *Chronicle* and complain about our name. 'Inherently racist in its implication that other cultures don't meet the same standards of normative behavior.' Someone actually wrote that in a letter to the editor. Normative behavior. I thought it should be our new name."

"You're kidding me."

"About the name, not about the letter. Welcome to PC city, hon, and I'm not talking about the computer industry."

"So the band broke up? Where did everyone go? Where's Crow?"

"*Crow* broke up the band. Said he was going in a new direction, literally and artistically, but it was really her fault."

Crow's mysterious female companion again. "Blond girl? With features like a china doll?"

"Blond, sure, but I don't know about any doll," Gary said, rubbing his chin, as if trying to stimulate growth in the wispy, halfhearted goatee there, a new affectation. "Unless you're talking Chuckie, from those slasher movies. She Yoko'ed us but good. Once

Crow met her, it was like I didn't even know him anymore. He suddenly wanted to do all this indigenous shit. He even asked me if I could learn to play the accordion. I told him he could take that Lawrence Welk shit and shove it up his ass."

"When was this?"

"Summer, I guess. Like it's not summer now. I remember it was hot. Then again, it's been hot since we got here in May. July? August? I don't know. A while. The other guys went back to Baltimore. I thought I'd give Austin a try. I mean, the winters here gotta be better, right?" He was pleading, his voice as urgent as any panhandler's. "A whole summer gone, and I haven't had a single steamed crab."

Tess had no patience for seafood reveries. "Where is Crow now? Is he in a new band? What's the name of this blond girl?"

"You know, I never knew her full name. She called herself Emmie, just one fucking name, like Madonna. She was performing under the name Lady M when we met her. But she had a place out in the Hill Country, I know that much. She and Crow crashed there sometimes. She said Austin wasn't the place to be anymore, and he believed her. He believed every stupid shit thing that came out of her mouth."

"Where's the Hill Country?"

"It's the area west of Austin and it's a pretty big place. LBJ's home," Maury put in. "You're going to need more than that to go on."

Gary glared at Maury, as if this strapping young Texan was responsible for everything that had gone wrong for him in the Lone Star State. "I know that. I'm not stupid. It began with a B."

"Boerne?" Tess asked, remembering the postmark on Crow's note to her.

"Naw, but somewhere like that. Bingo? Boffo? Blanco! He's in Blanco, OK? Or near there. I remember because of the White Album. But I think the town was called something like Two Sisters."

Tess was still mystified, but Maury nodded, smiling. "Now that's something to go on. Twin Sisters's a small enough place so a stranger might stick out."

Two lucky breaks in fifteen minutes—finding Gary, finding a lead. Tess just hoped she hadn't blown her serendipity account for all eternity.

"Okay, I'll head down there tomorrow."

"But what about dinner tonight?" Maury put in plaintively.

"Sure, fine, your pick."

"Barbecue. Chili dogs? Barbecue."

"Barbecue's good here," Gary said, his tone grudging.

Maury inspected the dejected drummer. He was wearing a Mencken's Cultured Pearl T-shirt with the sleeves ripped out and his arms were scrawny and sunburned. He had managed a haircut recently, but that only called attention to the white stripe on his bright red neck. "You want to join us? My treat, because I hate to hear of someone having a bad time in my hometown. Don't you know this is Eden?"

"Yeah, well, the snake and the broad with the apple have already been here and gotten me kicked out," Gary said. "But I could go for some barbecue, I guess."

There was precious little that was white about Blanco County. The hills were brown, with outcroppings of rock, the highway black, the cloudless sky above so blue, and so huge that Tess felt paradoxically claustrophobic, as if a gigantic sheet had been thrown over her. It seemed she could drive for days and days and never arrive anywhere.

Still, it was a relief just to be alone for a while, no one but Esskay for company. Not that solitude had come easily. Maury, sensing a payoff might be near, had wanted to continue on his whole Bwana trip. She had wanted to confront Crow alone. Perceptive Keith had told Maury that he had to cover the store while Keith ran errands that afternoon. She had left him sulking behind the counter, pretending to read a new comic book.

The town of Blanco wasn't much more than a small grouping of buildings and a sign warning that the speed limit had dropped. Tess, still wedded to her Old Western version of Texas, had expected a dusty Main Street flanked by late nineteenth-century buildings with porches, maybe a saloon. It passed by in less than five minutes, and in another five minutes she had found the dance hall and convenience store that seemed to be the sum of Twin Sisters.

The girl behind the counter was bright-eyed and friendly, a little too happy to be working as a cashier in the local convenience store. Just the kind of personality Tess had hoped to find—an outgoing busybody who engaged every passerby in conversation. The photograph of a boy in a football uniform was taped to the cash register.

"How're you doing today?" the girl asked, her voice as loud and enthusiastic as a big puppy on the loose.

"Fine, just fine," Tess replied.

Experience had taught her it was better to come at things slantwise. People trusted you more if you didn't seem too focused. She grabbed a Coke, then tried to find some regional specialty among the junk food. Alas, another aspect of American life gone totally generic. While some of her favorites were missing—Goldenberg Peanut Chews, Fifth Avenues, Clark Bars—there didn't appear to be any local equivalents to take their place.

"You looking for something in particular?" the clerk asked.

"In a manner of speaking. I want something I've never had before."

The girl's eyes widened, as if this was a strange, almost subversive thing to say.

"I mean, candy-wise," Tess explained. "What's the point of traveling if everything is the same wherever you go?"

"We've got some of these Mexican candies here by the cash register, pralines and such. These ones look like the Mexican flag." The girl held up what appeared to be a block of solid sugar, striped red, green and white. The red had faded, as if the candy had been sitting out in the sun for a very long time. "And you could always have a Big Red, I guess, instead of that Coke."

"What does Big Red taste like?"

"Truthfully?" The girl looked around, making sure there was no one to overhear her. "Ground-up pencil erasers. But it is local."

"I guess I'll stick with the Coke. And a moon pie. I can't get that back home."

"Really? There are places where they don't have moon pies? Imagine that."

Yee-haw. If she saw a swimming pool, she'd probably call it a "cement pond." But Tess held her tongue and put her money on the counter. "So I guess life is pretty quiet around here."

"Yeah. They say movie stars are moving out here, but I've never seen one. Of course, they're all up closer to Fredericksburg way, but you think we might get a little one. Like Pauly Shore."

Tess laughed. The girl had a spark of wit to her. Maybe she'd escape Twin Sisters after all, if she could avoid getting knocked up by the football hero boyfriend.

"As it happens, I was up in Fredericksburg, looking for someone," Tess said, pulling out the two photographs. "Not a movie star, but maybe you recognize him?"

"I know this one," she said, pointing to what Tess now thought of as the "Ed" picture. "He came in and bought groceries last month, just before school began. I remember, 'cause I work the earlier shift in the summer. He was staying up at the Barretts' place."

"Is Emmie Barrett a young woman with blond hair?"

"Oh, no'm." Tess didn't find the shortened version of ma'am any less painful. "But I know the blond girl you're talking about. I saw her, too, but she stayed in the car."

"What did she look like?" Tess was counting on a woman to come up with something more precise than a china doll or Yoko Ono.

"Blond, like you said. Big eyes, or maybe they

looked big 'cause her face is so skinny and small. She looks as if she hasn't been getting enough to eat, to tell you the truth."

Could there be more than one blond woman in Crow's life? Tess couldn't decide if she would prefer this to the idea that he was traveling with some chameleon who appeared differently to everyone who met her.

"You remember the car?"

"Yes'm, because it was a real nice Volvo, but he counted his money out careful-like, as if he wasn't sure he would have enough to pay for the groceries and the gas." Crow had driven a Volvo, a castoff car from his parents, complete with the private school stickers of his privileged youth. "He was polite, I'll say that for him. A lot of the new folks coming through here aren't very nice."

Yeah, yeah, yeah, spare me another anti-Yankee diatribe, Tess thought. "The Barrett place—could you tell me how to get there?"

The girl's eyes, already so bright, seemed to shine with excitement. "Is he in trouble?"

"Not at all," Tess assured her. "I've been hired to find him because—because he has a huge windfall waiting for him. Only heir to a large—well, I probably shouldn't say anymore."

"My *good*ness. Well, sure, I guess there's no harm in telling you how to get up to the Barrett place, although I haven't seen him for more'n a month, it seems to me now. Here, let me draw a map for you. You know what a Ranch Road is? They're paved, it's not as rugged as it sounds, but they're not on all the maps."

* * *

Many minutes of chatter later, Tess emerged with the directions and a second moon pie. The Barrett place, as the helpful cashier had told her, was a weekend place owned by an old San Antonio family. Twenty minutes from the convenience store, she turned her Toyota onto a gravel driveway. A small limestone house stood at the end of a long fieldstone path. There was no car in the drive, Volvo or otherwise.

But he had been here. She trusted her information. More importantly, she trusted her feelings, and she could sense his presence here.

She walked up the path and tried the front door. Locked. She walked around to the rear, which had a small patio with a pool, overlooking the hills. Hill Country—she got it now. It really was quite pretty here—endless vistas of soft hills, blue sky, a temperature of eighty-five this late in October. The only ugly note were the gnarled and stunted trees, which bent toward the ground like sour old women. Some were pecans, Tess could see the nuts coming in. The others were a mystery to her. Cottonwoods? Maury had been prattling about something that sounded like Wee-satches as they drove around Austin, but she hadn't paid close attention to his travelogue.

The back door was locked, too. Tess went to the Toyota and returned with a glass cutter from the old-fashioned picnic hamper she kept in her trunk. She had been accumulating the tricks of her trade— the gun, the lock picks (which she couldn't quite master), and this sweet little glass cutter, her favorite by far. She removed one pane, complimenting herself on her neatness, put the piece of glass aside, reached in and unlocked the door.

The house looked unused. No, the house looked as if someone wanted it to look unused. An important distinction. Covers over the furniture, no dishes out, garbage emptied, nothing in the old-fashioned refrigerator except ice—in trays and caked on the sides. Dusty cans of pork and beans and succotash were the only things in the cupboard. But Tess was convinced that the house had been inhabited, and fairly recently.

She opened the cabinet below the sink, found a wrench and took apart the pipe. She had dropped enough earrings down the drain to know how to do this quickly and efficiently. Exactly what she had expected—a few pieces of pulpy bits that had been washed into the sink, rotted and ripe-smelling, but evidence that people had been here, and not that long ago.

She wandered through the small house, hopeful of finding more clues. Weekend houses were such strange places, sterile even when they weren't rented out to others. A line from a favorite short story surfaced in the strange little swamp of her mind: something about the secrets of summer houses, which no real house would deign to keep. Not only could she find no traces of Crow, but she really couldn't discern anything about the owners. Rich, presumably, because they had this place. Yet the house wasn't opulent, far from it. It looked sad and lonely to her, not so much neglected as disowned and forgotten.

She left the house, wiping her fingerprints from

the surfaces she remembered touching, putting away her tools. What now? Where now? She found herself drawn back to the view. The sun was sinking below the hills, and the shadows were purple. In the violet light, she noticed a shed in a grove of trees that looked as if it had been converted into a pool house.

She walked over and tried the old wooden door. It was stuck, probably swollen from years of moisture and heat. She yanked harder, and it recoiled on her, almost knocking her off her feet.

What the door couldn't do, the smell accomplished. She fell to her knees, retching reflexively. For here was something much more pungent than a few carrot peelings: a nice, ripe human body in brand-new blue jeans and a denim shirt, a gaping hole in the chest, the face blown away for good measure, as if this was someone so reviled he had to die twice.

6

The sheriff held a metal wastebasket beneath Tess's chin. It was the third time she had thrown up in the hour she had been here, and his courtly manner was wearing thin, exposing the hard little kernel of his personality. The first two times she had gotten sick, he had let her leave his office and visit the ladies' room, a secretary posted outside the door. Such niceties were now officially over.

"Is that it?" Sheriff Kolarik asked.

"Probably. I haven't eaten that much today."

"Remind me to be thankful for small favors."

He meant it to be funny, but it didn't quite come off. The sheriff was young, no more than thirty-five or so. Maybe even younger. He had shiny black hair, shinier in the band where his hat had rested, and blue eyes that were almost too bright. Medium height and weight, not exactly the iconic Texas sheriff that pop culture had taught Tess came in two varieties—pot-bellied redneck and Gary Cooper. But his face was tanned and the sun had etched lines at the corner of his eyes and mouth. He also had a deep crease across the bridge of his nose, as if he squinted too much. That crease seemed to be growing deeper the longer Tess was in his office.

"Now tell me again what brought you to the old Barrett place," he suggested in a would-be friendly tone.

"I told you. I got lost and I stopped to ask directions."

"All the way from Baltimore, Maryland. I'd say you were lost."

He was looking at her PI's license, which was on his desk along with her cell phone and every other piece of plastic from her wallet, even her Nordstrom credit card, a relatively new link in her identity chain. Jackie had convinced her to start wearing makeup this fall, taking her to the M.A.C. counter and buying her the darkest lipstick Tess had ever used. Paramount. She seldom applied it, but she liked knowing she had it in her purse, in case a lipstick emergency came up. This little black tube was also rolling across the sheriff's desk. Esskay was sleeping in the corner, unperturbed by the day's events, although the sheriff had threatened to take her to the nearest hospital and have her X-rayed. He had heard of people smuggling things in dogs, he had told Tess. She had countered that one would probably use a fatter dog for such an operation, as opposed to one on which you could count each rib.

"Theresa Mon-a-ghan," the sheriff said. He hit the G hard, but something in his smart-alecky smile told Tess he knew better. "What brings you down this way, Miss Mona-ghan?"

"Vacation."

"You must be doing well. Most folks who work for themselves don't get to take many vacations. I know. I used to be one of them."

Tess pretended the interest he obviously expected of her. Baltimore or Blanco, in a bar or behind bars, the one thing men wanted to do was talk about themselves. "Really? What did you do?"

"Started a software company, then sold it for a lot of money. I'm a millionaire, and not just on paper. I moved out here thinking I'd take it easy, got bored in about six weeks and ran for sheriff. I spent one hundred thousand dollars on my campaign, and the only reason I won was because the incumbent died the day before the general election. That was six years ago. They like me now. Returned me to office with sixty percent of the vote last time around."

He leaned across the desk toward Tess, hands clasped as if he were praying. "You see, they like me because I don't take shit from the outsiders who are moving here. Converts make the best adherents, you know. I hate outsiders more than any fourth-generation Hill Country type ever could."

Message received: She wasn't to treat him like some local yokel, nor should she contemplate filling out a change-of-address card anytime soon.

"So, let me rephrase my question. You sure you're here on vacation? Or is there something going on in my county I should know about, something that would bring a private investigator all this way? Something that has to do with that ripe ol' boy you found?"

Against her will, she once again saw the vivid image of the body in the shed, its face missing, along with most of the chest. If it was Crow, her job was done. That was the possibility that had first made her nauseated. She grabbed the metal trash can, just in case.

"I'd like an answer, Miss Monaghan."

But she knew in her heart that it wasn't Crow. Death and rot could do a lot to a body, but the frame she had seen in the shed wasn't his. The legs had been thicker, shorter, with the cuffs of the jeans rolled up over a pair of fairly new-looking cowboy boots. Even if Crow had gone Texan with a vengeance, he couldn't find a pair of jeans so long that he'd be forced to roll them up over a pair of cowboy boots. Besides, the boots had been tacky, overdone. Cowboy Crow would have preferred something more authentic.

"Miss Monaghan?" Sheriff Kolarik handed her a paper towel to wipe her face, but he was clearly out of patience with her. "You going to answer my question?"

Yet Crow had been there, she was sure of that. Surer still that the sheriff must not know.

"I'm on vacation. I was looking for a shortcut to the LBJ ranch when I got lost."

"You think that's going to butter me up, throwing around LBJ's name? Well, I'm a Republican," the sheriff said, as if everyone should know this fact. Software millionaire turned sheriff, he probably had been written up in some of the national papers. Tess couldn't help wondering if there was any corner of the world where oddity was allowed to flourish for its own sake, unchronicled and unknown.

"Look, if you don't trust me, call Martin Tull.

He's a detective in Baltimore City's homicide division. He'll vouch for me."

"He'll say you were on vacation, will he, and looking for the LBJ ranch? He must know you pretty well, to have such a detailed itinerary."

"No, I mean—he'll tell you that I can be trusted. In fact—" She tried a winning smile, then realized it wasn't the most appropriate expression under the circumstances. "We met over a dead body, Martin and I."

Sheriff Kolarik opened up her M.A.C. lipstick. "Kinda dark," he commented. "This other body you found—was it on someone's private property almost a mile from the road? You see, trespassing is the issue here, ma'am, not homicide. Marianna Barrett Conyers doesn't get up here much from San Antonio, so we keep a close eye on her property. She's good people."

"I got lost and I stopped to ask for directions," Tess repeated. "After I realized no one was there, I wandered around the property, just because it was so pretty. As for the guy in the pool house—well, once I got downwind, it was hard to miss him."

"Hardly any breeze blowing today, Miss Monaghan. You sure you weren't looking for something else? Maybe a little souvenir to take home from your 'vacation'?"

"He didn't need any breeze, he was, as you said, pretty ripe." She widened her eyes, hoping she looked innocent. "He must have been dead a real long time, don't you think?"

"You do know your dead bodies, Miss Monaghan."

She sensed a trap, despite the sheriff's bland intonations. "Not really. I just watch *Homicide* a lot." Then, as an inane afterthought. "It's filmed in Baltimore, right in my neighborhood."

"That show's no good. None of those cop shows are. Although I like Chuck Norris in that Texas Ranger one. They filmed a scene up in Kerrville once. He's a little-bitty fellow, but all those actors are." The sheriff held his thumb and forefinger apart, in an approximation of Chuck Norris's little-bittiness.

"I don't know," Tess said. "Some of the guys on *Homicide* are pretty tall." The conversation was stupid, but safe. Then again, every minute she spent here gave the chatty convenience clerk more opportunities to tell someone about the inquisitive Yankee who had come in looking for local candy and some dark-haired fellow, and left with directions to the old Barrett place.

The sheriff also seemed anxious to get back to business. "So anyway, you find this body, which you know, from the smell, has been dead a long time because you watch a lot of television, and you called 911 on your little cell phone. Why do you have one of those things, anyway? You running drugs through my county?"

"The Baltimore drug market doesn't have to look to Texas for its supplies."

"Yeah, everybody's on crack up there, right?"

A conscious self-mockery edged his every word. The sheriff was playing with his role, Tess realized, shifting in and out of the stereotype as it suited his purpose. He was joking now, and testing her to see if she got the joke.

"Just about. Although heroin's making a comeback. It's sort of like the rivalry between Coca-Cola and Pepsi."

He opened his desk drawer, rummaged around, and pulled out a pack of Dentyne, took his time unwrapping a piece. "But even though you had a cell phone, you said you went inside the house, right, to see if there was a phone connected there, right? Did you notice that pane of window cut out of the back door?"

"Of course I did." Tess sensed he was trying to lead her someplace, someplace she didn't want to go. She had admitted to being in the house in case she had left a print behind, but she wasn't fool enough to admit to being the one who had broken in. She straightened up, throwing her shoulders back and showing her Cafe Hon T-shirt to what she hoped was full advantage. It was the one T-shirt she had brought from home, back when she thought she was making a quick overnight trip to Charlottesville. She and Crow had bought their Cafe Hon shirts together, and she had donned hers that morning, thinking that it would remind him of the times they had shared. She had been so sure that she was going to find him today.

"And the reason you just didn't use your cell phone to begin with—?"

"The roaming fees on my service are really high."

"Uh-huh. Now here's the thing I'm wondering. Who cut the glass?"

Tess wondered if it was possible to leave too few fingerprints behind. Did he need a warrant to open her trunk? She had the presence of mind to hide her tools in the spare tire well, and she put her gun there, too, as she still wasn't sure if her license to carry was good in Texas.

"Who cut the glass, Miss Monaghan? You can tell me."

"But I don't know."

"Well, who do you think? What would be logical?"

"The dead guy?"

The sheriff pretended to think about her answer. "Okay, I see what you're saying. This guy was trying to break in when someone came along, shot him, and then put him in the shed. Or maybe Mrs. Conyers was up here from San Antonio one weekend and shot a prowler, then forgot to mention it to me."

Tess had been nauseous so long now that it was beginning to seem normal to her. She wondered if her stomach would flip and jump inside her for the rest of her life. "I thought it was the Barrett place."

"Really?" He grinned, sure he had her. "Who told you that?"

"You did. Remember? You asked me what I was doing up at the old Barrett place."

The sheriff had a poker face, but his body was not quite as disciplined. His chest seemed to collapse a little, and he rubbed his index finger and thumb together, almost as if he had felt the fabric of her shirt in his hand, only to have her wriggle free.

"Barrett was her maiden name. The Barretts go way back in this county. They go way back in Texas."

"What's that—thirty, forty years?" Of course, no one in Tess's family had arrived until the 20th century was well under way, but the sheriff didn't know that.

"Texas was a free-standing republic in 1836."

"That's right," Tess said agreeably. "You seceded from Mexico so you could have slaves, right?"

The sheriff was not impressed that she knew this particular bit of Texas history. "Now here's the thing. That old boy up at the Barretts' wasn't killed there. No blood. No blowback. You know what that is, don't you? You shoot a man in the face with a rifle, there's going to be brains and stuff everywhere." He held up the trash can, but Tess shook her head. She had nothing left. But moon pies, through no fault of their own, would be forever banned from her diet. "So he was killed somewhere else, maybe not even in my county, and left here for me to clean up. Now that kinda pisses me off."

"I can see that."

"You got any idea who that ol' boy is, by the way?"

"*No*," she said, hoping it was the truth.

"So you didn't go poking around in his pockets." The sheriff grinned at the way her mouth thinned and tightened, her gag reflexes working again. But she just shook her head and swallowed.

"Well, given the condition of his body, we'll have to send him to the medical examiner, but his papers say he's Tom Darden, a recent guest of the state prison system over to Huntsville. A San Antonio boy. Cops down there tell us he's been hanging out with an old buddy of his, Laylan Weeks, who was sprung at the same time."

The sheriff leaned toward her, hands clasped in that prayerful position again, trying to look kind and concerned. But whereas a genuine good ol' boy might have been able to pull this off, this technocrat was nothing more than a virtual Bubba. Tess stared back at him, unmoved, determined to say nothing unless necessary.

"Now if you happened to have a glass cutter and you happened to use it to get into the house after you found ol' Tom, that wouldn't be quite the same as breaking and entering, see? We'd call that a mitigating circumstance."

His words offered no comfort to Tess. Who needed legal terms unless one was going before a judge?

"I've thought of something," she said suddenly.

The sheriff smiled.

"I guess his *buddy* had the glass cutter. The one that the San Antonio cops said he was running around with, since they got out of prison?"

"Laylan and Tom weren't burglars. According to what I've been told about them, they're the kind of boys who'd put their fists through the glass, and enjoy doing it."

"People change in prison. I mean, that's the point, isn't it?"

"Are you asking me or telling?"

She met his eyes directly. "Just guessing. That's legal, isn't it?"

"It depends on what kind of guesses you make."

"Here's one: I'm guessing you don't have any reason to hold me and I'd like to go now. Unless you're going to detain me and charge me. In which case, I'd like to call a lawyer."

"Why would I charge you?"

"I don't know. That's what I've been wondering

for the almost two hours you've held me here. I got lost. Okay, I trespassed up on the old Barnes place. Fine me, I'll pay it."

"Barrett."

"I found a dead body and I called the police. *The sheriff.* I guess it's true, no good deed goes unpunished."

"Did you know Tom Darden or Laylan Weeks, Miss Monaghan?" The sheriff was no longer taking the time to mispronounce her name, and what little drawl he had was gone, replaced with a clipped, precise voice. "You one of those girls who likes bad boys? Did you hook up with these two and find you were over your head? Because they're pretty bad. They've done things that you don't want to know about."

"I've been in Texas for less than seventy-two hours. I haven't had a chance to make any new friends." She stood up, reached for the Dentyne pack he had left on the desk. "I have been staying with some friends of my aunt up in Austin, and they'll be wondering where I am. So if you don't mind—"

"I'll want a number where you're staying up in Austin," the sheriff said. "And one back home."

"Sure," Tess said. She gave him her own home phone number. Let him talk to the mechanized version of herself. As for Keith's number—well, if the sheriff called there, Keith would tell him she had gone back to Baltimore. Because that's what she planned to tell Keith. Her work was done, she was heading home, taking the scenic route, stretching the 1,600-mile trip over several days. Let the sheriff call out the highway patrol in every state between

Texas and Maryland. They'd never find her there—because she'd be here.

Even as the sheriff had tried to pry information out of her, he had provided her with the next lead she needed. The Barrett place, the last place Crow had been, a place where a convict's body lay rotting in the pool house, belonged to one Marianna Barrett Conyers of San Antonio, just eighty miles south of Austin according to the sign posts she had seen that afternoon.

Maybe she'd get to see the Alamo, after all.

7

The front desk clerk at the Marriott in downtown San Antonio took one look at Tess, with
her wrinkled T-shirt and unraveling braid, and announced he had nothing for her. Esskay's presence
probably didn't help her cause, but the dog had
howled so piteously when Tess tried to leave her in
the car.

"No room at the inn. No room at any inn," he said,
showing off his teeth in a ravishing smile. He was
a handsome young Latino, a type Tess had always
found attractive, perhaps because it was in such
short supply in Baltimore. But this man's charm was
perfunctory and impersonal, a wall with no foot-
holds.

"There has to be a hotel room somewhere," she
said. The highway into the city had been one long
red blur of No Vacancy signs, so she had headed for
downtown, assuming the larger, expensive hotels
would be more likely to have rooms available. So
far, she had been turned away at three of them.

"Sorry. La Posada came early this year."

"La Posada?"

"La Posada. The inn. Around here, it's the reenactment of the Mary and Joseph story. The kids go from hotel to hotel on the Riverwalk, getting turned away. At least they get hot chocolate at the last hotel. All I can give you is some candy." He pushed a dish of brightly wrapped sour balls and Hershey kisses across the counter.

Tess sighed and, hating herself for it, called on those powers granted every reasonably attractive woman between the ages of thirteen and death. Her eyes widened, her voice sweetened, the coffee cup on her Cafe Hon T-shirt expanded just a little bit. "Are you sure there's *nothing* you can do for me?"

"Oh, there's a lot I could do for you," he said amiably, without a flicker of interest. "I just couldn't find a hotel room to do it in."

Aware that it would be hypocritical to be insulted—she had put the ball into play, after all—Tess rested her upper body on the counter and tried not to whimper audibly. The long day, with its singular events, was beginning to take its toll. All she wanted was a place to sleep for a little while. A place with room service, where she could shower and put on CNN at full volume, hoping it would drown out the night's sounds and the day's images.

"What's the deal, anyway?" she asked. She had been shooting for plaintive, but ended up whiny. "Why are all the hotels full?"

The clerk thawed a little then, as if he had been merely waiting for her to drop the bullying and bullshit. "There's a medical convention in town and then the All Soul Festival starts up mid-week. You won't find a room anywhere downtown. Especially not with *that*," he said, jerking his chin at Esskay. The dog reared up on her hind legs and propped herself on the front desk next to Tess, as if she were going to demand to speak to a manager. Instead she helped herself to a hard candy from the dish.

"She'll never be able to eat that," the attendant said. But he must have liked dogs better than humans. He stroked the dog's snout and scratched behind her ears, crooning something in Spanish.

"She eats charcoal briquets, too," Tess said. "Look, isn't there anywhere I can find a room? It doesn't have to be downtown. All I need is a place with a phone and a bed, something clean and safe."

Esskay coughed up a gnawed piece of red candy. Cinammon, Tess guessed. She didn't like spicy things.

"How loose are your standards on cleanliness and safety?" the attendant asked, as he looked for something to wipe up the pinkish drool on his counter. "I know a place maybe fifteen minutes from here, on Broadway next to the park. Look, I'll even call ahead for you, make sure they hold something."

"Great," Tess said. "What's it called?"

"La Casita. Ask for the daily rate. It's a better deal."

"As opposed to the weekly?"

He stifled a laugh. "As opposed to the hourly."

Mornings were quiet at La Casita, in marked contrast to the nights. Tess woke to the sound of a local news program, coming in on the television's only working channel. The television was bolted to the stand, just in case anyone developed a hankering for a 15-year-old Samsung *sans* remote.

Tess rolled out of bed and put on fresh clothes, taking a perverse pleasure in the spareness of her surroundings. Her clothes, her toothbrush, her copy of *Don Quixote*. It was Friday, she realized as she pulled on that day's allotment of underwear. She'd have to buy some Woolite, or drop in at a laundromat soon.

For a hooker motel, La Casita was nice enough, a Southwestern version of the Route 40 motor court that Tess had camped outside not even two weeks ago. Funny, it seemed like months had passed since that day, although in the wrong direction. When she cracked open the door of room number 103, the warm Texas autumn was so much like summer that she felt as if she had gone backward in time.

"Is it safe to walk around here?" she asked the elderly Vietnamese woman who sat in the front office, behind a Plexiglas shield with a pass-through for keys and money.

"Very safe, very safe," Mrs. Nguyen said. "Even in the park, very safe. Chris Marrou on Channel 5 *said*. You can walk to the river from here, walk to zoo, ride in the little cars on the wires, the ones above the trees."

"Sounds good."

Mrs. Nguyen shook her finger at her through the bullet-proof glass. "But don't talk to strangers, bad boys who ask you to go for ride, drink beer. They not good. Not good. They do things to girls who go with them. Chris Marrou *said*."

Although Tess didn't know this local oracle, Mrs.

Nguyen's warning made her feel cozy and cared for. She headed up Broadway, in order to get her bearings before trying the park. The neighborhood around La Casita wasn't seedy, but it had a jumbled look to it, as if it wasn't quite sure what it was, or what it wanted to be. There were inexpensive ethnic restaurants, the familiar fast-food chains, some upscale antiques stores, a secondhand book store, and the clothing store opened by Selena, the young Mexican-American singer killed by her own fan club president a few years back. Maybe Tess would go back to Baltimore with a sequined halter.

Within a few blocks, she came to a large museum set back from the street. The Witte Natural History Museum, according to its sign. She and Esskay walked around this and found themselves in a shadowy lane parallel to Broadway, on the park's edge. The zoo must be nearby—she had been able to hear a lion's roar last night. At least, she hoped it was a lion. Where was the river, though? If it were like Austin's Town Lake, maybe she could rent a scull somewhere. She missed rowing, her day felt unfinished without it.

But the San Antonio River proved to be a narrow, sluggish channel, smaller and shallower than the streams back home. "I thought everything was supposed to be bigger in Texas," she scoffed to Esskay. She'd be running and jumping rope for exercise as long as she was in San Antonio. She scouted a route and found a long, steep hill that ran above an amphitheater and past a Japanese-style garden.

Funny—she was worrying about running for exercise, when she should be worried about the fact that she was on the run. She would have to call Kitty, or Kitty's machine, and leave a detailed message about what to say if a certain sheriff called. Keith would play his part perfectly, for he truly believed she was heading back to Baltimore.

At the foot of the park, on a street called Mulberry, she stopped at a convenience store and bought breakfast—a large cup of coffee, a pint of orange juice, and a bag of Fig Newtons—and some dry dog food, dog treats, and a spiral-bound map book. It occurred to her she had gone almost five days without a bagel, and this single fact made her feel truly dislocated.

Back in the gloom of La Casita, she and Esskay stretched across the synthetic flowery spread and nibbled on Fig Newtons together as Tess paged through the phone book, which was thicker than she had expected. Even so, she found what she was looking for easily enough. Marianna Barrett Conyers lived on a street named for a sock, Argyle. There was no husband's name twinned with hers, and no coy initials to disguise the fact of a woman alone. Tess liked that in a woman, but only because it made a private investigator's job easier. *She* wouldn't have her own home number in the phone book for anything. Like most people who made their livings invading the privacy of others, she had become intensely protective of her own.

"Don't people know how easy it is to find them?" she asked Esskay. The dog appeared to think about this for a moment, then nudged Tess with her nose, demanding another cookie. Tess gave her a liver treat instead.

"Most people," Tess amended. "Everybody but the one person we want to find."

As it happened, Marianna Barrett Conyers wasn't quite that easy to find. According to the map, her house sat somewhere among a curving grid of streets in a place known as Alamo Heights, but Tess kept ending up on a long, narrow road below a flood plain, which took her away from the neighborhood and into another, similar-looking one on the wrong side of the highway. Finally, after she had crossed back for the third time, she found the right house.

It looked shy, if a house could be called that. The stucco exterior had been painted a soft olive green, the trim just one shade darker, allowing the house to disappear into the trees and plantings around it. Don't notice me, the house murmured. Drive on by, leave me alone.

A maid in a gray uniform answered the door, a tiny Mexican-American woman brandishing a broom. She looked at Tess as if she were a piece of dirt she wanted to sweep away as quickly as possible.

"You want to see Mrs. Conyers? What for? Who are you? She know you? I didn't think so. What do you want?"

Although the maid barely came up to her collarbone, Tess found herself taking a step back, out of arm's length, if not broom's length. "It's about what happened up at her country place," she said when the maid finally ran out of breath. She assumed Sheriff Kolarik had been in touch by now, that she need not go into too much gory detail.

"They've been here. She knows. It's got nothing

to do with her. Goodbye. We don't want any." The maid started to close the door on her, as Tess braced it with her foot. She didn't want to come on too strong, but she wasn't leaving without making her best effort.

"There are still things that have to be . . . discussed." Tess was trying to imply an official role without claiming one. "I was the one who found the body, you know."

"Really?" The maid was intrigued, but only for a moment. "So what?"

A voice called out from somewhere within the house. "Oh, let her in, Dolores. I guess I can stand two callers in one day."

Reluctantly the maid opened the door so Tess could pass, watching her to make sure she wiped her feet. Tess had thought she looked neat and professional, in her narrow, ankle-length skirt of blue plaid and a simple white T-shirt. She had even borrowed an iron from Mrs. Nguyen and gone to the trouble of putting her hair up. Dolores's sour gaze made her feel grubby and mussed.

Although the pale peach walls of the foyer were unadorned, the small study to which Tess was escorted looked as if a particularly ghoulish souvenir shop had exploded among the plain furnishings. Tess couldn't understand why anyone as wealthy as Marianna Barrett Conyers appeared to be would fill her home with such tacky, morbid things. One item might have suggested a certain camp sensibility, but this was true overkill, a virtual gallery devoted to death and rot.

A life-sized skeleton in 1890s garb walked a skeleton dog, grinning mouth clamped on a cigar, a corseted lady friend at his side. Other skeletons gazed from old woodcuts, while the built-in bookshelves held even more of their bony kin. There was a skeleton Mexican mariachi band, a skeleton bride and groom, a skeleton typing maniacally at a desk, her fluff of cotton ball hair standing on end, her head bouncing on a coiled spring of a neck.

Yet the skeletons proved to be the least ominous offerings here. A bright sun leered from the wall, a gaudy ceramic cathedral rose in the corner. But the most hideous piece by far was a flat-chested mermaid, wings sprouting from her bony shoulder blades, face frozen in a Munch-like scream. Just having this thing was in her house would give her nightmares, Tess thought.

"Do you like her, my little la sirena?" asked the woman sitting in a wing chair near the window.

Tess's high school Spanish was no help, but the context was obvious. La sirena, the siren. "Well, she's literally neither fish nor fowl, isn't she?" Tess took a seat on carved pine chair. The furniture, at least, was normal. "Interesting. All your things are . . . so interesting."

"Yes, I've been collecting for years." It was hard to see the woman's face, for the trees around the house kept the room dark. She had a glass of ice water at her side and a book in her lap, but Tess didn't see how she could read a single word in such deep shadows.

"I'm Marianna Barrett Conyers," the woman added, as if Tess might not know whose doorbell she had rung.

"I'm Tess Monaghan. I found the body, up at your country place yesterday."

"Yes."

Yes, what? Yes, you're Tess? Yes, you found a body? Yes, I have a country place?

"I told the deputies that I had gotten lost. That's not exactly what happened."

"Yes." A little less emphatic this time, more of a question.

"I was looking for someone. Someone who's been staying at your house."

She merely nodded at this piece of information and took a long sip from her water glass. Marianna Barrett Conyers was probably in her late forties, not much older than Kitty, but she seemed to cultivate the dress and aspect of an older woman. In Tess's admittedly limited experience, upper-class women knew how to be young and they knew how to be old, but few settled comfortably in their middle years. They either clung to a kittenish, jejeune look, with a little help from a friendly plastic surgeon, or they chose to mummify themselves prematurely. Mrs. Conyers's hair was set in stiff, careful waves, and her makeup was expertly thorough. Not just a little lipstick and mascara, but the whole deal, from foundation to eyebrow pencil. For all that, she was a woman better described as handsome rather than pretty, with blunt features that looked like a hasty first draft for a face.

"You were looking for someone," she repeated, as if thinking about this. "But you didn't tell the sheriff that."

"No."

"Why not?"

Tess needed only a second to come up with a plausible lie, but she had a feeling Marianna noticed that second. "My relationships with my clients are privileged."

"You're a lawyer, then?"

"No, but I work for one."

"A private investigator."

"Yes."

"Not from here."

"No."

"This reminds me of a game," said Marianna, closing her book and resting her chin on her palm. "Twenty questions. How many do I have left?"

"How about if we take turns and I ask a few? Did you have anyone staying at your house this summer?"

"Obviously I had at least one guest, the gentleman who was staying in the pool house." She smiled, pleased with herself.

"Did you have any *invited* guests?"

"Not precisely."

"Imprecisely."

Whatever delight Marianna had found in this conversation had disappeared as quickly as it had arrived. She was bored now, uninterested.

"My goddaughter has a key, she's allowed to come and go as she pleases. Someone might as well get some use out of the place. I haven't been up there for years, and I don't have any children of my own."

"Is your goddaughter a young blond woman named Emmie, who somtimes goes by the name of Dutch?" Tess decided to leave out the other details, the contradictory descriptions of china dolls, psycho bitches, and anorexic waifs.

"Dutch." Marianna smiled. "She hasn't used that name for years."

"She was using it up in Austin."

"Oh, yes, her music thing. Her real name is Emily Sterne. Emmie to the family. Why are you looking for her? Did . . . did something happen in Austin?"

"I'm not looking for her. I've never met her." Tess pulled out the photograph of Crow, the more recent one, the cutout with the words "In Big Trouble" above his head. "This is the man I want to find. He was in Twin Sisters with her, last I heard."

Marianna barely glanced at the photo. "And you're looking for him because of this—because it says he's 'in big trouble.'"

"Partly, yes. His parents haven't heard from him for more than a month, and they're worried."

"Parents always worry."

"I thought you said you didn't have children."

"No, but I had parents, didn't I? Did you think I came out of an egg?" Tess had touched some nerve. "Even Athena had parents, despite coming out of her father's head fully formed. It was Aphrodite, the goddess of love, who appeared out of the ocean with no explanation. She was the one to be feared, if you ask me. No, I had parents, and I caused them plenty of worry in their time. Yet here I am, a middle-aged woman, my life so safe and boring that it must be beyond their wildest dreams. They live in one of those senior residences. 'Assisted living.' Wonderful term. As if the rest of us can muddle through without assistance."

Tess tried to pull the conversation back on track. "This young man—his parents aren't overly protective. But he's never gone so long before without being in touch."

"I wish I had listened to my parents," Marianna muttered, reaching into a thick pile of newspapers in a leather-and-wood rack by her chair. She sorted through them, stopping to search what appeared to be a tabloid entertainment section, the kind that almost every newspaper publishes for the weekend. Tess noticed that the cover on one mentioned the All Soul celebration, the thing that the Marriott clerk had blamed for filling all the hotels. But Marianna rejected that one and kept going, almost to the bottom of the pile before she found what she wanted.

"Context is everything, don't you think? Miss— what was your name again, dear?"

"Tess Monaghan."

"Where are you from, anyway? I can't place your accent."

Tess hadn't known she had an accent. She definitely didn't have the drawn-out O's and misplaced R's of a typical Baltimorean. Then again, Marianna didn't have the Texas drawl she had expected. So far, no one here had sounded like what Tess thought a real Texan might.

"I'm from Baltimore."

"I could tell you weren't from the Southwest before you said a thing, by the way you reacted to my friends." She gestured to all the grinning skeletons. "You don't really like them, that's apparent. Not even my little mermaid."

Tess tried not to wince at the gruesome mer-woman. "She's not so bad."

"Context is everything," Marianna repeated. "You see my art and it makes you think of Halloween and other morbid things, but it's really all quite whimsical and sweet if you understand the Mexican traditions. Hopeful, even."

If you say so. But Tess just nodded politely.

"You see a photograph that says your friend is 'in big trouble' and you assume he must be."

Marianna was still flipping through the pages of the newspaper section. Finally she stopped, holding out her hand. Tess understood she wanted the photograph of Crow. Marianna took it and placed it down over the page in front of her, and turned it so Tess could see. Then she pulled the card away, and all was revealed.

It was as if the clipping she had been carrying was part of a jigsaw puzzle. For Crow now stood with three others, in what was obviously a publicity shot for a band. And "In Big Trouble" was part of a head-line: LITTLE GIRL IN BIG TROUBLE AT PRIMO'S TONIGHT. To Crow's right stood a blond woman with big eyes and a short bob. Her various personalities could not be discerned, but she was extraordinarily pretty. Beautiful, even.

"That's Emmie, of course."

"Of course." Tess placed an index finger on the young woman's likeness, as if that might tell her more about who she was, or where she was. "Did they call her Dutch because she looks like the boy on the Sherwin-Williams paint can?"

"The paint can?" Marianna laughed. It was a short,

not particularly infectious laugh, the laugh of a woman who rationed amusement to herself. "Oh no, the nickname isn't about being Dutch. The Sternes are German. Their family goes almost as far back as mine in San Antonio. The family cook, Pilar, called her Duchess when she was a baby, because she acted so imperious, and we shortened it to Dutch. I remember, she wasn't quite two, and she was so bossy, she tried to tell every-what to do. Pilar finally said, 'You'll be a duchess soon enough, for now you will listen to me.'"

She kept laughing, as if this were the funniest thing in the world. Tess felt the laugh went on a little too long and that it was a little too loud. It felt forced, artificial, like a middle-school girl on a giggling jag.

"I don't get it," Tess said. "Why would she be a duchess?"

"See, you need more context. San Antonio has a celebration, Fiesta, each spring, and girls are named to a court called the Order of the Alamo. There's a queen, a princess and all the rest are duchesses. Lollie and I were duchesses together almost thirty years ago. As it turned out Emmie was a princess—the Court of Dramatic Illusions, or Arabian Dreams. Something about dreams, I'm almost positive. Her dress will go to the Witte Museum."

Except for knowing what the Witte was, Tess was thoroughly lost. The Court of Dramatic Illusions, duchesses, princesses?

"Lollie?"

"Emmie's mother. She spoiled her so. Everyone did. First Lollie, then her cousin Gus, who raised

Emmie after Lollie died. Pilar was the only one in the family who ever stood up to that little girl."

"How did Emmie's mother die?"

She hadn't meant for the question to sound cold and rude, but apparently it came off that way.

"In an accident," Marianna said stiffly. "A car accident. She hasn't had a happy life, Emmie. Both her parents were dead before she was three and she never even knew her father. Lollie ran off with him at the end of her junior year in college and came back to San Antonio six weeks later, the marriage annulled, Emmie on the way. He was from El Paso, from a good family, but he was a careless man. Died in a hunting accident." Marianna frowned. "I never figured him for Lollie, not even in a momentary lapse. He was rather crude, really. Reckless. My latest mistake, she called him. That's what she called all her boyfriends. My latest mistake."

"How old is she now?"

"Emmie?" Marianna had been lost in her own thoughts, and needed a second to count up. "Twenty-three. She came into her trust fund five years ago. Gus wanted her to go to college, of course, but she wouldn't hear of it. She wants to be a singer. She is talented. A major record company tried to sign her when she was seventeen. Gus wouldn't give his consent. Perhaps that was the beginning of the end for them—they had a falling-out when she was eighteen and refused to go to college. But she seems happy. She bounces back and forth between Austin and San Antonio, changing bands and styles almost every month, it seems to me. She's very committed to her work, but she doesn't particularly care about commercial success."

It's not hard to keep your artistic integrity when you have an inheritance, Tess thought. "So now she's in a band with Crow?"

"Crow? Oh, your friend. Apparently so. You saw the photo. Although she changes band mates and band names almost as often as she changes clothes. Little Girl in Big Trouble was last month's incarnation. Who knows what she is today?"

"Did you know she and Crow were using your place this summer?"

"No. As I said, she's free to come and go as she pleases."

"Did you tell the sheriff that she had a key, that she might have been there?"

"Why should I?"

"Because a man was found murdered on your property."

"A man murdered somewhere else, according to the sheriff," Marianna pointed out. "Just another coincidence, Miss Monaghan, another situation requiring context. You think the two things are related because they're connected in *your* mind. You're like the old fable about the seven blind men, each trying to describe an elephant from feeling one part of it."

Tess took the newspaper from Marianna's hands.

"Is Little Girl in Big Trouble playing somewhere tonight?"

"I wouldn't know. I kept that because of Emmie's photo, but the paper is a month old, as you can see.

I don't recall seeing a listing for them in today's paper, though." She frowned, gave a convulsive little shudder. "I hate that name. I hope she has changed it by now."

"What's wrong with Little Girl in Big Trouble?"

"She took it from a headline in the paper, an old one from when the local press was more, well, colorful. She thought it was funny. I think it's bad luck to make fun of people's pain."

A strange superstition for someone who sat in a room full of skeletons. "About Dutch—Emmie—and Crow. They're in this band together, but are they, well, together-together?"

"Are you asking me if they're romantically linked? I don't know. I'm not Emmie's confidante in these matters. No one is. She's always been very private."

"But what do you think?"

"What do I think about what?" Marianna's smile was borderline cruel and Tess felt like a mouse being batted back and forth between a cat's paws. It was as if the woman was forcing her to say the words, to face the reality she was just beginning to realize she so dreaded.

"Are they in love?"

"I hope so," Marianna said, her voice strangely fervent. "I truly hope so."

8

Primo's, the bar where Crow's band had last played, was a local place, but it was so cheesy and soulless that it might as well have been part of a national chain. Tess's own neighborhood back in Baltimore had more than its share of these desperately zany places, where fun had to be planned and delineated with great care, and where the antibacterial cleansers overwhelmed the yeasty beer smell that a bar should have. They even had the same "theme" nights: Ladies' nights, mambo nights, Jamaica nights, Super Bowl night, cigar nights, two-for-one shooters, bottomless maragaritas.

Yet every night was the same. These bars were the cruise ships for Generation Whatever, the sullen young things for whom Tess had babysat when she was in her teens. Now that they had attained their majority—or, in the case of Primo's, attained the fake IDs that claimed they had attained their majority—they didn't know how to do anything but watch, complain, and repeat punchlines from the sitcom of the moment. *Kids today*, she thought contemptuously, eyeing the morose happy-hour crowd.

"The manager here?" she asked the bartender, who was whistling as he worked. At least he seemed to be enjoying himself. He winked and gave her a raffish smile as he jerked his head toward a nearby door.

"In there," he said. "And if you want to be his friend, I hope you're packing some raw meat in your bag."

The man wedged behind the desk in the tiny office was startlingly huge, three hundred pounds plus. He didn't get up when Tess entered, a lack of politesse for which she was grateful. She couldn't help thinking the desk functioned as a retaining wall for his girth and that if he stood, his huge stomach would come rolling toward her like a tidal wave.

"Yeah, they played here," he said, barely glancing at the page from Marianna Barrett Conyers's newspaper. A nameplate, a dusty pink lei looped over one end, provided the name he had neglected to give, Don Kleinschmidt. "Now they don't."

"Weren't they any good?"

"They're great, if you want some chick up there singing stuff nobody's ever heard of and nobody can dance to. All the little girls want to be Fiona fucking Apple these days. Which is okay, if you want your own goddamn Lilith Fair every night. But chick music doesn't bring the guys in, and the guys are the ones who drink. If I wanna sell cranberry juice, I'll get me a Snapple franchise."

Kleinschmidt lit a cigarette and looked around for an ashtray. A bright orange oval one sat on some bracketed shelves on the wall to his right. He could have reached it if he stretched. Apparently, Klein-schmidt had decided that a man's reach shouldn't exceed his grasp, for he flicked the ashes into a half-empty glass of Coke instead, then dropped the hand holding the cigarette behind the desk, as if fearful that Tess might demand a puff. Such stinginess seemed instinctive to him, Darwinian even. He hadn't gotten to his current size by sharing.

"I need a band that plays covers, dance tunes," he continued. "Oldies like 'Wooly-Bully,' 'Louie, Louie,' and whatever crap is on the radio right now. If the band has a girl singer, she can make like Alannis every now and then, but it's gotta be familiar. People come here to hear music they already know and eat food they already like. The only strange they want is on their pillow, after they leave. Get me? Get me?"

She got him. "And this band, Little Girl in Big Trouble, couldn't do that."

"*Wouldn't* do it. They said if they were going to play crap, there were people in town who would pay them more money to do it. So they walked. Prima fucking donnas."

"The girl was difficult?"

"No, it was him, mostly." He tapped a ridged, nico-tine yellow fingernail on Crow's face. "Fast Eddie here. He didn't like me talking to the girl. He didn't like anyone talking to her. Jealous little schmuck. Al-most started something with a customer one night. That was the end of it, you wanna know the truth. We might have worked out our artistic differences, but I draw the line at trying to beat up customers."

Pacifist Crow must be on on a real Sir Galahad trip

with his new girlfriend, trying to impress her. "Do you know if they're playing anywhere else in town?"

Kleinschmidt smirked, sucking on his cigarette, then dropping it behind his desk again. His mouth was tiny but full, a child's pink rosebud, incongruously pretty. It made him look as if he had just eaten a small boy, who was now trapped in those mounds of fat. *Don't be a fatist*, Tess scolded herself. Kleinschmidt would be disgusting at any weight.

"What's the information worth to you?" he asked.

It would have been easy enough to slide a twenty his way, even a fifty. Tess's per diem was based on the understanding that the occasional bribe was one of her operating costs. But she hated the idea of giving this man anything.

"How about if I don't come back here tonight and help the cops pick out all the underage kids at the bar? How much is that worth to you?"

Kleinschmidt shrugged and stole another puff from his cigarette. "I can't be checking IDs too closely. Trinity University is our bread and butter here on St. Mary's Street. I'm flexible with the chronologically challenged. That's why I'm still here after fifteen years, while almost every other place along here has bit the dust."

"I'm waiting," Tess said.

He sucked on his cigarette as if it were a straw in a glass with just a few drops of soda left. "Last I heard, they were playing at the Morgue."

"The Morgue?" First Marianna's house of horrors, now this. Tess was beginning to think San Antonio was one death-obsessed burg.

"Not morgue-morgue. Newspaper morgue. The developer picked up the old *San Antonio Sun* building cheap, thinking he'd make it into a mini-mall. You know, shops on the bottom, professional offices up above. But he couldn't get the right mix of tenants. So now it's like five music clubs in one. There's a big room downstairs for headliners, then lots of little rooms that can change their personalities to fit whatever nostalgia craze is under way."

"How do you change a room's personality?"

"That's the beauty of it—the decor is totally minimal. All he needs to do is frame a few front pages to change the era. Like, a disco room, with front pages from the seventies—Watergate, Nixon resigns, blah, blah, blah. Eighties? Stock market crash of '87. He's making money hand over fist, the lucky bastard. I heard he based it on someplace up north."

"We had something like that in Baltimore, the Power Plant. But it went bankrupt. Now the Inner Harbor has all the usual theme restaurants—Hard Rock Cafe, ESPN Zone, Planet Hollywood. Anne Tyler was being whimsical when she wrote *The Accidental Tourist*, but it's come true."

"Yeah, the more people travel, the more they like to stay at home. They got a point. I mean, you ever heard mariachi music? I pay those guys to *stop*."

They smiled cautiously at each other, pleased they had found something on which they could agree. "So do you think this band is still at the Morgue?"

"Could be. All I know is that Fast Eddie isn't my problem anymore. It's Friday night, go check out the scene yourself. You'd have a better time here, though. You know what we say, 'Primo's is primo!'" He dropped the butt end of his cigarette into the dregs of his Coke, where it sizzled and sank.

"Maybe some other time."

Kleinschmidt eyed Tess thoughtfully. She couldn't help feeling he was wondering what she would taste like broiled, with a baked potato on the side. "You look like the demographic I really want—out of college, a little more money to spend than some of these kids. What would make you come here?"

A knife at my throat. But Tess, long the sounding board for Kitty's money-making schemes, couldn't help being engaged by the question. "I don't know—something pop culturish, slightly ironic and totally self-referential. They may call us Generation X, but we're more like Generation Self-Obsessed. Which makes us exactly like the boomers, come to think of it. How about . . . lunchbox night?"

"Lunchbox night?"

"Everyone brings their lunchbox from fifth grade. In this age range, you'll probably get a lot of *ALF*, *The Cosby Show*, *Family Ties*. You could give prizes for people who can sing the theme songs, play TV trivia. What was the name of Cosby's youngest daughter, that kind of stuff."

"Lunchbox night. I *like* it! And lunchbox sounds kind of dirty, if you say it right."

"I hadn't thought of that."

"Well, that's what separates the true entrepreneur from the rest of the population," Kleinschmidt said, smug as a Cheshire cat. "I know how to take an idea and *run* with it."

"Without ever getting out of your chair," Tess said.

The Morgue stood at the intersection of Broadway and McCullough, two streets that began their lives parallel, then somehow managed to meet. Tess, who knew Baltimore so well that she could visualize its every joint and connection, had gotten lost for the second time today, and it made her grumpy. What kind of place had parallel streets that met? For that matter, what was with the street names here? Who was Hildebrand, for Christ's sake, or MacAllister? She wanted streets named Paca, Calvert, and Charles. Those were good names. Here, it was Austin, Houston, Milam, and according to her map book, one called Gomer Pyle. Well, Gollll-eeee.

Back in Baltimore, it was eleven o'clock—the perfect time to leave another cryptic message on Tyner's machine. Here, it was ten o'clock, early in clubland, but late enough so the band should be well into its first set. She wanted them to be onstage, wanted a chance to watch and study Crow without him seeing her. Then—well, she hadn't figured that part out yet. Technically, all she had to do was tap him on his shoulder, tell him to call his parents, and start driving back to Baltimore as fast as she could. If she really pushed it, she could be in her own bed by Sunday night.

But there was still the little matter of a dead guy up on the property where Crow had recently stayed. She wasn't buying into Marianna Barrett Conyers's theory of context, coincidence, and elephant-patting, not just yet.

She paid the ten-dollar cover, had her hand stamped, then lingered for a moment in case anyone wanted to see her ID. As someone who had looked twenty-one when she was fifteen then twenty when she was twenty-nine, Tess wasn't used to looking her age. It didn't seem that long ago that she had been scrounging up fake IDs and now she was flicking her braid at convenience store clerks, practically begging them to challenge her right to buy a six-pack.

"Where would I find Little Girl in Big Trouble?" she asked the young man who had taken her money, a broad-shouldered blond who was trying, without much success, to effect a bored, East Coast ennui. "The punk room?"

"I'm afraid I don't know any band by that name." She unfolded the newspaper photo for him. "Oh, our eighties band, the Breakfast Club. They're on the third floor. Pure pop for now people. Not as hot as it was a year ago, but still a good time if you're in the right mood. You know—'I want my MTV.'"

"Money for nothing," Tess finished for him, pretending to be in on the joke. Truth was, she felt stranded between the Morgue's bipolar sensibilities of nostaglia and irony. She had been an adolescent in the eighties and the memories—Madonna, rubber bracelets and bulimia—could still chafe. It didn't help that two of the three were still going strong, and that rubber bracelets had attempted a small comeback not that long ago.

But although the eighties were twice-over over, the eighties room was enjoying a boom time on this particular night. Couples who looked to be in their late thirties were packed into the small space, dancing gleefully to music they had probably scorned when it was new. The tune was catchy and as familiar as a toothpaste jingle. Tess needed a few seconds to identify it, then hated herself for knowing it at all.

"Wham," she said to herself, her eyes adjusting to the sudden darkness of the room. Goddamn Wham. George Michael and that guy whose name no one could remember. Wake Me Up Before You Go-go. This was Big Trouble indeed, for someone who had fancied himself a cutting edge musician just six months ago.

Her eyes went to the girl first. Woman, technically, but she was playing the vulnerable waif for all it was worth, skinny limbs exposed and fragile in her torn party frock. The outfit was a little anachronistic, first-generation Courtney Love, more early nineties than late eighties. No smeared lipstick, though, and no roots—this blond hair was real. Yes, Emmie "Dutch" Sterne was the real thing, all right.

She sang prettily but perfunctorily, as if her mind were somewhere else. A doll, yes, but more the windup variety than the china type. Still, she caught one's eye and held it. Emmie had that ineluctable quality called charisma. No two people remembered her the same way, but everyone remembered her.

A burst of harmony on the chorus, a man's sweet tenor. Head down, Tess let her eyes track to the right and saw the new Crow. With his long hair gone, the sharp, thin planes of his face were revealed. Yet even as his face had narrowed, his shoulders had broadened, his body thickened. He wasn't fat, far from it, but his boyish gangle was gone. He looked *good*—even in that ridiculous jacket and skinny tie, and with his hair moussed into a ruffled coxcomb.

She raised her head a little higher, feeling slightly voyeuristic, a peeping Tess hidden behind the bouncing dancers. She noticed she wasn't the only one watching in this way. A few partner-less women stood along one wall, eyeing the band's male members with bird-dog intensity. Wake me up before you go-go, yes indeed.

What is it about women and musicians? Over the brief course of her relationship with Crow, Tess had stood in dozens of clubs and watched little girls sigh over him and the other boys in his band as if they were Mick Jagger and John Lennon combined. To tell the truth, she had sighed herself in her time, had found herself nodding and smiling at some semi-attractive stranger just because he had a guitar, stood on a stage, and sang someone else's words. It didn't work the other way, for some reason. Men might lust for a female rock singer as they lusted for anyone, but the music, the performance, was incidental. Sure, there were men here tonight who were staring hungrily at Emmie, but not because she was singing. As Kitty had said, there were men who specialized in damaged goods, and Emmie Sterne was putting out the I-am-screwed-up vibe for all it was worth.

For women, the music was the point. You date a musician and—well, what had Tess thought? That Crow would serenade her from the alley below her Fells Point apartment, that her life would turn into some MGM production number? She still wasn't sure. All she knew was that the reality of dating a musician wasn't the same as the prospect. There was nothing like the feeling you had when you stood in a dark club and watched a man lean close to a microphone and imagined the microphone was your ear. Or your mouth. But the only way to hold on to such anticipation was not to act on it.

New song. Wham segued into Culture Club. "Do You Really Want to Hurt Me?" For a brief, paranoid moment, Tess thought Crow had seen her in the crowd. Who wants to hurt anyone? She had thought she was being so honorable last winter, breaking up with Crow when another man had filled her line of vision. She had hoped the small hurt would be better than the large-scale betrayal that seemed to loom. Now she wondered, and not for the first time, how monogamy worked. Did there ever come a time when you were impervious to stirrings for another person, or did you just learn to ignore those feelings? But if you pretended they didn't exist, weren't you a hypocrite?

In the Bible, if you felt it in your heart, you were busted. Might as well do the crime, because you were going to do the time. But in fairy tales, it was the test that mattered—one couldn't avoid temptation, but one could avoid giving in. The heart triumphed, time and again. Only how could the heart hope to make itself heard over the screeching chorus of one's hormones?

"We're going to take a break, folks. See you in fifteen." Emmie's speaking voice was huskier, rougher than her singing voice. The couples in the room didn't applaud, for that would require letting go of each other. It dawned on Tess that the real purpose of the Morgue was providing people with a series of semidark caves in which to grope each other. No wonder it was such a success with conventioneers.

Tess walked to the front, head down, as if Crow might not recognize the top of her head. His back was to her, anyway. He was crouching over a speaker, fiddling with the connection.

"Piece of crap," he said dispassionately. The two other guys in the band had already left the stage and been embraced by their ladies in waiting, the human coolie cups who had the honor of holding their beers throughout the set. Emmie stood where she was, twirling with a lock of hair, appraising Tess with the unabashed stare of a child. She didn't seem particularly surprised, or threatened. Probably lots of ladies tried to approach Crow between sets.

"Hey," Tess said to Crow's back.

"*What?*" he said, not turning away from the troublesome speaker, his voice irritable and impatient.

"Nice set," she said. "It's not Poe White Trash, but then, what is?"

Not one of the more immortal lines after a silence of almost six months, but it got his attention.

9

He turned on his heel, but still in a crouch, so he was eye-level with her knees. When he glanced up, there was an unguarded moment, and some unidentifiable emotion flitted past. Whatever it was, it was quickly overtaken and vanquished by wariness, a most un-Crow-like expression.

"Tess Monaghan," he said flatly, in the tone of someone diagnosing a rash to which he was prone.

"Hi, Crow. Only I hear it's Ed these days. Sometimes Eddie."

"Eduardo in these environs." He stood up, sticking his hands in his pockets, lest she try to reach for one.

"They called you Crow back there?" This was Emmie. Tess kept expecting her to move forward, to stake her claim with an arm around Crow's waist, or a hand in the small of his back, but her interest was polite at best. She didn't even seem to expect an answer to her question, and Crow didn't give her one.

"This isn't what I do," he told Tess.

"You have another job?"

"I mean—" He waved his arm at the emptying room. "Wham songs, for Christ's sake. Boy George, Culture Club. You spin me right 'round."

"Don't forget Manic Mondays, 'Til Tuesday Tuesdays, and it's Friday, I'm in love," Emmie put in, singing the last, the title of a Cure song, one that a Baltimore radio station, in a display of great originality, had been playing every Friday for almost a decade. "We're still working on themes for Wednesdays and Thursdays."

"But if we ever move to the seventies room, we always have the Bay City Rollers to fall back on," Crow said. "S-A-T-U-R-D-A-Y night! S-A-T-U-R-D-A-Y night!"

There was something nervous in their chatter, like children who had done something wrong, and were still trying to assess if Mommy knew.

"So what brings you to the Alamo City?" Crow asked. "A convention of—what are you now, anyway?"

As if he didn't know she was a licensed investigator. Then again, his letter had come to Tyner's office, not hers. Suddenly, she was angry that he didn't know all she had accomplished over the past summer—the new business, getting on her feet financially, solving a murder case everyone else thought had been solved long ago.

"My Toyota brought me here," she said. "Along with your parents' retainer."

This had the desired effect. "My parents hired you? I'm 24-fucking-years old and my *parents* are paying people to come look for me just because I don't want to take their checks anymore? They're only proving my point—I have to disappear if I'm ever going to be truly independent. What more do I have to do? Leave the country? Change my name? As for hiring *you*—well, that's beyond insulting."

"I happen to be a pretty good investigator, as evidenced by my ability to find you in three days in a state where I didn't know one goddamn person."

"How *did* you find us, anyway?" This was Emmie, and although she spoke in the same spaced-out, affectless tone, she couldn't quite conceal her interest in Tess's answer.

"I found Gary, Crow's old drummer, in Austin. He told me you had left Austin for Twin Sisters. That led me to Marianna Barrett Conyers's place, and that led me to Marianna Barrett Conyers."

"My godmother would never speak to some stranger," Emmie said with swift conviction. "Especially not about me."

"She didn't tell me much about you. In fact, I think she led me on a bit of a wild-goose chase." Tess was remembering how deep Marianna had dug into her pile of newspapers, providentially finding one almost a month old. She had to have known Little Girl in Big Trouble had already taken on a new incarnation. Obviously, she wanted Tess to run into a dead-end at Primo's, or at least a cul-de-sac.

"Marianna worries about me," Emmie said. "She worries about everything."

"Funny. She didn't seem too concerned that I went to Twin Sisters to find Crow, and discovered a dead body instead."

Ignorance, although a natural state for much of

the population, is incongruously tough to fake. But Emmie and Crow seemed truly stunned by this information. His mouth gaped a little, and he stole a quick look at Emmie, who was staring at Tess in wide-eyed dismay. Tess, now used to the dim light of the eighties room, saw for the first time how blue Emmie's eyes were, as blue as the flowers on the postcard Crow had sent his parents. Blue-bonnets. But you didn't notice the eyes so much as the shadows under them. Not bags, just shadows, dark as bruises. Strangely, they only made her more beautiful.

"A body?" she asked. "At Marianna's place? But we haven't—it *couldn't* . . ."

"We haven't been there for weeks," Crow put in. "Weeks and weeks. We stayed there after we left Austin, before we found a place to crash in San Antonio. It had the advantage of being free, but it was a little far to commute once we started getting gigs down here."

A young Mexican-American security guard came over, carrying a cup of water. "I thought you might be thirsty, Miss Sterne."

She took the glass without looking at him, her gaze still fixed on Tess. "Thanks, Steve. I sounded like crap, didn't I?"

"Oh no, you were great," he assured her. "Better than ever. You need anything else?"

"I could use a smoke. A joint would be better."

"Not in here," the guard said a little nervously. He wasn't much older than Emmie—perhaps twenty-five or twenty-six—and he had a moon-round face shiny with sweat. "Remember, the manager said—"

"Relax, Steve, I don't have any contraband on me.

I'm going downstairs to the main bar, so I can buy a pack off the bartender. Do we have time?"

The question was for Crow. "Sure," he said. "No rush."

She jumped off the stage, landing lightly, threading her way quickly through the crowd as if worried someone might try to stop her. The security guard watched her go, then retreated into the backstage shadows.

"So what are you going to do?" Crow asked. "Call my parents, tell them where I am?"

"That's what they paid me for."

"Give me a week. I'll call them a week from today if you don't tell them that you found me."

"That doesn't seem right somehow. They're worried about you, all they want to know is you're all right."

"And all I want is a chance to prove I can take care of myself," Crow countered. "What's seven days in the scheme of things? Look, I promise. You can go home, and I'll check in with them next Saturday. I bet you're missing Baltimore already, aren't you? Missing home, and all your little routines. Besides, Esskay's probably pretty lonesome."

"Esskay's not even two miles from here, snoring at a motel on Broadway."

"Really? I wouldn't have minded seeing her."

The implication was clear that he did mind seeing Tess.

"I could ask you the same thing, you know. What's seven days? Why can't your parents know now that you're safe and sound?"

Crow rolled his eyes, as if maddened that he had

to explain himself to her. "There's a guy from a record company, someone who's interested in the band. He's coming in for the All Soul festival and he's going to listen to our *real* music, in this after-hours place we play. It would be nice to call home with good news."

"What if he doesn't sign you?" The question came out crueller than she had intended. She couldn't help being skeptical. Then again, Emmie had been offered a record contract once before, according to Marianna. Maybe she wouldn't be so reluctant to leave Texas, now that she had Crow at her side.

"I'll still call." Crow sighed, and his shoulders slumped a little. "I'll call and give them my number, and we'll take it from there. But I can't take their money anymore, Tess. And they can't *not* send it. That's their peculiar weakness. They love me too much to let go. I've had the longest adolescence in history. It's gotta end."

Tess thought back to the house in Charlottesville, the carefully preserved boyhood room. From the beginning, from his very conception, Crow had been central to his parents' lives. Perhaps he had been too central? Tess began to see some advantages to having parents who converted your room to a sewing room the moment you left home.

"I have to tell your parents I found you," she said slowly, thinking as she spoke, trying to figure out a way to make everyone happy. "They paid for that information, they deserve it."

"Okay," he said, throwing his hands up dismissively. "Okay. Guess I was crazy to think you wouldn't let me down. *Again.*"

"They also deserve a son who's more considerate of them, but I can't help them with that."

"You do what you have to do."

"I always do."

"You always did," he agreed. "You know your way out of here? San Antonio's a little tricky to navigate. Where you headed?"

"On Broadway, near the zoo."

Crow made a face. "That's not so far from us. What are you doing, living on the cheap so you can pocket more of your per diem? I knew it didn't ring true when you started getting all holier-than-thou about wasting my parents' money."

That hurt, if only because it came so close to the truth of the person she had once been. *I'm not that cheap anymore*, she wanted to tell Crow. *I make good money now.*

But all she said was: "It was the only place I could find last night."

"It's easy enough to get to from here. Just go up Broadway."

"I *know* that."

"Tess—"

She waited. It occurred to her it was only the second time he had used her name.

"I love my parents, I never meant to hurt them. Please make them understand that. I hope—I hope they're going to be proud of me, that they'll understand why I needed this time to be on my own."

On your own, with Emmie. But she merely nodded.

Her stomach reminded her that she had not eaten anything since late afternoon, when she had polished off the rest of the Fig Newtons. She stopped at an all-night taco stand on Broadway, a bright pink one, only to be overwhelmed by the unfamiliar choices. Baltimore had not prepared her for the range of possibilities in tacos. What was carne guisada? Carne asada? Barbacoa would be barbecue, of course, but the sign said this was served on Sundays only. She settled for a fajita, feeling wimpy and defeated for settling for something she could have gotten back home.

Even so, it was so much better than anything she had ever eaten in Baltimore that she ordered two more. Charm City's inability to serve a decent taco remained one of its eternal mysteries. However, the Mexican beer, a Bohemia, was an old friend. Dark and flavorful, it smoothed the jagged feelings that seeing Crow had aroused.

What had she expected? What had she *wanted*? For him to fall into her arms and declare his undying love for her? For her to ride to his rescue, extricate him from whatever mess he gotten himself into, and thus settle the old debts between them? She wasn't sure. Something between the two. But Crow was fine, caught up in nothing more than the inevitable rebellion against one's parents, even if he had come to it much later than most. The pictures in his parents' home may have suggested unfinished business between the two of them, but that was five months ago. Some fruit flies lived longer than Crow's passions.

She looked down at the beef that had fallen from her tacos, and the image of the man in the pool house boomeranged into her consciousness. How quickly Tom Darden had been dismissed by Emmie and Crow, how incurious they had been. She believed Crow's mystification, believed him when he said he knew nothing about the man, or how he had come to be there.

Emmie—Emmie was another matter. In Emmie's case, it wasn't clear if it was the body that had caught her off guard, or the body's location "at Marianna's place?" she had asked, her voice scaling up.

And neither one had bothered to ask whose body it was.

10

A telegram—now there was a concept. In a world of cell phones, e-mail, faxes, and beepers, Tess knew Western Union existed only because it advertised its money-wiring service on television. But did it still do telegrams? She couldn't even find a Western Union in the telephone book, just a list of "offices" at the local grocery chain, HEB.

The closest one was only a mile up Broadway, but it seemed more like a food amusement park than a grocery store. In fact, groceries seemed an afterthought here, what with chefs whipping up pasta dishes on demand, a full menu of cooking classes, a walk-in-humidor, and a wine section that needed two aisles just for South America. Tess scuffed her feet on the rough floors—painted, a helpful clerk told her, to create the feeling of an old European market—filled with an intense and sudden hunger for things she had never heard of. She was enraptured, she was repulsed, she wanted to get a little cot and set up housekeeping, preferably near the flowers. Baltimore's upscale grocery stores—Eddie's and Graul's and Sutton Place Gourmet—were pathetic compared to this temple of food. She couldn't decide if the grandeur was driven by the Texas phenomenon of big-bigger-biggest, or whether it was the inevitable over-compensatory impulse of a founder who had been born with the moniker of Henry E. Butt.

Eventually, she shook off the store's decadent spell and asked someone where she could send a telegram.

"It's cheaper to call," the girl at the front counter said, examining her nails. She had on a new kind of polish that could be peeled off, and she was slowly liberating her synthetic talons from a coat of celery green. "I mean, you can buy a long distance card at the ice house. I got one there last week. It had a picture of David Robinson on it."

"No, it has to be a telegram," Tess said. No one could talk back to a telegram, ask it questions, or track its number through Caller ID.

"It's like my first week," the clerk said. "I don't know how to do everything."

"I'm patient," Tess lied.

The clerk sighed dramatically and rustled around until she found the form she needed.

Tess began to dictate: "Crow found—stop. Will call soon—stop."

"Why do you keep telling me to stop?" the girl asked fretfully. Then, as an afterthought: "You're sending a telegram because you found a crow? Don't they have those where you came from?"

"You say stop to indicate the end of a thought," Tess said, although everything she knew about telegrams she had learned from old movies. "It's like a period."

"Are you *sure?*"

Eventually, they collaborated on a mutually acceptable document to Charlottesville, Virginia. It read, in its entirety: *Crow fine. In Big Trouble name of new band. Will call in one week. Staying here till then.* The last line had been a last-minute inspiration, and Tess wasn't sure where it came from, or even if it was true. But seven days seemed little to spare to make sure that Crow wasn't going to use the time he had requested to run again. Besides, she wanted to see where the local authorities were going with the investigation into the death of her Hill Country pal.

"Where's the library?" she asked the girl.

"Enchilada Roja, you mean?"

Now that was Tess's kind of Spanish. "You call your library the red enchilada?"

"Yeah, and it didn't get its name for nothing. It sticks out on the skyline north of downtown, like a sore thumb. Or a big red enchilada, I guess. You can't miss it." She smiled for the first time. "They got computers there. You could zap your friends an e-mail, if you have an AOL account."

"Just send the telegram, okay?"

Enchilada Roja was easy to spot on the horizon, but it seemed to keep shifting as Tess drove toward it. She took several turns through a warren of one-way streets before she found her way into the pay parking lot outside the gleaming new library. Outside and in, it was the antithesis of her beloved Enoch Pratt—gorgeous appointments, state of the art computers, even a room dedicated to genealogical research. The only thing in short supply was books. The shelves yawned with empty spaces.

"Do you keep a lot of your collection in the stacks?" Tess asked the librarian who showed her where to find the local newspapers.

"What you see is what you get," the young man said. He had a long silky ponytail and Bambi eyes. Tess noticed the periodical section seemed unusually crowded, with a large number of high school girls peering at the librarian over the tops of *Teen People*, but her guide seemed oblivious to his fan club. "I guess they thought if they built the building, the books would take care of themselves."

At least civic thinking was the same everywhere. Float the bonds for the construction projects and hope everything else took care of itself. Tess settled down with a stack of local newspapers, looking for any mention of the body in Marianna Barrett Conyers's pool house.

The Blanco paper was a weekly, so its cycle had yet to catch up with the story. The New Braunfels paper reported the discovery on page one, but its focus was on public safety. A killer, believed to be dangerous, was still at large, the paper warned its citizens. *As opposed to non-dangerous killers?*

The *San Antonio Eagle*'s front page was full of pie-in-the-sky dreams for a new basketball arena which would transform the city's northeast side into a land of milk and money. Close your eyes and you're in Baltimore, Toto. Tess had to search the skimpy local section for a short item, which said only that a body had been found on the property of Marianna

Barrett Conyers of Alamo Heights. It was noted the apparent victim, ex-felon Tom Darden, also had made his home in San Antonio, before he was sent away on a kidnapping charge twenty years ago, along with Laylan Weeks. The sheriff had mentioned Weeks, too, Tess recalled. "The infamous Danny Boyd case," the paper called their crime, but the reporter didn't bother to explain the infamy for those who hadn't been around twenty years ago. In fact, the article's emphasis seemed to be on the terrible inconvenience of having a corpse in one's pool house, especially a body as undesirable as Darden's. He had been found, the nonbylined piece added almost as an afterthought, by a drifter.

"A *drifter*!" Although Tess spoke aloud, in a rather emphatic tone, no one shushed her. Perhaps this was because no one could really hear her in the happy Saturday morning bustle. The teenage girls were whispering and giggling, while small children trotted in circles, shouting for their parents. Adolescent boys hunkered in front of the computers, playing games, probably trying to figure out how to bypass the cyber blocks and download porn. Who needed Chuck E. Cheese when there were libraries around?

Before she left Enchilada Roja, Tess used the computer's Netscape browser to glide home to the Baltimore *Beacon-Light's* Web page. She had never thought she would miss the *Blight*. The *Eagle* was a little gaudy for her tastes, although she recalled Marianna had said something about its tabloid days, suggesting it had once been more sensational still. The *Blight's* Web site was a mess, done on the cheap, but it was a joy to read about meetings and crimes set in places she could visualize, in a typeface she knew. A robbery on Lombard Street, a homicide on Lanvale, a fire on Waltherson. It all combined to make her homesick.

She stopped at a laundromat, then, against all odds, found her way back to Broadway and La Casita, her home away from home. Someone was sitting on the curb in front of her room, arms hugging her body as if she were cold on this sunny, breezeless day. Tess couldn't see the face, but the hair was butter yellow in the sun and cut in a Dutch-boy bob.

"Hey," Emmie said.

"Brace yourself," Tess said, stepping around her with her duffel bag of clothes and unlocking the door. "I'm going to release the hound."

Esskay came bounding out of the motel room, greeted Tess as if they had been separated for days, then began inspecting the stranger on the curb. Emmie hunched her shoulders, as if frightened of dogs, but held her ground.

"I thought you might have left by now," she said.

Thought or hoped?

"I could," Tess said. "I've done what I was hired to do."

"What was that, exactly?"

"Find Crow."

"Oh." She appeared to be thinking about something, but her expression was inscrutable. "We're not together."

"Pardon me?"

"Ed and I. We're not together. We were—at first, up in Austin—but now we're not."

Tess held up her hand, traffic cop style. "None of my business."

Emmie was still sitting on the curb, hugging her knees to her chest, scratching her shins. She had drawn blood, Tess noticed, but she kept scratching, oblivious. There was scabs on her calves and pale, thin scars that would probably never quite fade.

"He keeps up with you, you know," Emmie said, after scratching a while longer. Esskay, usually so friendly, was keeping her distance from this visitor, as if even she could smell the craziness on her.

"What?"

"He has a file, of newspaper clippings. There aren't that many, maybe three or four."

"I haven't done much to write about."

"No, I guess you haven't." Emmie didn't sound rude, merely factual, the way children do before grown-ups school them in the art of the polite lie. "Have you ever killed someone?"

"What?" Tess felt as if she was saying this a lot.

"I mean, you've been in some real strange situations, but I don't recall if you ever killed someone. Have you?"

"No. I've seen someone die. I've seen dead people. But I haven't killed anyone."

"Hmmm." Emmie frowned. "And you can remember it, I suppose, all the gory details. All the blood. Assuming there was blood. Would you like to go to lunch?"

"Excuse me?" Tess had thought she was bad about jumping from topic to topic, but Emmie's synapses were misfiring like the cheap caps that kids play with on the sidewalk.

"Lunch. Aren't you hungry? Ed said you could eat a lot. You know what? I'm going to start calling him Crow. It suits him."

"Does Crow talk about me often?"

Emmie gave this serious consideration. "Not so very often. Sometimes. When it's so late that it's early, and we've played really well, so we're all drained, and he's had a couple drinks maybe, and we go to Earl Abel's for pie, and the sun is just coming up—his memories come up, too. Is it true you ate the same thing for breakfast every day?"

"Well, not *every* day."

"Do you think that means you're naturally monogamous?"

"*What?*"

Emmie held her fingers to her mouth, as if to taste the blood rimmed beneath her fingernails. "I would think someone who could eat the same thing for breakfast every day would be pretty dependable. Then again, maybe that's the kind of person who just loses it, you know. Goes postal, burns down the house, hits the road because she suddenly realizes she can't face another bowl of Frosted Flakes. So, do you want to go to lunch or what?"

"Why not?" At least it was a question she understood.

Tess wasn't sure where she had expected Emmie to take her to eat, but this lunch counter at the old-fashioned drugstore, the Olmos Pharmacy, was a pleasant surprise.

"Get a milkshake," Emmie instructed her. "They're the best in the world."

"My grandfather made the best shakes in the world, at his lunch counter." But Tess added a shake to her order of grilled cheese and bacon. She had never seen a milkshake served this way: The counter woman set small plastic tumblers of whipped cream in front of them, then left behind the sweating metal container from the old-fashioned Hamilton mixer. Emmie poured the thick concoction over the whipped cream, stirred, then dug into hers with a spoon. Although it was possible to coax the thick liquid up a straw, it wasn't very easy. A spoon was definitely the way to go.

"This was my high school hang-out," Emmie said. "The local malt shop. Isn't that sweet?"

"You make it sound as if that were forty years ago."

She nodded dreamily, licking her spoon. "It feels that way. We lived in Olmos Park, on Hermosa. Handsome street. Now here's a riddle—Can ugly things happen on a street called handsome?"

Emmie's crazy act was beginning to seem just that, an act. "I think I drove through there. I kept ending up in Olmos Park when I was trying to find your godmother in Alamo Heights."

"San Antonio is tricky that way."

It sounded like a warning, but Emmie's face was all innocence as she dipped her spoon in and out of her malt. She was not what Tess expected. She couldn't say what she was exactly, just that she wasn't what Tess had expected.

"Why are we here?" Tess asked her.

"That's a pretty big question, isn't it? One of the biggies. Why are we here? The thing is, we are here, right, and we just have to make the best of it, until we're not."

"No, why are we having lunch? Why did you come find me today? *How* did you find me, for that matter?"

"You told Crow you were staying at La Casita. Crow tells me everything."

"Everything?"

"Everything I want to know. I asked him this morning if he knew where you were."

"Why?"

"I told you. I wanted to tell you there's nothing between us. Between Crow and me."

"Okay, I know. So what?"

"Sew buttons," Emmie said, blowing into the straw in her water glass, making bubbles like a little kid.

"Emmie, do you know a man named Tom Darden, or Laylan Weeks?"

Tess had deliberately omitted any context with the names, but Emmie's face was a careful blank. "No. Who are they?"

"Darden is the man I found at Marianna's place. Weeks is the person they think he was with before he died. They're from here, but they've been in prison for a pretty long time."

Emmie put on a pretty pout of concentration, as if thinking hard. "Did they go to Alamo Heights High School?"

"I don't think so."

"Then I guess I don't know them."

"Do you know what brought me here?"

"Now that's another one of those big questions, isn't it?"

Tess pulled the clipping of Crow from her date-book. "I know now this was cut out of an old news-paper ad, and the headline is nothing more than a fragment of the band's old name. But it doesn't mean he isn't in big trouble. He sent me this for a reason."

"You think Crow sent this to you?"

"Who else?"

Emmie sucked her metal spoon clean, then tried to hang it from her nose. It fell to the counter with a noisy clatter. "It never works with these spoons. I don't know why I keep trying."

"Is he in big trouble, Emmie? Are you?"

"I'm *fine*," she said sharply.

"Did something happen while you were staying at Marianna's place?"

"*No.*" She gulped the last of her shake. "I have to go. We've got a late night tonight. I need to catch a few hours of sleep."

"You playing the Morgue again?"

Emmie nodded. "But on Saturdays, we have an afterhours gig in this really cool place, Hector's. It's like a shack under the highway and most of the people who hang out there are bikers. But a lot of people come there just to hear us now. We're not the Breakfast Club there, we're Las Almas Perdidas. The Lost Souls."

"Not more eighties music?"

"Original stuff. And covers, done in a conjunto style, with a little bluegrass mixed in. You'd be sur-prised how an accordion and a fiddle can make an old song sound new again."

Yes, Tess would. "Well, let's get me back to La Casita, so you can have your siesta."

"When are you going back to Baltimore?"

"Not sure." She was less sure of everything, the more time she spent here. "Do you want me to leave, Emmie? Is that the point of this excursion? Or are you trying to figure out if I know anything?"

"I just wanted to talk to you a little. I feel as if I know you. I know you and Crow knows—actually, he doesn't know as much as he thinks he does. But that's another story, for another day."

They drove back to La Casita in Emmie's little Nissan Sentra, not the type of car Tess would have picked for a crazy rich girl. Emmie was an unexpectedly competent driver, too, focused and aggressive, with none of the dreaminess or abrupt shifts that characterized her conversation. Tess alternated between studying Emmie and studying the landmarks. She was beginning to get her bearings.

"It's like a bow-legged woman," she said.

"What?" Emmie asked, for once the one caught off guard.

"San Antonio. It's laid out like a bow-legged woman with her legs crossed at the ankles. That's how the parallel streets of Broadway and McCullough come to intersect. Here on Hildebrand, we're about waist-high. Now that I understand that, I think I'll be able to get around better."

"Sure, on the north side. But there's more to San Antonio than the north side. The streets and highways around here are like dividing cells. They come together and break apart, they change names abruptly. Don't be fooled into thinking it's an easy city to know."

But when they stopped at the next traffic light,

Emmie glanced over at Tess, and seemed to take pity on her. It was as if she knew how vulnerable it made Tess feel to be in a place where she didn't know everything and everyone.

"A bow-legged woman," Emmie said. "That's not bad, actually. Hildebrand is waist-high, you're right, and your motel is just above the knee. She must be a very fat woman, don't you think, with big thighs spread far apart? Yet her ankles are very dainty. Her best feature." Emmie laughed happily. "Yes, you might even say it ain't over until the fat lady crosses her ankles."

Tess said nothing, she was too busy looking out at the window, grimly memorizing landmarks. They had passed one college on the right, now another was on the left, where they were turning by the Southwestern Bell Building and heading down the fat lady's left leg, Broadway. And here was La Casita. Home sweet home.

"Thanks for the milkshake," she told Emmie.

"Milkshake?" she asked, as if she had forgotten their trip to the pharmacy. "Oh, de nada."

Tess checked in with Mrs. Nguyen before going to her room. "I still don't know when I'm leaving." Actually, she still didn't know why she was staying.

"No problem," her landlady said, eyes fixed on a Mexican soap opera as she ate a slice of pizza. "Your friend find you?"

"Her? She's not really a friend."

"Not your girlfriend. Boyfriend."

"I don't have a boyfriend," she said stupidly.

"Not boyfriend boyfriend. Boy. Friend. He came by, he had a picture of you, with your black dog.

That's how I know he knows you. I told him you gone off, he asked me if he could see the dog. So I let him in the room. But don't worry, I watch him. I watch him carefully. Very nice boy, very handsome, he patted the dog on the head. Younger than you, yes?"

"Ye-e-e-sss." The milkshake seemed to lurch in her stomach, as if it was going for one more spin in the Hamilton mixer. "And you watched him the whole time?"

"Whole time," Mrs. Nguyen said, nodding vigorously. Then her head stopped in mid-bob. "Except—"

"Except when, Mrs. Nguyen?"

"When the pizza man came, I had to go get my purse. No more than two minutes. Maybe three. Very nice boy. He said goodbye, I locked your room. The dog looked happy to see him."

The world's greatest watchdog bounded up when Tess opened the door to her room. Whatever Esskay knew, she wasn't telling. But she had something on her breath, some liver-ish treat that Tess hadn't given her. Heck, Charles Manson could drop by if he brought a treat. Esskay had her priorities. And she would have remembered Crow. Her long-term memory was much better than her short-term one. She still remembered the exact spot where she had once seen a cat sunning itself on a windowsill.

The room looked normal, and Tess had so few possessions that it didn't take much time to inventory everything there. Her bag of laundry was on the bed, her copy of *Don Quixote* on the nightstand. Her knapsack was there, too, seemingly untouched.

She took out the false bottom, made sure her gun and cell phone were nestled there. This past summer, in a particularly hellish forty-eight hours, her gun had been stolen and her phone had been flung across five lanes of traffic on Interstate 95. A tailor had designed a black flap that attached with Velcro strips, but it would only fool someone who glanced inside the knapsack without picking it up. The weight would have given away its secret contents.

No, if Mrs. Nguyen hadn't mentioned her gentleman caller, she would never have known someone had been here. But someone had, and it felt as creepy as a real break-in, or a burglary. Creepier, because she knew who the perpetrator was, yet couldn't begin to guess at his motives.

LAURA LIPPMAN

11

Hector's was not the type of place listed in the yellow pages, or in San Antonio's Chamber of Commerce magazine. But Mrs. Nguyen, embarrassed by her uncharacteristic lack of vigilance on Tess's behalf, called a cousin whose daughter had a friend who knew a guy who sometimes hung out with bikers. A family scandal, as it turned out, and Mrs. Nguyen was on the telephone for quite some time, clucking over the shame of it all, even as she passed keys to the La Casita regulars and kept one eye on her Mexican soap operas.

Finally, she rang off. "It's ice house, out in the country," she told Tess from her side of the bullet-proof glass. "Way out Pleasanton Road."

"Ice house?" It was the second time today Tess had heard this strange term. The HEB clerk had claimed you could buy a phone card at one.

"Like package store, but with places to sit, maybe a pool table. But it's not a nice place, not for nice young lady."

"No problem. I'll just take my gun."

"Good idea," Mrs. Nguyen said, nodding vigorously, although she certainly never needed a gun. *Her* office was an impenetrable fortress—Mrs. Nguyen not only had the protection of the glass, but she slipped into a back room to make change or run credit card receipts, locking the door behind her.

"I was *joking*, Mrs. Nguyen."

"But you got gun, why not take it? Is legal here, to have guns. Except maybe not for you. And maybe not in bars. They usually have signs, saying no guns. But you take yours, and keep in car. Better safe than sorry."

At home, Tess had found it irritating when the people in her life—Kitty, Tyner, her parents—pulled this protective stuff. Here, she felt lonely without their scolding. She agreed to be careful.

A few miles south of Loop 410, San Antonio seemed to disappear, and darkness swallowed Tess's Toyota. And while the sky was crowded with stars, they provided no light. It was hard to believe there was anyone or anything outside the path of her headlights, much less some biker bar that turned its stage over to an avant-garde polka-bluegrass band at closing time. Then Hector's suddenly surfaced like a mirage from the shadowy, flat countryside.

It wasn't much to look at: a low cinderblock building dwarfed by an enormous patio outlined in Christmas lights. No sign, but it must be the place, judging by the mix of vehicles in the lot—a few motorcycles, mostly Harley-Davidsons; some banged-up, castoff family cars, the kind driven by college students; and a smattering of expensive foreign cars, which probably cost more than Tess made in a year. *Someone was slumming*, she thought. What was the point of having money if you couldn't lord over people who didn't?

She checked her watch. It was a few minutes shy of 2, and customers were lined up along one end of the patio, at a long waist-high refrigeration case on wheels. A portable bar.

"Still serving?" she asked when her turn finally came. The bartender was an older man with thick, long sideburns that had probably cycled in and out of fashion several times over the years he had worn them.

"Sure," he said, unscrewing the cap on a generic cola and pushing it toward her, then pocketing the five dollars she handed him.

"No change?"

"Monopolies are a bitch, ain't they?"

"Don't gouge, Sam," a woman's clear voice cut in. "Either give her some change, or give her a beer."

"She with you, Kris?" The bartender sounded contrite. "Sorry, I didn't know. I thought she was one of those new kids who keeps showing up, ever since the band got written up in the *Eagle*." He exchanged the cola for something called a Shiner Bock. "Any friend of yours and Rick's is a friend of mine."

He moved to the end of the bar, to wait on another customer. Tess noticed he was pulling the beers from plastic coolers, not the metal ones built beneath the portable bar, and taking only cash, no credit cards.

"Loophole in the liquor law," explained her defender. "After two Hector's is a private social club, for members only. If Sam doesn't know you, he won't sell to you."

"So am I member now?"

"Yeah, that's why you didn't get any change from your five dollars. Beer is two dollars a bottle, and you can get set-ups—cokes, ginger ales, tonic—for a dollar. There's also food, although this isn't much of an eating crowd. Just bags of chips and pork rinds, and fresh tamales when Sam's wife gets inspired."

Her newfound friend was a blond, perhaps twenty-five, in an embroidered white blouse and dangling silver earrings. The costume was clearly meant to be Mexican, but on this milk-fed, apple-cheeked girl, the effect was more St. Pauli girl on her night off.

"Well, thanks," said Tess, who was unused to the kindness of strangers. "You made this out-of-towner feel pretty welcome. I'm Tess Monaghan."

"Kristina Johanssen," the girl said, thrusting out her hand. "Hector's can be pretty overwhelming on first visit. But you're in for a treat. How did you hear about Las Almas Perdidas?"

It took Tess a beat to recall this was yet another name for Crow's band. "Actually, I go pretty far back with them. The guy—Ed—used to be in a band up in Baltimore, Poe White Trash."

"You *know* Ed Ransome?" Kris asked breathlessly. "Really know him?"

"We worked together in my aunt's bookstore—"

"Too cool. Enrique—" Kris grabbed Tess's hand in hers, which was warm and sweaty as a little girl's, and all but dragged her to a nearby table, where a tall, bored-looking man sat. He was as dark as she was fair, and wore clothes that looked more suitable for a country club dance—white shirt, blazer, khakis. "Enrique, this woman knows Ed Ransome."

"Try not to get so carried away, sweetheart." Enrique's drawl was a surprise, the first genuinely Texan accent Tess had heard. It didn't seem to belong with the flan-colored skin and the Aztec warrior profile. "It's not like he's Willie Nelson or Merle Haggard. Hell, he's not even Freddie Fender."

"Oh, Enrique." While Kristina's vowel sounds were Midwestern flat, she trilled the R in her beloved's name with admirable skill. "You and that country music. Just my luck to finally find a Mexican boyfriend, only to discover he has the soul of LBJ."

"I think of myself more in the Kennedy mode, darlin'," he said, stretching out his long legs. His studied preppiness ended at his feet, where he wore well-shined black cowboy boots instead of tassel loafers. "Handsome, charismatic, great political future, women falling over me."

Kristina snorted. "You're more likely to defend a Kennedy than be one."

"I can only hope one of them runs afoul of the law in Bexar County," he replied placidly. "The case probably won't be as challenging as some of the capital murder cases I've tried, but then the check won't bounce, either."

Kris turned back to Tess. "This is my boyfriend, Enrique Trejo. I'd like to say he's usually not this obnoxious, but the fact is, he's a much bigger cabron most of the time. That means asshole."

"*Rick* Trejo," he said, holding his hand out to Tess. "And as long as we're having this little Spanish lesson, I wish I could introduce Kristina as *mi novia*, my betrothed, which sounds far more elegant than girlfriend or old lady, but she keeps refusing my pleas to make her an honest woman."

"*Enrique.*" Kristina punched him on the arm—not some little fake girl punch, but a good, solid thump. "Don't involve strangers in our private life."

"Excuse me, but who brought this woman over to me? Miss, Miss—what is your name?"

"Tess Monaghan."

"Miss Monaghan, can you imagine why any woman in her right mind wouldn't marry me? I'm an attorney—"

"Well, there's one reason," Tess said.

"I'll ignore that. Lawyer jokes demean only those who tell them. As I said, I'm an attorney, with a thriving practice and the best winning streak of any criminal lawyer in the county. I'm handsome. Not being vain, just stating the facts of life as my mother has explained them to me."

"She does," Kristina put in. "She almost swoons every time he stops by. '*Oh Ricky, que guapo.*' She calls me la flaquita—the little skinny one. And I'm not even skinny by most people's standards. She thinks he can do much better than some Wisconsin gringa."

"And yet I don't want to do better," Rick said, pulling Kristina into his lap. "I'd settle for you, sweetheart. So what do you say? Say yes right now, and I'll let you have this goddamn punk conjunto music at the reception and you can walk down the aisle in one of those stupid Oaxacan dresses you love so much. I'll wear a guayabera, I'll let you fill our house with crap from your gallery. But you have to say yes right now."

"Shhh." She clamped a hand over his mouth, but she was laughing. Tess had never seen a more mismatched couple, or a happier one. "They're about to start."

The band emerged from the building at the edge of the vast patio. They had shucked their eighties costumes from the Morgue, and their eighties ennui along with it. This was an inspired, revved-up group, and the audience fed its energy. Emmie was right—the accordion, as wielded by the keyboard player, reinvented old songs and made the new ones soar. Tess felt a strange surge of pride, watching the couples get up to dance, hearing the slap of tapping feet on the poured concrete floor. Poe White Trash had never been this good. Crow had found his muse in Texas. *Or in Emmie.*

For she was the one everyone watched. She wasn't holding anything back and her full voice proved a huge, powerful thing with a life of its own. Tess finally understood why the voice was spoken of as an instrument. This was a separate entity that happened to live inside Emmie. As the set progressed, the voice seemed to grow stronger and stronger, while Emmie looked frailer. Her voice was like an incubus, drawing all the strength from her and she surrendered to it gladly, joyously.

After a fast thirty-minute set, the band broke, and while Crow disappeared inside Hector's, Emmie mingled with the crowd. With the men in the crowd, at any rate, flitting from table to table, bumming smokes from surly biker types. The surlier, the better.

Tess spotted the same moon-faced security guard from the Morgue, puppy eyes fixed on Emmie. He had it bad, she could tell—his dark skin was flushed with his yearning, his eyes had the same fixity of purpose that Esskay brought to a biscuit. Tess caught his eye and, feeling sorry for anyone lost in such a hopeless crush, waved for him to join them. He hesitated, then started walking over, keeping his gaze on Emmie as long as possible.

"Tess Monaghan," she reminded him. "I saw you last night."

"Steve," he said, stopping as if he smelled something very bad, then jerking his chin toward Rick Trejo. "I didn't know you were with him."

"We just met. They kept the bartender from gouging me for a generic cola."

"Yeah, Mr. Trejo is a real stickler for legal technicalities. It's the big issues he's not so good on. I gotta get back to work. Enjoy the rest of the show." And he shouldered his way back through the crowd, until he was back at his post near the stage.

"What was *that* about?"

"He's a cop," Rick said. "Steve Villanueve."

"A rent-a-cop, you mean. I met him at another club last night."

"No, he's a city patrolman. A lot of them do security work for extra dough. Mr. Villanueve is a good cop, but he's young, and he takes things personally. A guy he pulled over for speeding last year ended up getting popped in a sexual assault. It's not my fault the judge threw out the case when he found out the victim had seen the suspect on television before the police brought her in to see a line-up."

"He raped a woman," Kristina said, her voice small and tight.

"He was *suspected* of raping a woman. Hey, I did it pro bono, sweetheart. Doesn't that make me a good guy?"

"He got arrested two months later for another attack."

"The band's starting," Rick said, his tone resigned. The happy couple suddenly seemed less happy. "Let's just listen to the music, okay?"

While the first set had been revved up and fun, a dancing set, Las Almas Perdidas was quieter and more contemplative this time around. Music to go to bed by, and you could define that anyway you wanted. These songs were slow, bittersweet. They could put you in the mood to grab a stranger, but they also provided a suitable soundtrack for going home alone.

After five songs, Crow spoke from the stage. His face was flushed from exertion, his voice ripe with what could only be called pride. No wonder he and Emmie phoned it in at the Morgue, Tess thought. They were saving their energy for their real music.

"We're going to close with something a little different, but give it a chance," he said. "We call this medley Sondheim con salsa."

He didn't even like the Broadway composer, Tess recalled, a little miffed. Sondheim was her passion, and Crow had often mocked her for it, damning it as too clever, the kind of music where the smart lyrics were there to form a barrier between the listener and the composer. Of all the things Crow might have carried out of the burning house of their relationship, Sondheim would have been her last pick.

Maybe it was intended as parody instead of tribute. The medley Crow had concocted drew on the considerable number of songs Sondheim had written for those on the verge of a nervous breakdown, thanks to love. "You Could Drive a Person Crazy." "Losing My Mind." "Not a Day Goes By." Was he making fun of the words by setting them to these new rhythms? No, with the help of Emmie's heart-rending voice, he was making them sadder still. Especially on the last, "Every Day a Little Death"—a song about surviving betrayal in a marriage. But the song could have been about any broken relationship, with its incantatory accounting of how lost love turns up everywhere in one's life. In buttons, in bread. In a sweater the color of sauteed mushrooms. In a greyhound's breath. In a bagel. In a neon Domino's sugar sign, blazing red across the harbor. No, that had belonged to her and Jonathan.

Tess wanted to turn away, embarrassed by the nakedness of Emmie's yearning, but it was impossible to take one's eyes from her face. As she rasped out the final words, her head dropped and her knees buckled a little, and it appeared she might faint. Out of the corner of her eye, Tess saw Steve start to move toward the stage. Crow was watching, too, but he didn't seem quite as concerned. Another second passed, and Emmie lifted her head, blew a kiss to the audience, and waved good night.

The patio lights came up and the audience erupted into a standing ovation. Without thinking, Tess jumped to her feet with the others, managing to upset the small metal table at which they sat. The resounding crash seemed to echo forever across the patio, and the people in the audience ducked reflex-ively. The sound of an overturned table was not unknown at Hector's, Tess thought, although it probably signaled the beginning for a fight, not some dumb woman's clumsiness. She was now the center of attention, and when Crow saw her, a smile broke over his face—a sunny, guilt-free grin, as if he had no memory of the trick he had played on her just that afternoon. He put down his guitar and the crowd parted, allowing him to walk straight to her.

"You're still here," he said.

"Evidently."

"You didn't rat me out, did you? You didn't tell my parents where I was?"

Maybe that was all he had wanted to know. But what in her motel room could have told him that?

"No," she said. "I made sure they know you're okay, but I didn't tell them anything else. You asked for seven days. You've got it."

"So why are you still here?"

Good question. One of the big questions, as Emmie might have pointed out. Why was she here? Tess had thought she was staying because she didn't trust Crow to stop running, and because she needed to know what he was running from, and if it had any connection to the death of some ex-felon named Tom Darden.

So why was she at Hector's? Because Crow had searched her room, because Emmie had dropped enough hints. Maybe Crow had wanted her here, so she would know that he wasn't spending his life cranking out bad music in some tourist trap. Why was anyone anywhere? It was past three A.M., and she had been up for almost twenty-one hours and she was fresh out of answers for even the easiest questions. She only knew she was standing in a little circle of light in the middle of some vast darkness, and Crow was grinning at her as if she had passed some test. She wondered what it was.

"You want breakfast?" he asked. "I could probably find a place where you can get two bagels, toasted, one with cream cheese and one without. And I'll make sure the waitress keeps your coffee cup filled to the brim, although she's more likely to call you honey than hon. But it would still be your usual, just like back in Jimmy's."

Finally, a question she could answer.

"I don't *want* my usual. I've driven sixteen hundred miles, crossed five state lines, and entered a new time zone. I want something I've never had before, in a place I've never been before."

Crow smiled. "I think that can be arranged."

12

They ended up Earl Abel's, the restaurant that Emmie had mentioned, the place where secrets came out as the sun came up. But Crow just ate ice and played with a piece of pie, while Tess was almost too weary to lift the forkfuls of German chocolate cake to her mouth. Almost.

"Still not much of a night person, are you? You row in the mornings still?"

"Oh, yeah," Tess said automatically, as if he had asked if she was breathing on a regular basis.

"Of course you do. You row in the morning and you eat at Jimmy's for breakfast. You walk Esskay twice a day, and you always take the same route. You hang out in Kitty's kitchen, you argue with Tyner. Same as it ever was. Same as it ever was."

"Not exactly." He might consider her life boring and static, but there were changes, significant ones. She just didn't know how to explain Jackie and Laylah, or even Detective Martin Tull, who had come into her life as Crow was leaving it. Nor could she explain the mix of feelings that came over her as she sat in her office, balancing her books. She felt a frisson of pride, yes, but also a suffocating sense that life was closing in too quickly, setting around her like a quick-drying concrete. She thought of her parents, going to the same jobs every day for almost thirty years now, of how moody and distracted Tyner had been as of late. Every bowl of porridge was too cold for him, every bed too soft. It wasn't that long ago she had yearned for such sameness and security, but now that she had it, she was beginning to see the charming precariousness of her old life.

"How did you know about Hector's, anyway? Not exactly your kind of place."

"Emmie mentioned it when she came to see me today."

"Emmie came to see you?" She had been wrong, Crow could fake ignorance exceedingly well. Tess decided to let it go, for now. She'd find out eventually what he had been doing in her room.

"Yes. We went to lunch together."

"She's a good kid."

"A little . . . odd," Tess said. She thought it was a polite way to describe someone who was several Prozacs short of a prescription, but Crow frowned and shook his head.

"She's a brilliant singer, fucking brilliant. You can't expect her to be without a few idiosyncrasies. That's what makes her an artist."

"If you say so."

Crow crunched a piece of ice. Other than his haircut and a new range of frowning facial expressions, he hadn't changed that much, either. He had always chewed his way through a glass of postper-formance ice in his Poe White Trash days.

"So, what did you think?" His voice was too casual.

"Of what?" Of *Emmie*?

"Of Hector's."

"The Shiner Bock was very good."

"No, of us. The band."

Tess hesitated. She thought the band was terrific, but she was reluctant to praise his new life, after the way he had mocked hers.

"At first, it felt a little over the top to me, too conscious of whatever musical style you were aping. I couldn't see that you brought out anything new in the covers you did. I thought it was gimmicky, blending all those styles. But then, I began to like it. It was like bluegrass and zydeco and—what did you call it?"

"*Conjunto*. Together."

"Conjunto," she repeated after him. "Anyway, I got used to it, and the differences weren't so jarring and I listened to the voices, and the instruments, and it all fit. It was the best performance I've ever seen you give." Then, grudgingly: "Emmie is extraordinary."

"Yes, she is."

"She told me—" But she didn't know how to finish that sentence.

"About her and me? I should have seen that coming, I guess, when she asked me where you were staying. Emmie is big into confession, but always on her own terms. It hasn't occurred to her yet that it's frequently hell for other people, when you always say exactly what you're feeling."

"Were you in love with her?"

He crunched another mouthful of ice. "We were a comfort to one another. Sort of the way I was a comfort to you, after Jonathan. A bookmark you put in your heart to keep your place, until you remember how to love again."

"That's not fair, Crow. I never thought about Jonathan when I was with you."

"Keep telling yourself that. Anyway, I was a comfort to her. Then, suddenly, she didn't need to be comforted anymore, not by me. We've been not-together now longer than we were together. But I feel responsible for her."

"Why?"

He started to say something, stopped, started over. "I don't know. Maybe I'm just a self-interested shit, who doesn't want to see her self-destruct when we've honestly got a chance to go somewhere with our music."

An uneasy silence fell. Tess was still smarting over his bookmark comment. It hadn't been like that, not quite.

"If you're so interested in Emmie's welfare," she said at last, "you might want to say something to her about her choice of men. I saw the guys she was cozying up to at Hector's. Men like that are not big on teases. She's going to get in over her head, and you're going to have to come on like Mr. Macho. I hear that got you canned at Primo's."

"Who says we got canned, Kleinschmidt?" Again, that strange twisted smile she still couldn't get used to seeing on Crow's face. "And who says she's teasing? Almost every Saturday night, she goes home with whatever guy has tattoos and piercings approaching the triple digits. I've tried to talk her out of it, but she assures me that she'll never get involved in anything that would make her miss Sunday breakfast at the Alamo."

"Breakfast at the Alamo—is that some code?"

"One of Emmie's many rituals. She likes to get some tacos and coffee, then sit in the gardens there and read the paper. She told me it started when she was a teenager, and trying to cultivate a reputation for eccentricity. An affectation that metamorphosed into a routine, you know?"

"Yeah, I do actually." Tess smiled. "Although I went the other way. I always tried to pass as conventional—school sports, jock boyfriends, bourbon choked down in finished basements with knotty pine walls."

"Whereas I had to do anything and everything to stand out—down to purple dreadlocks." He noticed, for the first time, that she was wearing her Cafe Hon T-shirt. "Or dying my T-shirt orange, because I couldn't have a Cafe Hon T-shirt like everyone else in Baltimore, oh no."

"I always saw you as this blissed-out boy who followed his heart."

"Was I?" Crow furrowed his brow, as if trying to remember someone they had both once known, many years ago. "I'd like to think so. I'd like to think there was a time when I just did what I wanted to do and didn't have to run it through eighteen different filters. A time when I knew what I wanted, and was sure of what I could do."

"What do you want right now?"

"I want—I want—" He was laughing, completely at ease for the first time.

"No thinking," Tess said. "Just say what you want, the first thing that comes to your mind. More pie, another cup of coffee? A Rolex, a new guitar, a chartreuse Cafe Hon T-shirt, a first edition of Poe's *Eureka . . .*"

"I want—" They were both giggling now, giddy as a couple of drunks.

"Say it, Crow."

"I want to make love to you."

All the other sounds of the restaurant seemed to disappear. Tess looked down at her plate. His voice had been low and sure, without a single teasing note to get them off the hook. She realized she was forking her cake in half. Not eating it, as Jackie would say, yet still obsessed with it. She didn't feel quite so tired anymore.

Crow wasn't finished. "I want to take you back to my house and take all your clothes off and put you in my bed and keep you there until we both walk funny, as if we'd been out to sea for weeks and weeks."

She wanted him, too, which surprised her, yet didn't surprise her. She wanted him because he had rejected her, and that left her feeling unfinished. A psychiatrist would say she only wanted the men she couldn't quite have, and she supposed her life so far supported this thesis. But now Crow was sitting here, saying she could have him. In which case, she shouldn't want him at all, right? So if she went with him, she was actually doing the right thing, right?

"What do you say, Tess?" Whatever filters Crow

had learned to put up between himself and the world were gone now. He looked younger and older, very pure, as if he couldn't tell a lie to save his life. Yet he had been lying to her right and left over the past twenty-four hours. Which made him a bum, which made him her dream man, which made her—Jesus, didn't her brain have an off-switch?

"Tess?" he asked again.

"I think that could be arranged," she said.

Earl Abel's wasn't even two miles from the duplex Crow shared with Emmie, but it took them a long time to travel those two miles. It was as if they were in such a hurry that they had to keep slowing down. First in the parking lot—Crow wouldn't even let her get her key in the door lock, he had to kiss her right there, much to the rowdy amusement of some college boys who had arrived at the restaurant after a long night of partying.

"Nail her, man," one yelled.

"Get a room," another called out.

"Nail her, then get a room," a third suggested.

"What about your car?" Tess asked Crow, coming up for air.

"Leave it. Let them tow it. I don't care."

When they were finally in her car, he kissed her at stoplights, holding her face in his hands until horns sounded behind them.

"My place is closer," Tess said, even as La Casita's flickering neon sign flew past.

"No," Crow said. Now he was trying to kiss her as she drove, lifting up her hair in the back, pressing his lips against her neck and her throat. "I don't want to feel like some John you picked up in Brack-enridge Park. Turn right here, onto Mulberry. Can't you drive any faster?"

She thought she was going pretty fast, but she was like a drunk who couldn't distinguish fifteen miles per hour from ninety-five. She was losing all her senses, except those Crow had engaged. His hand was under her T-shirt now, on the small of her back.

"How much farther?" she asked.

"Left here, then right on the second street, Mag-nolia Drive. I'm at the end of the block."

But once the car was parked, Crow simply began kissing her again. It was as if he didn't want to risk letting go for even the moment it would take to run up the walk. She wasn't so sure she wanted to leave the car yet, anyway. The truth was, it was delicious to neck in a car again, to feel sixteen again. She could have been parked in front of her parents' house, testing the boundaries as she had done back then, wondering how far she would dare to go with her father not-sleeping just yards away. *One more minute*, the boy would ask. *Just a little more. Can I—? Will you—?* And she assented, silently, always silently, for if she spoke of what she was doing, she would betray how conscious it was, how much she craved it, how she was really the one who was set-ting the pace, pushing them further and further on each date. Part of her wanted to keep going. Part of her yearned for Patrick to come charging out of the house and yank her from the car, and back into the safety of her childhood. When he didn't, there was nothing to do but keep pushing forward, until she found herself on her back in the Enchanted Castle.

Sixteen had really been too young, she knew that in the split-second it had taken her high school boyfriend to finish. With the loss of virginity, a girl lost her best reason for saying no. From that moment on, she had to choose, and choose carefully, there was nothing between her and her desires. That had been the terrifying part, not the sex itself.

The strange thing was, it was no less terrifying now.

And then, with the suddenness of a nightmare, she was sixteen again and the thing that had never happened was happening—the car's doors were being thrown open, and there was yelling, and heavy, thick arms reached in from the darkness to drag the two of them apart.

"Put your hands up and step away from the car," an amplified voice called from beyond a bank of lights. The light was so bright that Tess couldn't see anything, but she was aware of running car engines and the sudden sound of a helicopter overhead.

"It's not what you think," she said, struggling against the arms that held her. Her braid had come loose at some point and her hair was flying around her head in snaky Medusa tendrils. Crow was lying in the street, a police officer's knee in his back, his hands being cuffed. Four other officers stood in a circle around him, and when Crow tried to raise his head, one pushed him back to the pavement with his foot.

"Leave him alone," Tess screamed. "He wasn't doing anything."

"Do you live here?" one of the officers asked impatiently. The one who had been holding her arms had finally released her, but she could still feel his bulk at her back.

"No, it's his place."

"Fine." He walked over to Crow, bent down, and took the keys from his pocket, using them to open the door. It seemed as if dozens of officers followed, although Tess later realized there were no more than six. Her sense of time was also off—it felt like hours passed, but her watch said only fifteen minutes had elapsed when they returned, toting a rifle bagged in plastic. A plainclothes officer had arrived at the scene, and they showed him their find with great excitement. But he shook his head, and although Tess could not hear what he said, he seemed angry and upset.

"Is this your shotgun?" the plainclothes officer asked Crow, now handcuffed and in the back of one of the patrol cars.

"I've never seen that before in my life."

"Do you have a search warrant?" Tess asked.

"We had a warrant for the arrest of one Ed Ransome and this was under the bed in what appears to be his room." The cop turned back to Crow. "And if this is the gun that killed Tom Darden, you're going to have a lot of explaining to do."

"Killed *who?*"

"Shut up, Crow," Tess called to him from the curb, where they had left her in the care of a big beefy police officer. "Just shut up and don't say anything until you get a lawyer."

The detective walked over to her. "You might want to heed the same advice, miss."

"Are you taking me in?"

"We've got a few questions to ask you. Unless you want to change your mind and file a rape complaint, then we'll make sure you get to the emergency room. How about it?"

It was first light now, a pale, ghostly rim of color showing at the horizon. Tess was aware of people streaming out on their lawns in bathrobes and nightclothes, staring curiously.

"Were you here waiting for us?"

"We had officers waiting here for him and officers following you. You threw us off when you left the restaurant in only one vehicle—but not for long."

"You brought the cops here? You brought the cops to me, to this house?" Crow called out from the patrol car. "Jesus, Tess, how fucking stupid could you be? I trusted you, and you screwed me again."

"I didn't—"

Two cops were pushing Tess into another patrol car now, slamming the door, so her protestations to Crow were cut off.

"I want a lawyer," she said, but it came out as a undignified whimper. Specifically, she wanted Tyner, and she almost cried at the thought of how far away he was. Lord help her, she'd give anything to hear that cranky old bastard screaming on the phone at her.

"You won't need one, miss," said the detective, who had taken his place in the passenger seat. "You're not being charged with anything. We'd just like to take you downtown and ask you what you know about your friend, Mr. Ransome."

"I know he couldn't kill someone under any circumstances."

The detective had sorrowful, cocker spaniel eyes. "Then maybe you don't know him quite as well as present circumstances would suggest."

13

Church bells were ringing in the distance before anyone bothered with Tess at the police station. They had left her in a room, not under arrest as far as she could tell, but not free to go, either, judging by the officer posted outside her door. At last she was in the famed "box," as everyone in Baltimore knew to call it since *Homicide* had become the city's official religion. She had spent the balance of the night in a plastic chair, her body desperate to sleep, her mind refusing. Talk about a mind-body problem. These two were like some long-married couple— the resentful insomniac mind kept jabbing the body every time it drifted off, hissing: *How can you sleep at a time like this?* Body begged wearily for its due, arguing that they would both be better off if they got a little rest. And so it had gone, all night long.

She was almost crazed with exhaustion by the time a man entered the room, carrying a wax paper bag and two Styrofoam cups of coffee. It was the sad-eyed plainclothes cop from the night before, the one who had arrived late, then ridden downtown with her. She remembered he seemed angry or troubled, but that might have been the fragment of a not-quite dream.

"Detective Al Guzman," he said. "Homicide. And you're Theresa Monaghan, according to your various licenses."

She nodded, letting the full version of her name pass. She wasn't going to form words until strictly necessary. The coffee was black and bitter—she usually took hers with a generous portion of half-and-half—but she needed the caffeine, so she sipped at it. Awful. The bag held an elephant ear and she broke off several flaking layers and dropped them into her coffee to sweeten it. Guzman watched approvingly, as a mother might watch a finicky child.

"Sorry for last night," he said. "You were caught in an unavoidable confluence of events, I'm afraid. Wrong place, wrong time. Wrong guy."

She let a lift of her shoulders pass for a reply.

"You know Ed Ransome before you came to Texas, or was he just, uh, a new friend? You can tell me. There's no law here against getting involved with the wrong man. Couldn't build enough prisons to hold all the women guilty of that crime."

It was a cornball thing to say, but he smiled as if he knew it was a cornball thing to say, and she found herself thawing a little. Guzman was not a handsome man, and his body was shaped like a squash, with its narrow shoulders and paunchy midsection. But he had a kind face that invited confidences and confessions—those big brown eyes and a glossy mustache whose shape mirrored the gentle, downturned mouth beneath it. Perhaps if she told him everything she knew, she would be allowed to go home and sleep. She thought longingly of La Casita, then remembered that Esskay was there alone. Maybe they would let her call Mrs. Nguyen at least, so she could feed the dog, get one of the hookers to take her for a walk. It would be so good to crawl into bed next to her.

But what was best for Tess wasn't necessarily best for Crow.

"I'm a private detective, which you know, since you've obviously gone through my wallet. Crow—Ed Ransome to you—is an old friend. An old boyfriend." That wasn't revealing anything, given the way the police had found them. Coitus interruptus by SWAT team. At last a form of birth control that was one hundred percent reliable. "His parents asked me to find him and I did. End of story."

"I think it's just the beginning," Guzman said, then waited, with those big brown eyes and that so very sad smile. He was letting the silence do the work, hoping Tess would rush into it out of nervousness. Exhausted as she was, she couldn't help admiring the technique.

"This is really good," she said. "This elephant ear. It's the best I've ever had."

Guzman followed her little sidestep effortlessly, the Arthur Murray of the box. "It's from Mario's, in El Mercado. You been there yet?"

She shook her head.

"I keep forgetting, you're not just another tourist. El Mercado, the River Walk, the missions—those are the places the tourists go."

"And the Alamo."

"*Claro que sí.* Not that I have much use for the Alamo."

"Why?"

"Do I look like John Wayne?" he asked. "Or even Fess Parker?"

"Oh, yeah—your people were on the outside."

"Not *my* people. My people run a shoestore in Guadalajara. Besides, there were Mexicans inside, too, you know. No, it just doesn't mean anything to me. There's a lot of stuff in San Antonio like that. This stupid All Soul Festival, for example. Gus Sterne's brainchild."

"Gus Sterne?" Tess had heard of the festival, and heard of Gus Sterne, the cousin who had raised Emmie until their falling-out. She hadn't heard the two were connected.

"Yeah, Gus Sterne. I know he raises all this money for scholarships, but to me, it's a sacrilege, using Day of the Dead as some hook for another week of parties and parades that also happen to promote his barbecue restaurants. Yet the City Hall folks, the tourism gurus, say it's a big deal. They say it's going to be bigger than the New Orleans Jazz and Heritage Festival one day. 'As if,' my twelve-year-old daughter would say."

As if she would say as if. That locution was only a thousand years old in teen-speak. Under different circumstances, Tess might have smiled at the thought of this streetwise cop who couldn't keep up with his own daughter's vocabulary.

"Anyway, I don't care," Guzman said. "I'll make some overtime."

"Umph," Tess said, hoping it sounded like a polite, neutral agreement. Her lips were covered with pastry flakes and there was no napkin she could see. The back of the hand would have to do. But then her hand was covered with pastry, which made her giggle. God, she was so fatigued, it was like being stoned. Where had she read that British secret service agents had to undergo seventy-two hours of sleep deprivation as part of training?

"I remember when I used to make overtime working cases, not pulling parade duty. The bad ol' days. Now the homicide rate's at a twenty-year low."

"Really." Although Tess couldn't put much energy in her reaction, she was impressed. Baltimore had fallen back from its body-a-day high, but not by much. In fact, the stats indicated Baltimore's killers were simply getting more efficient: fewer shootings, but a higher fatality rate. Way to go, kids. If you can't bring up your reading scores, at least you're improving as marksmen.

"It gives us time to solve cases," Guzman said. "Old ones, as well as new ones. Today's technology can solve yesterday's murders. We cleared a twenty-five-year-old case last month. I was counting on Tom Darden to help me clear another one, one almost as old. You remember Tom Darden? You made his acquaintance up near Twin Sisters, as I recall. Stocky fellow?"

Not so stocky with his chest hollowed out by a gunshot blast, Tess thought. Somewhere in her body, a warning signal was going off, or trying to go off—it seemed almost as far away as the city's church bells. *See?* her body screamed at her mind. *You should have let me sleep, then we could cope with this.*

The mind replied testily: *Oh shut up and make some adrenaline.*

"You know who Tom Darden is, Miss Monaghan?"

"He's the man I found."

Guzman smiled approvingly, a teacher with a slow student who had finally, after much prodding and many hints, come up with the right answer.

"That the only time you've ever seen him?"

"As far as I know. I don't really know what he looked like when he was alive."

Another smile, another nod. "Good point. They keep making bigger and better guns, but there's still nothing like an old-fashioned shotgun for ripping open some guy's face, is there? That gun we found under your friend's bed, it was old, but it could do the job, couldn't it? A beauty. Matches a gun that belongs to Marianna Barrett Conyers. I just talked to her on the phone. She confirmed that she keeps it up at her weekend place. What do you want to bet that it's not there anymore?"

Tess said nothing, but in her mind she was making another quick inventory of the limestone cottage. No bullets in any of the drawers she had pulled open, no locked gun cabinet, but she recalled a rack above the fireplace. Empty, it hadn't registered as being of any significance. Could have been a plateholder for all she knew, or some other piece of decorative bric-a-brac. A gun rack. Go figure.

"Don't get me wrong," Guzman said. "I'm not going to shed any tears over Darden. In fact, I was counting on watching him die one day. I just thought it would be through lethal injection, a few more years down the road. The thing is, I wanted to talk to him first about some old business, and now I can't do that. And although I'm indebted to your friend, I can't really let it go, you know? Even lowlifes have rights."

Tess started to nod, then stopped, not sure what she would be agreeing with.

"Unless—" Guzman paused as if struck by a sudden brainstorm, only he was a little too stagey. "Unless, of course, your friend killed him in self-defense. I can see that. He's staying up there with Emmie Sterne, and this bad guy breaks in. Your friend gets scared and grabs the gun. Bang, bang, bang, lots of blood and screaming. Everybody panics. It's natural. He stashes the guy in the pool house, cleans up real good, and hits the road. Then you come along, looking for your old buddy, and you find the body. Only you don't bother to tell the sheriff why you're really there. That how it happened?"

"If it did, wouldn't it be a matter for Sheriff Kolarik? His county, his body."

Perhaps the slow student was moving a little too fast now. For whatever reason, Guzman was no longer smiling and nodding at her.

"Believe me, Sheriff Kolarik would love to have you return as a guest of the county. Problem is, we know where Darden was found, but we don't know where he was killed. He was last seen alive in San Antonio, about two weeks ago, with his old buddy Laylan Weeks. Sheriff Kolarik doesn't mind if I make a few inquiries down here, seeing as the weapon appears to have shown up and all. Under your friend's bed. And seeing as Tom Darden might be the link to something where the stakes are a lot bigger."

"I hate to undermine your theory, but Crow Ransome doesn't know how to use a gun." At least, he hadn't when Tess last saw him. Or had he? Perhaps his knowledge of firearms had been something else he had mentioned in passing. *My father abandoned a shot at the Nobel Prize to run off with my mother the famous sculptor and, by the way, I'm a crack shot.* It was possible. Anything seemed possible just now. "He's also not stupid enough to hide a murder weapon under his own bed. Who hides anything under the bed, anymore? I haven't put anything there since I was twelve and trying to read *Lolita*."

"That Russian book they made into the dirty movie on Showtime?"

Tess decided not to challenge his characterization. "Yeah."

"Man, I'd jump up and down if my twelve-year-old was trying to sneak a book like that. The only thing she has under her bed is a stash of makeup that her mother won't let her wear until she's sixteen."

"If you want her to read a certain book, all you have to do is ban it. Better yet, hide it wherever you hide your own contraband—my mom used the linen closet. Your daughter will find it there and start sneaking it out, gulping it down when you're out of the house. Leave a little Balzac behind, and she'll take it from there."

"Naw. Estrella doesn't know our hiding places."

"If you've got a twelve-year-old in the house, she knows where everything is. Including the dirty videos and drugs. Well, no drugs in a detective's house, I guess. But the videos and the booze, even contraband chocolates."

Guzman blushed. "Yes, well. Anyway, you came looking for your old boyfriend. Why did he go missing in the first place?"

The postcard with Crow's picture, the one that had started this whole mess, was in the pages of Tess's datebook. She worried for a moment that some police officer might be pawing through it even as she and Guzman spoke, then remembered the datebook was back at La Casita. With Esskay and the double bed with the polyester spread, which suddenly seemed the most wonderful bed in the world to her.

"He was trying to strike out on his own, make it as a musician. Nothing sinister."

"How did he hook up with Emmie Sterne?"

"They met in Austin." Had she just been lulled into telling Guzman something he didn't know? "Or maybe here. I'm not sure. She was looking for a guitarist, he was looking for a singer."

"What about Gus Sterne, her cousin. He have any connection to this band?"

"Not to my knowledge. Someone told me they were on the outs."

"Yeah? Everyone in this town loves her cousin, and she hates his guts? That's pretty strange, don't you think?"

"I'd say it was about par for the course as families go."

Guzman extended his index finger, as if awarding a point.

"So you know the whole story about Emmie Sterne, then? The poor little princess, orphaned before she was even three years old? A daddy she never knew, a mommy she barely remembers."

"Marianna Barrett Conyers told me how both Emmie's parents died in accidents." If he had already spoken to Marianna about the shotgun, he knew she had been there. She wasn't giving him anything new.

"Accidents?" Guzman did a double-take, neat as any professional comic. "I suppose you could call it that. I mean, rich people have fancy words for everything, so why not? Horace Morgan shot his head off after his wife left him. I guess you'd call that an accident. Meanwhile, Lollie Sterne died in a really big accident. An accidental triple homicide that Tom Darden was going to help me solve."

Tess suddenly remembered where she had learned that invaluable bit of trivia about British secret service agents and sleep deprivation: It had been on the VH1 "popup" video for Duran Duran's "A View to a Kill." Gee, if only VH1 had provided more invaluable training for the up-and-coming private investigator. For example: what to do when you got hit with a fact so important, so central to everything that you had been doing, that it felt like someone had slapped you across the face with a wet towel.

"Emmie's mother was murdered?"

"Uh-huh." Guzman was really enjoying himself now. "Killed in what looked like in a botched robbery at her restaurant, Espejo Verde. It was a big deal. If you were older, I bet you'd remember it. Some local sleaze even got a book out of it. I was the first cop on the scene." He waited, as if used to people reacting when they heard that fact. "Someone had heard a child crying from the restaurant late on a Monday night, when it was supposed to be closed. It was Emmie, in a playpen in a room off the kitchen."

"Where were . . . Could she?" Just trying to form the right question made Tess felt queasy and prurient. Emmie's strange preoccupation with dead bodies and blood suddenly made more sense. Everything about Emmie suddenly made more sense.

"Her mother was in the dining room, along with the cook. One shot each. The third victim, a man, had been left in the kitchen. Technically, I shouldn't have touched anything, not even Emmie, but I couldn't leave that baby alone in there. My oldest boy had just been born. She wasn't crying, she wasn't even awake, but there was blood on her. Not much, just streaks on her arms and hands. As if she had crawled through it."

"The killers put her back in her playpen?"

"I don't know. There's a lot of stuff we don't know about Espejo Verde, things as basic as the motive. It looked like a robbery, but the weekend receipts would have been in the bank Monday morning, and the restaurant was closed Monday nights. Even two robbers as stupid as Darden and his buddy Laylan Weeks should have known that."

"Are you sure they did it?"

Guzman shrugged. "They were lowlifes, they ripped off convenience stores for beer money. Then, out of nowhere, they get popped for this botched kidnapping and get sent away to prison. They dropped some hints, in Huntsville, like they knew something about Espejo Verde. Twenty years is a long time, you run out of stuff to say, and they might have been bragging, trying to seem tougher than they were. But they were the only leads I had, and now one is dead and the other is missing. Meanwhile, the rifle that probably killed Darden just happens to be in the house where Lollie Sterne's daughter lives."

Tess wasn't really paying attention. She was thinking about a crying toddler, traces of blood on her baby hands. Jackie's Laylah had lost her biological mother at an even younger age, but she hadn't seen anything, and the child psychiatrists were already heaping sermons on Jackie's head about how and when to tell her about her past.

Guzman was still talking to her, she'd better listen.

"So you see, when Tom Darden turns up dead on a ranch where Emmie Sterne has been known to go, and a gun from that ranch ends up under your friend's bed in the house he shares with her—well, a person has to make some connections, don't you think?"

"Only if Emmie knew about Darden and Weeks." Her response had been automatic, but something twitched in Guzman's face, and she knew she had found a weak spot. So she pressed. "She doesn't, does she? The family doesn't know about this lead you developed. You probably sat on it, waiting, hoping to surprise them with an arrest."

"I'm not telling you everything we know," Guzman said sullenly.

"And I don't know anything. It's Emmie Sterne you need. Not me, and not Crow."

"Good idea. Do you happen to know where we can find her? There are only two roads into that neighborhood, and I've had a cop stationed at each one all night, waiting for the two roomies to come home. You swam into our net eventually. But she never came home."

Breakfast at the Alamo, Tess thought, but she didn't volunteer the information. At this point, she wasn't sure if finding Emmie would help or hurt Crow.

Guzman was still waiting for her answer, allowing another silence to fill the room, when the policeman who had been watching the door poked his head in and motioned to the detective. The two left the room together, shutting the door behind them. Tess couldn't make out the words, but she heard Guzman's voice getting louder and angrier. The door opened again, and his kind face had been transformed into a furious one.

"You can go," he said curtly.

"Go *where?*" Her car was at Crow's duplex, which she wasn't sure she could find again. She knew the place was close to La Casita, somewhere in the folds of the park, but she didn't remember much from the trip, except the feel of Crow's hands on her body, his mouth on her neck.

"An officer will take you to your car."

"No, we'll take her, Detective." Rick Trejo was leaning against the door jamb. He wore the preppy clothes and cowboy boots of the night before, but Tess was sure these were different, cleaner versions. He was freshly shaven, too, and his face had the smooth, rested look of someone who had enjoyed at least a few hours of sleep. If she hadn't been so relieved to see him, she might have hated him for looking so well-rested. She hated everyone who had slept in the last eight hours.

"It's no trouble," Guzman said.

"I'm sure it's not. I'm sure you'd love to have her in a patrol car just a little while longer, ask her a few more questions. I'd prefer to have her come with me and my client. It's her choice, of course. But if she's free to go, she's free to choose how she goes."

"Yeah, well, tell your client not to leave town anytime soon. I bet we have him back down here before the week is out."

"Detective, you can talk to him anytime you want—as long as I'm with him. I only hope you won't drag him down here again unless you're prepared to charge him." Trejo smiled at Guzman. "Cheer up, buddy. It's not my fault that the DA says you fucked up. He sounded kinda mad, by the way. Not that I talked to him. I just could hear how loud he was screaming when your boss was on the phone with him. C'mon, little Yankee gal. *Vamanos.*"

Tess, thoroughly confused, followed him. She felt guilty somehow, as if she had chosen the slick lawyer over the earnest cop, but she didn't see what choice she had.

"How did—" she began to ask in the hall.

"Not here," Rick said quickly. "We'll talk in the car."

"He's not charged with anything?"

"The search was no good. They had a warrant for his arrest, but they didn't have a search warrant, and they didn't have any reason to enter the house—Crow was outside, remember?"

She remembered.

"If the shotgun had been out in plain view, things might be different. But it wasn't. And the gun was all they had, which wasn't much to begin with—you can't match shotgun pellets the way you can bullets. The DA knows they can't use it, so they're going to have to build a case without it. End of story. For now."

Crow was sitting in the lobby with Kristina, who was beaming as if bailing out her favorite musician was the realization of some long-held dream. Crow looked dazed and frightened, yet grimly resolute. Tess had a feeling that Guzman had not been so kind and gentle with him.

"How did you know we were here?" Tess asked Rick.

"I have sources," Trejo said. "There are people here who let me know when there are, um, interesting cases in which representation might be required."

"He pays people," Kristina said.

"Kristina—that would be illegal. I simply am a generous man with a very long Christmas list. Anyway, Sam from Hector's called me, after Crow called him."

"We have to go," Crow said, rising to his feet. "It's already past eleven."

"Go where?" Kristina asked.

"In the car," Rick said, before Crow could say anything more, indicating the desk sergeant with a slight lift of his chin. "Let's confine all our chatter to *the goddamn car.*"

Once in the car, a Lexus the same flan color as his skin, Rick wanted to take a meandering course through downtown to make sure the police weren't following them. Crow was much too impatient for that.

"We don't have time," he said, pressing his hands against the glove compartment as if he could push the car through the streets. "She's probably already gone."

"Who's gone where?" Rick asked.

"The Alamo," Crow said, which didn't answer Rick's question, but told Tess everything she needed to know. "Just drop me off at the Alamo."

"Let's show a little discretion, okay? I'll let you off at Rivercenter Mall. Where you go from there is your own business. Just make sure you're not followed."

Crow didn't ask Tess to accompany him, but when he leaped from the car, she was a half-step behind. He scurried ahead, trying to lose her, but he couldn't break into an all-out run without attracting attention, so she had no problem keeping pace. At last, she could feel a little adrenaline moving through her body.

They left the mall by another entrance, Crow practically jogging now, a determined salmon swimming upstream through the schools of sluggish tourists. In less than a block, they were behind the walls of the Alamo, in a pretty, shaded garden. Crow stopped at a bench, then turned in a circle. He was looking, Tess knew, for a bright blond head, and there were plenty of those to be seen. But it was just a group of Germans passing through, eyes and mouths round with reverential awe. Who had told her, some time ago, that Germans loved the whole cowboy-frontier thing? It had been Crow.

"She's not here," he said. "She's not here."

"Maybe she's back at the house?"

"The cops would have gotten her, then. No, she's gone, and now everything's ruined." He looked at Tess balefully. "Everything's ruined because of you. You brought the cops right to us. All I needed was a week to make everything okay and you wouldn't even give me that. One goddamn week. Why couldn't you stay away? Why did you have to come to Hector's and set all this in motion? You know, I keep thinking you won't disappoint me if I don't ask for too much. But I'm always wrong."

With that, he turned and walked away. She could have run after him. She could have caught him, too, and told him it wasn't her fault, that the cops had simply made the same connection she had, from Marianna to Emmie to him. But she knew he was determined to be alone, or at least without her. Unsure of what to do, or how to hook up with Rick and Kristina, she sank onto a bench and looked around. So this was the Alamo.

It was pretty, although smaller than she thought it would be.

14

There comes a point when it's simply too late for sleep. Tess was now so tired that the only thing she had going for her was momentum. A book, Guzman had mentioned a book about the triple murders. He hadn't given its title, but his tone had indicated that its ambitions fell short of *In Cold Blood*. The library, even if open on Sundays, might not have such a book. Nor would a new bookstore.

But Mrs. Nyguen's near-neighbor, Half Price Books, was a possibility. Tess and Esskay dropped by after their walk that afternoon.

"That dog can come in here only if it can read," said the clerk, who appeared to be in training for angry young manhood.

"She can," Tess said, feeling perverse. "Show her a bag with 'kibble' written on it, and she'll go crazy."

He called her bluff, producing a brown bag and a black marker from behind the counter.

"Make the letters large and plain," Tess said. "Her eyesight's not so good."

When the clerk held up the bag, Esskay began

leaping around the store in a frenzy. What the clerk couldn't know was that Tess bought Esskay's food from an old-fashioned feed store in Fells Point, and it came in brown bags just like this, with black markings.

"Gee, now you've got her all worked up. Anyway, I'm looking for this book about this triple murder here, about twenty years—"

"*The Green Glass?*" Good, she had made his day, given him another reason to sneer. "We got all you could ever want. Cases of 'em. It's a pretty sleazy book, though. Sloppy, too. The guy didn't even get the name of the restaurant right. Espejo Verde is the Green *Mirror*."

"How come you have so many in stock?"

"It was a local book, and the publisher went bankrupt a few years back. My boss bought his stock, which included more than two thousand copies of that piece of trash. Turns out Gus Sterne ordered the bulk of the first print run, sat on the books for two years, then shipped them back and demanded a full refund. The publisher couldn't cover the loss, and that started his slide into bankruptcy."

"Interesting." And slightly at odds with the portrait Guzman had sketched of Gus Sterne as the patron saint of San Antonio. "Why go to all that trouble?"

"I think he wanted the guy to know the boxes had never been open, that he screwed him on purpose. See, Sterne apparently told the guy he would take an order of twenty-five hundred and sell them through his barbecue restaurants, even do some advertising—if he could get a one-month exclusive on it. The guy was a small-timer, he didn't know how things worked."

"Why did Sterne want to keep the book from distribution?"

The young man leaned forward, his initial antipathy toward Tess forgotten. He might not like providing service, but he obviously loved sharing gossip. "I always heard he wanted to make sure that his little cousin, the dead woman's daughter, never saw a copy. Because of the photos, you know? They are pretty gross. That's why the boss won't even put it out on the floor."

"Can you sell me a copy?"

"Sure." The clerk looked at her shrewdly. "But it's a collectible, you know. Twenty-five bucks. Cash."

Tess left Esskay behind the protective glass, curled around Mrs. Nguyen's ankles, then walked across the street to the Vietnam, the one Broadway eatery Mrs. Nguyen never patronized. ("Why should I?" she asked. "I make that myself.") Midafternoon on a Sunday, the tiny, almost decor-free restaurant was a blessedly quiet place, and the wait staff seemed unperturbed by the braided Occidental who lingered there, drinking sweetened iced tea long after her lemon chicken was gone.

The paperback for which she had paid twenty-five dollars had sold for two dollars when it came out, and that was still a dollar more than it was worth. *The Green Glass: An Inside Look at San Antonio's Unsolved Triple Homicide* was a failure even on its own low terms. Much too late to be a quickie book—it had been published almost five years after the murders—and without the virtues found in great true-crime writing, it was a shallow, vapid piece of work, with more padding than a training bra. Then there was the bonus of those black-and-white photos from the murder scene. Yummy.

The writer, a local journalist named Jimmy Ahern, spent the first hundred pages explaining—repeatedly—how important the Sternes were in San Antonio, and how common tragedy was in the family. "Bad luck stalked them," he had written, "as relentless as any serial killer." It was one of his more inspired lines.

The Sterne money had started in meat: They had been butchers whose small shop had grown into the supplier for the city's finest steakhouses after World War II. August Frederick Sterne and Loretta Anita Sterne—Gus and Lollie—had been first cousins, raised as brother and sister by their grandparents when both sets of parents had been killed in a private plane crash off Padre Island. Lollie—"the vivacious blond beauty," as Ahern wrote reflexively at every mention of her name—had married Horace Morgan of El Paso while in college, but they separated while she was pregnant with Emmie. He had not left a note when he committed suicide in his family's hunting camp, which freed Ahern to speculate freely that he was despondent over Lollie's desertion.

Meanwhile, sober, serious Gus had skipped college and gone straight to work at Sterne Foods. This made him "the last of the self-made men," although Tess couldn't see how bypassing school to run your grandparents' business qualified one for Horatio

Alger status. But Gus had put his mark on Sterne Foods, convincing his cautious grandfather to move away from supplying other restaurants and to start their own steakhouses.

A string of small diners had followed, then a successful German restaurant that Gus had tried to take national. That venture had failed so miserably that the privately held company almost had to seek outside investors. Then Lollie opened Espejo Verde and its cash flow, although relatively modest, helped Sterne Foods regain its footing. "People flocked to Espejo Verde not just for the food, but for Lollie, whose vivacious blond beauty drew them like moths to a flame," Ahem had written. Torturous prose, yet Tess thought she understood what he was trying to say. Emmie had that same quality.

"Lollie brought a new brand of showmanship to San Antonio's restaurant business, and a new kind of flair to her family's business." Sadly, Ahern didn't provide many examples of that showmanship, although he did note that Lollie once had her hands insured by Lloyd's of London for one million dollars. A publicity gimmick, it was intended to counter another restaurateur's bitter claim that she was a spoiled rich girl who spent all her time in the dining room, playing hostess, while others prepared the meals for which she was celebrated. "But nothing could dim Lollie's success—until the night of December third."

Cue the spooky organ music. Now that she finally had arrived at that seminal event, Tess found herself less than eager to read about the murders. She skipped ahead to the inevitable "Where are they now?" epilogue at the book's end. Five years after the murders, Gus had started the Barbecue King, with such great results that the Sterne fortunes had quadrupled, and he was one of the city's leading philanthropists. The baby christened Emily Sterne Morgan was now known as Emmie Sterne, although she had never been formally adopted by her cousin. Patrolman Al Guzman had made detective. Marianna Barrett Conyers had become a virtual recluse, who would never speak of the night in question. That was Aherne's phrase, the night in question. Tess couldn't see how Emmie's godmother figured into the story, even if she had been Lollie's best friend. More padding on Ahern's part, she assumed.

Sighing resignedly, Tess flipped back to the descriptions of the murder, which took up the middle third of the slender book. Ahern's prose puffed and panted, but his ability to describe blood in varied ways could not disguise the fact that he had no first-hand information—and that the investigation of the crime had stalled almost immediately. The murder scene was all Ahern had, and he kept returning to it. The word "grisly" figured largely.

Lollie had been found near the door, killed by one shot to the back of the head. The cook, Pilar Rodriguez, was nearby, also killed execution style. Frank Conyers, chief financial officer of Sterne Foods, was in the kitchen, where he had been going over the books at a long wooden table. Nearby cans of gasoline and a pile of rags indicated that the killers had planned to burn the restaurant, perhaps to hide their handiwork. Their failure to go through with this part of the plan could only be attributed to Emmie, not quite two, in her playpen in Pilar's small bedroom off the kitchen. She had blood on her hands, elbows, and right cheek, but it wasn't hers. Police had never said how Frank Conyers had been killed, only that he had been stabbed instead of shot.

Tess's tired mind caught the name on the second mention: Frank *Conyers*. Because everyone used all three names when they spoke of Marianna—and because "Barrett" seemed to provoke so much more awe and respect than "Conyers"—she had missed the connection. *Frank was Marianna's husband.* She had not only lied about the circumstances of Lollie's death, she had neglected to mention her own husband had been involved in the same "accident." But why? The book said only that Marianna, Gus, and virtually everyone in their social set were at a Monday Night Football party, watching the Dallas Cowboys play the Redskins. "The party at Gus and Ida Marie Sterne's home on Hermosa had a 'South of the Border' theme," Jimmy Ahern had written, probably cribbing from the society columnist. "The menu included fajitas, borracho beans, and, ironically, a guacamole salad made from Lollie Sterne's very own secret recipe."

Just holding this book in her hand made Tess feel dirty. She would have tossed it into a trash can on her way out of the Vietnam, but it was hard to throw away something that had cost twenty-five dollars. She still couldn't fathom why Marianna had misled her so thoroughly, but Tess could see why Gus Sterne had tried to kill this ugly little book, as well as its publisher. The Barbecue King. She was reminded of another king, who had tried to rid his country of spindles so that Sleeping Beauty might not prick her finger. Ah, but there was always a spindle waiting somewhere in the kingdom, in some forgotten tower. In the end, kings could never protect their princesses.

A ringing phone woke Tess from a not very restful sleep. Her mind seemed to be stuck, like a video machine playing back the same scene over and over again. She kept hearing Crow's words, yet it was the black and white photos from the old murder scene that ran across her mind. *Ruined everything, ruined everything, ruined everything.*

"Hello?" she asked the receiver. Then she figured out it worked better if you picked it up. "Hello?" With the curtains drawn, the room was dark, so the bedside clock proclaiming it was eight o'clock wasn't much help. She could have been sleeping for four hours, or sixteen, or even twenty-eight.

"Why do you sound so groggy?" Kitty asked.

"Napping," Tess muttered, looking at her watch, still trying to anchor herself in time and space. All her instruments agreed: She was in La Casita on Broadway in San Antonio, Texas, a city of a million-plus souls, few of whom seemed to like her very much. Esskay was stretched out on the bed next to her. It was the last Sunday in October, unless it was Monday. And if Kitty were on the line, demanding to know why she sounded groggy, deductive reasoning meant it must be a time when normal people are awake.

"How'd you find me, anyway?" she asked her aunt. "I didn't even wait for the machine when I called you yesterday."

"I starred-69 your ass, as the expression goes. Maybe I should be the detective in the family."

"You want my business, it's yours. What's up? Everyone okay?" The Sternes' tragic history had reminded her how fragile family happiness was, how quickly an unknown and unexpected evil could shatter everything one loved.

"Tyner called, so did Pat. I'm not sure which one is more furious with you."

"Pat?" Her mind was still cluttered with the weekend's events.

"Patrick Monaghan, your father, my brother. Remember him? He seems to hold me personally responsible for you being in Texas. I tried to tell him you sneaked out without letting anyone know where you were going, but he wasn't mollified. And Tyner's over here every hour of the day and night, wanting to know if I've heard from you. I am not your answering service, Tesser. Call these people—and talk to them, not their machines. Write them postcards. All they want to know is that you're okay."

"Okay," Tess said, but she wasn't agreeing so much as repeating Kitty's last word back to her.

"You *are* all right, aren't you?"

"Sure, yeah. Just tired."

"Did you find Crow?"

"Found him—" She stopped to calculate. Friday, Saturday, Sunday. Had so little time really passed? "Two days ago."

"And he's fine?"

"More or less." Probably less than more, what with a corpse in a pool house, an unexplained shotgun under his bed, a missing femme who might be fatale in every sense of the word, and some bad-ass ex-con on the loose who was likely to be miffed about his dead buddy, assuming he wasn't the one who had killed him. Then there was the part about her hormones kicking in at a most inopportune moment, but that was so much more information than Kitty needed.

Tess heard a high-pitched babbling on Kitty's end of the connection. "Is Laylah there?"

"Yes, Jackie dropped her off. She has a date."

"Jackie has a *date?*"

"Dinner with this nice man who was interested in hiring her for a capital campaign for Sinai Hospital. She says it's business, I say you don't wear a backless red dress unless there's some pleasure involved. Wait, Laylah wants to talk to you."

A brief silence, then Tess heard Laylah's snuffly little breaths as she panted into the phone. Laylah felt that telephone communication was largely telepathic. She just held on tight and thought lovely thoughts, until they flew through the line.

"Hey, Laylah, it's Tesser."

No response. Laylah knew the piece of plastic that Kitty held to her face wasn't Tesser.

"No, really, it's me. Esskay is here, Laylah. What does Esskay say? What does the doggie say?"

More snuffly breaths. Then, suddenly, clear as a bell: "Hey, hey, Esskay. Go yo' way. Hey, hey, Esskay."

It was a fragment of the sausage company's hotdog

jingle, the one that Cal Ripken had been pretending to sing all summer long on the Orioles' radio broadcasts. Tess laughed so hard she almost fell off the bed. She was still laughing, and Laylah was still repeating the jingle, very pleased with herself, when Kitty took the phone back.

"She takes after you, Tesser. Your first sentence came from a commercial for pork products, too. 'More Parks sausages, Mom—please?'"

"Bullshit," Tess said, but she couldn't stop laughing, and her room at La Casita no longer seemed quite so dark. Somewhere, there was a place she knew, a place where people knew her. She'd get back there eventually. She could be there the day after tomorrow if she really wanted. Get in the car right now and drive without stopping. Steal a cat nap somewhere in Tennessee, and pull up to Kitty's bookstore early Tuesday. Part of her longed to do just that.

But she wasn't finished here yet. Finding Crow had proved to be only the beginning. Now she had to save him, too. From what, she wasn't quite sure. His own good intentions, some twisted sense of honor, a trouble much bigger than anyone had anticipated? She rummaged through her bag and her pockets until she found the card Rick Trejo had given her. No answer at his home. On a hunch, she called the office number. He picked up on the first ring.

"Working on a Sunday night?"

"I'm the hardest working man in show business." And happy to be so, judging by his cheerful, upbeat voice. "What can I do for you, sweetheart?"

Stop with the stupid endearments for one thing. But it was hard, for some reason, to take offense. The sensible-seeming Kristina put up with Rick Trejo and she was, well, a sweetheart.

"They're not finished with him, are they?"

"Your friend Crow? Not by a long shot. Screwing up the search was a temporary setback. Guzman is a good detective. When he's pissed, he's a great one."

"Crow couldn't kill anyone."

"You don't have to convince me, baby. But he knows something. Got any idea what it is?"

"Not a clue."

"Well, don't hold out on me. That's rule number one. My hunch is that Emmie Sterne is neck-deep in some shit, and he's trying to protect her. Our best-case scenario is that she's the one who stashed the gun under his bed, then called the cops and fingered him."

"Why would she do that?"

"Because if she killed that guy, she needs a fall guy. And because she is *crazy*. Big-time, fucked-up, welcome-to-the-snakepit crazy. Of course, a lot of the old-money Anglos in this town are, but I guess she comes by her nut-house shtick legitimately."

Tess thought of the photos she had seen, and the sad legacy of the Sterne family, where everyone ended up orphaned. Although Gus Sterne had a little boy, according to the book. Clay, a year younger than Emmie. He had beaten the family curse, made it to adulthood with his parents alive.

"I don't think Crow would stand by if he thought Emmie was a cold-blooded killer. Only she knows what she's up to."

"Or where she is," Rick pointed out.

"Hire me," Tess said. "I'll find her. I'll go back to

her godmother, for one thing, and find out why she was so determined to mislead me—sending me to the wrong place to find the band, glossing over the family history."

"You're not licensed to work in this state."

"There's got to be a way around that."

"Yeah. You could work for free. After all, my client is officially indigent."

"His parents have money."

"He says if I call his parents, he'll find someone else to be his lawyer. And, baby, I want this case. Trust me, they can come into court with a video of Mr. Ransome offing Tom Darden, and I can get a jury to let him walk."

"I thought the goal was to keep Crow from being charged at all."

"The goal is to win. I'll take it in the early innings or in the bottom of the ninth, with bases loaded, two men out. If you think finding Emmie Sterne is going to help, you go for it. But bear in mind, it could hurt, too. We could end up with two coconspirators pointing fingers at each other, with the race on to see who can cut the fastest deal with the DA. Ever think about that?"

"It doesn't make any sense," Tess insisted. "There's no reason for Emmie Sterne to kill Darden. Guzman told me he thought he could link Darden and Weeks to the murders, but he never told the families that he was working that angle."

"I know, I know," Trejo said. "I talked to him, too. I can't decide if this helps us or hurts us. Then again, anything we don't know can hurt us. I tried to impress that fact upon Crow when I caught up with him later today. He swore he was telling me everything he knew."

"And?"

"He lies pretty well, but not well enough. Sometimes I wonder if I'm ever going to have a client that starts off telling me the truth. Probably not. Even the criminal attorneys who represent the white boys in white collars probably have to listen to a lot of lies in the beginning."

"Probably."

There was a moment of silence on the line, as Tess and Rick were lost in their own abstract musings—he on his class of clientele, no doubt, she on Crow's loyalty. One of his greatest strengths, but strengths could become weaknesses. Why was he so insistent on protecting Emmie? Why was he upset when he couldn't find her in the Alamo?

Time was a factor, and not because some record producer was coming to town. All I needed was a week. What could happen in seven days? God could create the world and take a day off. An ordinary mortal could work forty hours, get shit-faced and still have a day left to recover. Personally, she had gone through a complete set of days-of-the-week underwear and done a wash. Anything could happen. Everything could happen.

"So where do we start?" she asked Rick.

"Darden's buddy, Laylan Weeks, is out there, somewhere. I've got an old client in town who might have some ideas about where to find him. I say we go looking for him. You can look for our crazy little lead singer on your own time. Man, I wouldn't mind being her lawyer. The baby found at the scene of the city's most famous unsolved homicide, now a murderess in her own right. That would pack them in."

"You're really doing a lot to change all those ugly lawyer stereotypes."

"Yeah, yeah, yeah." She could tell Rick was distracted—clacking away on a computer, eating a sandwich, slurping down something that had to be loaded with caffeine. She wouldn't be surprised to find out he was on a treadmill and watching television, too. "Man, listen to me, I sound like a friggin' Beatles song. You know, I don't even like *their* music that much. Give me Waylon Jennings any day. The way I see it, God proved his existence by keeping him off that plane, the one that went down with Buddy Holly and Richie Valens."

"You're saying God could save only one musician, and he chose Waylon Jennings over Buddy Holly?"

"No, I'm saying God knew Richie Valens had to die. If only he had gotten to him before 'La Bamba.' You know how many times I've heard that goddamn song? The movie came out just as all my sisters were hitting their teen years. I've got five sisters. Every goddamn quincenera they played it! *I'm not a sailor. I am the captain.* Could you explain those frigging lyrics, please? Give me 'Pancho and Lefty' any day."

"The Willie Nelson song?"

"He sang it, with Merle Haggard. Townes van Zandt wrote it. And he died a few years back, died way too young. So I take it back. God doesn't know shit about music."

Tess had to laugh. Rick's ferocity about the smallest topics seemed to her an excellent harbinger for someone who might end up protecting Crow's life, given Texas's mania for the death penalty. "Are you always so adamant about everything?"

"*Always.* If you can't know your own mind, what can you know?"

Tess had no answer. But a corollary occurred to her: If you could know your own heart, would you then know everything?

15

Tess was jumping rope in her room on the next morning when the pounding started. She assumed it was the hooker next door, who couldn't sleep through her hopping. Even with the carpet muffling her slow double-bounce jumps—she was much too tired to jump proper pepper-style, like a boxer—La Casita did seem to shake a little each time she landed. Too bad. After all, Tess had slept through her noises last night, which were much louder and less rhythmic than rope-skipping. But as she continued jumping, she realized the pounding was coming through the door, not the wall. She had a guest.

"Some guard dog," said Rick Trejo, using his soft leather briefcase to shield his double-breasted suit—Armani, or a darn good copy—from Esskay's affections. "You ready for our meeting?"

"Where's Crow?"

"He's a loose cannon, and I don't need the hassle of shuttling artillery around San Antonio. Besides, it's my understanding you're not his favorite person right now."

There was a question in Rick Trejo's eyes, one she didn't want to answer. "I wasn't expecting you for another hour."

"I moved things up. I was going to eat breakfast first, but it's better to talk to this guy on an empty stomach."

"Give me five minutes to get ready."

In six minutes, she was out of the shower, in fresh clothes, and plaiting her wet hair. Rick Trejo, who seemed to have a talent for making himself at home in the world, had removed his jacket and was stretched out on the bed with Esskay. They were watching the local news segment that came at the end of each thirty-minute chunk of the national news.

"Fatuous," he declared. "If it bleeds it leads, indeed. The dip in the homicide rate has sure been hard on local news here. We're seeing a lot more car crashes and freak accident footage. Is your news this bad?"

"As a point of local pride, I would have to pit Baltimore's television news against any major market for sheer awfulness."

Rick tried to change the channel, only to find that the television set had no other channels.

"Nice place," he said. "I can see you're accustomed to traveling in style. Oh well, Channel 5 is good enough. The important thing is, Guzman played fair. He didn't leak the fact that Crow had been questioned to the *Eagle* or the television stations."

"How could he? Crow wasn't charged. I used to work for a newspaper. We never would have identified someone unless he had been charged or named in a warrant."

"You don't know the *San Antonio Eagle*, querida. They have ways with punctuation. When in doubt, just put a question mark at the end of the headline. 'Is there a killer cop in San Antonio?' 'Is the mayor's marriage falling apart?' Sometimes, they get so carried away, they ask questions where simple statements of fact will do. 'Is Governor George W. Bush elected easily to a second term?'"

"Was there?"

"What, a George W. Bush? Believe me, he's all too real."

"No, a killer cop."

"In fact, there was, a long time ago. He's dead now, killed by his partner, who was then acquitted. And the mayor's marriage was falling apart, but he put it back together again, just like Humpty Dumpty. So maybe the reason the *Eagle* doesn't get sued is because it asks the right questions." He glanced at his watch. Not a Rolex, but it might as well have been. Its gold casing was no wider than a dime. Funny, how small had become a status symbol in some things. Tess bet Rick Trejo had a cell phone the size of a credit card. "Let's go. Although I don't know why I'm in such a hurry. It's not like he's going anywhere. But the earlier in the day we talk to him, the less stoned he'll be."

"Sounds like a classy guy, this ex-client of yours."

"Sweetheart, you don't know the half of it."

As Rick Trejo's car headed west along Commerce Street, Tess was quickly disabused of any notion that she had begun to get her bearings in San Antonio. The trip had been familiar for a few blocks—she recognized downtown, caught a glimpse of the police station where she had spent Sunday morning—but then they passed under a freeway, and it was as if they had entered a different city. A different country, really, with signs in Spanish and rundown bungalows painted in once-bright Southwestern colors, now faded from the harsh sun.

"Welcome to the *barrio*," Rick said. His Spanish always sounded faintly ironic, as if he were mocking himself. Or mocking others' ideas about him.

"It's not so bad," said an ever-competitive Tess. "Baltimore's slums are much worse."

Trejo smiled. "Actually, some parts of the west side are very nice. I grew up on this side of town, my parents still live here, in as nice a neighborhood as you could ask for. But I'll let you walk through the Alazan-Apache Courts at midnight, see how 'not bad' you think it is."

He headed south, then west, south again—she could tell only because his dash had a built-in compass, as well as an inside-outside themometer—and finally stopped the car in a small business district. There was a group of men hanging on the corner, and a little chorus of hisses went up when Tess got out of the car. She hissed back at them, which was met with a great whoop of delight.

"Ignore them," Rick said, rounding the corner. "They're harmless. Just day workers waiting for someone to come by with a job for them."

"But it's so rude," Tess said.

"Yeah, well, after we talk to this guy, you'll be begging for that kind of rudeness."

They walked up a shady street, to a house where

a shirtless man sat on the steps of the front porch, drinking a beer. The house and garden were well-tended but shabby, usually the signs of an older woman living alone. Yet here was this seemingly able-bodied man who could have made the small repairs it needed.

"A little early for a beer, Al," Rick said.

"And good morning to you, *abogado*. You come all the way over here just to see what I'm having for breakfast?"

He was small, with narrow shoulders and a thin, sly face. Tess watched his dark eyes shift, saw his gaze follow a group of children walking down the street. He held his tongue between his teeth, in the un-selfconscious style of a little boy concentrating on a task.

"Stop it, Al," Rick said.

"It's legal to look, isn't it? I know, I know—the priest says it's a sin to even *think* it, but the judge's law is different from the church's law. The judge lets you think all sorts of things, as long as you don't do them. The priest lets you do things, as long as you confess to them. Is this your girlfriend? She's a little big for my taste. I like them flatter-chested. But you know that."

"This is Tess Monaghan, who's working on a case with me. Tess, this is Alberto Rojas, a former client."

"Nice to meet you."

To Tess's relief, Rojas didn't offer his hand. Although he looked clean enough, he had a too-sweet smell, as if he had to douse himself in cologne and deodorant soap to mask a terminally sour body odor. Trejo put one shiny loafer on the lowest porch step, but didn't come any closer to his one-time client. "How long you've been out of Huntsville, Al?"

"You should know." His words came out wet and soft, as if there was too much moisture in his mean little mouth. "You was my lawyer, for all the good it did me. My mama paid you all that money, and for what? I still went to prison."

"For two years. They wanted to put you away for twenty, remember? They were going to put you in there for a good long time, and all but plaster a bumpersticker on your ass that said 'Honk if you love baby rapers.' Instead, you were convicted for grand theft auto."

"So next time," Rojas said, "I won't steal no fucking car."

"No next times. You gave your word. Remember? You sat there in my office and cried in front of your mama, and said you would learn to control yourself if you got a chance. Besides, your neighbors all got letters. They know you're back in the neighborhood, they know what you did to that little girl. The elementary school has your picture up, the bodega, the ice houses. You'll never get near another child."

"It's a big city, *abogado*. There are many schools, many bodegas, many ice houses. Parks and playgrounds, too."

"Which is why you have that thing on your ankle." Tess looked down and saw the cuff used for electronic probation peeking beneath the hem of Rojas's loose gabardine slacks.

"Yes, more of your good work, Counselor. You were really looking out for me."

"In fact, I was. You make any friends in Huntsville?"

"I was a nice boy. My size, you have to be."

"There were two men from here, Laylan Weeks and Tom Darden, pulling a long haul for kidnapping. You know them?"

"Huntsville is a big place, bigger than some cities."

"Yeah, but all the boys who like little boys and girls manage get to know one another, don't they? I did a little checking on Darden and Weeks. There was a rumor that they took this kid, Danny Boyd, for sex, not money. It was hushed up for the kid's sake, but the story's still out there. You know anything about that?"

Rojas smiled. His teeth were as brown as the beer bottle he was sucking on. "They told everyone who would listen that they were in it for the money."

"So you knew them."

"A little. From afar. They liked to tell everyone that they were big, bad hombres who had done terrible things, important things." He sucked on the bottle—didn't drink from it, just stuck the long neck in his mouth and popped it in and out of his cheek. "Personally, I always thought they were full of shit."

"So I guess you didn't make any plans to catch up with them when you all came home to San Antone."

"Like I said, we weren't really friends."

Rick pulled out a twenty-dollar bill. Rojas took it, rolled it tight as a cigarette, then blew through it, making it sound like a kazoo.

"The cops gave me fifty," he said.

"The cops have already been here?"

"Oh, yeah." He smiled at Rick's consternation.

"They even asked the same kind of questions, but they were nicer to me. Much more respectful."

"What did you tell them?"

"How can I give to you for twenty what I gave to them for fifty?" Rojas asked sweetly, as if he were a man who dedicated his life to such questions of fairness and ethics. Trejo pulled out another twenty, and a ten, which Rojas tucked into his waistband, like a stripper saving tips in a G-string.

"They said they had money coming to them, when they got out. They said they were set for life."

"You told the cops all this."

"Maybe." Rojas had now unfurled one of the twenties and was edging it in and out of his teeth, like a wide piece of dental floss. Tess felt sorry for the unsuspecting cashier whose hand might one day close over this bill. "Maybe I told them more, told them about the things that Darden and Weeks bragged about, the things they never got popped for. I don't know, *abogado*. Every day is the same for me, you know. I just sit on the porch and watch the little children go by. It's up to me to put some variety into it. Variety is the spice of life. Or so they say."

A woman's shadowy form appeared at the screen door. "Quienes son, Alberto?" she called sharply.

"Señor Trejo, my wonderful, wonderful lawyer, and some *grandota*," Rojas replied. "Remember Mr. Trejo? The one you paid all that money, so you could have me back home, chained to you like a little monkey?"

A torrent of Spanish poured out of the woman. At first, Tess thought Mrs. Rojas was berating Rick, but she soon realized the angry words were for her own son. They didn't seem to affect him at all. Smiling, he stood, pretended to hand one of the twenties to Rick, then snatched it back, still smiling.

"Wouldn't it be funny, *abogado*, if I used this very bill to get a little girl to come into the yard?" he said. "There are a few who walk by my fence every day. All I have to say is, 'Want to make some money? I'll give you twenty bucks. Come around to the back of the house, I have something to show you. Shhh, shhh. Don't tell. It's our secret. C'mon, it will feel so good. You make me feel good, then I'll make you feel good. But don't tell anyone. They wouldn't understand. Grown-ups don't want you to know how good you could feel. But I do. I do.'"

He turned and climbed the porch steps, whistling a pretty little melody, letting the screen door bang behind him. His mother's harsh, frantic words rained down on him, but Rojas didn't seem to hear her.

"My money's on his mother," Rick said, his voice light, his fists clenched at his side. "She'll never let him out of her sight again. I can only hope she outlives him."

"How could you represent someone like that?"

"Because it's my job," he said. "And because his mother goes to church with my aunt, and I couldn't say no when my aunt asked for a favor."

"Still—"

"The police caught Al driving a stolen car, then coerced a confession out of him about the assault on a neighborhood kid. The confession was inadmissible, and I got it thrown out. I have to defend all my clients to the best of my ability, Tess. I have to fight for the Al Rojases of the world as hard as I'm going to fight for Crow. Would you have it any other way?"

For the first time in their short acquaintance, Rick's speech had lost its slightly arch, ironic quality. Tess scuffed her toes along the sidewalk, thinking about what he had said. She wanted to protest: *But Crow is innocent.* Nothing came out.

Back in the car, speeding away from Mr. Rojas's neighborhood, she said: "So Texas has a Megan's law, too."

"A what?" Rick had been lost in his own thoughts.

"A Megan's law. One of those laws designed to inform people when a child molester moves into the neighborhood. That's some small comfort."

"Such laws don't apply to Rojas. Didn't you hear? He had a real sharpie for an attorney, who pleaded him down to grand theft, auto. He's got no record as a child molester."

"So how did those fliers go out with his photo? How did the school find out about him, and the local shops?"

"I really couldn't say, although I do happen to have a brother-in-law who owns a print shop near here. Someone might have dropped off a photo of Rojas, told him when he was coming home, given him a mailing list."

Tess smiled. "Of course, a lawyer could never do anything like that, even to a former client, because he would risk being disbarred."

"Of course." Rick started to whistle, then stopped abruptly when he realized the melody he had picked up was Rojas's sprightly tune.

16

They had breakfast at a west side cafe, a dingy place that didn't look open from the street, and didn't look particularly safe from within. Rick recommended something called migas, and the combination of cheese, eggs, and sausage was so good that Tess quickly regained her lost appetite. Rick had been right—an empty stomach was the only way to talk to Al Rojas.

"Sorry you didn't like it better," he said, pushing away his half-eaten meal even as Tess was wiping her plate clean with a flour tortilla. She wasn't embarrassed. After all, that's what the jump-roping was for.

"I've never had anything like this. Most Mexican food in Baltimore is so . . . perfunctory. I mean, you know you're in trouble when the best place in town has something called 'Los Sandichos' on the menu. And the Mexican place near my house has a wait staff of Estonians. Here, I could make a meal from the tortillas alone. They're incredible."

Rick looked puzzled. "They're flour and lard. You could make them yourself. Anyone could."

"Theoretically." She also could solve simple physics equations if she put her mind to it, but that didn't mean she was going to start anytime soon.

He paid the bill, helping himself to a handful of pralines and bright candies. The same "Mexican candies" the clerk in Twin Sisters had offered her, only fresher-looking here.

"Something's bothering me," he said as they walked to his car.

"Rojas?"

"Darden and Weeks. Twenty years is a long stretch, and Texas has an overcrowding problem. I wonder why they didn't get parole."

"Ask Guzman."

"I'd be happier if Guzman didn't know what we're thinking about. Guess I could call someone on my Christmas card list, see what they know."

Rick headed back into the city, stopping in yet another neighborhood Tess had never seen, an old-fashioned business district surrounded by a residential neighborhood. The houses were large and gracious, but most of them had been converted to apartments, or made over into businesses. Rick bounded up the steps of a hot pink Victorian.

"Y Algunas Mas," Tess said, reading from the hand-painted sign over the door. "Se venden milagros."

"And Something More," Rick translated, his lips twitching slightly at her Spanish pronunciation. "We sell miracles."

"Funny motto for a criminal law practice."

"Law practice? Oh, this isn't my office. It's Kristina's shop."

Inside, the old house's large rooms were crammed with the same hideous skeletons that Tess had seen at Marianna Barrett Conyers's house, hundreds and hundreds of them, leering cheerfully at her from every direction. But that was just a portion of Kristina's eclectic collection. The crowded store also held a menagerie of brightly painted wooden animals, huge black pots, carved saints and papier-mâché monsters that might have crawled in from one of Hunter Thompson's better drug trips.

Kristina was pushing one of these papier-mâché creatures toward an older woman, who was trying not to recoil. "Oh I don't know," the woman said nervously. "I do love the little skeleton mariachis you told me to buy, Kris, but this—" She gestured weakly at the figure in question, which looked like some strange cross between a blowfish and a bat—"well, it's so large."

"It's a museum-quality piece," Kristina said. "The curator from the San Antonio Museum of Art was in here looking at it the other day."

"For the museum?"

"For his *private* collection."

"Oh, I just don't know," the woman repeated. She walked around the thing, as if it might become attractive from another angle. Tess realized the woman, despite the wealth and class indicated by her clothes and manner, yearned desperately for Kristina's approval. But she just couldn't come to terms with the monstrosity before her.

Finally, Kristina took pity on her customer, putting the blowfish-bat on the counter and picking up a notebook-sized piece of tin, with a faded painting of a virgin. Still not Tess's idea of art—it reminded her too much of the Jesus-Kennedy kitsch hung in the living rooms and kitchens of her Monaghan relatives. But it looked genuinely antique, and had the advantage of not inducing heart attacks.

"It's a Virgen de Guadalupe, an exceptionally nice one, possibly eighteenth century," Kristina said, catching Tess's eye. "Do you know the story?"

She shook her head. "I've got a Catholic name, but not the character-building torture by nuns that usually goes with it."

"It's doubtful any Baltimore nun would have told you this story. In the 1500s, a peasant, an Indian, one of the Indians indigenous to Mexico before the conquest, saw a vision. The *virgen*—" She used the soft h sound of the Spanish pronunciation, Tess noticed—"appeared before him and told him in his own language to gather rose petals in his cloak, then take the cloak straight to the bishop. He was to show the petals to no one but the bishop. When he arrived and unfurled his cloak, the rose petals were gone and her image was in their place. The Virgen de Guadalupe."

"Oh she's *darling*," the woman cried. "How much, Kristina?"

"This? It's only seven hundred dollars."

Tess watched in disbelief as the woman handed over cash, then left with the carefully wrapped treasure. Rick, who had been uncharacteristically quiet, burst into laughter as soon as her Chevy Suburban pulled away from the curb.

"You are so good, it's scary," he said. "I mean, how many times have you done the bait-and-switch with one of those *alebrijes*. It's genius—one of your ladies comes in, you show her something new and so damn ugly that she's scared to buy it. Then you offer her one of the antique pieces that costs ten times as much, but has the virtue of being something that won't give her indigestion. And she leaves, feeling like she's let you down. Do you tell them that the story has been discredited? That the bishop in Mexico had to step down when he agreed there was no historical evidence that this 'miracle' ever happened?"

"Look, running a folk art gallery may not be the lofty practice of the law, but it has its moments," Kristina said coolly, sticking the cash in an old-fashioned cash register that had been painted bright red and studded with tiny silver charms.

"If you married me, you wouldn't have to be a shop girl," he said.

"I like being a shop girl, especially given that I'm one of the owners. And it's not a shop, it's a gallery." But she was smiling.

"Phone?" he asked, smiling back at her.

"What are you asking? Do I have one? May you use it? Be more specific, please."

"May I yank it out of the wall in a show of brute force that will fuel all your stereotypical fantasies about Latin men, so that we end up coupling right here, as Tess watches the door?"

"No, but you may use the phone," Kristina said in a fake-prim manner. "For a local call."

Rick took the portable from its base, disappearing into the curtained storeroom behind the counter. Tess suddenly felt shy. She might have met Kristina first, but she now felt more comfortable with Rick, given their shared sense of purpose. As for Kristina, she was one of those poised people who didn't need to fill silences with blather. She moved around the shop, tickling her objects with a feather duster.

"I was in a house with a lot of cra—a lot of stuff like this," Tess said, making conversation. "Emmie's godmother, Marianna Barrett Conyers." *Emmie's godmother, who described the death of Lollie Sterne as an accident, and neglected to mention her husband had been involved in the same "accident."*

"One of my best customers," Kristina said. "I take new shipments to her for private showings. She has a great eye, and she doesn't haggle."

"Do you know her well?"

"No. I don't think anyone knows her very well, except her maid. She's so reserved. I call her the Duchess of Euphemism—she has the most tactful way of telling me she loathes something." Kristina gave Tess a knowing look. "You could pick up a few pointers from her."

"Huh?"

"I can tell just by the way you stand here, holding yourself, that you hate my things. It's as if you're scared you might catch something."

"Well, they are creepy."

"Not to me. I love every piece. They brought me to San Antonio. Four years ago, my senior year at Wisconsin—I was an art history major—I came down here for spring break. We were supposed to fly to Padre Island, but the charter plane had some mechanical problem, and we were stuck here for a day. I went into a gallery like this one, down in the

King William neighborhood—Tienda Guadalupe— and I saw this wooden cross, studded with milagros."

"Milagros? I thought it meant miracles."

"It does, but it also refers to these charms, like these things on the cash register. See? Little hands and limbs, babies and hearts. They represent things you pray for. Anyway, I thought that cross was the most beautiful thing I had ever seen. When I held it in my hand, I felt something, something warm. It was the wildest sensation. I bought it and took it back to Wisconsin. The day after graduation, I moved here. I didn't know a single person and people laughed at my Spanish, it was so fussy and academic. But from the start, I was at home here. Total GTT."

"Gone to Texas," Tess said. "Crow said the same thing, in a postcard he sent to his parents."

Kristina laid down her feather duster. "You don't get it, do you?"

"His dad explained it to me. Something about what fugitives carved on their doors."

"No, I mean the *feeling*. I was meant for Texas. Listening to Almas Perdidas, I sense Crow is, too."

"Maybe," Tess said. Crow was under some spell, but she couldn't figure out if it was San Antonio's or Emmie's.

Kristina just smiled and went back to dusting, tickling the long nose of a banana yellow ferret. Rick walked through the door, portable phone in hand, his voice in that winding-up mode that one has when trying to end a call, while the person on the other end drones on and on.

"Uh-huh, uh-huh. Thanks. Surest thing. We should. No, we definitely should. Okay, okay. Uh-huh. Thanks." He inched the receiver that much closer to the base. "Definitely. Till then. No, I mean it."

At last, he hung up. "My source gave me a lead on a retired detective who worked the Darden-Weeks case, knew these guys as well as anyone."

"Was that the detective?"

Rick rolled his eyes and pulled at his collar as if it were choking him. "His wife. She says he went to Las Vegas on a charter, won't be back for two days. Probably trying to get away from her for a while. She talks a blue streak. Gave me a complete blow-by-blow of her health, her husband's health, their dog's health, what she had for breakfast this morning— English muffin with raisins, a little Sanka. Jesus. He probably goes gambling just to have some peace and quiet for a change."

"See?" Kristina said. "That's how marriage works. I bet there was a time when he told her he loved her, and couldn't be without her, and now he's reduced to playing blackjack to get away from the sound of her voice. That's what marriage is, Rick. The death of romance."

"That's not what marriage to me would be like," he said, circling her waist and kissing her neck. Kristina never missed a beat in her dusting.

"*Two* days," Tess complained, feeling awkward. "What do we do until then? I don't want to sit around La Casita, watching Esskay sleep."

"Look for Emmie," Rick said, still holding fast to Kristina, who continued to ignore him. "That's what you said you wanted to do in the first place. Got any ideas where to start?"

"In fact, I do," Tess said, eyeing the skeletons, which seemed to be laughing at her. "I think I'll see if the Duchess of Euphemism would like to take tea with me this afternoon."

17

Marianna Barrett Conyers was in the garden behind her house when Tess returned to Alamo Heights early that afternoon. Given the trees and the high stone wall, the garden was as dark as the interior of the house. It seemed unlikely that the sun ever penetrated here. Yet Marianna wore a large hat and was carefully applying sunscreen to her face and hands. She sat at a wrought-iron table, an authentic version of the ones that had come back into style. A blue-rimmed pitcher of iced tea and matching glass completed the Martha Stewart perfection of the scene.

"It's one of the things I've done right, taking care of my skin," she volunteered, although Tess had asked for no explanation, had not yet even reintroduced herself. "I never sunbathed like the other girls."

Marianna held out her tube of Estée Lauder sunscreen to Tess, whose face was tanned and freckled from a summer's worth of rowing. Tess shook her head. Too little, too late. Although now that she was thirty, she probably should get serious about moisturizer. Not that Marianna's complexion was particularly impressive. Her pores were large, her color was uneven, and age spots had begun to creep along her jawline.

"You'll be sorry," she said. Marianna wasn't good at playfulness, and the warning sounded almost too ominous.

"Probably," Tess agreed. "Did Lollie Sterne sunbathe?"

If Marianna was startled by the question, nothing in her face betrayed this. She capped her Estée Lauder tube, then rubbed her hands together to absorb the extra lotion. When she was done, she patted the cushioned chair opposite her, inviting Tess to sit. Commanding her, really. Tess didn't like being directed by anyone, but she wanted Marianna to think she was in control of the situation, at least in the beginning. So she sat.

"You've been busy," Marianna said.

"Very," Tess agreed.

"How old are you? Twenty-seven? Twenty-eight?"

"I was thirty in August."

"Still young. Too young to know there are stories you will grow weary of telling. Especially when it's the only story anyone knows about you. Or cares about."

Tess smiled and nodded. She had no idea where Marianna was heading with this.

"I am a survivor. Not in the new sense of the word, which implies triumph over self-inflicted adversity, followed by public redemption in the chapel of some talk show host. I am a 'survived by.'"

"Survived by whom?"

"No one, that's just it. I'm the one in the list at the end of the obituary. *So-and-so is survived by.* I'm the official mourner, and my past is as noisy as Marley's chains. I am Frank Conyers's widow, I am Lollie Sterne's best friend. That's the sum and total of who I am. People no longer remember that my father's people were related to William Barrett Travis, the commander at the Alamo. Distantly, but related nonetheless. They don't recall the things my father did for this city, how almost every building here has a foundation poured by his concrete company. There was a time when I would have given anything to be known as someone other than my father's daughter. Be careful what you wish for."

"By withdrawing from the world, you made it worse," Tess said. "You've frozen yourself in time. If you want to compare yourself to a Dickens character, try Miss Havisham."

Marianna shook her head impatiently.

"If you want to listen to my story, then you have to *listen.* Don't you know how many reporters have tried to get me to tell this to them? Usually at this time of year, too. Right before what they call the 'anniversary.' As if I might be having a cake and a party. They called the first year, and the second. The fifth and the tenth, the fifteenth and the twentieth. It's not just the local media, either, but reporters from Dallas and Houston, and *Texas Monthly.* *Unsolved Mysteries* even showed up on my doorstep one time.

This year, the twenty-first will probably be a little quieter than some. But someone will come by. Someone always does."

She stopped, her eyes fixed on some spot in the garden wall. Tess knew to leave the silence alone.

"And then one day, someone shows up who doesn't know anything. A young woman with an accent as flat and matter-of-fact as she is. A young woman whose ignorance allows me, for a moment, to *not* tell the story I thought everyone knew. Yes, I rewrote history for a day. Horace dead in a hunting accident. Well, it happened in a hunting camp. Lollie, Frank, and Pilar, dead in a car accident." Suddenly, brightly: "Did they tell you they tortured him?"

"Who?"

"My Frank." She held a finger to her lips. "Only we're not allowed to say how. That's something only the killer knows."

Jimmy Ahern's book had hinted at details about Frank's death that had never come to light, but Tess had assumed he was a bad reporter.

"I'm sorry, I didn't—"

"—know. You didn't know. Exactly. That was your charm."

Charm. The Duchess of Euphemism had struck again. What Tess had been was stupid, even arrogant.

"So you knew who Tom Darden was all along."

"No, I was truthful on that count. When you came here on Friday, Tom Darden was nothing more than a corpse on my property. Yesterday was the first I heard that he was thought to know something about how Lollie and Frank . . . died." She smiled ruefully. "You should understand the Sternes and I have not been kept informed about all the developments over the years. Perhaps we should have been less critical of the police investigation. But they made such a mess of things, at first."

"How so?"

Marianna looked weary and pale beneath her careful makeup. Tess was beginning to understand why she had permitted herself the lies that allowed her to avoid this topic, at least for one afternoon.

"Small things. Probably unimportant things. But when it's you, and it's your husband—or your first cousin, and the servant who all but raised you, in the case of Gus Sterne—there are no small things. All I know is they never came close to making an arrest, and they didn't seem to have many satisfactory explanations as to why. Now the detective tells me Darden and this other man were in prison all these years, so the case 'lacked urgency.' Well, it never lacked urgency for *me*."

"What about Emmie?"

"What about her?"

"Could she have known about Darden?"

"I'm sure Emmie would like to see justice done, but Lollie's death has never preoccupied her."

Tess leaned forward. "I thought today was the day you weren't going to tell lies. If people associate you with your husband's death to the exclusion of almost everything else, then the murder of Emmie's mother must be the central fact of her existence as well."

"That sounds logical, but it didn't work that way. Emmie didn't have a before and after. Her life is all aftermath. She never knew Horace, and she accepted the family's explanation that he died in a hunting accident. When Lollie died, she was only two. The truth is, she doesn't even remember her mother. She's like a child who had a bad dream and woke up to find herself safe and warm in a house where everyone loved her. Gus did a very good job of protecting her while she was growing up. It was her mother's absence that scarred Emmie. Gone is gone."

"However you want to explain it, she's clearly disturbed. Did she ever get professional help?"

Marianna sipped her tea. Tess had worded the question as carefully as she could, but it obviously was too blunt for Marianna's sensibilities.

"When she was a teenager, Emily began . . . acting out in various ways," Marianna began cautiously. "She saw various counselors and doctors. One decided she could recover Emily's memory of what happened the night of the murder. I'm sure she thought she'd solve the crime and be a big hero. At any rate, she put Emily under hypnosis. When Emily couldn't remember anything, she became hysterical, convinced something was wrong with her. Gus gave up on doctors after that."

"How was she 'acting out'?" Marianna's habit of casting other's words in invisible quotation marks was catching.

"Pardon?"

"You said Emily was sent to all these doctors because of her behavior. What was she doing?"

"Oh, typical adolescent rebellion. Truthfully, I think Gus over-reacted. His son, Clay, is so well-behaved, he makes normal children look out of control. Emily is a Sterne through and through, very headstrong. Clay's genes were watered down by his mother. She was a Galveston girl, pretty enough, but weak-willed. I think eating all that shellfish thins the blood."

"'Was'? Is she dead, too?" *Jesus, how many "accidents" could one family have?*

"Oh no, she and Gus divorced about ten years ago, and she settled in California. Another blow for Emmie. She ended up losing two mothers before she was thirteen."

"I don't imagine it did much for her son, either."

Marianna lifted one shoulder in a tiny, ladylike shrug, as if Clay's problems were of little interest to her.

"Would Emmie go to her uncle if she were in trouble?"

"I told you the first time we met that they haven't spoken for five years."

"You told me lots of things the first time we spoke," Tess reminded her.

Marianna Barrett Conyers's face had a way of clicking off abruptly, like a coin-operated television set in a bus station.

"Waste your time if you like. Sterne Foods is on the Austin Highway, not that far from here. It runs off Broadway, near an old Mobil Station, the one that was a dress shop. You'll find it easily. But don't be surprised if you have trouble getting in. Security is very tight just now."

"Why does a restaurant chain need security? Is someone trying to get the recipe for the secret sauce?"

"I wouldn't know." And Marianna Barrett Conyers tilted her face toward a nonexistent sun, her part of the conversation clearly over.

Tess liked roads that told you where they went. Back home, it was York Road, Frederick Road, Harford Road—not to be confused with Old York Road, Old Frederick Road, and Old Harford Road. They weren't the fastest routes to their namesakes, but they were always more interesting than the interstate. Here, it was Fredericksburg and Blanco and Castroville. And if the Austin Highway was no longer much of a highway, it seemed cheerful about its demotion. Tess stopped for lunch at a place called the Bun and Barrel, on the theory that any restaurant configured to look like its namesake was always worth a visit. Although only the barrel was present here, and it was just a little decoration on the roof, the theory still held. It was almost two when she finished her burger and drove a little farther up the highway, to the fortress that was Sterne Foods.

One of the older buildings along this stretch of road, it had a fierce spick-and-span quality. The squat stucco rectangle was blinding white, with a red trim that was so shiny it looked wet. The cyclone fence—and the razor wire stretched across the top—shimmered in the midday sun. The grass was bright green and sharply edged, the flower beds severely symmetrical. No risk of E. coli here, Tess thought. Sterne Foods put the process in processed foods.

The only scruffy note was a slow-moving line of protesters in front of the fence. With union members on both sides of her family, Tess automatically assumed these were disgruntled workers. But their placards told of a much deeper dissatisfaction with Sterne Foods. SAVE YOUR OWN SOUL—DON'T EAT MEAT, READ ONE SIGN, COWS DON'T DESERVE THE DEATH PENALTY. HUMANITARIANISM DOESN'T STOP WITH HUMANS. And, a little mysteriously, CHRIST-MAS IS CARNAGE. Tess couldn't let that one go.

"Christmas? It's not quite Halloween."

"It's from *Babe*," said the picketer, a stringy woman with yellow-orange skin, the color of an expensive pepper. "You know, the movie about the pig who wants to herd sheep."

"A classic," Tess agreed. She and Esskay had watched it on video several times. "So what's your beef with Sterne Foods?"

The picketers looked alarmed, as if even the meta-phorical use of the word was forbidden to them.

"We've been out here every day for a year, since the city gave Gus Sterne permission to stage the All Soul Festival," said the stringy woman, who seemed to be the leader. "He calls it a celebration of food and culture, but it's really just a way to promote his chain of barbecue restaurants. Oh, sure, he'll give all the profits to local charities, but he's still respon-sible for the slaughter of hundreds of thousands of cows. He's made his millions off animal genocide, but no one ever talks about that."

"Eating meat is legal."

"That doesn't make it moral. Or safe."

A young man leaned into the conversation. "Cig-arette smoking was acceptable, too, once. We want to marginalize meat eating in the same way, with additional taxes and more truth in labeling."

Tess had a sudden image of the office building of the future, with workers standing in little clusters, some smoking, others hunched over roast beef sandwiches.

"You didn't pick an easy state to start your fight, I'll give you that much."

She had meant to appease the group, but the stringy woman took offense.

"We aren't interested in easy battles. San Antonians think it's not a celebration unless meat is consumed. We're petitioning city hall for meatless, cruelty-free venues at all the major festivals here."

"Life is cruel. Existence is predicated on destruction."

"Those are very fancy rationalizations for being a flesh-eater," sniffed the human yellow pepper. *I wouldn't want to be in the Donner Party with you*, Tess decided. Although her lack of body fat would probably doom her early on, she'd be much too lean to support those left behind.

"I had a cheeseburger for lunch," Tess announced sunnily. "Medium rare."

Some of the people in the group took a few steps backward, as if they might catch something from her, but the stringy woman held her ground.

"This isn't a joke," she said. "We're willing to go pretty far to press our agenda. I wouldn't plan on having too good a time at the All Soul Festival, if I were you."

"Oh, be off before someone drops a house on you, too!" Tess muttered, pushing past the pickets to a small guardhouse that bisected the wide drive into Sterne Foods. An automatic fence separated her from the guard, and she hooked her fingers into the mesh, rattling it to get his attention.

"I'd like to see Gus Sterne," she said.

"You got an appointment?" asked the guard, barely glancing up from the sports page.

"No, it's a personal matter."

The guard shook his head. "Uh-huh. That won't work."

"Pardon me?"

"Oh, this crazy sports columnist, Robert Buchanan, he thinks the Texas Longhorns need more offense. He is so retarded. Where do they get these guys? I could write a better column."

"About Gus Sterne—"

"Sorry. No one gets in unless they're on the list. You want to see him, you have to call, get an appointment first, and show two forms of ID when you show up here. Fact is, he's pretty busy right now, what with the festival and all the traveling he's been doing. You won't be able to get an appointment for a week, maybe two."

Even as the guard spoke, a silver Lincoln Continental convertible was gliding down the hill. The gate began to slide open automatically and Tess jumped back, surprised by the sudden movement. The Lincoln was possibly the largest car she had ever seen. Brand-new, it would have been gross, the kind of stereotypical excess expected of Texans. But this car looked to be at least forty years old, which lent a certain dignity to its oversized proportions.

The same could be said of the broad-shouldered man behind the wheel, a man not much older than the car he drove. His shoulders were broad, his hair blond running to silver. As a young man, he had probably been handsome in a coarse, almost too-obvious way. Age had improved him.

One could only hope it would do the same for the young man in the passenger seat. His lines were as blurry as a second-generation photocopy. He hadn't gotten his face yet, as Kitty might say. His profile was mushy, his shoulders narrow and round, and his posture was noodle-limp.

The gate was open all the way now, and the guard lifted his hand in a gesture that was halfway between a wave and a salute. The picketers seemed confused by the sight of the car—instinctively jumping out of the way, then drawing close again as it waited to make a left turn into the heavy traffic. The driver paid no attention to them at all, but the younger man scrunched down in the passenger seat until he almost disappeared. The Lincoln caught a break in the traffic and slid smoothly into it.

"Well, you got your wish," the guard said.

"What?"

"You *saw* Gus Sterne. You just didn't get to speak to him. And li'l Gus. Excuse me—Clay." The guard grinned. "He's a watery-looking kid, isn't he? It's like he came out of the oven before he was baked through. Clay's a good name for him. Play-Doh would be better."

"He's young."

"He's *my* age," the guard said, with a truly proprietary outrage, as if he owned the year in which he was born. "Twenty-two, just graduated from UT. I hear he wants to go back and study something like history, but Daddy says the only way he'll pay for any more school is if he goes for an MBA, or a law degree. It's pretty funny if you think about it. Gus Sterne has a foundation that sends all these poor kids to college, but he won't let his own son go back. Poor baby. He wants to go be a history teacher, and his daddy's making him run a multimillion-dollar business."

"Everywhere I go, I hear Gus Sterne's a pretty nice guy. Practically a saint."

"He's fine as bosses go. But you get used to making rules for other people, you start thinking you're better than them, that you know best all the time. I could have had me one of those Sterne Scholar gigs, then I read the fine print. You wouldn't believe all the requirements attached. Not only a B average, but you had to do volunteer work, too. Man, I'd rather work for the guy than take his charity. Fewer strings attached."

Tess pulled out the photograph of Little Girl in Big Trouble, the one from the newspaper. "I'm looking for a girl, Gus Sterne's cousin. Emmie Sterne. This is her. Blond, kind of small and frail looking."

The guard shrugged. "I don't remember her coming to the gate. But she looks like she'd have fit right in with that gang at the foot of the driveway, and I don't pay them too much attention, long as they keep moving and don't block the path of any cars."

"Are they the reason security is so tight?"

"Big part of it. I think they're all talk, but you never know. Meanwhile, no one gets in, unless Sterne's secretary phones and tells me they're okay."

"What about the cops?"

"Even they don't get in, unless I'm told it's okay."

"No, I mean, have they been here recently?"

"Some captain came by a month ago, but I think it was to go over the parade route. Like there's anything to go over. We only have about twenty parades a year in this town, and they all go the same way. Down Broadway, past the Alamo. Hey, I get to work security for the All Soul parade. I'm gonna drive the car."

"What car?"

"That sweet silver Lincoln you just saw. Pretty cool, huh? Too bad I can't really open it up, but you gotta drive slow, so the boss and his son can do the big wave from the backseat." He did a passably good imitation of a prom queen's wave. "I'm going to wear mirrored sunglasses, and a little wire in my ear. I'm gonna be Secret Service, practically."

Tess nodded absently. It had been silly to come here. If Emmie had decided to pull the prodigal daughter routine, Sterne Foods wouldn't be the site of their tearful reunion, despite the surplus of fatted calves on the premises. To go home again, you have to go *home*. Hermosa Street, she had said. A handsome place, the shrine of Saint Gus, who had come to believe that he always knew best.

Which, in Tess's experience, made him a very dangerous man indeed.

18

Esskay was behind the bullet-proof glass in La Casita's office, enjoying leftovers—it looked like she had the grease-soaked red and white remains of a KFC bucket in her mouth—while Mrs. Nguyen watched one of her Spanish-language soap operas.

"She cried," Mrs. Nguyen said sheepishly. Tess assumed she was referring to some character on her soap opera, *El Corazon de la Noche*. But Mrs. Nguyen was nodding her head toward Esskay.

"Women complained, so I had to do something. Very strange, this dog. Doesn't make a bow-wow sound. Sounds more like someone in pain." She did such a good imitation of Esskay's plaintive howl that the dog looked up, puzzled and intrigued. "*Everyone* complained, up and down the block. Man at the antiques store, and people at used bookstore, too."

"Good job, Esskay," Tess said. "In a motel full of hookers, you're the one who gets busted for being too noisy."

"Not hooker motel," Mrs. Nguyen corrected swiftly. "Businesswomen. Like you."

Tess started to object, but Mrs. Nguyen had a point. After all, she was working out of a room at La Casita, charging hourly rates. And providing her clients with far less satisfaction.

"If you like her company, feel free to let her out of the room anytime," she told Mrs. Nguyen. "In fact, you can baby-sit her this evening. I've got to drive over to this house in Olmos Park, on Hermosa. You know the neighborhood?"

Mrs. Nguyen nodded her head in vigorous approval. "Rich."

"Gated?" That would be a bitch and a half.

"No, no gates. But rich. Very rich."

"Are the streets busy? Is there a lot of traffic?"

Mrs. Nguyen thought about this. "The street that goes straight through is very busy, but lots of the streets go round and round, go nowhere. Hermosa is one of those, not so busy."

In other words, an impossible place to do surveillance, especially in a twelve-year-old Toyota with out-of-state tags. Tess sighed. Even in a nice car, it was difficult to keep vigil in a residential area. Rich people were quick to call the cops at the sight of anything out of the ordinary. She would have to think of some other way to watch the Sternes' house for evidence of Emmie.

Not that she was particularly confident she would find her at the Sternes'. It was just the only place she could think of to look. Because when you really were in big trouble—big-time, get-a-lawyer, warm-up-the-electric-chair type trouble—the past would be forgiven, family feuds forgotten.

Crow's in that kind of trouble, some second-guessing voice in her head taunted her, *and he's still keeping his family at arm's length*. But perhaps this was the proof that Crow didn't grasp just how much trouble he was in.

Mrs. Nguyen had turned her attention back to the television. Esskay appeared to be watching, too, studying the small figures moving across the screen with bright eyes and pricked ears, as if they were little Spanish-speaking rabbits.

"Do you understand Spanish?" Tess asked.

"A little."

"Then why not watch the ones in English?"

"Because this way, I can make up my own story. My stories much better than theirs. See, this girl—her name is Maria—she's having problems with her husband. She thinks he's not in love with her any-more. But what she don't know is, he lost all their money, and he don't want to tell her, so he works a second job, to make the money back. He away every night, so she thinks he has a girlfriend. She cries boo-hoo-hoo." Mrs. Nguyen's fake crying sounded a lot like her imitation of Esskay's barking. "And he thinks maybe he's not the father of her baby, be-cause she act so funny."

One of La Casita's businesswomen came in just then, dressed for success in what appeared to be a halter made out of a shower curtain. She greeted Mrs. Nguyen in Spanish, Mrs. Nguyen answered in Vietnamese as she handed over the key. *Mrs. Nguyen's life was more interesting than any soap opera in any language*, Tess decided. Couldn't she see that? Probably not. No one ever sees the drama of his or her own life. In our own heads, we were all normal and rational, doing things that made sense. Even Emmie Stern.

San Antonio's October days were not only hotter than Baltimore's, they seemed to last longer, too. The city must be farther west in its respective time zone, surmised Tess, ever the geography dunce of West Baltimore Middle School. Tonight, that suited her purpose. It was still light when she parked her car at a Stop 'n' Go on the boundary of Olmos Park, and the air had cooled a little. Perfect jogging weather. Too bad she had jumped rope and done fifty push-ups that morning, but she figured fast-walking wouldn't be that taxing—depending on how long she had to do it. It was the only way she could think of to make repeated passes by the Sterne home without drawing too much attention to herself. The house sat near a long, curving road called Contour Drive, and Mrs. Nguyen had told her people often jogged there.

"Woman killed there once, in front of her baby," she had warned Tess darkly. "It's true! Chris Marrou said. Take your gun." But Tess had decided packing a .38 while exercising would draw too much attention, even in Texas.

She walked east on Olmos Drive, then north toward Hermosa. The blocks were long and irregular here, it took more time than she would have liked, and ten minutes had gone by before she made her first pass by the house. In a neighborhood of big, beautiful houses, the Sterne home was perhaps the most impressive, a stone mansion with the kind of green lawn that only chemicals and a full-time gardener could have maintained. A new wing appeared to have been added fairly recently—the attached garage, connected to the house by an enclosed breezeway, was made of slightly different materials, although the addition blended in nicely. It also was constructed in such a way that one could come and go without being seen, Tess noticed. Emmie's little Nissan could be parked in there right now.

She had slowed down, almost stopped, as she examined the Sterne homestead. That wouldn't do. She sped up, turning onto Contour Drive.

She wondered if the police were ahead of her here, too, as they had been with Al Rojas and Marianna. The police wouldn't need to pretend to fast-walk through the neighborhood, they could walk straight up to the door, ring the bell and demand a search if they had any reason to believe that Emmie was there. If she was, wouldn't her uncle hand her over? After all, he was Mr. Good Citizen, so beloved that he was going to have his own parade. Emmie could run to him, but she probably couldn't count on hiding with him.

Unless he was willing to keep her under wraps until he had his big day. Maybe Gus Sterne didn't want to ride down Broadway in his Lincoln Continental with people whispering about the latest Sterne scandal. He wouldn't obstruct justice, but he might slow it down a little.

Tess was so caught up in her thoughts that she

overshot the block where she needed to turn and circle back toward Hermosa. Now she was confused. This was no standard, rectangular grid, as she recalled from the map. Instead of doubling back, she continued on to the next street, Stanford—there was no discernible pattern to the names here—and headed up a street called El Prado, still lost enough in thought that she didn't immediately register the silver Lincoln.

The car was ahead of her and, of course, moving much faster. But there couldn't be two perfectly maintained silver Lincolns in the same neighborhood, not with a vanity license plate that read: BBQKNG. She kept her pace steady until it turned onto Hermosa, then decided to sprint. Runners often put on a burst of speed on at the end of their workouts, she reasoned, why not a fast-walker? She didn't think she looked too suspicious—until she stopped abruptly at the edge of the Sternes' property, where she hoped to catch the garage door going up, and a glimpse of Emmie's car beyond it.

The garage door was still down, the Lincoln left in the drive. "Dammit," she said, loud enough so a woman gardening across the street looked up at her. Tess bent over in what she hoped was a realistic-looking spasm of a pain, grabbing her leg as if it had just cramped up. With great show, she dragged herself to the curb and massaged her calf, all the time studying the Sterne house.

Was the Lincoln in the driveway because the garage was occupied? But they were rich people, they probably had many cars. Even as Tess watched, the garage door began to rise, revealing a glimpse of a

Chevy Suburban and a small sports car. She didn't recognize the make, but it clearly was not Emmie's blue Nissan. The young blond man she had seen in the Lincoln convertible was coming down the drive, holding a plastic bottle of something bright green.

"Drink this," he said. It was a sports drink, a brand Tess found particularly vile.

"Thanks, but I prefer water after a run."

"You're cramping up, right? This helps."

What could she say? She took the bottle from him and forced down a swallow. Perhaps if she had been sweating, it wouldn't have been so bad. As it was, it was like drinking an over-sweet limeade with a tablespoon of salt.

"Better?" he asked.

"Mmm."

"So, are you going to keep circling our house, pretending to workout, or did you get to see what you wanted?"

"I'm not sure what you mean." She lifted her brows, trying to look as stupid as people sometimes assumed she was, what with the girlish braid and the overripe body that nature had given her to cart around. Sometimes she toyed with dying her hair blond, curious to see if people could condescend to her even more.

"I saw you outside the office today."

"What office?"

Clay Sterne was young, but he couldn't be fooled by the pretty little pout of consternation that Tess thought she did so well. "You were at Sterne Foods, about mid-afternoon. You were talking to Javier as we drove by. My father pointed you out to me."

"Why?"

For some reason, Clay blushed. "He thought you looked . . . healthy. All things considered."

"Healthy?"

"Robust." Clay's blush deepened. "I mean—he just thinks I should pay more attention to the world around me."

Tess knew exactly what he meant. "Your father should be pointing out women closer to your own age."

"Oh, it's not like he would want me to go out with someone like you."

"Someone like me?" Tess echoed. She suddenly felt as if she were in some fifties melodrama, the one about the waitress from the wrong side of the tracks, knocked up by the ne'er-do-well scion.

"Well, you know, radical."

How could someone project a political stance on someone after such a fleeting glimpse? Tess took the time to put herself in the passenger seat of the silver Lincoln, surveying the scene from Clay's vantage point.

"You think I'm one of the *vegans*."

"Aren't you?" Eye contact was not Clay's strong suit. He kept his head down, studying the grass. His blond hair was a shade darker than Emmie's, although his pale skin had the same bluish cast. His eyes appeared more gray than blue, but that might have been the effect of his silver wire rims, or the twilight. He also had those heavy dark circles beneath his eyes.

Tess was sprawled on the ground, still playing the part of the injured runner. She struck her quad muscle with a balled-up fist. "You could probably build a muscle like this with beans and grain, but I didn't. The only meats I don't eat are sweetbreads and scrapple."

"Scrapple?"

"If you don't know, you don't need to know."

Clay Sterne's smile was sweet, although he held it tight and close, the way a little old lady holds her purse on the street. "So if you're not with them, why were you at the office today? Why are you here now?"

To her dismay, Tess found herself without a ready lie. Even if she had one, she might not have used it. For some reason, she would have felt guilty lying to this young man. Like his cousin, Clay made one want to tread carefully, to protect and coddle him. The young Sternes were so very fragile. Emmie knew it, and used it. Clay didn't have a clue.

As she sat there, nonplussed, flexing her toes so her calf muscles winked on and off, Gus Sterne came out of the house and down the front walk.

"Supper's almost on the table, Clayton."

He was big, bigger than she had realized. Almost six-five, and large-boned, the thickness of middle age just beginning to settle at his waist. The extra ten or fifteen pounds were not unflattering, but Gus Sterne had refused to acknowledge them, so his dark green polo and khaki pants were just a fraction too tight. Frat boy going to seed.

"It's the woman from the office," Clay said to his father, in the manner of a little boy showing off an exotic butterfly he couldn't wait to impale on a pin. "The one who was talking to Javier. But she's not one of them. She eats meat."

Her fake cramp forgotten, Tess jumped to her feet, brushing grass from her jogging shorts.

"It's nice to meet you."

Gus Sterne nodded. "My pleasure. Who are you?"

"Tess Monaghan." Her voice scaled up, as if she wasn't quite sure.

"Is there something I can do for you?" His voice was pleasant, but wary. Maybe he was worried this was an ambush and her vegan friends were about to rush him from the bushes across the street and drench him in blood.

"I'm a private investigator from out of town, working with a local attorney. We're trying to find your niece, Emmie Sterne—"

"My cousin," Sterne corrected. "Emmie is the daughter of my first cousin, Lollie Sterne. That makes her my first cousin, once removed. Very much removed. We've had no contact for five years, by her design."

"But if she were in trouble—I mean, if she knew someone who was in trouble—"

"I think you had it right the first time," Sterne said dryly. "You might as well know the police have already been here, Miss Monaghan, and told us all about Emmie's latest adventure. A dead man at her godmother's place, and the murder weapon discovered under her roommate's bed. I wish I could say I was surprised."

"Has she contacted you?"

"No, and I don't expect her to. Being on the run from the law, a suspect in a killing, at the very least an accessory—those things aren't grave enough for Emmie to break her vow never to speak to me again."

"Where else would she go?"

Gus Sterne looked weary. The blue-black circles under his blue eyes were puffy, as if he had not been sleeping well.

"I'm sure I don't know. Trying to think the way Emmie does is a lost cause, Miss Monaghan. Succeed, and you'll be as crazy as she is."

"Dad!"

"I'm sorry, Clay, but we have to stop pretending. Emmie is a very sick girl. We can talk about the reasons forever, but we can't change the reality." He turned to Tess, anxious to explain his side to a new, apparently neutral party. "People assume Emmie was shaped by the horrible events of her childhood. But even when she was too young to understand what had happened to her, she was a spoiled, reckless child. She tried to drown Clay once, you know."

"That's not fair, Dad. She was only four at the time." Now it was Clay pleading his case before Tess. "We were playing Moses in the bulrushes. She honestly thought the wicker basket would hold me."

"Right, a sewing basket was going to carry you down the Blanco River. It sank less than three feet from our dock. But at least Emmie admitted what she did back then, without falling back on excuses. By the time she was a teenager, she'd scream and sob when anyone tried to thwart her. *I can't help how I am. I crawled through my mother's blood. I saw her dead body, even if I can't remember it, the memory is there.* I wish I had a dollar for every time I heard that lament."

"It's not a bad reason, as reasons go," Tess said.

"True. But Emmie wants it both ways. If she

can't control her own actions, she needs to be locked away until she can. I was happy to pay for whatever help she needed. She wasn't willing to take it."

"Dad—"

"Clay, you don't know half the things that girl put me through."

"Yes, I do," Clay said. He was not as small as Tess had thought at first, it was just that Gus Sterne was so large. "I know more than you think I do."

"Have you been in touch with Emmie? You are strictly forbidden—"

"I'm twenty-two, Dad. I'm of age. I can drink, marry, go to war, and even talk to anyone I please. But, no, Dad, I haven't talked to Emmie." He was speaking to Tess now. "And I don't know where she is. Dad's right about one thing. This is the last place she would come. After all, there's been a restraining order against her for five years. She's not allowed within one hundred feet of this house, the office, or anyone in the Sterne family. But I guess that's old news, here in San Antonio. Not supposed to talk about it, not right now. Can't rain on the King of Barbecue's parade by reminding him how much he's hated by the girl he raised like his very own daughter—" Clay choked a little on the last word, as if he found it distasteful. "No, we just can't have Emmie crashing this party, can we, Dad?"

"Clay—"

"Do you know that my father was a King Antonio *twice*? He's presided over two Fiestas, but it still wasn't enough for him. He had to make up his own event and crown himself king, forever and ever.

Everybody loves Gus Sterne—everyone but his ex-wife and his blood relations."

Except for uttering his son's name, Gus Sterne had not tried to speak throughout this rant. Now Clay looked at his father expectantly, as if he feared a blow. As if he would welcome one.

"Finished?" his father asked, putting a hand on the young man's shoulders, which were still heaving with emotion.

Clay flinched and nodded at the same time.

"Then let's go have our supper, son. Manuela made the hunter's stew you like."

"With veal?" Clay asked.

"With veal."

Tess watched them go down the walk. Gus's big arm lay lightly across his son's round shoulders, yet Clay walked as if the weight were crushing him.

19

Technically, Tess awoke to the phone the next morning, but it was really Tyner's voice that roused her, its volume unaffected by the distance it had to travel. As she was no longer sitting in the back of a patrol car, she wasn't quite so nostalgic for the sound.

"You sure have made a mess of things here," he began. No hello, no how are you. Tyner liked to surge into a conversation the way rowers jump across the start in shorter races. "How is that everyone knows to call my office since you skipped town?"

"I changed the message on my machine, then used call forwarding, activated long-distance. Isn't technology great?" She drew out the vowel sound in the last word until it became two, three syllables, the way the women here did in the impossibly glossy grocery stores. *Look at this mango. Isn't it great? Look at these tuberoses. Aren't they great? Look at all that Gulf Coast shrimp isn't it greaaaaaaaaaate?*

"Trust me, it wasn't that great when Mr. Cesnik showed up on my doorstep, yelling about sausages."

"Pierogies," Tess corrected. "Cecilia's dad, remember? I told you about him. He added a little restaurant to his tavern this summer, started serving authentic Polish food. He did so well that Casimir Cudnik, his biggest competitor, copied him. But he's using frozen pierogies, and passing them off as homemade. I did a Dumpster dive two weeks ago and found the boxes. But you know, Cudnik could accuse us of putting them there. I guess it doesn't constitute proof. What do you think?"

"I don't give a damn about pierogies, frozen or fresh. You have a business to run, and you better come back here and run it. Why are you still there, anyway? Kitty told me you found Crow last week."

"Crow wasn't the first thing I found here," Tess sighed. She was beginning to understand Marianna's reluctance to repeat the same story over and over again.

Still, it was strangely clarifying to rehash everything for Tyner. She worked in a simple, chronological order, and in her mind she saw one of those old-fashioned movie maps, a dotted line tracking her progress from Charlottesville to Austin, then to Twin Sisters and San Antonio. Tyner listened without interrupting. When he wasn't shouting, he was a wonderful listener.

"So Crow has gotten himself mixed up in these murders, old and new," Tyner said at last. "And he keeps giving you every indication that something's going to happen this weekend, but you don't know what, or why."

"You got it."

"Has it occurred to you that Crow is being reticent

about Emmie not out of misplaced chivalry or blind love, but because he's involved, too?"

"Crow would never be mixed up in a murder," she said, hoping her voice conveyed more conviction than she felt. "This is a guy who couldn't put out a mousetrap."

"It wouldn't be so very hard to justify killing a man like Tom Darden, if you believed he was a killer."

"But that was information Emmie didn't have, only the cops."

"This detective, Guzman, said *he* didn't tell the family members what he suspected. But there are few true secrets in the world. San Antonio sounds like a small-big city, just like Baltimore."

"I wish I were in Baltimore," Tess said.

"Why?"

"Because then I could go to the Brass Elephant, rest my head on the bar, and moan softly until Victor made me a double." A Victor double was another bartender's quadruple. "Then I'd call Feeney over at the *Beacon-Light*, and he'd help me figure it out. He always has little bits of information stored away, like a squirrel."

"So all you need is a South Texas Feeney," Tyner said.

"Too bad I don't know one. There was this old hack, Jimmy Ahern, who wrote that book I was telling you about, but I haven't seen his byline in the *Eagle*. He's probably dead, or retired. On the other hand—" She felt like a deep sea diver, going after a tiny pearl somewhere deep in her memory banks. "I do know a reporter down here who helped me, when

I was doing that background check on Rosita Ruiz. He might still be around. A. J. . . . . Sheppard."

"Now you're thinking." Tess knew if she could see Tyner on the other end of the line, he would be tapping his forehead with his index finger. Add that to her list of reasons to be glad the videophone had never caught on.

"Silly me. I thought I was thinking all along."

He wasn't finished with her. "Now, how are your workouts going?"

"They're going. No shell, and no river even if I had one, but I'm jumping rope, running, doing push-ups and situps."

"How far did you run yesterday?"

"I didn't run yesterday, exactly—"

"Six miles," Tyner said. "Interval training. Are there any hills around there? I always imagine Texas as flat and dusty."

"Actually hillier than Baltimore in some places. In fact, San Antonio is really a very pretty city. But Tyner—"

"Six miles," he repeated. "Meanwhile, I shall handle the pierogi wars of East Baltimore."

"Hearing footsteps" is not an empty sports cliché for women joggers in lonely places. Tess, who had been running for more than half her life, never felt as vulnerable as she did on a deserted path, an unseen runner closing the gap, breath ragged and hard, feet striking the ground harder still. Was it someone trying to pass you? Or someone trying to *catch* you? Fifteen years of uneventful runs didn't keep Tess from worrying about the worst-case scenario. Bad luck overtook most people eventually. She could only hope it wasn't coming up on her left flank as she pounded down a path in Brackenridge Park.

She drifted to the right, the protocol for allowing a faster runner to pass. But the unseen runner was slowing down now, content to stay even with her. In her peripheral vision, she caught a glimpse of a man just about her height, a little stocky through the torso, with short, thin legs working very hard to match her stride for stride. She was dogging it, running a nine-minute mile, but the pace was clearly taxing him.

"Mind if I join you?" he asked, and she had to make eye contact then. It was Steve Villanueve, the bouncer who was really a cop.

"Be my guest. You live around here?"

"No, but I like to run here in the mornings. In the summers it's worth the drive to have the shade. How much farther for you?"

She glanced at her watch. "At least twenty more minutes."

He tried to look enthusiastic. "Great."

"Let's pour it on."

She increased her speed, heading for the long steep hill she had noticed on her first day here, the one behind the curious Japanese-style garden.

"These are the Japanese Tea Gardens," Steve said as they climbed. Talking-while-running obviously wasn't easy for him, but he seemed determined to make the effort. "They've come full circle. They began as the Japanese Gardens, then the name was changed to the Chinese Gardens after Pearl Harbor. Then they were the Sunken Gardens, which really made no sense. They finally gave up and went back to the original name. Who knows, maybe"—a few quick, almost asthmatic pants—"Texas will be Tejas again in my lifetime."

Tess nodded. There's a school of thought that you should be able to hold a conversation while running, if only to prove you were working at an aerobic rate, instead of an anaerobic one. But it wasn't a mandate. For her, part of the pleasure of working out was the quiet, the time to think and recharge.

"They get good concerts down in the amphitheater sometimes." Another pause, another round of harsh breaths. "The first concert I ever saw was when I was just four years old. Some born-again Christian group with Little Ricky as the drummer. You know, Little Ricky from the old *I Love Lucy* show? Babalu!"

Tess tried to think of something to say, if only to be polite, but nothing occurred to her.

"They were probably awful, in . . . retrospect." He groped for that last word. There was a slight hesitation to his speech that couldn't be explained by his panting, an exaggerated deliberateness, like a cured stutterer. She wondered if English was his second language. Unlike glib Rick, whose self-mocking repetoire of accents ran from redneck hick to Frito Bandito, Steve tried to speak in a bland newscaster's tone. "But it was the first concert I ever saw, and I loved it. Got a guitar, of course, like every other boy in America, but I couldn't play a lick. Can't sing, either. Or dance. Born to be a fan, I guess. Someone has to be, right?"

They crested the summit. One of the great ironies in running is that going downhill simply punishes the parts of the body that had it easy on the ascent. Gravity pulled on her quadriceps, teasing them, testing them, setting her up for a fall. Gravity was a bitch, in Tess's opinion, a much bigger enemy than time. It was gravity that pulled the body apart, made everything droop and fall.

"So do you do security for the money or the access?" she asked Rick, trying to give him a chance to breathe.

"Both, I guess. I like the money. I like the music."

"Especially Emmie's."

She glanced at his face. The deep color in his cheeks wasn't purely from exertion. "Emmie's good."

A short silence, as they hit bottom. "Want to knock off early?" he asked. "We could grab breakfast on Broadway, near where you're staying."

Tess stopped abruptly. "I didn't tell you where I was staying."

"Sure you did—" He had stopped, too, and was bent over, his hands on his knees as he sucked in air greedily.

"No, Steve, I'm very careful about such things. My father's training. I've never listed my home address in the phone book, and I wouldn't casually broadcast my whereabouts in a strange city. I suppose you could have gotten it off the police report from this weekend—"

"Oh, were you down at the station?" he asked. His acting was on a par with his running.

"—but that still doesn't explain why you're here today, chatting me up, trying to get me to go to breakfast. Guzman's idea? Or is this a little ad hoc plan concocted by a patrolman who wants to move up to detective?"

"I don't want to write tickets forever," Steve said, straightening up. "Besides, Guzman has his ambitions, too. If I could help him solve the triple murders, everyone would get what he wanted, and that would be a good thing." The last sounded like a child repeating something an adult had told him. "Guzman was so close, until Darden turned up dead. Now the other one, Laylan Weeks, has vanished without a trace, and Emmie is missing, too. He thought . . . I thought . . ."

"He thought he could send you to spy on me, the way you've been spying on Emmie at the Morgue and Hector's. Did you work at Primo's, too? Didn't Emmie ever get suspicious, seeing you at every gig? But I guess that's what the whole lovesick-puppy thing was about. You pretended to have a crush on her because it made it plausible that you'd be hanging around, watching her every move. She thought you were a groupie. You're really a spy."

"Doing my job," he pleaded. "Just doing my job."

"Consider it done," Tess said. "I'll make you a deal—you stay away from me from now on, and I won't let Guzman know how badly you botched this particular assignment."

"You'd go to Guzman?" He was scared. The sweat on his brow was fresh, his round cheeks were flushed anew. She couldn't blame him. She wouldn't want to be on Guzman's shit list either.

"If I see you anywhere near me, I'm on the phone to him. But if you stay away from me, this will be our little secret. Now scoot. I still have a real work-out to do."

He backed away from her, then turned and began sprinting toward the path that wound along the zoo. His bright white, perfectly plain T-shirt became smaller and smaller, until it was little more than a tiny flag of surrender, waving at her from a great distance. Tess felt like a bully. It wasn't the worst feeling in the world.

20

A. J. Sheppard had agreed to meet her for lunch, once he determined she was paying. Apparently *San Antonio Eagle* reporters didn't have the kind of expense accounts taken for granted by those reporters at Baltimore's *Beacon-Light*. He named a place on San Antonio's River Walk, and when Tess demurred—she wasn't a tourist, after all—he had been insistent. "When you get home, it's all anyone will ask you, anyway. Did you see the Alamo? Did you go to the River Walk?" He was strangely emphatic on this point, in the manner of a person who is strangely emphatic about the smallest matters. In the end, it was easier to concede.

The little district of restaurants and shops, a flight of stone steps below the real city, was pretty and picturesque. A cleaner Venice, decided Tess, who had never seen the real thing. The River Walk had begun life as a one-time WPA project, according to an old travel guide she had found in the nightstand at La Casita, then been pulled back from the edge of ruin in the early sixties. Not unlike Baltimore and its Inner Harbor project. American cities seemed in a constant state of such rediscoveries, waking up again and again to the reality that the old downtowns were aesthetic marvels, well worth preserving. The only thing Tess couldn't understand was why such developments seemed predicated on having bodies of water nearby. Not that you could really call the San Antonio River a body of water. More like a small limb.

From a patio table at Siempre Sabado, she studied the passersby, trying to pick A. J. out of the crowd. The only thing she could be sure of is that he would not be wearing a conventioneer's badge, like so many of the others she spotted here. Come to think of it, she had no idea what he looked like nor how old he was. Their fleeting acquaintance was based on exactly one telephone call seven months ago, a call he had promised to disavow. On the phone, he was loud and braying, like a deaf old man who thought he had to shout to be heard. His accent was comically broad; he would not have been out of place on *Hee Haw*. Try as she might, she couldn't get any visual image to adhere to that voice, except for a straw hat and a corncob pipe. This morning, when she had asked what he had looked like, even he seemed stumped. "I'll find you," he said at last.

He did, swooping down on the table like a sudden change in the weather.

"Monaghan!" He pumped her hand with a vigorous up-and-down motion, as if her arm were the lever on an old-fashioned water pump. He was a tall, lanky man with something on his face that was either an early 5 o'clock shadow, a weak beard, or crumbs from his breakfast cereal. He wore a jacket over his blue jeans, and a reporter's notebook was sticking out of his back pocket, tenting the jacket. He pulled out the notebook and threw it down on the table with a loud smack, yelling for a waitress. The staff regarded him tolerantly, if not fondly.

He squinted at her. "I thought you'd be a tough old gal, with a fedora and a trench coat, and here you are, looking like some damn cheerleader. How old are you, twenty-one?"

"I'm thirty," she said, a bit sharply. He looked about thirty-five or forty and she wanted him to know he shouldn't patronize her.

"Excuse me. Never knew you could insult a lady by underestimating her age." He picked up the menu but didn't bother to open it. "You drink at lunch?"

Tess figured no one would ask that question unless *he* drank at lunch. Why not? she thought. She'd sip, he'd slurp, she'd have an edge. This was not, after all, her buddy Feeney, who owed her so many favors, and who would sit on a story at her request. She'd have to tread carefully here.

"Do they have good margaritas?"

"They're the only reason to come here. That and the view. Food's pretty mediocre, compared to what else is out there. If there was any truth in advertising, they'd call it Casa So-So." He waved frantically at the waitress, his long arm slashing the air. "Two frozen margaritas."

"On the rocks for me." Frozen margaritas went down too easily.

The waitress brought the drinks and a basket of

chips, with a thin, brown sauce new to Tess's taste buds. She poked the edge of a chip into it, like a shy swimmer dipping her toe in the ocean. It might be mediocre to Sheppard, but it was still awfully good by her standards.

"Tess Monaghan," A. J. said, drumming his hands on the table. "Tess Monaghan, private eye. How'd you get into this private investigator gig, anyway? I thought you worked at a newspaper up in Baltimore."

"I was working for the paper as an investigator when we spoke. But I was a reporter at the *Baltimore Star*, before it folded."

"That thing we *didn't* talk about last winter—boy, that ended pretty badly, didn't it?"

"Yes." The image of the body in the ditch was always there, waiting for moments like this to clutch at her. The white T-shirt had been so bright against the winter-brown land, the blue plastic grocery bags had looked like a bier of roses.

"This related?"

"No. I'm on a missing person case of sorts."

"Something in it for me? Remember, the newspaper is your friend. A story might flush out some leads."

"*No.*" Perhaps she was a little too quick. But one of the few honorable things Guzman had done was not go to the media. Well, maybe not honorable—he had his own agenda, as evidenced by Steve Villanueve's botched surveillance and interrogation—but the bottom line was there had been no leaks. She wanted to keep it that way.

"I mean, I'm more interested in poking around in your archives. I thought you could help me."

"Sorry, our library is closed to the public. But if you tell me what you need, maybe I can get it for you."

He was persistent, she had to give him that. "Aren't your archives searchable on the Web?"

"Only for the last two years, and it will cost you two bucks an article to pull up more than the headline. Before then, most of the paper is stored in shoeboxes."

Tess laughed. Every newspaper reporter she had ever known took a perverse pride in denigrating their employer's resources.

"No, literally," A. J. said. "That was the old system. Shoeboxes. The old publisher cut a deal with Joske's department store, and he got these shoeboxes really cheap, which they stacked on top of each other. One day a whole wall of 'em fell over on one of the librarians, and the workers' comp claim convinced the company to modernize. Even if you could get in there, you'd never be able to find what you want."

"Probably doesn't matter, anyway. The good stuff never gets in the paper."

"Amen."

"I mean, this guy I'm looking for . . . Tyner Gray—he's a lawyer, disappeared with his partner's money." The lie was fun to tell, even if Tyner wasn't there to hear his name taken in vain. "I don't think it's the first time he disappeared down here, he might have even been living a double life. But as you said, the juicy stuff never sees print anyway."

He nodded, having forgotten that she was the one who had expressed this sentiment, not him. He had only seconded it. "Tyner Gray. Doesn't ring a bell."

"Oh, he's a small-timer. Probably never crossed your screen." She paused, trying to decide if she could make the transition she needed without sounding too forced. "I got excited for a moment when I saw the item about this guy, Tom Darden, whose body was found in the Hill Country. Because Gray had used the name Darden once. But I don't think there's a connection."

"Can't see that there would be, given that Darden was locked up for the last twenty years."

"Yeah. The paper called it the 'infamous Danny Boyd case,' but I've never heard of Danny Boyd. Should I have?"

"Not unless you were around here two decades ago. Even then, there are plenty of folks who don't know what happened. 'Infamous'—that's a kind of a code."

"Code for what?"

A. J. glanced at the tables around them, as if he were planning to break a confidence. "It was before my time, but everyone knows that Danny Boyd's kidnappers molested him. But we couldn't print that detail, because he had been identified when he was snatched, and, of course, we don't identify victims of sexual assault. Especially when he's a rich man's little boy. So it became the 'infamous' Danny Boyd case. It's a wink at the reader, you see, a tip that there's something salacious we can't tell." He sighed. "Of course, given recent events, it's hard to remember those innocent days when there were things that newspapers didn't deem fit to print."

"I knew there was something," she said happily, as if this were a game they were playing. Read Between the Lines, Win Cash Prizes. Much better than Wingo any day. "Maybe it's the ex-reporter in me, but I always can tell if the reporter is holding something back when I read the paper. This may make me sound cynical, but I figure this Sterne guy, who's getting so much press for this All Soul Festival, can't be as saintly as he's made out to be."

"Gus Sterne? Actually, what you see is what you get, in my experience. A little arrogant, maybe, but basically a good guy for someone with that much money and that much clout."

"Still, everyone has skeletons in their closets." She was pushing too hard, A. J. was wary again. "Hey, I've been in some San Antonio homes. People here have skeletons on their bookshelves."

He smiled, but the good ol' boy veneer was gone, revealing a much shrewder man than she wanted to deal with.

"You got a lead on the murders? Because if you do, all bets are off."

The murders. Thousands of people had been killed in this city over the last twenty years, and many of those cases must have gone unsolved as well. But there was no doubt what "the murders" were.

She was grateful for the interruption of a short, plump man with an old-fashioned flash camera, who stopped at the table and asked if the gentleman would like a photograph of the beautiful, beautiful lady, to remember this magic moment always. A. J. waved him away impatiently.

"Well?" he asked Tess.

"I never heard of Lollie Sterne before my work brought me to Texas," she said, pleased to have the truth on her side, at least momentarily. "It's her daughter, Emmie Sterne, I'm looking for. I have a friend who was in a band with her, and she skipped out on him, owing him some money. End of story."

"How does that connect to the murders?" He had drained his frozen margarita and waved for another, but the drink hadn't dulled his senses as much as Tess had hoped. People who drink at lunch also tend to have a pretty high tolerance.

"It doesn't. I'm cruising for a little dirt on the Sterne family. My client really needs this money." She was beginning to buy into her own story, always the mark of a good lie.

"And you think Gus Sterne will pay his cousin's debt, if you can dig up something on him?"

"Knowledge is power."

"Then you should know they're on the outs."

"Yeah, but I figure if I go to him this week, just before his big day, tell him that Emmie has ripped off this guy and I'm willing to go to the press with the story—"

"He'll make good on her debt to avoid the bad publicity." A. J. drank from his margarita glass. He didn't use the straw, and his healthy slurp left a little pale green mustache on his upper lip. "I like how you think. But it's still a stretch. The *Eagle* won't touch the story. For one thing, it's Gus Sterne. Besides, you can't expect a guy to bail out the woman who tried to burn his house down."

Tess, who had just bitten into a tortilla chip, inhaled too sharply, and the chip lodged in her throat. Eyes watering, nose running, she gulped water, trying to wash it down. She recalled reading that people had died this way, choking to death on lethal little tortilla triangles that got stuck in the trachea.

A. J. was enjoying all her levels of discomfort. "You really don't know what you've stepped in, do you? Yeah, Emmie Sterne tried to burn ol' Cousin Gus's house down. What was it—four years ago, five?"

"Five," Tess said faintly. *They had a falling-out, five years ago.* Marianna, the Duchess of Euphemism, had struck again, backed up this time by Gus Sterne's own evasive half-truths. Clay had hinted at the rest of the story, but she had thought he was just being a petulant brat.

"So you do know. Sterne convinced the cops not to press charges, and our weak-kneed publisher really undercut us on the story. You couldn't read between the lines there, because there were no lines, except for a short on the fire itself. The insurance company wasn't so easily appeased, but they straightened it out eventually, and as long as there were no criminal charges, the paper wouldn't make it public. Gus thought he was doing the girl a favor, having her judged incompetent and packed off to some ritzy mental hospital for a few months. I hear she didn't see it that way. But she was damn lucky, I'll tell you that. If Sterne and his son hadn't gotten out of the house in time, she'd have been in prison for a double homicide."

"Emmie tried to burn his house down? The one on Hermosa?" *I grew up on Hermosa. Ugly things can happen on a handsome street.* Then the new looking garage and the adjoining wing had not been an addition, but the part of house that had to be rebuilt after the fire.

"She said it was an accident, but if a Girl Scout had made that little campfire, she'd have gotten a merit badge for her use of accelerants."

"When did this happen? What time of year?"

A. J. raked a chip through the salsa, took a bite, and made another pass. A double-dipper, that figured.

"It was hot. I remember I was heading up to New Braunfels to go tubing on a Saturday afternoon when I heard about the fire on the police scanner I keep in my car. June? July? No, late May, early June. I was covering higher ed at the time and it was one big blur of commencement speakers. I still remember the rack card the city editor wanted to run, before the story got spiked. 'Murder Girl in Big Trouble.' Murder Girl! You gotta love it. The noun-noun construction is what makes it an instant classic. Like Sewer Boy or Glue Dog."

In Big Trouble. Emmie's band was called Little Girl in Big Trouble. Tess was barely listening to A. J. now, but he assumed her furrowed brow meant she wanted a more in-depth explanation.

"Sewer Boy was a kid who fell into the city's sewer system when someone stole a manhole cover. Didn't surface for twenty-four hours. The headline said: 'Sewer Boy Still Missing.' Glue Dog was this puppy some huffers got hooked on inhalants. The county took him away. 'Glue Dog Taken from Torturers.' That was a rack card, put over the boxes to pump up street sales. Now that we're the only game in town, we're more respectable, don't have to work so hard to sell the papers, because what else are they going to buy? Truth be told, we used to be a helluva lot more fun."

"Emmie was in a band called *Little* Girl in Big Trouble."

"Really? That figures, that's the original."

"The 'original'?"

"Little Girl in Big Trouble. It was the headline, on one of the folios, back when the murders first happened. I wasn't at the paper then, but I've heard the story. A month after the murders, the investigation was going nowhere, and the story had dried up along with it. There were three newspapers then, and the *Sun* was beating the *Eagle*'s ass. The *Eagle* reporter, Jimmy Ahern—"

"The one who wrote the book."

"Yeah, right. Anyway, he was desperate for a scoop. So he sort of goosed the story a little bit."

"What do you mean?" She wondered if it was a mistake to admit she was familiar with Jimmy Ahern's oeuvre, but the fact didn't seem to have registered with A. J.

"He had a source—at least, he said it was a source, but I think it was a voice in his head, or at the bottom of his bourbon bottle—who said Emmie was the link, the key that could unlock the murders. He got a little carried away and suggested she was a *suspect*—Little Girl in Big Trouble. Slapped a question mark on the end of the sucker and it led the paper. Turned out that the source really said Emmie couldn't be ruled out as a *witness*, despite her age. Wrong on both counts. Oh well. We ran a correction. Eventually."

Tess had thought she knew every permutation of newspaper fuck-up possible. "The *Eagle* printed a two-year-old was a suspect in a murder case?"

"She was there, she had blood on her." A. J.'s tone was mildly defensive. "At least, she did until the well-meaning social worker scrubbed her up at the station. *Adios, el evidencio!* I mean sure, they assumed the blood was from the victims, but the killer might have hurt himself, and his blood might have been on the baby. There were bloody fingerprints on her T-shirt, too—until the social worker threw that in the washing machine. It's a shame. Twenty-one years ago, you couldn't do shit with that, but if they even had a photograph of the print today, they might be able to blow it up, match it to every fingerprint on file nationwide. Yep, Espejo Verde was the most compromised murder scene of its time."

"Is it still around?"

"What?"

"Espejo Verde."

"The building is. Sterne Foods shuttered it, put a cyclone fence around it and it stands to this day on the river in Baja King William. The area is pretty hip now, and I'm sure a lot of people would like trying to run a restaurant there. But the Sternes won't sell."

"Could you tell me where it is?" Tess said. "I'd like to go see it."

"What's the point?"

"I don't know. Just morbid curiosity, I guess." And a hunch Emmie Sterne might be staying there. She had to be somewhere.

"C'mon, don't waste your time. Have another drink, order an entree."

"I'm not hungry."

"Then let me have another drink, and my cha-lupa, and we'll go."

"*We'll?*"

A. J. leaned over the table, his eyes in a squint so narrow they might as well be closed. "Look, stop fucking with me. There's a rumor going around town that Emmie Sterne is a big girl in big trouble these days. Unfortunately, the cops aren't talking. The DA's office also has a black-out on information. But something happened over the weekend. I know, because a cop got disciplined for making a bad mistake, and the union rep is just busting to tell me about it, how unfair it was, and what an asshole Al Guzman is, how he's going for this guy's balls to cover his own ass. Only he says he can't, until next week."

That time frame again. "I told you, it's no big deal, a bad debt, nothing more. After hearing all this, I'll probably tell my client to forget it."

"Then there's no problem if I want to accompany you on your little sight-seeing trip."

Tess was saved from answering by a brief commotion on one of the bridges spanning the narrow river. A man and a woman—tourist types, even Tess's inexperienced eyes had learned to pick them out here—were arguing heatedly. Drunkenly, too, judging by their liquid posture. The words were inaudible from this distance, but the body language spoke volumes. Arms windmilled, middle fingers saluted. Tess tensed up, ready to act if the man shoved or hit the woman. Her peculiar brand of sexism also dictated that she would never sit idly by when a man struck a woman.

The woman grabbed a fistful of the man's hair. He pushed her away, clambered onto the railing.

"I'd die for you, that's how much I love you," he screamed at the woman. "I'd fucking die for you."

And he jumped. The woman screamed, but everyone else seemed surprisingly blasé. It turned out the water was not even chest deep and the man bounced to the surface, stunned and sputtering. "Neeeeeeeeeeeil!" the woman screamed, and jumped in after him. They embraced in the water until a passing tourist boat fished them out. Just another beautiful love story.

"He's lucky we had some rain this fall," A. J. observed, helping himself to another chip, double-dipping yet again. "Otherwise, they'd both have broken their legs. Want another drink?"

"We already have a second round coming."

"I believe in planning ahead."

Espejo Verde. The Green Mirror. Tess had expected something fancier than this plain, dull green cinderblock building next to a muddy-brown river. Especially after seeing the other side of the King William neighborhood, which was full of restored Victorian mansions that almost lived up to A. J.'s rhapsodic descriptions. This area below Alamo Street—Baja King William, A. J. kept calling it—had some nice houses, too. In particular, she liked the purple one with the pink porch, which A. J. said had the local historical society up in arms. But Espejo Verde, even in its glory days, had been plain at best.

"What was the big attraction?" she asked.

"I always heard it was the food. Authentic Mexican, Mayan dishes like cochinita pibil. And Lollie Sterne.

She was one of those people who made a party wherever she went. People liked to be around her."

Tess got out of A. J.'s car, an old Datsun that, in the tradition of reporters' cars everywhere, was a rolling garbage can. The restaurant's windows were literally shuttered, the patio ceiling had been culled of its fans—by scavengers who left behind ragged wires, little snakes hanging overhead. But there was no graffiti, and few other signs that anyone had dared to tamper here. It wasn't a place where one would trespass lightly. She imagined the neighborhood children, the stories they must tell each other about the ghosts that roam the grounds at Espejo Verde. Did they hold their breaths when they ran past, or was there some other delightful, shivery ritual to keep its evil spirits at bay?

The fence was padlocked, but Tess twisted the Master Lock and it came open in her hands. Someone had been here and closed the lock without pressing it down, so it only looked as if the chain was fastened.

"That's trespassing," A. J. said uneasily, as she opened the gate, which creaked in appropriate horror-movie fashion. But the sky was bright, the street was busy. What harm could really come to them here?

"I'm not a reporter, I don't have to follow the rules. Look—the door lock's rusted off."

After a moment of hesitation, A. J. pushed ahead of her into the old restaurant. The first things they saw were their own wavy images, reflected in a huge funhouse mirror, its surface cracked and speckled, its verdigris frame caked in dust. The Green Mirror, the restaurant's namesake. Beyond it, the room was musty and dark, with a strong smell of decay to it, but surely that was just her overactive imagination. Tess studied the empty space, trying to envision a two-year-old girl playing among three corpses until she was smeared with blood. She saw Guzman, a young patrolman when he had walked in here twenty-one years ago, and she almost felt some empathy for him. His face had probably been cleanshaven then, his stomach not so soft, his mouth not so sad. No one was ever tough enough to see something like that.

But the baby had been in her playpen, off the kitchen. How had she gotten there? Who would kill three people, only to hold a little girl in their bloodied arms, and put her to bed? What had Emmie seen, what might Emmie know? Was she on the run because she had killed someone, or because her tangled mind held the secrets to what had happened here? Recovered memory therapy was a fragile science, if a science at all. But Tess remembered things from when she was two. Okay, she remembered telling a dog to get out of their yard, but it was there, it had happened.

"She's not here," Tess said out loud. "This is the last place she would come."

"What are you talking about?" A. J. asked.

"Nothing."

He hadn't waited for answer, pushing through the old swinging door into the kitchen. He came back so fast that it was like watching a cartoon character getting caught in a revolving door, then spat out again.

"Don't," he said, holding up one hand to wave her

away, while he held the other to his mouth, trying to swallow whatever had risen in his throat. Tess ignored him and tiptoed to the door, although she wasn't sure why she was worried about being overheard. She cracked it just enough to see the cowboy boots at the end of a long wooden table, the dark stain all around the body, an orange T-shirt with what appeared to be brownish splotches draped over a chair. There was something about the head, something odd—no, she wouldn't go any closer. She backed out of the room and went to sit on the floor next to A. J., who had lit a cigarette with fumbling hands, then appeared to have forgotten about it. It hung from his gaping mouth, his lips white, his face the same color as the margaritas he had been drinking.

"You never get used to seeing dead bodies," Tess said.

"I've seen plenty of dead bodies," he retorted, as if this were a point of pride. "I've seen guys on the table, in mid-autopsy. I saw a guy in a trash compactor once. But I've never seen a guy crawling with maggots, his head all but sawed off. And I've never stepped on a guy's fingers."

"His fingers?"

"All ten of them, arranged by the door so they were pointing toward the guy. As if you might not notice him otherwise."

21

Minutes went by, six-hundred-second minutes in which A. J. and Tess just couldn't find the will to get up off the floor and walk out into the bright sunshine, where they would have to face the consequences of their discovery. The smell seemed to worsen as they lingered, taking on a life of its own and wrapping around them, jeering at them. Still they sat, their legs too rubbery to use just yet.

"According to the laws of osmosis, you're supposed to get used to it," Tess remarked.

"I don't think the laws of osmosis apply here," A. J. said, taking short, shallow breaths and trying to pull the neck of his shirt over his nose, so he looked like a kid playing bandit, or that weird guy with the sweater from the old Bazooka bubblegum cartoons. "The question is, who should we call first? The cops, or my photographer? You got a cell phone?"

"No," Tess lied. "You?"

"At the office. I didn't count on writing today. Guess I'll be filing after all."

"You can't write a story. You're a witness."

"Who are you, the ombudsman? I'm a reporter with a first-person story on a murder at one of the most notorious murder scenes in the city. Wonder who that is in there. But even if it's nobody, it's a story."

Nobody indeed. He might be a dead, decaying stranger, but Tess had no doubt they had found Laylan Weeks, Tom Darden's pal. Which meant he was no longer a viable suspect in Darden's death. Which meant Crow and Emmie were.

A. J. stood up, his legs shaking hard enough to make the change in his pocket jingle. "Guess I'll walk up to that ice house on Alamo and make the call."

"Do that, and the cops will be here and have it roped off before you get back," Tess said quickly. "I'd hold my ground, if I were you. Let me walk to the gas station. I'll call the paper, they can get another reporter and a photographer out here. Then I'll wait fifteen minutes and call the cops, like a good citizen. Your guys will already be in, and you'll have told them what you saw. So if you get held up at the cop shop, giving a statement, your paper still gets the story."

A. J. thought about her proposition. Tess knew he wasn't bothered about waiting to call the police, he was just trying to figure out the best way to keep control of the story. He wanted to keep his exclusive, and maybe prevent the local television stations from getting it for the early news. Once the call went out on the police radio, his advantage was lost.

"How about if I give you the beeper number for a photog? The city desk might send one of those hungry youngsters who—well, let's just say there's not always a healthy respect for territory. We'll get the photog in and out, with a statement from me, before the cops get here. Then I'll have the photog call the cops, report it as a break-in."

"Sure," Tess said, suppressing a smile. "Write the number on the back of your business card."

"Do you think—I mean, can't I wait just outside the door, but inside the fence? I don't want to stay in here—" Tess knew he was about to say "alone," then felt sheepish. "I mean, I think it's better if I'm outside when the cops come."

"I do, too," she assured him. "I'm off."

She shouldered her knapsack and felt her phone pressing into her back, beneath the bag's false bottom. Too bad she had to double-cross A. J. He was a nice enough guy, but he put his interests first, which forced her to do the same. She walked briskly down the block until she was out of sight, then broke into a jog. She had to run almost a mile up Alamo Street before she found a cab to take her back to her car.

She called Rick Trejo from the cab's backseat, then the *Eagle* city desk. The person who answered the phone was either very young or very old—the voice was cracked and quavery, which could be from tentativeness or overuse. At any rate, the woman on the other end was blessedly dull and asked no questions when Tess left word that A. J. Sheppard was having car trouble, and probably wouldn't be in for the rest of the afternoon.

"You didn't call the cops? Jesus, Tess, what were you thinking?"

"That we could use a head start."

"Why?" Crow asked. He was sprawled in the only chair in the duplex's living room, his guitar in his lap. "I've been here all day, I obviously didn't sneak down to this restaurant and murder some guy I've never even met."

"Trust me, it's not today you need an alibi for," Tess said, remembering the smell and A. J.'s description of the maggots.

Rick paced the small living room. Tess realized she had finally made it inside Crow's house. The shotgun duplex was charming in a funky, retro way, or could have been. It had old-fashioned built-in bookcases and a huge fireplace, which had been converted to gas. The wood floors needed refinishing, but were basically sound, the windows large and numerous. But there were no domestic touches, no indication that Crow and Emmie had considered this anything but a way station to wherever they were headed.

"If Tess is right, and that's Laylan Weeks in Espejo Verde, the police will want to question you again," Rick told Crow. "I wouldn't be surprised if they find a way to charge you this time, if only to coerce you into finally telling them what you know."

Crow ran his fingers lightly over his guitar strings, humming softly to himself. He was like a little kid who puts his hands over his ears and chants to avoid hearing what he didn't want to hear.

Tess leaned toward him. "You do know something, don't you, Crow?"

"I know Emmie's not going to surface until she's good and ready. All we can do is wait."

"You'll be waiting downtown," Rick said.

Crow looked unconcerned. "Big deal, so I spend the afternoon down there. They'll take me in, they'll try to get me to tell them something, they'll let me go because I don't have anything to tell."

"You better be prepared for the reality that you could be charged and held without bail," Rick said. "It's a homicide rap, you're from out of state. They'll argue you're at risk for flight. You could be in jail until your trial comes around."

"They can't do that."

"If there's one shred of physical evidence to tie you to that scene, they can. Someone's already tried to frame you once, and only police incompetence kept it from working. Why wouldn't they do it again?"

Tess saw a flash of orange in the gloom of the Espejo Verde kitchen, and then remembered Crow happily dying his Cafe Hon T-shirt in her sink, until his hands were bright yellow and the sink had a permanent ring. It had been that same mango-y color, almost exactly, as the stained cloth she had seen. "I used to have a Cafe Hon T-shirt," he had told her Saturday night.

"I can't be in jail this weekend—"

"Why, Crow?" Tess asked. "What's going to happen? What's Emmie going to do?"

"Nothing," he said, and his eyes went dark and flat. "But we've got all these gigs. The Morgue paid us in advance, and we'll have to give it back if at least three-quarters of the band doesn't play Friday and Saturday. And I don't have it, okay? It's already gone, blown on frivolous things like food and gas for my car."

"You won't have to worry about those things if you're in jail," Rick said. "If you do get charged, and I can get bail, will your parents be able to cough up the money?"

"Call my parents and I fire you," Crow said firmly. "I don't want them bailing me out of anything, literally or figuratively. Besides, if you're right, there's not going to be any bail."

Rick glanced at his watch. "I have to call the cops. Better I call them before they call on us."

Crow smiled, a bitter, downturned smile. "I'll brush my teeth so my breath will be kissing-fresh for the interrogation."

Rick picked up the phone, which sat in a curved niche in the wall. "Detective Guzman," he said into the receiver. Then, to Tess, as he waited to be put through. "You should have called me from there. It looks bad, the way you handled it. As if you assumed he was guilty."

He made her feel like a child, and she answered in a child's whiney tone. "I'm tired of talking to cops. I'm tired of finding dead bodies. Let A. J. give them the blow-by-blow. He saw everything. Besides, as long as Crow surrenders, what's the big deal? There's no reason we should assume he's involved in this."

"I just hope Guzman sees things your way," he said. "If he ever picks up. I hate to think of how many minutes of my life I've spent on goddamn hold. I want those minutes back. When death comes for me, I want back every minute I was on hold, in traffic jams, and behind people with eleven items in the ten-items-or-less line."

For all its windows, the living room was fairly dark, perhaps because it faced north. Crow's neighborhood was quiet in the late afternoon, and Tess became aware of the sounds around her—Rick's tuneless humming, the wind moving through the trees, a car moving slowly down the block, bushes rustling, a burst of barking from what sounded like an entire kennel of dogs a block or two away. The steady, muffled sounds of traffic from the nearby highway.

Then she became aware of the sounds she wasn't hearing—running water from the bathroom, Crow's footsteps as he moved about the rear of the house, gathering his things.

"Rick—"

But he was hearing, or not-hearing, the same thing. He dropped the phone, even as Guzman's voice came on the line. They ran down the narrow hall to the bathroom, a large old-fashioned room with a vanity flanked by high built-in cabinets and small square windows bracketing the vanity's mirror. The window closest to the door was up, and the screen had been pushed out on the ground below.

"The car's still there," Tess said, pointing to the Volvo with Maryland tags.

"Only because his key ring is in the front door. And with the park nearby, he can get a good head start on foot," Rick said. "I just wish I'd known he was going to do 'Norwegian Wood' for his encore."

"Norwegian Wood?"

"Sure. This Crow had flown." And he laughed mirthlessly at his own bad joke, while Tess just stared at the empty space where a screen had once been, where Crow's body had been only minutes ago. It was such a small space, even for someone as slender as Crow. It couldn't have been easy to slide through it without making too much noise, to drop to the ground without a thump that would draw their attention.

Such a small space, yet it reminded her just how big trouble can be.

22

"Obstruction of justice," Al Guzman said, as if reading from a mental grocery list. "Accessory after the fact. Criminal trespassing. What else? There's gotta be more. Maybe I'll have your car towed down to a garage, make sure it meets our safety standards, check your dog's license, impound it if you don't have your rabies certificate number. Then again, if there was a felony charge for being *estupida*, I'd have you on a dozen counts of that."

Tess regretted not following Crow out the window. She was persona non grata at SAPD, the city's most unwelcome visitor since Santa Anna, to hear Guzman tell it. Rick was sulking, convinced that she had put him at risk for possible disbarment. A. J. Sheppard, who had sat a long, lonely vigil at Espejo Verde, only to be picked up by the cops, no longer wanted to be her new best friend. As for Steve Villanueve, who glimpsed her in the hallway, he just shook his head sadly.

"So what do you think?" Guzman demanded.

"Would your boyfriend come back for you if I lock you up? Or is he running toward the border with Emmie Sterne? I guess what I'm really asking is if you were a willing accomplice or a dupe."

"C'mon, Guzman," Rick said, rousing himself from his funk. "She was trying to help. She kept the story out of the media for the short term, no easy trick when one of the most aggressive reporters in town is on the scene. By calling me and asking me to meet her at Ed Ransome's apartment, she was trying to ensure he turned himself in. I was on the line with you when he went out the back window. What do you think, I was calling you to chat? Besides, how far could he get? He left his car and, according to him, he was low on funds."

"Low on funds? I think not. He's got his trust fund money, if my hunch is right. If not, then maybe he's got fifty thousand dollars that he took from Tom Darden and Laylan Weeks. Which makes their deaths capital crimes, by the way. Death penalty crimes, which isn't something we take lightly here in Texas, Miss Monaghan. We put more prisoners to death last year than any other state in the union. Year before last, half of the death row prisoners executed in the United States were executed right here in Texas."

"You must be very proud," Tess said.

"Go back to the fifty thousand dollars," Rick said, giving her a will-you-shut-up look.

Guzman had a chair, but he preferred to sit on the edge of the table, well into Tess's personal space. He was astute, he had figured out that such closeness made Tess feel nervous. And when she felt nervous, Tess was inclined to blurt out whatever occurred to her, as she had just demonstrated.

"We've had Darden and Weeks under surveillance since they got out of prison two months ago," Guzman began.

"Not very close surveillance, apparently," Tess said. She really couldn't stop herself. If only Guzman would move even an inch away from her, she might be able to have an unexpressed thought.

"I'm not talking day in, day out. They weren't the smartest two ex-felons around, but they'd know if we were on their ass, and they'd have gotten some slick little defense attorney to come after us for messing with their constitutional rights. After all, they paid their debt to society. Ran up a bigger debt while they did it, but that's how it works."

"As a professional devil's advocate, I have to point out that they did their time—twenty years," Rick put in. "If you ask me, the person who represented them ought to be in prison."

"Hey, I got no problem locking up lawyers," Guzman said meaningfully. "Anyway, they were always talking over at Huntsville how they had this money coming to them. The usual brag. *Someone owes us fifty thousand dollars for this thing we pulled, we'll get paid when we get out, going to buy us some new motorcycles.* But, lo and behold, they come out, and pretty soon they're flashing money all over this town, paying cash for all sorts of things. New Harleys, hundred-dollar tabs at Hector's."

Tess and Rick exchanged a look.

"Yeah, Hector's," Guzman said. "Biker bar south

of the city, where a girl named Emmie Sterne and a guy named Ed Ransome happen to play in an after-hours band."

"If they were making a big show of how much money they had, anyone could have killed them for it," Tess offered. "They probably didn't have the sweetest friends in the world."

Guzman pretended to think about this. "Yeah, right. Darden and Weeks come out of prison, score a bunch of money somewhere, and someone kills them for it, then stashes one body outside a house in Twin Sisters, where Emmie and her friend happened to spend a few weeks this summer. Then the other guy shows up at Espejo Verde. Pure coincidence. By the way, how close did you get, Miss Monaghan? Did you get a good look?"

"Not very."

"You see something kind of orange on the table? More red than orange, I guess, but it started out gold?"

The T-shirt, the goddamn T-shirt.

"It happens to be a shirt from someplace called Cafe Hon in a place called Bal-tee-more, Maryland." He put a lot of Latin spin on those last two words, as if it were a ridiculous-sounding place for anyone to be from. "You know anyone with a T-shirt like that?"

"I do, for one. Lots of people have Cafe Hon T-shirts," Tess replied. "They put them in local hotel rooms, like Bibles or terry-cloth robes. It's practically a city ordinance that you're not allowed to leave without one."

But to her knowledge, there was only one the color of a mango.

"Do you know how Frank Conyers died?" Guzman asked. The question sounded random and sudden, but Tess doubted the detective ever said or did anything without having a reason.

"Everyone knows about the triple murders, Guzman," Rick said in a bored voice. "He was killed with Lollie and the cook that night."

"Not when, *how*. You see, Lollie and the cook, Pilar Rodriguez, they died nice and neatly, as these things go. Bullets in the back of the head. Frank Conyers was carved up as if someone was trying to make menudo out of him."

"Menudo?" asked Tess.

"Tripe stew," Rick said.

"They disemboweled him," Guzman said helpfully. "See, I was trying to be nice, but Trejo here made me spell it out. Conyers's throat was slit. So was Weeks's. Conyers was disemboweled—"

"So was Weeks," Tess finished for him.

"You saw?"

"I guessed. What about the fingers, though? Does that correspond, too?"

Guzman frowned. "No, that's a new touch. But it's the other stuff that intrigues me. We never made the details of Conyers's death public, yet someone knows. Someone who Darden and Weeks were going to lead us to this summer."

"A third person?" Rick asked.

"Three bodies, three killers. It has a nice symmetry to it, doesn't it? Or, at least—no, that's all I'm going to tell you right now. You already got more than you ever gave. I'm not telling you another thing until you tell me where to find Ed Ransome and Emmie Sterne."

Tess said dully, "Crow's gone, God knows where. If I knew where Emmie was, I'd have been there already. And you'd have been right behind me. Unless you were right in front of me. From what I can tell, the cops have been surrounding me like bookends all week. I go someplace, you've been there. I look behind me, and you're there. If I stopped suddenly, one of your guys would step on my heel."

Guzman sighed and—finally—moved away from her. Not by much, but at least she no longer felt as if he were all but sitting in her lap.

"I don't know what to do with you, Theresa Monaghan," he said. "Maybe I should lock you up, maybe I should have you under surveillance. It all depends on if you're crazy like a fox, or just *stupid* like a, like a—like a hamster." He continued to scrutinize her, as if her animal orientation might be found in her face.

"And?" she said at last, losing the stare-down.

"Go home," he said. "Don't wear yourself out on your little exercise wheel."

23

Thursday morning. Tess had been in Texas nine days. She sat in the garden at the Alamo with a Peanut Buster Parfait and thought about everything she had accomplished.

She had found Crow, only to lose him again.

She had found two dead men, both so ripe they might have forever changed her relationship with soft cheeses.

She had learned to say "Good morning," "Good dog," and "You are the father of my baby" in Vietnamese. (People were always saying that last bit in Mrs. Nguyen's private telenovela, and she was kind enough to translate.)

She had experienced coitus interruptus by SWAT team.

She had stumbled on a Dairy Queen in a downtown San Antonio mall and convinced the vacant-eyed adolescent at the counter that she had a medical condition requiring her to consume soft ice cream, hot fudge, and peanuts at eleven in the morning.

Yes, travel was broadening. She'd have to do it

again sometime, perhaps at the end of the next millennium.

She saw a flash of blond hair and dared to hope—but no, Emmie wouldn't come here. Emmie was on the run, a trail of dead men in her wake, their ill-gotten gains now her iller-gotten gains. Crow was on the run, looking for Emmie. Or on the run from Emmie, because he had the fifty thousand dollars and she wanted it. That was another one of Guzman's theories. If Emmie and Crow weren't in this together, then they were at each other's throats. Emmie and Crow had conspired to kill her mother's suspected murderers, then fallen out over the unexpected cash bonus. Tess wasn't satisfied. Why would a girl with a trust fund bother to fight over a sum less than the yearly payout on a million-dollar lottery ticket? What did Emmie know about the night her mother died, if anything? What did someone think she knew?

And how could Crow kill anyone, under any circumstance? No one changed that much in five months.

But he would keep quiet to protect someone. Especially if he thought the act was morally defensible.

Especially if he was in love.

Oh, sure, he had been convincing enough in his thwarted seduction of her the other night. But you could sleep with someone while you were still in love with someone else. You could do it quite enthusiastically, even. Tess knew this from firsthand experience. What had Crow said? He had accused her of using him as a bookmark, a way of keeping her place while she tried to figure out how she felt about watching the death of a man who didn't quite belong to her, and never would. A man she didn't quite love, and never would. Just because Emmie was through with Crow didn't mean Crow was through with Emmie. Lovers seldom finished at the same time.

"You're thinking too much," Rick had said when she tried to break down Guzman's theories on the way home from the police station. Happy to be a lawyer still, all he wanted to do was find Crow and turn him over to the authorities, then start preparing his case. But Rick's method of finding Crow was to sit back in his office, doing his other work, waiting for the phone to ring. Sure, they were still going to see that detective this afternoon, the one who had been involved in the original bust of Darden and Weeks. But what did it matter, now that Weeks was a corpse, too? Tess wanted to *do* something, go somewhere, ask some questions. Unfortunately, her inherent bias toward action was proving less than constructive, except as a way of drumming up business for local mortuaries. She felt as if she were flooring a car in snow and ice. The tires spun, the snow melted, taking you down to the ice, where there was no traction, so you went nowhere. So you floored it again, and the tires spun, and the snow melted, and you went nowhere.

Again she thought she saw a blond head, the same white blond as Emmie. It couldn't be.

It wasn't. It was Clay Sterne, disappointment naked in his face.

"She's not here," Tess said.

"I didn't come to see her," he shot back.

"You don't have to worry, Clay. I won't tell your father you were here."

"I do what I want to do, not what my father tells me."

Tess nodded. "Is that why you're living at home, preparing to take over a business you can't stand, instead of going for the advanced degree you want?"

He sat on her bench, keeping as much distance between them as possible. "I'd think you were an extraordinarily good detective if I didn't know Javier had such a big mouth. Okay, sure, it's no big secret. I'd rather be getting a Ph.D. in history, but someone has to run the business, and I'm it. The last of the Sternes."

"You and Emmie."

"She's not a Sterne. And she's not here."

"Not a Sterne?"

"My father never adopted her. He took her in, she used the family name, but she's still Emily Morgan on her birth certificate and driver's license. Bad joke on her mother's part, naming her that."

Tess must have looked blank, for he added, "Emily Morgan was the so-called Yellow Rose of Texas, the beautiful 'mulatto' slave with whom Santa Anna was supposed to have dallied before the battle of San Jacinto. Serious scholarship doesn't really support the story—Emily Morgan was more likely a free black woman who didn't 'dally' with anyone—but never mind. You couldn't have a song called 'The Free Black Woman of Texas.'"

"Still, she is a Sterne. She's Lollie's daughter."

"My dad made the business what it is, anyway," Clay said, his tone argumentative, almost aggressive.

"Yes. Although it was faltering, right, twenty years ago?"

The question surprised him, but only for a moment. "If you're going to read Texas history, you might want to try something with a little more depth than *The Green Glass*. May I suggest T. R. Fehrenbach? Not politically correct, of course, but still a good place to start. By the way, the Mexicans were on the outside here, the Texans on the inside."

"Fine, mock me, if that makes you feel better. Besides, not all the Mexicans were on the outside."

"What?"

"I went through the exhibit here. You think I was going to come all this way, sit in the garden at the Alamo, and not walk through the place? Some of the defenders were Mexican. There were women and children here, too. I never knew that. Some scholars have questioned whether the battle really was important, while others say it provided Sam Houston the opportunity he needed at San Jacinto. The legend has William Barrett Travis drawing the line that separated the men from the boys, and Davy Crockett going down swinging Old Betsy. But it's been suggested by one historian that Crockett begged for his life, tried to pretend he was just passing by, and was executed on the spot."

Clay gave her a suspicious look. "You didn't learn all that here. The Daughters aren't big on some of the, um, newer theories."

"I went to the library. I didn't read Fehrenbach, but I did manage to skim a few books on the subject. Not because I care if Jim Bowie had a broken leg or venereal disease—"

"Typhus, more likely."

"Not because I care," Tess repeated, "about anything that happened in 1836. But because I want to know where your cousin is, and I thought the answer might be in where she used to come, and history was all I had. Breakfast at the Alamo, Clay. What was that all about?"

He looked around the garden, as if the answer might be posted, like one of the sign boards in the Long Barracks. "It was just some ritual she had. She was very susceptible to rituals. One of her many, many psychiatrists diagnosed obsessive compulsive disorder."

"Was that the same one who tried to recover her memories of the murder through hypnosis?"

Again she had surprised him. "I don't think so. They were all hacks, if you ask me. The thing is, she wasn't crazy then. I'm not sure she's crazy now . . . just disappointed."

"Disappointed?"

"In life. Isn't everyone?" He looked around, frowning. "Personally, I don't care much for the Alamo. It's too accessible."

"Do you think history should be hard to get to? That it doesn't count if you can just walk over on your lunch hour, or on your way to the post office or the mall?" *Or after a trip to the Dairy Queen.*

"I think historic sites shouldn't be places that you zip through on your way to the gift shop to buy a ceramic ashtray."

He looked so serious when he said this that Tess couldn't help laughing. Clay flushed. He was literally thin-skinned, so pale and transparent that his skin was almost blue when he wasn't blushing. He was just twenty-two, she reminded herself, a young twenty-two at that, although he didn't look quite so gangly and spindly away from his broad-shouldered, bigger-than-life, Texas-sized father.

"I'm sorry, you're right," she said contritely. "History is serious. All history, not just wars and elections, but family history."

Clay's eyes darted, anxious to be anywhere that wasn't in her direct gaze.

"I know about how Emmie tried to burn the house down, Clay. A reporter from the *Eagle* told me." The same reporter who has the page one exclusive today on the discovery of a body at Espejo Verde, but she didn't want to go into that.

"It was an accident," he said automatically. "The fire, I mean."

Tess made a neutral noise, not bothering to let him know she had already been told otherwise. "Were you two close, growing up?"

"Sometimes. We're only a year apart. That's okay when you're younger. When we got to high school, it was . . . different. She was part of this very fast crowd, and she did the whole Goth thing. Dyed her hair jet black, if you can imagine. Smoked pot, screwed around. My father had a fit."

"Was she jealous of you?"

"Jealous? Why would she be jealous of me?"

"Because you're the 'real' son, and she was merely a cousin. Because you're the well-behaved, dutiful straight-A student type, and she's always been so troubled. I imagine your father and mother treated her a little differently than they treated you."

Clay shook his head. "My parents divorced when I was in junior high school. I don't see her much. Truth is, she treated me and Emmie exactly the same—with complete indifference."

Tess had forgotten about the divorce, the "Galveston girl" who had retreated to California. It was one of the rare bits of truth Marianna had let slip. "I'm sorry."

"Why? It's just more history. The social history of the latter part of the twentieth century. Half of all marriages, etc., etc." He paused, stuck on his own statistic. "I've never quite believed that, actually. What does it mean? Does someone like Elizabeth Taylor skew the results? Do you count Richard Burton twice? Even if you don't, in her case, one hundred percent of marriages end in divorce. See, that's the problem with anecdotal evidence."

"Not one hundred percent. Seven-eighths, not quite 90 percent."

"Huh?"

"Mike Todd died in a plane crash. So, divorced seven times, widowed once. Nick Hilton, Michael Wilding, Michael Todd, Eddie Fisher, Richard Burton, Richard Burton, John Warner, Larry Fortensky. So far."

Clay looked genuinely aghast. "You shouldn't have that in your brain. It's taking up space where something useful might go."

"I don't seem to have much say about what gets lodged in there," Tess said, hitting her head lightly with her palm, as if to shake out the offending factoid. "Nope, it's stuck, right next to the lyrics from the theme song from *The Flintstones*. Then again, you'd be surprised at the kind of information that proves useful. Why, I bet there are things Emmie told me the one time we talked, or even you and your father, which seemed meaningless, but may yet help me find her."

She had thought her bluff hit just the right note of implicit menace, but Clay wasn't impressed. "Sounds like urban archaeology to me. But at least they have a reason for doing things the way they do."

"What do you mean?"

"There's a hotel down Alamo Street, the Fair-mount. It used to be an old flophouse, on the other side of town, and they moved it from one site to the other over two days. I think it made *Guinness*—not the largest building ever moved, but the largest one ever moved on rubber tires across city streets."

"Now that's the kind of stat Baltimore specializes in. Distinction through compound modifier." The longer she stayed in San Antonio, the more she saw how much the two cities had in common. "But what does it have to do with archaeology?"

"They were clearing the site when they realized the land was essentially a trash pit from the battle of the Alamo. Broken china, weaponry, even an un-fired cannon ball. But the hotel move couldn't be delayed. So, toward the end, they just began shovel-ing it all up and carting away truckfuls of dirt, to be sifted through later at the University of Texas–San Antonio. Not an ideal way to work, but sometimes it's all you've got."

"Is there a point to the story, Clay? Is there a big pile of dirt I should be sifting through somewhere?"

He was suddenly, inexplicably, quite angry. "I'm

saying that you can dig forever, but all you're going to find is garbage. Even if you did find something of significance, you wouldn't really know where it fit without years of study. You can't just come someplace and get to know it right away. You can't come into a family, any family, and think you know them because you heard some gossip, or read some sleazy book. You don't know my dad, or me, or Emmie. You don't understand anything you've seen. You're just a dumb, gawking tourist. Too bad there's not a gift shop for you to visit. At least you might leave with a nice keychain for your troubles."

And with this, he pushed himself off the bench and ran for the exit, toward the very wall a handful of men had scaled when William Barrett Travis had drawn the line that separated the men from the boys. Assuming, Tess thought, that had ever really happened.

24

"He lives on Bikini."

"Huh?"

"This detective, Marty Diamond," Rick Trejo said, heading up Austin Highway. Tess realized she knew where she was, for once.

"He lives in a bikini? You mean he hangs around the house in one?" Tess envisioned a too-brown old man, greased-up and dessicated at the same time, his stomach cascading out of a tiny magenta swimsuit. It wasn't an image that sat well on a late lunch from La Calesa. Rick had given her another taco tutorial—actually, the menu had been *Mexican-*Mexican according to his lexicon, the same sort of food that Espejo Verde had served. Despite that unhappy association, it had been all she could do not to stand up on the breezy patio and belt out: "How Long Has This Been Going On?" One thing was certain: She was never going back to ground beef, cheddar cheese, and chopped lettuce in an Old El Paso shell.

"Bikini is the street name," Rick said. "All the

streets in this subdivision have some kind of Hawaiian theme. Waikiki, Molokai. Lots of retired military around here. I think the Pacific Rim theme makes them feel at home."

The houses in this northeast-side neighborhood were small ranches. Some had fallen on hard times, but most were fastidiously maintained. The lawns, in particular, seemed a kind of fetish here. Tess wondered how much work it took to keep one's yard so green and lush in a climate like San Antonio's. Rain hadn't threatened once in all the time she had been here.

They were on Molokai now. A witch, two tiny skeletons, and some cartoon superhero that Tess didn't recognize were walking down the street with Mylar bags.

"It's Halloween," she said. "I'd completely forgotten. Lots of tricks, but no treats at La Casita."

Rick grunted. He was in a rotten mood and had been preoccupied throughout their lunch, barely touching his food. Tess had finished his *carne tampiquena* for him. He had mentioned a fight with Kristina, but Tess didn't understand how that could bother him. Bickering seemed to be a cornerstone of their relationship.

"He must have a good porno name," she remarked, just to be saying something. "Our detective friend, Marty Diamond. A good porno name, but not a good soap opera name."

"What?"

"Don't you know how to get your porno name? You take your childhood pet and the name of the street where you lived as a child, and that's your 'nom de nekkid.' I don't have a good one unless I cheat and take the cross street where I currently live. Then I'm Tweetie Shakespeare. What's yours?"

"Your dog's name is Esskay," Rick pointed out.

"You weren't listening. *Childhood* pet, childhood street. I think those are the rules. Besides, I said I was cheating. The porno names are problematic. But the soap opera names always work. That's middle name plus current street. Then I'm Esther Bond. So boring. Sounds like the old lady who runs the dress shop and never gets in on one of the big plots."

"I'm . . . Midnight Zarzamora." He scowled when Tess laughed. "I think it's pretty."

"Oh, very pretty. But you're going to need implants."

He was turning onto Bikini now. Two blocks in, a paunchy man with a cigarette was standing in his driveway. He had a bristly gray flat-top, a baby blue Banlon shirt that hugged his bulging stomach, and baby blue suede loafers that no one would ever dare step on. Even if Tess hadn't known it was Marty Diamond, she would have known that this was a man who had spent most of his life in uniforms, official or otherwise.

"Even my own house is no smoking," he said when they got out of the car. "So I stand out here and smoke, and then I see some weed I missed and I want to start dragging out all my gardening stuff."

"Detective Marty Diamond?" Rick asked, offering his hand.

"That's me. You the lawyer? I've heard a lot about you."

Diamond didn't take Rick's outstretched hand.

Rick didn't take the bait, although Tess thought his good ol' boy accent seemed a little more pronounced when he spoke again. She couldn't tell if Rick used this way of speaking to mock people or to ingratiate himself. A little of both, probably.

"This is Tess Monaghan, a private detective from Baltimore who's been assisting me."

Diamond glanced at her dismissively, then turned back to Rick. Tess couldn't tell if she had been disqualified on the basis of her gender or her hometown. "Let's go sit out back, so I can smoke when I want to. Although I hope you won't be here too long. I got things to do today."

Sure, Tess thought. Smoke a few more Merits, yank out a few weeds, count a few more clouds as they go by. Marty Diamond was a busy, busy man.

His wife fussed around them at first, bringing out a tray of iced tea no one touched, offering trick-or-treat candy no one wanted. A yippy little Yorkshire terrier dogged her every step. Mrs. Diamond was a small, bird-like woman who seemed innately tentative—in her words, in her movements. Yet she had been so voluble when Rick had called earlier in the week. Part of the reason they hadn't canceled this appointment today was because he dreaded another drawn-out conversation with her. It had seemed easier to go through with it.

"We wanted to talk to you about an old case—" Rick began.

"You the girl who found Darden?" Diamond asked abruptly.

"And Weeks," Tess replied. Rick was very big on

hierarchy, as it turned out, and insistent on conducting this interview. She didn't care. They were just doing this to be doing it, to fill time so they wouldn't feel so useless.

"I hear Guzman's not one of your biggest fans." He was addressing Rick again. Tess glanced at him, and Diamond smiled, showing his surprisingly nice teeth, not at all stained or yellowed. Dentures, probably. "Yeah, I still got some friends downtown. Not many. And they're not Guzman fans, so don't worry, but they brought me up to speed on what's happening. That new breed is a little righteous for my taste. No offense. I mean, it's not because they're Mexican that they're so holier-than-thou. Guzman wants to be chief someday. He has *ambition*."

Steve Villanueve had said almost the same thing, but his tone had been admiring. Diamond made it sound ridiculous, contemptible.

"You were in homicide?" Rick asked.

"Robbery."

"How did you get involved with Darden and Weeks?"

"We knew those guys a little, they liked to hit convenience stores and drive-in restaurants. When the kidnapping came down, they put together a task force, with the feds, the sheriff's department, and a couple of our guys."

He leaned back in his chair, patting his stomach as if it were something separate from him, a big round cat he had suddenly found in his lap. "Yeah, we didn't figure them for something like this at all. This was for big stakes, not a weekend's worth of beer money. On December 16, two guys jump out of a car on the north side, grab this kid out of his stroller, right in front of his nurse. Danny Boyd. Dad was a big airline executive. Everyone assumes it's a kidnapping, because the guy's loaded. But three days go by, and the note doesn't come, no one makes contact. Lucky for us, the nanny is the greatest witness ever. She remembers the make of the car and gives us a partial on the plate. She was a smart little beaner, I'll give you that." A not-quite-conciliatory look at Rick. "Sorry. Didn't mean anything by that."

Rick ignored the apology. "Didn't you have to let the feds run the show? They usually pull rank in kidnapping cases."

"Oh yeah, the feds were hot for it—at first. But when we got the kid back and had the guys in custody, and it looked like a loser, they weren't so eager to prosecute. They kicked it back to the DA about three months in. It was a tough case. They only take the easy ones, those guys."

"Yeah, tell me about it," Rick said agreeably.

Diamond lit another cigarette. "Cowbirds. They'll take your nest, but they won't leave anything behind but their own shit."

"Still, you had an eyewitness, you got the kid back. Sounds to me like you had a pretty good case." Rick grinned, and for the first time today seemed wholly himself. "Not that I couldn't have gotten them off, but the DA obviously had plenty to work with. I'm surprised the feds backed away."

"We didn't exactly *get* the kid back. They gave him back. On day five, two guys walk into the Pig Stand restaurant with a little blond boy. They order a lot of food, and eat most of it."

Tess noticed Diamond used the present tense, as if he were narrating an episode of *Dragnet*.

"Already, they're kind of suspicious-looking, these two dark-haired bikers toting this golden-haired little kid around. Then one gets up and goes to the men's room. Second one follows him a few minutes later. Like a waitress isn't going to notice that these two dirtbags just left a toddler alone at the table. They went out the bathroom window, the manager called the cops on them for walking the check, and we found Danny Boyd, making mud pies with the ketchup. Unharmed, as far as anyone could tell."

"'Ransom of Red Chief!'" Tess said. "Only he was so little, he couldn't have been that mischievous. Maybe those two thugs just couldn't handle changing diapers?"

"O. Henry lived here for a while," Rick offered. "Not far from the Alamo."

"Really?"

"There's more." Diamond seemed miffed by their interruptions. He was enjoying himself, the very act of telling the story loosened him up, the way a drink might have freed the tongue of another man. Tess could tell he was more at ease with them. Or at least with Rick. After the one question about Darden, he hadn't acknowledged her presence at all.

"So we have a problem. No ransom demand, no real evidence, car's gone, the feds are washing their hands of it. And wouldn't you know, the star witness can't ID these guys after all. Oh yeah, she had the car cold, but she couldn't pick these guys out of a lineup. They're claiming some other guy left the kid with them. The only thing we had going for us is that their court-appointed attorney is this do-gooding little Mex who's coasting on affirmative action." Another sly look for Rick. "No offense, Counselor. You're good at your job—too good, according to my buddies. But this girl was an airhead."

"Go on," Rick said.

"I mean, she was one dumb cu—cookie." Tess's turn for that pretend look of contrition. "So we tell her that the doc who examined little Danny couldn't rule out sexual abuse. Which is true, 'cause you can never rule out fondling and shit, even though you can't prove it, neither. But why would they take the kid otherwise?"

"Everything's done for sex and money," Rick said.

"Exactly," Diamond said, not catching Rick's ironic tone. "So we tell 'em we might go for a moles-tation charge on top of the kidnapping if they didn't plead out. We play them against each other, tell Darden that Weeks is fingering him, tell Weeks that Darden says it was all his idea. They agreed to make full confessions on the state kidnapping charges—they don't want that baby raper shit on their record. They thought they'd get a lighter term for pleading out. They should have remembered judges in Texas are elected. District Judge Bailey gave 'em twenty years when they went before him. And that's what they served. They were model prisoners, but every time they went before the parole board, they got shot down. They picked the wrong guy's son to mess with, that's for sure. The Boyds moved away, but Daddy Boyd made sure those guys stayed in for their full term. Now they're dead. Can't say I'm surprised, or sorry."

"And that's it?" Rick asked.

"Isn't it enough?"

"Of course, it's more than enough," Rick back-tracked, trying to soothe Diamond's feelings. "To be honest, when we called and asked to see you earlier this week, we thought you might give us a lead on Laylan Weeks. But the case has altered, as they say."

"Is it true what they say about Weeks's body?"

Tess realized he was speaking to her for the first time. "I think it's supposed to be a secret."

"Sure, to the public. Cops gossip, too, you know. I hear Guzman thinks he's going to solve the Espejo Verde murders and be a goddamn hero. That guy's in love with the technology of crime-solving. But he's not a good cop. He's got no instincts for people."

Tess looked down at her datebook, which she had held open in her lap during their conversation, doodling on that day's date. She had drawn the figure of a child, sitting in a booster seat.

"Tell us about Danny Boyd."

"What's to tell? His daddy was rich and his ma was good-looking. Lucky for him, he looked like ma. She was a cute little thing, blond, blue-eyed, very hot. Did you know women get sexually excited when they're upset like that? It's a medical fact. All that adrenaline, and Mrs. Boyd didn't wear a bra."

Diamond closed his eyes, enjoying some private memory.

"And he was two years old?"

"Thereabouts. Maybe younger, maybe older. He could walk, he could talk, but we weren't going to court with his testimony, if you know what I mean."

"We know," Rick said, standing. "We won't take up any more of your time."

"Good luck with whatever you're working on. It's hard for me to know which side to root for in this one. Don't go for lawyers much, as a rule, but I sure do get tired of reading about the great Señor Guzman in the *Eagle*."

"Detective—" Tess began, her voice artificially sweet. "That little dog is so cute, does he have a name?"

"Cute? If you say so. Drives me crazy. That's her Butchie."

Butchie Bikini. Now that was a name for a porn star. Behind Diamond's back, Rick grinned broadly, momentarily cheered.

They hadn't even left Diamond's street when Tess asked: "How could you put up with that?"

"With what?"

"With beaner this and Mex that and the sneering way he called Guzman 'Señor.' He was goading you the entire time we were there."

"Which is why I ignored him."

"You shouldn't let stuff like that go by," Tess said, thinking of how Jackie believed in confronting anyone, even prospective clients, who made the mistake of saying something racist in her presence. "It's like . . . letting someone litter, or pour toxic waste into the water system."

"Look, he's some old fart on a policeman's pension whose only hobby is killing weeds and trying to get lung cancer. My car probably costs more than he paid for his house. I win."

"As in, the one with the most toys, etc., etc."

"Most toys, most power. A person who really has power over you doesn't have to pull the kind of penny-ante shit he was trying. We had to be polite to him because we thought he might have something for us. That's the up side to getting nothing. We don't owe him, and we don't have to go back."

Tess thought back to Diamond, how he had slobbered over Danny Boyd's mother, with her big blue eyes and blond hair. Danny had taken after his mother. A cute little boy, a rich man's son. Blond hair, blue eyes.

"I'm not so sure we came away empty-handed."

"What are you talking about?"

"Danny Boyd. He doesn't fit. He never fit. It's like trying to hammer the wrong jigsaw puzzle piece into place. Why do two convenience store robbers suddenly upgrade to a high-stakes kidnapping?"

"Because they had just killed three people in a botched robbery and they needed the money to get far away," Rick shot back.

"I thought of that. But they didn't ask for any money. They took a kid, then tried to give him back, and they were so broke they walked their check at the Pig Stand, whatever that is. You think we could get the original police report on the kidnapping? I want to check something out."

"Legally, we're entitled, but I bet the cops won't make it easy for us," Rick said. "As it happens, I now realize I know the 'do-gooding little Mex' who represented Darden and Weeks. She's an attorney with a nonprofit, does environmental law now. And, no, she wasn't well-suited to criminal law, but she's the kind of anal-retentive Harvard grad who keeps her records forever. Chances are, she picked up a copy of the complaint, preparing to depose the nanny if it came to that. I know her pretty well."

"She still a friend, or did it end badly?"

"Darlin', she's ages too old for me." Rick smiled. "She's more of a mentor-mama figure to me than anything else. Besides, all my ex-girlfriends love me. It's the current one I can't keep happy."

It was dusk before the bell rang on the fax machine in Rick's office, a small but posh suite of rooms on the twentieth floor of a downtown office building. Tess stared out at San Antonio, watching the way the city began to glow at sundown. The sky almost seemed to part, the east going black while the west was still full of rosy clouds, the McAllister Freeway running between them like a dividing line. It was really a very pretty place in its own right, a lovely place of hills and old trees and gracious homes. There was nothing here to dislike, and much to admire. It was not, in the end, that different from Baltimore. A small big city, provincial and anxious, eager to please. Its only flaw was that it wasn't home, and she was so homesick.

She held Jimmy Ahern's *The Green Glass* in her hand, her thumb marking the page. In the end, the proof had been in the padding. All those little details that he had thrown in so frenetically, trying to puff the book up to full-length. How had the cops missed the motive buried there? Not that it would matter, unless she was right about this, too. She needed A plus B before she could get to C.

At the high trill of the fax line, she turned and watched two pages peel off the machine, falling to the floor where they rolled and shimmered like shiny snakes. When she didn't move Rick leaned over and picked them up, handing them to her facedown so she could have the first look.

"Well?" he asked as she scanned the old report.

"The Boyds lived on Shook Avenue."

"So your hunch was wrong."

"My hunch was dead-on," she said, looking up with a victorious grin. "The Boyds lived on Shook, but the kidnappers grabbed Danny on Contour Drive, less than a block from Gus Sterne's house on Hermosa. A little blond boy, out with his nanny, the same age and description as Clay Sterne, just outside the Sterne house. Sure, the Boyds never got a ransom demand. Because Gus Sterne did. And never told anyone."

Rick rubbed his eyes. "I'm totally lost," he confessed. "Why did Darden and Weeks have it in for this one family?"

"They didn't. They took Clay because Gus Sterne said he would pay them to kill Lollie and then reneged on the deal. They were just trying to get him to pay up. And if they had taken the right kid, things might have worked out differently all around."

25

They left a message for Al Guzman to meet them at the Liberty Bar, where Rick and Kris were to have dinner.

"If she shows," he said glumly, parking next to a lopsided old house that made the Tower of Pisa look stable. But once inside, Tess felt like Brigham Young regarding Utah. The long old-fashioned bar, the worn wooden floors, the smell of fresh-baked bread, the decadent chocolate cake beckoning to her from a sideboard—it was at once homey yet untamed, a place to seek comfort or adventure, depending on one's mood.

"Do you come here a lot?"

"All the time." He looked wistful. "Kris and I have had some of our best fights here."

They took a seat in one of the neon outlined windows overlooking the street. Older ghosts and goblins roamed the sidewalks here, and many of them had spilled into the bar. A devil brandished his pitchfork at a curvy vampire, while a doleful-looking man with an accordion was walking around in huge rubber chicken feet.

"Strange costume," Tess said.

"Old story," Rick said. "Suffice to say, a woman who dances with the man with chicken feet will live to regret it."

The waiter, dressed as a safari-bound Groucho Marx, greeted Rick with a familiar smile and a curious look for the woman who was not Kristina. He left them with fresh bread as they studied the specials on the menu. Pork chops, meat loaf, pasta, eggplant puree on parmesan toast, and—she couldn't help laughing at this—a "Maryland-style" crabcake that was billed as one of the house specialties. No crab for her, Maryland-style or otherwise. But everything else looked wonderful. Everything. Tess, whose Irish roots often had to fight to be heard over the domineering Weinstein genes, had found her inner Molly Bloom. Yes, her taste buds sang out. Yes, yes, yes.

She was not so far gone in her own appetites that she didn't notice how glum Rick still looked.

"Not to pry—" she began.

"You?" But she had gotten a smile out of him. "You're a professional pryer."

"It's just that you and Kristina bicker all the time, and you both seem to enjoy it immensely. So how did you end up having a *fight*-fight?" She was feeling very warm and wise. Now that she had all but solved the triple murders, she was ready to tackle anything. She could see herself on the radio, dispensing brisk, no-nonsense advice about love and marriage, or telling people how to manage their stock portfolios, repair their cars, build small nuclear weapons with household items.

"Honestly, I don't have a clue. It started out about there being no two percent in my fridge, and the next thing I know, she's slamming doors and saying I'm not serious about our relationship."

"You're the one who wants to marry her."

"She says the marriage talk is a joke to me, that I'd never mention it if I thought there was a risk of her saying yes. At least, I think that's what she said. I kind of zoned out in the middle part, somewhere between the two percent and 'you son-of-a-bitch.' I was reading the sports pages when she started in on me. That columnist Robert Buchanan, man, he pisses me off. I mean, I'm not saying he should be a homer for the Spurs, but he could cut them a little slack now and then, you know?"

"When Crow and I were together, *I* was the one who buried my nose in the paper while he prattled." She remembered Charlottesville, the discovery of all the things she hadn't heard—assuming they had ever been said. "Just more proof that I'm not very feminine."

"Wouldn't say that. Wouldn't say that at all."

The compliment was automatic, mindless. Rick was still in his funk, while Tess's mind was racing, making connections someone should have made long ago. The fire at the Sterne house, the fire that was never started at Espejo Verde, despite the gas cans found there. Did Emmie's act prove that she knew the man who raised her was responsible for her mother's death, or was it just a coincidence? And all those psychiatrists, how scared Gus Sterne must have been when one had tried to recover Emmie's memories from the night of the triple murder. You could see how everything fit together if you took a step back. Guzman had been too close, for too long.

The paunchy homicide cop came into the restaurant as she was thinking about him. There was a split second before he spotted them, and Tess used this opportunity to study him. His eyes were so active, like a camera on a motor drive clicking away. She saw skepticism on his face, a hint of amusement at his surroundings. But the primary impression was of someone who made a constant inventory of wherever he happened to be, whether it was a restaurant or a murder scene.

Then he saw them, and his face was instantly more guarded.

"This the kind of place you hang out in?" he asked Rick, sitting down and helping himself to a piece of bread, reaching for the butter, then pushing it away. "Kind of girly, isn't it?"

"The food is good and they've got Shiner Bock on draft. Besides, Tommy Lee Jones always brings the out-of-town press here for all those profiles they're forever doing on him. If it's good enough for Tommy Lee Jones—"

"Then it's good enough for Tommy Lee Jones," Guzman finished. "Now what have you and this particular out-of-towner cooked up for me tonight? You going to tell me where to find your client?"

"I'm going to tell you why you don't need to find him." Tess had intended to be cool, to make Guzman work harder for what she knew, but she couldn't hold back. "Crow didn't kill anyone. Neither did Emmie."

"Yeah?" He was intent on his bread, which he had decided to butter after all.

"Seriously, you've got to listen to me. I know one of the first things police do in any homicide is look to see if anyone benefits from the murder, financially or otherwise—"

"Oh, you mean like that whole motive thing? You know, I knew there was something I forgot." He slapped his forehead with the palm of his free hand. "Twenty-one years on a case, off and on, and I forgot to check if there was a motive."

"No need to be sarcastic, guy," Rick put in. "She's assuming you did your job. So tell us, were there life insurance policies on the victims?"

"Okay, yeah, we checked that. Lollie Sterne's daughter was her beneficiary, while Frank Conyers left Marianna about five hundred thousand dollars. She's probably got more change rattling around in her sofa than that. The cook, Pilar Rodriguez, was the kind of old woman who kept her money in her mattress, so she didn't need an executor for her estate."

"There was a corporate policy, too, one that Lollie took out as a publicity stunt. It paid one million dollars if her hands were damaged. I'm assuming death counts as damage. That policy paid off, and Sterne Foods, which was about to be forced into seeking outside investors, was suddenly in very good financial shape."

Nothing registered on Guzman's face. Not surprise, not even mild interest. He just helped himself to another slice of bread. When he did speak, his voice was so mild that he might have been inquiring about the weather. "Why not just torch the restaurant, if you need insurance money? Why kill your cousin, and two other people?"

"Arson might have been the original plan," Tess said. "It was a Monday night, the one night the restaurant was supposed to be dark. Darden and Weeks came with gasoline. But the building probably wasn't worth nearly as much—"

"Fifty thousand, as a matter of fact. Yeah, I checked that, too."

"So I think the intent was just to cover their tracks after they killed Lollie. But they couldn't go through with it, because of Emmie. They couldn't kill a little girl."

"They could shoot two women in the head, and torture a guy, but they couldn't let a baby burn up? I guess everyone has their limits."

"It's consistent, though. They didn't hurt Danny Boyd, either, when they realized they had the wrong little boy. They could have killed him, or left him by the roadside. Instead, they tried to abandon him someplace relatively safe and got caught for their trouble."

"Wrong little boy?"

"Darden and Weeks meant to kidnap Clay Sterne. Check the arrest report. He was grabbed a half-block from the Sterne house."

Finally, she had Guzman's attention. She could almost see his mind opening beyond his intense dark eyes, taking in the new information and examining it from every angle.

He spoke slowly, deliberately, thinking out loud. "When Darden and Weeks were picked up for the kidnapping, they hadn't yet been linked to the triple murders. That was a lead we developed while they were in Huntsville. So at the time—"

"No one made a connection between the Boyd kidnapping and the murders. And even when they became suspects, the reason for the kidnapping seemed obvious—they took Danny Boyd to generate quick cash for their getaway. It all made perfect sense." She tried to find a smile that was conciliatory, without being smug or cocky. "Unless you know they intended to kidnap Clay Sterne. Two boys, both blond, about the same age."

She hadn't expected Guzman to start high-fiving her, but she had thought he would be more gracious. Instead, he chewed his bread, staring over her shoulder at the Halloween night crowds.

"So you're saying Gus Sterne hires these guys—to kill his cousin, a woman who was like a sister to him—because he needed money to keep Sterne Foods going, and then was crazy enough to think he could get away with not paying them?"

"I'm saying Gus Sterne was naive enough to think that he could pay these guys for their work, and they would go away. Once the job was done, I'm sure they blew it all, then demanded more money. There's about a two-week lag between the two crimes. They blackmailed Sterne, he balked, and they decided to take his son, to show how serious they were. Instead, they ended up with Danny Boyd and they went to prison, hoarding their secret because they still planned to cash it in. You said they obviously had money when they got out. That could have been hush money from Sterne."

"Okay, I'm with you so far. I don't believe a word of it, but I'm with you. So who killed Darden and Weeks?"

"Gus Sterne," Tess said, trying not to sound too triumphant. "He learned the hard way that you have to do these things yourself. He killed Darden and Weeks, and tried to frame Emmie for it. So the gun shows up under the bed, Crow's T-shirt ends up at the murder scene. But it's all credible, because everyone knows she's crazy enough to do anything. Whereas no one would believe Gus Sterne, San Antonio's great benefactor, could be responsible for his own cousin's death."

Guzman smiled. Worse, it was a fatherly smile, sweet and sorrowful and kind. The smile of someone who knows he has no choice but to disappoint you.

"It's not a bad theory," he began, and Tess knew then how bad it must be, that she had missed something crucial, that the devil, as always, lurked in the details. "But there are a couple things you couldn't have known, either of you. You, because you're not from here, and Rick because he was just a kid when some of this happened."

"Fourth grade," Rick confirmed. "I remember the cops coming to school after the kidnapping, reminding us not to get into strangers' cars."

"So you can't know that Gus Sterne was almost destroyed by his cousin's murder," Guzman said. "His business got much worse before it got better, and he neglected his wife, which probably set him up for the divorce that came a decade later. I saw this guy at the funeral—I did the motorcade. He was a zombie, a wreck. He sobbed, and he didn't care who saw him. Finally, he pulled himself together for the kids, for Clay and Emmie, and he turned Sterne Foods around by sheer will."

"You can grieve for someone whose death you caused," Tess said stubbornly.

"Yeah, but not for someone whose death you ordered," Guzman said. "A person who contracts a hit is a strange combination—a cold-blooded wimp. But, okay, let's say Gus Sterne's the greatest actor since Barrymore, that he faked out everyone. You still lose your motive, because he didn't use the insurance money to bail out the company. Yeah, we knew about the Lloyd's policy. It paid off to the corporation, sure—and Sterne used every cent of it to set up a foundation. A foundation in Lollie's name, not his. Neither he nor the business got a penny of it. Maybe it's just me, but I don't think anyone has three people killed because he's itching to set up a scholarship fund."

"Remorse?" Tess offered, but it sounded weak even to her. Guzman shook his head impatiently.

"Now let's talk about that other crime-solving favorite, opportunity, as it applies to the deaths of Darden and Weeks. As you know, the coroner can only come up with a range of time they've been dead. It's pretty interesting, actually, they use the maggots to date the corpse—"

"I've read about this, I don't need all the details," Tess said firmly. She was still planning to eat something after Guzman left.

"So, anyway, all we've got is a range. But the range says one thing: Gus Sterne couldn't have killed either guy. Because, as those who read the *Eagle*'s business section know, Gus Sterne returned Sunday from an international restaurant expo in Tokyo, where he had been for the last two weeks."

"Have you seen his passport?" But it was Rick who jumped in, and he was too quick, too glib, a lawyer falling back on his instinct to match the other side point for point. "For all you know, the paper ran something from a press release. An article doesn't prove he was in Japan."

Rick was given the kind smile, too. "Well, if it comes to that, I'll check the airlines. In the meantime, if your client shows up, please remember I've got dibs." He stood, leaving behind a five-dollar bill for the half-loaf of bread he had consumed, waving Rick's hand away when he tried to push the bill back to him. "Ethics policy, Mr. Trejo. Can't have it get out that I let a criminal attorney stand me to even a slice of bread. I'm sure you understand. Drive safely."

The plunge from cocky conviction to abject humiliation is a fast, sickening one, and it doesn't mix well with alcohol. Tess drank anyway. She drank and she got maudlin, although she tried to disguise it at first.

Rick saw through her and hitched his chair closer, and his attempts to comfort her hurt almost as much as Guzman's fatherly smile. She must have looked very foolish indeed if Rick was trying to be genuinely sweet to her, with none of his usual smart-alecky comments or taunts. She drank bourbon, her appetite forgotten.

"Slow down," Rick said, as she drained her glass for the third time. "It's not a contest."

"Just my luck. This is one thing I do really well."

The Liberty was not quite as bustling as it had been when they had arrived an hour ago and she could hear the music over the speakers. She knew this melody. "That Lovin' You Feeling Again," the voices of Emmylou Harris and Roy Orbison entwined like a bower of wild roses. He gave her his love. She had wanted his heart. And some goddamn 2 percent, most likely. Tess hummed the last few bars as Orbison's yodel faded away.

"See, you do like country music," Rick said. His mouth was close to her ear, but it was all very brotherly and proper. A friend comforting a friend, nothing more. But she could change that. She knew, with a swift and terrible sadness, the power women have in such situations. Most women knew. How a look, a tone, the tiniest change in body language, the slight pressure of a knee or a hand, could transform such a platonic moment.

"I like *you*," she said. She wondered if this were true. She was in that gray space where she was still aware of what she was doing, but drunk enough so the alcohol could be her excuse if she kept going. Did she want to keep going? Rick had put his arm around her to comfort her, and it was still there. Rick was mad at Kris. Tess wasn't mad at anyone but herself, and she was so sick of her own company. She had not been with someone for such a long time.

"Have something to eat," Rick said. "A slice of chocolate cake, at least."

Of course, Rick belonged to Kristina, so it would be wrong, and she didn't really like him—not that much, not in that way. But if no one knew, if they just went to his car, parked in the shadows at the edge of the lot, and made out like teenagers, would it be so wrong? It would just be between Rick, Tess, and her karma. If no one knew, no one would be hurt.

"You son of a bitch." It was Kristina's voice, coming through the window. What a pretty picture they must have made for her, framed in the red neon that bordered the windows. "You goddamn son of a bitch."

"You're late," he said, confused by her anger. For he, after all, was still innocent, a guy doing nothing more than a good deed, who had no idea how close he had come to cheating on his girlfriend. But if he had yet to gauge Tess's intentions, Kristina had seen through her immediately. "Two hours late. I didn't think you were coming."

"So you start all but making out in public with whoever is convenient? Well, *fuck* you."

"We weren't making out," Tess said. *Just contemplating it.*

"You go, girlfriend," a man in a Mae West outfit hooted in falsetto, as the ghosts and witches surrounding Kristina nodded and yelled their support.

"You know, Kris, you're worse than any redneck racist," Rick yelled through the glass. "You see me with my arm around some woman—around Tess, who isn't my type at all, as you damn well know—and you think I'm on the verge of going to bed with her because I'm this hot-blooded Latino who can't keep it in my pants. But if I were to get jealous of you in the same situation, I'd be paranoid. The bottom line is you don't trust me. You don't want to marry me, and you're desperate to find an excuse, any excuse, so you can go running back to Wisconsin and marry some thick-headed Swede like yourself, and have lots of milky white children."

"I'm *Norwegian*, you asshole."

With that, Kristina ran across the street to her car. Rick bolted from the restaurant, and soon Tess saw his Lexus zipping past the window. She did the only thing she could think of, given the circumstances. She summoned the waiter, asked for the check, then inquired if it was difficult to catch a cab in this part of town.

Five hours later, in the grip of a guilt-induced insomnia, Tess finished Volume 2, Chapter 74, of *Don Quixote*. Or *Don Quijote*, as some of the new translations insisted. She had been working on the book so long that her copy was obsolete. Over the years, Kitty had tried to replace this worn, broken-back edition with newer, fresher versions, as if a new version was all it would take to get Tess to finish it. What she had needed was being spared the knowledge that it was so very good for her. The novel's virtue had always been the sticking point, as Don Quixote himself might have said.

"Death came at last for Don Quixote, after he had received all the sacraments and once more had disavowed his books of chivalry . . . Don Quixote was born for me alone and I for him; it was for him to act, for me to write, and we two are one . . . *Vale*."

Finishing it was strangely sad, sadder than finishing sex, which could be very sad indeed. The little death, as the French called it. No, what was really sad is what had driven her to finish it, how she had almost allowed herself to do something truly wretched because she was feeling sorry for herself. She was alone, more alone now that the book was finished. She had done something she had long meant to do, which should have filled her up, but instead it emptied her out. What would she put on next year's list, when she outlined her goals in a black and white composition book, her fall ritual for almost twenty-five years now? Perhaps: "Stop trying to sleep with other people's boyfriends."

It was three A.M., four A.M. in Baltimore, but she had to talk to someone. Kitty would understand. She would understand the book and all the varying types of sadness weighing Tess down.

She came on the line within two rings, her voice fresh and alive, as if she hadn't been sleeping at all.

"Tesser! Are you okay?"

"Physically. Spiritually, I think I racked up a few demerits tonight." The story spilled out, and Kitty listened, as was her great gift, saying nothing until Tess finished.

"You have to apologize," she said, her tone gentle but firm. "She doesn't have to forgive you, but you have to apologize."

Tess had hoped for something a little closer to absolution. "If you think about it, I didn't really do anything—"

"You would have. I love you, sweetie, but you've always had a covetous streak. Sometimes, I think you'd rather borrow someone else's boyfriend than have one of your own."

"Well, sure, there was Jonathan, but I'm not like that anymore."

"Apparently you are, and you're using the same

rationalizations. You were feeling sorry for yourself. Just like when you got mixed up with Jonathan. Remember, you two had broken up, it was only after you lost your job and he got engaged that you started sleeping with him again. Have you ever stopped to think what would have happened if he hadn't died? He'd be married to someone else by now. He wasn't yours, honey. He still isn't."

Tess came close to making an angry reply. Unfortunately, Kitty had the advantage of being right.

"You're right, I have to apologize," she agreed. "I'll start with you, in fact. I'm sorry I called in the middle of the night. It was self-centered and thoughtless. But I felt so alone, and I needed to talk."

"Oh, I wasn't asleep, Tesser. I was having a little snack."

Tess smiled, happy to know things were back to normal in some quarter of the world. Kitty's pre-dawn snacks were never eaten alone. "So I guess the UPS man kept wearing his shorts."

"Well, no—" Kitty sounded uncharacteristically flustered.

"Is it someone else? Is he right there? Or are you in the bedroom, waiting for him to bring you cold cuts on that white wicker tray?"

"No, I'm downstairs. What would you think if I moved my bedroom downstairs, into the big store-room behind the kitchen, and moved the office upstairs?"

"Why would you do that? You'll be running up and down all day."

"Kitty!" It was a loud voice, a familiar voice, a voice that always made Tess feel as if she should drop and give someone twenty. But now there was a softness to the voice, a warmth that Tess had never heard before. "Do you want capers on your bagel, or just the smoked salmon?"

"Just the smoked salmon."

"That's Tyner! You're sleeping with Tyner!"

"We've spent a lot of time together in the past two weeks," Kitty said. "He started coming over at first because you hadn't called him. Things progressed from there."

"But—*Tyner*!" Esskay sat up in bed, instantly alert at the sound of any word beginning with a T, which meant "treat" in her limited vocabulary.

"He's very nice," Kitty said.

"Tyner!" Tess repeated. One of the hookers banged on the wall and told her to be quiet.

"We'll talk when you get home, sweetie." A muffled exchange. "Tyner wants to know when that is, by the way."

"I'd say sometime before hell freezes over, but it apparently just did. You're sleeping with Tyner! He's old! He's cranky! He's Tyner, for God's sake!"

"We'll talk when you get home," Kitty repeated. "I love you."

"Tyner!" Tess screamed to the empty line, and the hooker banged again, and Esskay wagged her tail harder, trying to wait patiently for this treat Tess kept screaming about.

26

Seven hours later, Tess pushed open the door of Y Algunas Mas and found Kris with her arms full of marigolds.

"From Rick?" she asked, and received a baleful look in return.

"I'm making an *ofrenda*. Tomorrow is Dia de los Muertos. Day of the Dead," A small silence, and then Kris lifted her chin. "Rick brought me yellow roses. Three dozen."

"I should be the one sending you flowers. Rick didn't do anything last night."

Kris turned her back on Tess, arranging the bright orange blossoms on what appeared to be an altar, although it was unlike any altar Tess had seen in her rare visits to church. In addition to the marigolds and votive candles, it had a round of bread with a cross slashed into it, a bottle of Diet Rite, a six-pack of Schlitz, an Art Deco cigarette lighter, a pack of Merits, candy skulls, and a photograph of a striking woman, circa 1950-something, judging by the hair and the sweater.

"He *said* he was trying to comfort you."

"He was." Tess paused. "Where that might have gone remains to be seen. It was up to me, and I'm not sure what I might have done."

"Up to *you*," Kris said, her back still to Tess, but the catch in her voice, the way she jerked her shoulder blades, hinted at the angry tears she was trying to hold back. "Who do you think you are, some sort of femme fatale who crooks her little finger and the men all come running? No offense, but Rick says he doesn't have the slightest interest in you, he wouldn't have fooled around with you just because he was mad at me."

"No, he wouldn't." Tess suspected this was a lie, but lies were greatly underrated when it came to making people feel better. "Look, I'm not one of those women who thinks women are inherently better than men. Obviously, *I'm* not inherently better. I felt crummy last night, and I would have reached for anything offering a little temporary oblivion. A drink, a joint, someone else's boyfriend. You have the solace of knowing nothing happened. But I'll never know what I might have done if you hadn't shown up."

She was still looking at Kristina's back, at the white blond hair, worn today in two plaits, exposing her milk-white neck and a narrow part as pink as a little girl's.

"Besides, what if I had? What if I had come to my senses, gone home and crawled into bed with *Don Quixote*? The book, I mean. I still thought about it. I lusted in my heart. Not for your boyfriend, not for Rick—although he's a great guy," she added hastily, as Kristina turned, green eyes narrowed at the in-ferred insult. "I just wanted to blot out my thoughts for an hour or two."

Kristina's lips twitched. "It didn't last quite that long."

"Did you—?"

She nodded. "Then he made me breakfast in bed this morning. And you can be damn sure he went out and got some two percent along with the roses."

Tess couldn't help feeling a small pang. So many people having sex and then breakfast, and she wasn't one of them. She hadn't even had breakfast this morning, because her stomach was jumping at the thought of this meeting.

"Well, I hope Rick persuaded you he was totally innocent."

"Oh, he sold you out," Kris said cheerfully. "Sang like a canary, to use the vernacular of his trade. Still, it's a relief to have you come in here and say more or less the same thing. I'm assuming he didn't put you up to it, because I can't imagine anyone making a more unflattering apology than you just did. I'll give you points for that. You didn't try to sugarcoat it, not much. It almost makes me think I could like you again. Almost."

Kitty was right: Tess had to apologize, but Kris-tina didn't have to forgive her. Still, it hurt that this open-faced, generous girl no longer trusted her.

"Tell me about that thing you're putting together, that old *frienda*."

Her deliberately mangled Spanish wrested a small smile from Kristina. "*Ofrenda*. It's in memory of my grandmother, who died last year."

"But why the beer, and cigarettes, and all the other stuff?"

"Because Day of the Dead is the day that people come back to visit us. So we have to have their favorite things, along with the traditional marigolds and *pan de muerto*—dead bread." She held up a pair of silver combs. "These were my grandmother's favorites. She also loved beer and keno—I used these Mexican loteria cards instead. Most of all, she loved her Merits, even if they did kill her. If she's coming back, she'll want a smoke. Day of the Dead isn't a time for lessons."

"Can anyone do this?"

"Sure. It's not like there's a licensing requirement." Kristina scanned Tess's face. "Is there someone you're missing? You could make a small one right here. I'd help you."

"Maybe . . . I'd need some things, though— ordinary things, like you have, but I'm not sure where I'd find them."

"I don't know what you need, but there's a Family Dollar store, and a liquor store on Main for starters. You go scare up whatever you think is appropriate, and I'll cover a card table with a cloth, put out the candles, flowers, and dead bread."

"I don't know—"

"C'mon, Tess. Maybe this is one time when it would be a good idea to act on your impulses."

She was back in less than an hour, arms laden as if she had been on a scavenger hunt. A bottle of mezcal, a Big Mac, a Hohner Marine Band harmonica. A bag of Domino sugar, to stand in for the neon sign they had watched from her terrace. The *Beacon-Light* had been the hardest item to find, and she had almost settled on a *New York Times* from a box. She had driven all over the city's north side, it seemed, before she found a bookstore with out-of-town papers.

Her collection of artifacts seemed paltry when compared to Kris's more elaborate *ofrenda*, and she looked around the gallery for things she might add. Her eyes fell on a ceramic taxi, driven by a grinning psychopath of a skeleton, a backseat full of terrified skeleton passengers, bony fingers clasped to their cheekbones in Munch-style horror, a devil perched on the trunk, watching the whole scene with great amusement. Kris nodded at the question in her eyes, and she added the taxi to the table of candles and flowers, although there had been no passengers. No witnesses, in fact, except her and the driver, who had not been smiling, not as far as she knew. It had been such a foggy morning, the air thick, like some animal's coat.

And although she hadn't seen the devil sitting on the taxi's fender, she had never doubted he was there.

"Do you have a picture?" Kris asked. "It's traditional to use one."

Yes, she had a picture. Two, really. A picture in her head, of a man airborne over a Fells Point alley, and another one that she kept in her datebook, a grinning head shot that could never quite blot out the first one. Perhaps that had been part of the problem. The literal photo, not the mental one. People blame the wiring in their heads for everything. But maybe it's all the *things*, Tess thought. The mementos, the sealed packages of love letters, the dates we keep in our heads—maybe these are what really weigh us down and keep us from moving forward. The photo in her datebook had been the unseen wedge between her and Crow, an amulet between her and the risk of caring too deeply, in a world where death, life, and other women were always out there. She took the snapshot out of a slender fold meant for business cards and propped it up on the *ofrenda*, against the taxi that had taken his life.

Jonathan Ross, dead at twenty-eight, killed because he was a better reporter than even he had known. It was for him to write, and her to act. Vale.

"Boyfriend?" Kris asked.

"No," Tess said.

She sat in a cafe she had noticed while driving around town on Mission Ofrenda. The name, Twin Sisters, had drawn her in. It was apparently literal, although the photos of the owners invited disbelief. One had dark corkscrew curls, the other straight blond hair. The menu showcased the same kind of striking contrast, with pastries and tacos mixed in with more healthful fare. Tess asked for a bowl of fruit, pointed to a sugar-topped muffin in the case. "Oh yeah, the Jewish coffee cake," the waitress said, and Tess was taken aback. But surely it was meant as a compliment?

She skimmed the *Eagle*'s weekend section, which provided a full schedule of this weekend's All Soul activities. She hadn't realized just what a big deal it was—B. B. King and Etta James were playing Saturday night, there was even a symposium on Robert Johnson. Meanwhile, the local listings claimed a band known as the Breakfast Club was still at the

Morgue, while Las Almas Perdidas was scheduled to appear at Hector's. Hard to cancel gigs while one was on the run, she supposed, stealing glances at a family enjoying a late lunch. School was out, apparently, a teachers' conference according to the scraps of conversation she could overhear.

The younger child, a freckled-faced boy, was playing air guitar with a lot of Pete Townshend gyrations, while his sister rolled her eyes beneath a mop of amazing pre-Raphaelite curls, beautiful hair that would probably be her complete despair for much of her adolescence. Mother and father exchanged fond, if tired, looks over their heads, and the looks carried so much history that it made Tess ache a little. She wanted to know how these people, barely ten years older than she, had arrived at a shore that seemed so impossibly distant. Who had given up what? Who had pursued whom, who had followed? Had they ever fought, or had second thoughts? Tolstoi had it backwards. Unhappiness was the same everywhere; it was the happy families who were unique.

Sighing, she went back to her paper. She noticed the date: Friday, November 1, All Saints' Day. Tomorrow was not only Day of the Dead, it was the Day of the Deadline, the day Crow's parents expected to hear from him according to a telegram she had sent about eight million years ago. She would have to call them instead, explain how she had found their son only to lose him again. Good news, though: She now had the San Antonio Police Department helping in the search.

Why had Crow wanted a week? At first he had said it was because some record company executive was coming to town for the All Soul Festival. But even after Emmie had disappeared, and the future of Las Almas Perdidas seemed more likely to be played out in the criminal justice system than on the radio, he had been fixated on that date. *You ruined everything*, he had said to her in the garden of the Alamo, the next-to-last time she ever saw him. *All I asked for was a week, and you couldn't even give me that.* And it was only when Rick had said he couldn't expect to make bail, that he might be in jail over the weekend, that he had gone out the window. After Emmie. Not because he knew where she was, Tess realized, but because he knew he had to find her before Saturday. Why?

When Tess was a little girl, she had gone out an open window on the second story of her parents' home. She had been trying to re-create Goldilocks's flight, which seemed suspiciously easy to her. Sure enough, she had broken her collarbone, which had somewhat dimmed her pleasure in being right.

Last night, she had gone sailing out the window again, confident in own theories, and been proven wrong. That had knocked the wind out of her in much the same way.

But nothing hurt more than the thought that Crow had not trusted her with whatever secret he was hoarding. She had to find him—again, and before tomorrow. What was the law of missing objects? They can be found in the most obvious places. Crow was not an object, but he was in a city he didn't know all that well, with no car and very little money, and a mysterious deadline fast approaching.

The only thing to do, she realized, was to retrace

her steps, as if she were looking for a set of keys, or a notebook, or her gym shoes. That was how you found things. Retrace your steps. Retrace them again and again and again. Think about the last time you saw or held the missing item. Retrace your steps. What you have lost is always there, you just don't always see it until the third, fourth, fifth time around.

Chris Ransome had said there was something unfinished between his son and Tess, an energy like a divining rod. It wasn't the kind of theory for which one won the Nobel Prize, but it was all she had.

27

Before setting out, she stopped at La Casita to ask Mrs. Nguyen to keep an eye on Esskay for the rest of the day. She found the two fast friends watching yet another telenovela—*Mi Amor, Mi Vida*—and sharing a bag of pork rinds.

"Don't let her have too many of those," Tess cautioned. Esskay gave her a smug look, confident that she could charm the birds out of the trees. Or at least pry the pork rinds from Mrs. Nguyen's fingers.

"Okay. When you coming home?"

"No idea."

"Better take a jacket."

"Jacket? It's eighty-five degrees out there."

"See the sky?" Tess glanced at the little slice of sky visible from La Casita's office. It was bright blue, with a few white fluffy clouds. "No, *other* sky," Mrs. Nguyen said. "Blue norther coming in, from the northwest. Much rain, cool weather behind. Temperature drop twenty, thirty degrees just like that." She snapped her greasy fingers. "Chris Marrou on Channel Five *said*."

"I'll take a jacket, Mom," she said.

"And your gun!" Mrs. Nguyen called after Tess. "Always good for a girl to have her gun."

The cool front was only a rumor as Tess drove, windows down, re-covering all the ground she had covered in the past few weeks. She drove down the St. Mary's strip, where Primo's was already advertising "Lunch Box Nite!" and a new band called the Urkels. But the creepy manager was at the bank, and the smiling bartender had no news of Crow. She circled the Morgue, a forlorn place in daylight, all its doors locked and bolted, even the back entrance off the loading dock. She found the duplex on Magnolia Drive, where Crow's Volvo was still parked in the back. Had he left his car because he knew where to rendezvous with Emmie all along? She didn't think so. She thought Crow had done what she was now doing, moving in ever-widening circles, trying to find Emmie by visiting what he knew of her past. But Emmie had the home-field advantage.

She headed to Hector's, much scarier at three P.M. than it had been at two A.M. No Crow, no Emmie, she was told. Not since last Saturday night. Did she know if they would be there tomorrow? Doubtful, very doubtful.

The rhythm of driving was addictive, she couldn't stop. As long as she was moving, she was doing something. No location, no matter how tangentially related, should be overlooked. She ate an early dinner at Earl Abel's, glided past the Sterne house on Hermosa, cut over to Austin Highway, and saw the lonely band of picketers keeping vigil outside Sterne

Foods. Her knowledge of San Antonio exhausted, she headed north, bypassing the town of Twin Sisters this time and going straight to the old Barrett place. She told herself she'd try Austin next, drive all night if she had to, watch the sun come up over I-35 and head back into San Antonio, repeat the whole crazy loop. Momentum was the only thing she had going for her.

Crime scene tape marked off the pool house at the Barrett place and a new pane of glass had replaced the one she had cut, but it was otherwise as she had first seen it. She shouldered her knapsack and walked around the house a few times before she peered through a kitchen window. There was a dark shape on the floor in the main room. Her stomach clutched—she really wasn't up for finding another body. But this shadow was flat and still, nothing more than the corner of a blanket, or a bedroll.

A bedroll? There had been nothing lying on the floor when she had made her first inventory of the house. She tried the door, found it unlocked, and stepped over the threshold.

"Hello?" she called.

"What do you want?"

The voice came from behind her. Crow stood in the doorway, backlit so she couldn't really see his face. The sky beyond him was unlike any she had ever seen—dark gray, with a stripe of navy blue on the horizon. A blue norther. She hadn't realized the term was so literal.

"You're alone?" she asked.

"Yes."

"I am, too."

"I know. I hid in the grove of pecan trees when I heard a car on the gravel driveway. I wouldn't have come out if anyone had been with you. Even Rick. I'm not turning myself in, Tess. Not yet."

"Not until tomorrow, right?"

He had come all the way into the house, and she could see his face now. He looked surprised and a little irritated. "How do you know about tomorrow? How did you find me?"

There was one answer for both questions. "Because I know you."

"You did once," he said. "Not anymore."

"No, it's the other way around. I know you better now than I ever did when we were together. Looking for you, I began to understand you, to find out things I should have known all along." His face remained guarded, closed to her. "There were times when I didn't understand you. But I always knew you wouldn't be involved in murder, Crow."

"Well, I'm *not*," he said, sounding at once angry and relieved. "But I can't go to the police, Tess. They'll keep me, thinking I can tell them where Emmie is. I can't. My only chance to find her is tomorrow."

"What is it about tomorrow? You've been fixated on that date since I got here."

"It's All Souls' Day—and the day of the All Soul Festival parade."

The parade, Gus Sterne's brainchild, his ego trip through the streets of San Antonio. "So what's Emmie going to do, Crow? She can't burn down a parade."

Instead of answering, he walked past Tess into

the main room, where he crouched in front of one of the built-in bookcases. From the lowest shelf, he pulled out a scrapbook, then sat on the bedroll, inviting Tess to sit by him.

"Do you know where we are?" he asked, opening the book. It was a pretty volume, with a moss green velvet cover and pale gray pages.

"On the old Barrett place, near Twin Sisters, somewhere between Austin and San Antonio, in the state of Texas, in the United States of America," she answered dutifully.

"We're at a trysting spot. Two lovers used to meet here. Two lovers forbidden to be lovers. They met here and they promised to love each other forever and ever, despite the world's disapproval, despite all the obstacles in their path. One of them broke that promise, and the other one can neither forget nor forgive."

He began flipping through the pages, and dust from pressed flowers rose into the air, their fragrance long gone. The first few pages were filled with photographs. A Polaroid, the kind taken in restaurants, of two men and three women, laughing over their margaritas. Tess recognized Marianna Conyers and Gus Sterne, guessed that she was looking at the long-dead Frank Conyers and the long-gone Ida Sterne. The third woman looked like Emmie—more correctly, like the woman Emmie was in the process of becoming. Lollie Sterne. Her obituary was pasted beneath the Polaroid and Emmie had circled her own name among the survivors, then written "Survivor's List?" in the margin in the same red crayon.

"She thought it would make a good name for a band," Crow explained.

"An odd photo to save."

"It's the only one she has. Gus couldn't bear to have photos of Lollie around, after the murder. He put them away, planning to give them to Emmie one day. For obvious reasons, that never happened."

Next page. A tall, handsome man with two blond children on tricycles. Emmie smiled into the camera with a charisma that had not yet soured into craziness. Little Clay stared at the ground, sulky and cross. Gus Sterne looked at Emmie. More family photos, clippings from the society pages, more fragile remains of old corsages. Gus Sterne and family at this gala or that. Ida was in some of these, then she disappeared, with no explanation or acknowledgment.

With or without her, the dynamic was always the same—Emmie looked into the camera, Clay looked away, features twisted into a pout or a frown, Gus looked at Emmie as if startled by a particularly lovely ghost. It was like watching a rosebud unfurl—Emmie looked more like Lollie with each passing year. Here she was as the princess of the Order of the Alamo, escorted by her grim-faced cousin. Emmie at a picnic. Emmie backstage, in costume for a school play. *Oklahoma*, given the gingham dress and the comical hat. The girl who can't say no. Every picture told a story. Every picture told the same story: A radiant young woman, an unhappy boy, an older man who could not take his eyes off the young woman.

"Jesus," Tess said.

"There's more," Crow said. She was barely listening. *Had Clay known his father and Emmie were lovers, or had he merely guessed? Technically, it wasn't incest, not by blood, but Gus had raised Emmie as his daughter, so it might as well be.*

Crow turned another page, to a glossy photo razor cut from a book. This was a famous image, one Tess knew: The old *Life* photo of a woman lying on the hood of a crushed car after jumping from the Empire State Building.

"The twentieth century's version of the Lily Maid of Astolat, who died for the love of Lancelot," Crow said. "That's Emmie's fantasy. She'll jump, and hit the hood of the car, the old Lincoln, and it will carry her down Broadway. I've told her dying isn't as easy as it looks, but she's determined. When she realized I intended to interfere with her plan, she decided to get rid of me. She's the one who put the gun under my bed, then called the cops."

"So you do think she killed Darden and Weeks."

"No. Emmie's not a killer. But she doesn't care about them. She doesn't care about anyone. Nothing is important to her, except making this grand, stupid, *insane* gesture."

"All for Gus Sterne."

Crow looked perplexed. "Who said anything about him?"

"You showed me the pictures." She took the scrapbook from him, flipped back to the earlier pages. "You told me about the two lovers who met here secretly. I put it together."

"You put it together wrong. Emmie wasn't in love with Gus, for Christ's sake. She's in love with *Clay*."

"Clay?" That raw, unfinished boy—someone was willing to die for him? But Tess was coming to realize that it was futile to try to understand who might love whom, or why. She thought of Kitty and Tyner, of Kitty and Keith, of Kitty and everyone. Of Rick and Kristina, even the squabbling couple on the bridge above the River Walk, comical to everyone, but not to one another. Lovers made sense only to themselves.

"Since high school," Crow said, answering one of her many unvoiced questions. "Gus found out and forbade them to see each other. Clay, dutiful as ever, agreed. Emmie didn't. That's when she tried to burn the house down. When she left the psychiatric hospital, she followed Clay to Austin and they started again, meeting here. Then, about a year ago, Clay suddenly broke off all contact, with no explanation. In May he moved back to San Antonio—and into his father's house. He chose Gus over Emmie. At least, that's how she sees it."

"May—that's about the same time a band called Poe White Trash arrived in Austin."

Crow nodded ruefully. "Yep. I was looking for a girl singer. She was in the market for an accomplice to her self-destruction. We both got more than we bargained for."

"Did she tell you her whole saga, or did you just figure it out?"

"A little of both. I knew about her mother's murder before I met her—she wasn't shy about milking her past, whether for publicity or sympathy. One night up here the two of us ended up on a real maudlin drunk, literally crying in our beer. I showed her my broken heart, she showed me hers. She told me she had a fantasy about killing herself in front of Clay. Later she denied everything, said it was the liquor talking. But I had already seen the scrapbook. Besides, liquor's a pretty good truth serum. I've never known anyone to lie when they were drunk." He looked at her. "Once, when you had a lot to drink, you said . . . someone else's name in bed."

She didn't remember this, but nor did she doubt it. "You know, liquor isn't so much a truth serum as it is a paint thinner. It strips a lot of stuff away, takes you down to the old finishes. I am so over my past, Crow."

"As of when?"

"As of this morning."

He had nothing to say to that. Some things were so stupid they had to be true.

"You know, she may have been exaggerating," Tess said. "Emmie's definitely a drama queen."

"No, she's going to kill herself, and she's going to make sure Clay sees the whole thing. When I couldn't talk her out of it, I thought I might at least be able to stop her."

"How do you know it's going to be at the parade?"

"I don't, for a fact. But Sterne Foods is a fortress, she can't get to him there. Ditto the house on Hermosa. Besides, she has to *jump*, that's part of the fantasy. Falling to her death, falling in love. The parade route has a nice tall building in a key spot." He frowned. "Although not necessarily tall enough. I've tried to impress that upon her. There's a real chance she'll only cripple herself. Or kill someone else, a spectator along the route. A child, even."

The wind was kicking up, but the chill Tess felt had nothing to do with the weather.

"Why did Gus care if Clay and Emmie were together, anyway? They were the children of first cousins. They could have married in most states."

"Gus said she would hurt him, and he couldn't bear to see his son hurt." Crow's face was sad and drawn in the strange gray-blue light. "As if you can ever spare anyone the hurt of loving anyone."

She reached for his hand, unsure whether to hold it or pat it. She ended up tugging on his index finger. "I'm sorry, Crow."

"Sorry for what?"

"Everything?" It still didn't seem like enough.

The rain Mrs. Nguyen had predicted started then, as heavy and sudden as any storm Tess had ever experienced. It clattered on the tin roof, cascaded from the pecan-clogged gutters. It was as if watery drapes had been thrown over the world, blotting out everything.

"My car windows!" She ran through the rain to roll them up. When she returned, soaked to the skin, Crow was still sitting on the bedroll. For some reason, he seemed more surprised to see her now than he had been when she first arrived.

"I thought you had just uttered the greatest exit line of all time. 'My car windows!'"

"Why would you think that?" she asked, squeezing water from her sodden braid.

"Because that's your style, Tess. Cut and run, with

a few banalities about the weather, or your inability to make a commitment."

"I was trying to be fair to you. I had met someone else—"

"Tess, there's *always* going to be someone else. Your sexual desires don't go away because you're with someone. How are you going to stay in a relationship for the rest of your life if you can't grasp that?"

Tess was shivering in her wet clothes. "I'm not sure I'm ever going to find someone I want to be with forever and ever."

"Then you probably won't." His voice wasn't unkind. "Look, I don't want you to drive while it's raining so hard. You don't know this area. The low-water crossings will be five feet deep, you could be washed away if you make a wrong turn. Stay the night."

She pulled her T-shirt away from her skin, and it made a rude smacking sound. "You don't want me to leave because you need a ride into town tomorrow."

"Maybe." But he was smiling now, pouring on the charm.

"If I take you in, you have to let me come along."

Crow hesitated, but only for a moment. He had no leverage, he had to see that. It was a package deal, Tess and the Toyota. "Okay. Emmie knows you, so she won't freak out. She likes you, in her own way. In fact, she used to study this photo I had, the newspaper photo of you and Esskay."

"The one you showed Mrs. Nguyen, so you could search my room at La Casita."

He wasn't listening to her. He was studying her

face, with his detached painter's eye, as if planning to sketch her yet again.

"Your hair is going to get all snarly if you let it dry like that," he said. "You better comb it out."

"I don't think I have a comb in my knapsack. I wasn't planning on a slumber party."

"I do. I have a toothbrush, too, if you want it." He left the room and came back with both, obviously proud of himself.

"You were ready to evacuate all along, weren't you?" Tess asked.

"No, but I had the presence of mind to grab a few things before I jumped. I had my choice of toiletries, I just didn't have any money or food. I had to sleep in Brackenridge Park the first night, then catch a ride up here with a crew of day workers heading for a nearby ranch."

"Didn't it occur to you this place might be under surveillance?"

"Of course. But that was the one good thing about you finding that second body in San Antonio—it shifted all the attention down there." He was all but preening. "I keep the lights off to be safe, but as far as I can tell, the sheriff's deputies haven't come near this place. I have to admit I'm kind of proud of myself. It's not every man who gets away from Tess Monaghan *twice*."

"Let me have the comb, before my hair dries from all this hot air."

He shook his head. "No, you won't do it right. I've seen you comb your hair. You just try to beat the tangles into submission. Turn around, little girl, and no whining. Or we'll just cut off all this hair and leave you with something more manageable."

It was what her mother used to say when she was younger. She didn't even remember telling him this fact, but he remembered. Crow remembered everything.

She sat on the edge of the bedroll, her back to him. He unplaited her hair, running his fingers through it to loosen it. Only then did he use the comb, and he was as gentle as he had promised. He took his time, curling the ends around his finger, lifting the heavy mass so he could comb the wispy ringlets at the nape. The rain was even heavier now, and it was hard to imagine the room could get much darker.

"You ought to wear your hair up," Crow said, twisting it into a pile on top of her head.

"My friend Jackie showed me how to put it up so I don't look like a spinster in a bun. But I don't do it so well."

"Jackie?"

"A new friend. She has a little girl, Laylah, whom you'd love."

"I love you," he said very casually. "I stopped for a while, but then I started again."

Her back was to him, which made it easier to tell the truth, but it didn't make it easier to know what the truth was. She couldn't say she had stopped and started again, because she wasn't sure she had really loved him the first time around. She couldn't say she would love him forever and ever—she had just admitted she didn't know if she'd ever get that right. But Crow wasn't asking for assurances about the past or the future, she realized. He would settle for now.

"I love you, too."

He put down the comb, burying his face in her hair and her neck, his arms reaching around her waist. He held her tight, like an exhausted swimmer coming to a branch or a boulder after a long, long time in turbulent waters. Yet he was in no hurry, this was distinctly different from the other night, just a week ago. He had still been angry with her then, she realized, his passion had been a mask for his fury. Crow held her, and she allowed herself to be held, her senses expanding. She was aware of the rain, of the darkness, of the grain in the floorboards beneath them, of the watery shadows on the walls. Finally she broke his hold on her, but only so she could peel the wet T-shirt away from her body and turn to face him.

She was home.

When morning came, it was as Mrs. Nguyen and Channel 5's Chris Marrou had prophesied—cooler, crisper, the kind of fall day that Tess would have taken for granted back in Baltimore. But she was beyond taking anything for granted now.

Blinking heavy eyes, she glanced around the house. A shower was running somewhere, and the dryer was thumping softly. Thoughtful Crow must have washed her clothes. His nurturing, once mildly oppressive, now seemed sexy. She wondered if they had time for him to nurture her a little more before they drove to town. She glanced at her Swiss Army watch, the only thing she had managed to keep on through the long night. Nine A.M. The parade started at one but they needed to leave soon if they were going to intercept Emmie.

Strange—the only thing in the dryer was a small load of dishtowels. Maybe he had hung her clothes up outside, under the now-brilliant skies. But she couldn't see anything from the windows. She knocked on the bathroom door, then pushed it open without waiting for a reply. Steam rolled out, as if the shower had been running for a very long time.

It had, and if Crow had ever been in it, he wasn't now.

She looked for her shoes, but they were missing, too. Naked and barefoot, she ran from the house, down the flagstone path to where her car had been. Gone as well, not that this surprised her. The shower and the dryer—those had probably been turned on in hopes of muffling the noise of an engine starting.

Back in the house, she saw what she hadn't seen before—her datebook open on the kitchen table, a message scrawled on today's date, November 2.

"I started this on my own, and I need to finish it on my own. Love, C. (Nothing here to eat but canned pork and beans, I'm afraid.)"

Damn chivalry. It wasn't enough for Crow to rescue Emmie, he had to spare Tess as well, leaving her with nothing but canned pork and beans and a blanket. But what could she do, naked, shoeless, and at least twenty miles out of San Antonio? If it was so important to him to play Sir Galahad alone, then so be it. She wandered back into the main room and, for want of anything better to do, leafed through Emmie's scrapbook.

Funny how one's perceptions change. Now that she knew the story, she saw the photos differently.

Clay was trying to hide his emotions, while Emmie didn't care if the world knew what she felt. Neither one of them had changed.

But how to explain Gus, with his sad eyes and haunted expression? What was he seeing? What was it that kept his eyes riveted on Emmie? Tess studied the Polaroid, the only image she had seen of Lollie alive. It was taken less than two weeks before the murders, according to the date stamped on the bottom. The five smiled, innocent of their destiny. Lollie sat in the center, the two couples on either side of her. Lollie, Gus and Ida, Frank and Marianna. Two were going to die, two were going to divorce, one was going to be widowed. The three women looked in the camera. The two men looked at Lollie.

The two men looked at Lollie.

Tess thought of the three bodies in Espejo Verde. Two had been killed hastily, quickly. One had been tortured, his death drawn out, his suffering the point of the exercise. *Everyone does everything for money and sex*, Rick had said, mocking the old robbery detective, Marty Diamond. But Diamond might have been closer to the truth than they realized. Sex and money, money and sex. And love. Some people killed for love, or thought they did.

The three women looked in the camera. The two men looked at Lollie. And a little girl had grown up, studying this photo, memorizing it, decoding it, until she finally recognized in her cousin's eyes a kinship only they could share. You had to be crazy to die for love. You had to be crazy to kill for love.

Emmie Sterne was crazy enough to do both.

28

Thank God for make-up sex—Rick and Kristina were still at Rick's house when Tess called from her cell phone, their voices as soft and rumpled as the sheets beneath them. But once Rick understood why she was calling, he asked almost no questions, just took down the directions and promised to get up there as soon as possible. He didn't even press for an explanation when Tess told him she needed a change of clothes for the ride into town.

They were there within an hour, both of them, and Tess couldn't help wondering if Kristina had decided Rick shouldn't make a solo house call to a naked Tess. She had brought Tess clothes, however—a pair of jeans that couldn't fasten over Tess's hips, and a baggy T-shirt. *Fashion Puta, She'll Do Anything for Clothes*, the legend read. No, Kristina wasn't taking anything for granted.

"This time, I'm calling the cops," Rick said, once they were back on the highway, heading toward San Antonio at a steady seventy miles per hour, a speed that would get them into town within thirty minutes, but wouldn't cause the Texas cops to look at them twice. "If you know where Crow is, and you tell me, I've got to call them, or face the consequences."

"But I *don't* know. All I'm sure of is that he's gone to find Emmie somewhere along the parade route."

"You're making a big leap, Tess, from suicide to murder. Remember, less than forty-eight hours ago, you were just as sure that Gus Sterne had killed Darden and Weeks. Now you think it's Emmie."

"It has to be Emmie."

"I gotta call the cops," Rick repeated.

"If I end up in an interrogation room for the rest of the day, nobody wins. Even the cops, with all their manpower, aren't guaranteed to find Emmie in time. But Crow knows where she is, and there's only one way to make sure she doesn't hurt him."

"How's that?" Kristina asked, looking back over the front seat at Tess, her eyes bright with excitement.

"We have to stop the parade."

Between the parade and the usual Saturday traffic, it took them twenty minutes to inch through Bracken-ridge Park once they left the freeway. Finally they reached La Casita, where Tess grabbed her running shoes and some jeans that fit, then checked on her all-but-abandoned child. Mrs. Nguyen and Esskay were watching the pre-parade coverage on one of the local stations and sharing a can of Pringles.

"Mrs. Nguyen—please, no more junk food. It's really not good for her."

"Oh, I only gave her one. Maybe two. We have a pizza coming." Esskay smirked at Tess.

She glanced out the windows. Broadway was bumper to bumper, and there was no place to park. "Can my friend leave his car in your lot—we probably can't get much closer to the parade route than we are here, and I don't need my space today."

"Sure thing, sure thing," she said, waving a vague hand, eyes still fixed on the empty street in front of the Alamo. "Chris Marrou said there are ten thousand people already downtown."

It was more than a mile up Broadway to the parade staging area and the sidewalks and streets were clogged with people, making it impossible to move quickly. By the time they found the staging ground and a parade worker showed them to the shaded underpass where Gus Sterne's silver Lincoln idled, it was twelve-thirty. Half an hour until the first marching band started down the street. Tess motioned to Kris and Rick to hang back—she didn't want Gus Sterne to know she had confided her suspicions in anyone—and walked over to the car.

Clay was in the backseat, reading a book. His father was nearby, in a knot of men who all looked like him, with their gray hair, florid faces, and navy blazers.

"What'd you do, pay God off?" one asked. "The weather couldn't be better, you son of a bitch."

"You son of a bitch," the others echoed, slapping hands and passing around a silver flask. Gus Sterne declined it with a shake of his head. He looked distracted and uneasy to Tess. It probably would make a man nervous, knowing two of his accomplices had been murdered in the past month.

Tess placed her hand over the pages of Clay's

open book, to get his attention. "You have to stop this."

He looked up. "I couldn't stop this parade with Sam Houston at my side. Besides, what's the big deal? I know it's just one big ego trip for my dad, but no one ever died from a little self-aggrandizement."

"Emmie is out there somewhere along the route. When the car goes by, she's going to kill your father, then kill herself. Can you live with that?"

He stared at her as if she had spoken in another language, and he hadn't caught every word. "Emmie? But where—"

"We don't know. That's why our only hope is to stop the parade."

They had spoken in low tones, but Gus Sterne suddenly moved toward the car and grabbed Tess by the elbow. "What is this nonsense? Stop the parade, because Emmie has made another one of her silly threats? I won't have it. That girl has exacted her last measure of insanity on this family."

"It's *not* a silly threat, and you know it. Otherwise, why would you step up security at Sterne Foods, and meet with police about the route? Darden and Weeks have already died for their part in the Espejo Verde murders. Now it's your turn."

Tess didn't know what emotion filled Gus Sterne's face then, she only knew she had never seen anything like it. It was ugly, it was evil, and yet it was also weak and pathetic, the look of a man who was almost relieved to hear his terrible secret spoken aloud.

His voice, however, betrayed nothing. "Get away from me, and get away from my son, or I'll have you arrested," he said softly, so no one else could overhear.

"You are interfering with a legal parade, for which there is a permit, and you are making demonstrably false, slanderous statements. Those who wish to protest this event have been given a small space at the corner of Broadway and Grayson. Join them if you like, but you're no longer welcome here. Javier—"

Javier, the gabby security guard who was to pilot the silver Lincoln through the parade, seized her by the arm.

"She'll kill herself, right in front of you," Tess called over her shoulder to Clay as Javier led her away. "But first she'll kill your father. It's awful to watch someone die. I know, I've seen it. To watch someone die and to know it's your fault, that you might have prevented it—I can't imagine living with that."

Javier was frankly dragging her now, up to the curb where Rick and Kristina waited.

"Crazy Yankee," he muttered, as if expecting Rick to commiserate with him, but he and Kristina were bent over the parade route from that morning's paper, marking the high buildings along the way. Their map was festooned with little red X's, far too many to canvass in the minutes they had left. Besides, once the parade started, police would keep the route clear and the sidewalks would be crowded with reviewing stands.

"There are four- and five-story buildings most of the way," Rick said. "All private businesses. You'd have to know someone to get in. Watching from those vantage points is considered a perk."

"Then again, the Sternes know everyone," Kris

put in. "She might have found an old family friend who let her into a private party for old time's sake."

Tess looked at the map, but it meant nothing to her. If it had been Baltimore, she would have known every building and its history, she could have figured out some association between Emmie and the place she planned to die. Here, she was lost.

"Is there anything near the Alamo?" It was Clay, still holding his book. He was trying to act very nonchalant, as if they should have expected him all along. But his cheeks were bright red, his voice shaky with the momentousness of what he had done.

"If I'm not in the car, she's got no reason to jump, right?" he asked as they stared at him. "And if she's not going to jump, then maybe she won't try to hurt Dad, either."

"It's a long shot, but I'll take it," Tess said. "You've given us more of a chance than we had five minutes ago. If only we could figure out where she is. You know her better than anyone, Clay. Where would she be?"

He looked at the route. "The television cameras are set up across from the Alamo."

"But there's nothing *there*," Tess said. "She can't jump from the Alamo, it's not even two stories. And the hotels in that area are too far back, right? I don't know how good a shot she is—"

"Pretty good," Clay said. "Better than I am, as Dad will be the first to tell you."

"Still, she has to be as close as possible."

Tess bent over the map again. The parade went straight up Broadway, past the Morgue, then wound its way through downtown. The Morgue, where

Emmie sang. The Morgue, which stood at the intersection of Broadway and McCullough, two streets that started their lives parallel and ended up perpendicular. A fat lady with her legs crossed at the ankles, Tess had said, and Emmie had agreed. *You could even say it ain't over until the fat lady crosses her ankles.*

She had confided in Tess as surely as she had confided in Crow.

"She's here," she said definitely, circling the Morgue. She glanced at her watch—twelve forty-five. "But even if I'm right, we barely have enough time to get there before the parade starts. I wonder if we can delay it, at least."

"You'd still need Dad's say-so," Clay said.

"I wasn't thinking of a *legal* delay," Tess said.

Rick threw up his hands. "I told you, I'm not risking disbarment for anyone. We know where she is, let's go to the cops."

"No!" Tess didn't want to think what might happen to Crow if the cops stormed the place. Emmie was too unstable, too unpredictable. "We can't be sure. Once the cops get involved, we lose all control. I might be wrong, I don't want this to be my only shot."

"Let me help," Kristina said eagerly. "After all, I can't be disbarred."

"Kris, I absolutely forbid you."

Kristina turned on him, wagged a finger in his face. "Get one thing straight—you're never going to tell me what to do, even when we're married, you sleazy shyster."

"Sleazy shyster! Sleazy shyster!" Rick stopped, his outrage momentarily forgotten. "I'm not going to marry a woman who speaks to me so disrespect-fully, I can tell you that much."

"Shut up, both of you," Tess said. "You can fight later. Now, Kristina, see that motley group of pick-eting vegans over there? I bet all it would take is a little rhetoric to get them out of the official protest area and into the street."

"Kris—" Rick yelled in vain, for she was already running full-speed toward the vegans, screaming "Meat stinks!" She didn't even wait for their reac-tion, just grabbed a hotdog stand and began running with it down Broadway, the confused and outraged vendor in pursuit. Kris stopped long enough to douse him with his own ketchup and mustard bottles, then resumed running with the cart.

Now the vegans had caught on, and they were at-tacking other meat vendors—hurling turkey legs to the ground, overturning steaming vats of ground beef at the picadillo stand, throwing buns at the hapless hamburger server. Spectators who couldn't care less about the politics of the food chain began scooping up the fallen treats. As the cops converged on Kristina and a sighing Rick ran to her aid, Tess and Clay slipped across Broadway, to the relatively deserted street that ran parallel to the parade route.

"Do you really think she'll do it?" he asked.

"You know her better than I do, Clay. What do you think?"

He didn't answer. They were running almost full out, but it still took ten minutes to reach McCullough. This side street was full of vendors and overflow from the parade, and no one seemed to notice the woman with the braid and the man with the book slipping into the parking lot behind the Morgue, where the door to the loading dock, tightly bolted yesterday, was now ajar, and a white Toyota with Maryland plates was parked illegally. Great, her car would probably be towed before this was all over.

Clay started to follow her inside, but Tess stopped him. "If you're there, she can still do it, right? She wants to die in front of you. She doesn't need a parade to do that. Wait here, and if I don't come out in fifteen minutes, I want you to get a cop and come find me. Okay?"

"Okay," he said reluctantly. "But if I'm there, if I can talk to her—"

"We can't risk it, Clay. Now help me with Emmie—think—roof, or the top floor?"

He didn't need more than a second. "Top floor. On the roof, the news and traffic helicopters could spot her. She's smart enough to have thought that through."

Tess took the stairs to the fourth floor, treading as softly as possible. The Morgue's various music venues went only as high as the third floor, and this area appeared to be a storage room, virtually unrenovated. She walked through old boxes and piles of newspapers, moving toward what her ears told her was the Broadway side of the building. The crowd was loud and restless, possibly because the parade was now officially behind schedule. The noise would be deafening once things truly got under way. She wondered how much time Kristina had bought them.

She tried a series of doors along the corridor. The Lady or the Crow. No. No. No. What if she was wrong, after all? She had bet all the time they had on this one hunch. She might have bet Crow's life on it as well.

The last door she tried was in the northwest corner and when she entered, there was Emmie, kneeling over Crow, pressing her hand against his stomach. When she saw Tess in the doorway, she held her hands up as if to ward off a blow. She wore white gloves. Once-white gloves now covered with blood.

"I'm so sorry." Emmie was almost babbling. "I wouldn't have hurt him, not for anything, you have to know that. I tried to tell you he was in trouble, but you were so slow to come. Why couldn't you come sooner?"

Tess pushed Emmie so hard that she hit the far wall, next to the room's only window. She knelt next to Crow and lifted his shirt. The wound was narrow, but deep, and he was losing blood at a sickeningly rapid rate. She took off his shirt and used it as a compress.

"You'll be fine," she said, hoping it was true. She should get her gun out of her knapsack, hold it on Emmie, so she wouldn't come at both of them with the knife. Tess looked around the room and saw the long blade lying on the floor, just a few feet from her. She couldn't get to it without leaving Crow's side. Meanwhile, Emmie seemed in no hurry to pick up the weapon and resume her attack. She sat on the floor, legs spread out like a Raggedy Ann doll, babbling to herself.

"You should have come sooner. I wouldn't have hurt him for anything."

"Go," Crow said, his voice weak. "Live."

"Not for anything," Emmie repeated in a low

moan. "Never, never, never." She beat on her skirt, as if trying to put out flames, but succeeded only in leaving her own bloody handprints behind. She was dressed like a princess, or a little girl's idea of a princess, in a long gauzy skirt over a pink leotard and leggings, her feet in flat ballet slippers. Those white gloves. "I never wanted him to be hurt."

Tess felt the pulse at Crow's neck. It wasn't strong, but it was steady. There was some hope. "Then why did you?"

"I *didn't*," she wailed, crouching in the corner like some strange animal. "But he said—and I promised, and I keep my promises, I always keep my promises, He was the one who broke his promise. He said no one would be hurt. Only bad people, he said. Only bad people, who deserved what they got."

The door opened, and Clay stumbled in, a police officer at his side. Good for him, he hadn't waited the prescribed fifteen minutes. They would need a cop to get an ambulance through the crowds, to get Crow the help he needed. The parade was starting, she could hear the strains of a marching band, blasting out something that sounded like "I've Been Working on the Railroad." She looked up hopefully into the face of the cop with the rifle on his hip.

Steve Villanueve took off his dark glasses.

"Don't feel bad, Tess," he said. "You weren't the only one who never stopped to think that Pilar Rodriguez had a family, too. Or that there was someone who loved her enough to avenge *her* death."

29

"Pilar Rodriguez was my family's cook," Clay said stupidly. Tess noticed he was still holding his book, a finger at his place, as if he might have time to finish a chapter or two before Steve killed all of them.

"Pilar Rodriguez was my *grandmother*." Steve used the rifle's long barrel to prod Clay into the corner where Tess crouched, her hand still bearing down hard on Crow's wound. The door was less than fifteen feet away on a diagonal, Tess judged. If she or Clay ran, they might make it before Steve got off a shot. But she couldn't leave Crow, and Clay seemed to be in a trance.

As did Emmie, who couldn't stop staring at her cousin. She chewed a knuckle, eyes wide, her back pressed so hard against the wall that she might have been nailed to it. It had probably been a year since she was this near to him, since he had been close enough for her to touch, to gaze into the shadowed eyes so like hers.

In a room full of people, Tess was clearly on her own.

"You did fool me," she told Steve. "I thought you were an overeager rookie, trying to win points with the boss. But you were miles ahead of Guzman."

He nodded curtly, too distracted by the events swirling around him to pay much heed to her fake praise, much less be taken in by it. Sweat beaded on his brow, and his round face had a flushed, feverish quality. He had looked like that when they were running together. Yet this day was cool, and the little room, away from direct sunlight, was cooler still.

"Pilar Rodriguez," Tess said, musing aloud. "No, I never gave much thought to her. 'The cook.' That's what Guzman, everyone, always called her. The cook."

"As if she were nothing," Steve said. "As if she weren't a person, too."

He was still looking out the window. He would have a very precise plan, Tess knew. He had probably written it down, gone over every possible scenario, then committed it all to memory. Tess suddenly realized he was the one who had put the gun beneath Crow's bed, left his T-shirt at Espejo Verde, hoping to be rid of him before today. He was that careful. He was so careful that any disruption, any unexpected contingency, would throw him off his stride. How flustered he had been in the park that day, when she had seen through him. Well, almost seen through him. Crow's appearance today would have kicked up the first stone in his path. Now here were Tess and Clay. Everything was falling apart.

"I don't remember her," Clay murmured. "I know her name, of course, but I don't remember her."

"I do," Emmie said. "She smelled like vanilla. She was the one who called me Dutch."

"She wasn't *yours* to remember," Steve said. "She was your employee. She cooked your meals, she took care of you, so she would have money for her own children and grandchildren. Money, but no time, because she worked six days a week, living in your house. She made the food that made Espejo Verde famous. So then she had two jobs. Before too long, she had a third job as well—babysitting, while Lollie Sterne fucked her best friend's husband in the little bedroom off the kitchen."

Steve leaned out the window, checking on the parade below. Even if anyone noticed him, it wouldn't matter. Why shouldn't a cop in a bullet-proof vest be watching the parade from such a vantage point? Why shouldn't he have a powerful rifle with a scope?

"I know that. We all know that," Tess said, although she wasn't sure what Clay knew, but he didn't seem surprised by anything he had heard so far. "Why so much talk? Go ahead, kill us. If my time is up, I don't want boredom to be the last thing I experience."

"You just wait," Steve muttered, still looking out the window. "You won't be bored much longer."

She looked down at Crow, now barely conscious. She thought she saw him try to jerk his chin toward Emmie, but that must be wishful thinking on her part. Was he trying to tell her something? Maybe she should be focusing on Emmie, instead of trying to fence with Steve. After all, one never knew what she might do.

"Why not jump right now, Emmie?" she asked

with elaborate carelessness. "Clay's here. That's what really matters, isn't it? Him watching you die. Everything else—killing Darden and Weeks, killing Gus—is gravy. Go ahead and jump. Because it's not really about avenging the death of your mother, is it? It's about you. It was always all about you."

"Not just me—"

"Clay, too, of course. But not Lollie, or her death. You never really knew your mother. But you knew Clay. You loved him. And he chose his father over you."

Emmie scratched furiously at her legs, but gloved fingers couldn't draw fresh blood through her pink tights. Clay looked at Tess with undisguised revulsion. She didn't care. She watched Steve's eyes dart nervously around the room. His plan was unraveling, slipping through his hands like so much string.

"Shut up," he said. "Just shut up."

"You do understand, Emmie, he's going to kill Clay," Tess continued in the most conversational tone she could muster. "He has to. In fact, I think he always intended to kill Clay. Oh, sure, he told you he would kill Gus, then let you jump in the confusion. With your body broken, and such an easy solution at hand—Gus Sterne's homicidal cousin finally does him in after years of trying—they won't look too closely at the physical evidence. I bet Steve even had you write a letter, confessing to everything, telling Guzman how you figured out that Gus Sterne was the man who hired Darden and Weeks to kill Frank Conyers."

"There is a letter," Emmie muttered, almost to herself. "But to Clay—I wrote you a letter, Clay. So you'd know, so you'd understand. I'd do anything for you, anything."

"Clay's not going to be reading any letters," Tess said.

"Stop talking," Steve ordered, waving the rifle at both of them. "I can't hear myself think, with all this chatter."

Tess looked at Steve. "How many fingers did you have to cut from Weeks' hand before he confessed, before he gave you the name that Emmie already knew? All ten or was that simply for show? Did you have to stuff Crow's T-shirt in his mouth to keep his screams from being heard, or did you and Emmie bring that back later, when your first attempt to frame Crow failed? Not that I blame you for your methods. After you killed Tom Darden, Weeks was your only chance to find out for sure if Gus Sterne had arranged the murders."

"I'll kill him," Steve said, pointing his rifle at Crow. "I'll put his brains in your lap if you don't stop talking."

"No, no, no, no, no," Emmie sang to herself, covering her ears. "No, no, no, no, no."

Tess took a deep breath, exhaling the way one does on a difficult weight exercise. "Go ahead," she said. "Show Emmie who you really are. Kill Crow. Kill me. My only regret is I'm not going to live long enough to watch you try to convince Emmie that Clay has to die, too, and by her hand. But he always was the target, wasn't he? That's why you dragged him in here when you saw him waiting outside. You don't want to kill Gus Sterne. You want him to live, the way you've lived. You want him to grieve."

"Steve?" Emmie asked.

"Don't listen to her. She's trying to turn you against me. I'm the only one who ever understood you, Emmie. The only person who doesn't think it's crazy to die for love."

"You're killing for it, not dying," Tess said. "There's a difference. If you want to die for love, I won't stop you."

But Steve was calming down now, taking time to analyze his options.

"Bring me the knife, Emmie. And her knapsack. She has a gun in there."

Another small mystery solved. "*You* were the man Mrs. Nguyen let into my room that day," Tess said. "Emmie gave you the photograph from Crow's things."

"One of the first rules of war is reconnaissance," he said, stumbling a little over the last word. "The knapsack, Emmie. Take it off her back and bring it over here. No—don't lift your arms. Let Emmie slide it off, one strap at a time. Keep your hands where I can see them."

Trancelike, Emmie did as she was told, dragging the knapsack behind her on the floor, holding the knife awkwardly in her right hand. But instead of returning to Steve's side, she suddenly threw herself, weeping, into Clay's arms. "It's all your fault. None of this would have happened if you hadn't stopped loving me. Why can't you just love me again?"

He put one arm around her and rocked her. "I do love you, Emmie. I'll probably never love anyone else the way I loved you."

Her sobs were wild, convulsive spasms, shaking

her whole body. "He's my father, isn't he? He loved Lollie, and she ran away from him when she got pregnant, then made up the story about Horace Morgan. That's why he won't let us be together."

Clay stroked her hair. "I wish it were that simple. No, your father really was some stupid El Paso boy who killed himself for love of your mother. But you're right—when they were our age, Gus loved Lollie, and she loved him. Then she stopped, but he couldn't help believing she would start again, even as they married other people, and went on with their lives. He always thought she would come back to him. Then one day, Lollie told him she had fallen in love with Frank Conyers, and he was going to leave Marianna for her. They were going to move up to Austin, open their own restaurant there. Gus thought if something happened to Frank . . ." Clay looked at Steve over Emmie's head. "He never meant for Lollie to die, much less Pilar. They weren't suppose to be there."

"But she did die, didn't she," Steve said. "That's all that matters."

"He made me choose, Emmie," Clay said, cupping her face with his right hand, his left still clasping his book. "When he found out we were seeing each other again, he told me everything he had done, and he made me choose. You or him. If I kept seeing you, he was going to turn himself in, confess to everything he had done. I couldn't let him do that. It's a death penalty crime."

"He was jealous," Emmie wailed. "He didn't want us to be happy because he could never be happy."

"No, he believed we would end up as he and Lollie

had, with one of us killing the other. He said it was our legacy, and we could never outrun it. You loved the way he loved, and he knew how that story ended. He saw himself in you. He wasn't far from wrong, was he?"

Tess remembered the look on Gus Sterne's face, the way he stared at Emmie as if he had seen a ghost.

"We could be together," Emmie insisted to Clay. "It's not too late."

An accomplice in two murders, and she still thought her future was as wide open as the window through which she had planned to jump up until five minutes ago.

"Don't let him go through with this, Emmie," Clay pleaded. "I'll make Dad tell the truth, face the consequences for what he's done."

"He won't," Steve scoffed. "He told you the truth to bind him to you, to make you do what he wanted. He'll never admit his crimes to anyone who counts."

"He *will* do the right thing," Clay said. He was trying hard not to cry, but a few tears slipped down his cheeks. "I'll make him. But don't kill my father. He's all I have."

A huge cheer went up from the street below, and Steve glanced out the window. In the split-second his head was turned, Tess saw Emmie slide the knife along Clay's spine, into the waistband of his khakis.

"Here comes Gus. You're up, Emmie," Steve said. "You can jump, or I'll kill you—but not before I kill your cousin. I've got no problem with letting Al Guzman wrangle over a mysterious quadruple murder for the next twenty years."

"*Please*," Clay said. Emmie broke their embrace and backed away from him. "We'll go to the police. My dad will confess. At the very least, he'll have to tell the grand jury."

"What grand jury?" Steve asked.

"The one that's convened whenever a cop is killed."

Clay hurled his book at Steve's face, and the young cop reflexively put up a hand to deflect it. "What the—" Steve didn't drop the rifle, but with one hand swatting at a book, there was no way he could get a shot off. He was thrown off-balance for no more than a second or two, but that proved to be all the time Clay needed. With a speed that surprised everyone, perhaps himself most of all, Clay pulled the knife from his waistband and ran forward, jamming it through the bullet-proof vest and into Steve's chest with one sure thrust.

Steve Villanueve died surprised.

Surprised that all his reconnaissance had not paid off. Surprised that bullet-proof vests only stop bullets. Surprised that all his careful planning had come to naught. He slumped to the floor, only a few seconds of life left in him, and nothing left to say.

"Clay, get the cell phone from my knapsack and dial 911," Tess called to him, for he was staring stupidly at the dead man at his feet, and she still had her hand pressed to Crow's midsection. "I just hope they know how to get an ambulance to us with most of Broadway blocked off."

Clay took the knapsack from Emmie, dug out the cell phone, and punched in the number. As he turned his back on the window, covering one ear so he could hear over the parade noise, Emmie began moving like a sleepwalker, her blue eyes empty. She stepped around Steve's body as if it weren't there, then clambered to the ledge behind him.

Later, Tess would wonder if she did the right thing. Wasn't Emmie Sterne entitled to her death wish? She was broken, and all the king's horses and men and money couldn't put Emmie together again. Did Emmie even have a life left to save, given that her fate was now a narrow destiny limited to a prison or a psychiatric hospital? But these questions came later, when there was time to think. In the moment, without the luxury of contemplation, she hurled herself across the room and caught Emmie by the knees just before she launched herself into the sky.

If Emmie had weighed a little more, she might have dragged Tess out the window with her. As it was, she kicked and twisted and screamed, begging to die, clawing at Tess's face. Clay dropped the phone, ran forward, and grabbed Tess, and the three fell backward together in a pile, even as a silver Lincoln glided into the intersection below.

They could hear the crowd cheering the benefactor who had brought them this beautiful day, this wonderful parade, all this good food and good music. Of course Gus Sterne waved back, they knew that without looking down. What they couldn't know was if he ever noticed those few spectators who had screamed and pointed upward as Emmie and Tess dangled above him. On Channel 5's early broadcast that night, Mrs. Nguyen would later tell

Tess, it was reported that two drunken women had been seen cavorting in a dangerous fashion on a window ledge in the old *Sun* building. No one was believed to be hurt. It had to be true. Chris Marrou *said*.

30

The emergency room at the county hospital was filled with the usual parade detritus. Children who had fallen on broken bottles, men who had fought over the stupid things that men fight over, pregnant women who had gone into premature labor. Guzman told Tess he could find her a quieter, more private place to wait, but she preferred to stay here, pressing a piece of gauze into her elbow, where a nurse had taken her blood at her insistence. She wasn't sure how these things worked, but Crow was going to need blood, lots of it, and she might as well make the first deposit into his account.

Guzman kept trying to get her to drink a soda, or eat a cookie, but she refused this offer, too. She couldn't imagine anything staying in her stomach, although she was achingly hungry. The last thing she had eaten must have been her breakfast of beans, cold from the can.

"You got a stab wound, this is the emergency room where you want to come," Guzman said. "They see a lot of stab wounds here."

"Humph," she said. *Tell the Chamber of Commerce to put it in the brochure.*

"Truth is, *I've* seen a lot of stab wounds, and your friend—well, if you're going to get a knife stuck in your belly, that's the way to go. If anything was hit, it was the appendix, and who needs that anyway? He did lose a lot of blood—"

"Tell me about it," said Tess. She had tried to wash, but the fingernails on her left hand looked as if they had rusted. "He was half-empty when they finally got him in here."

"Now if you were an optimist, you'd say he was half-full."

To her own surprise, she almost laughed, but it was a mirthless, barking sound that veered dangerously close to a sob. She bit her lip. Whatever happened, she didn't want to cry in front of Guzman.

"You know, I don't think I've ever heard you laugh," Guzman said.

"You still haven't."

Guzman scratched his head. "That's fair. Yeah, I guess that's fair. We haven't been having a lot of fun, have we?"

He walked away, toward a bank of phones at the end of the hall. He had been going back and forth to the pay phones since arriving here. Damage control, Tess assumed. The press was all over the story, they just didn't know what the story was. The paramedics had put the call out as an officer down, and every newsroom in town had jumped when that code went across. According to the television bolted high on the waiting room wall, four people were in custody for the stabbing death of an off-duty police officer.

It was easier, Guzman had told her, not to try to set the record straight tonight. They'd atone on Sunday morning. Until then, let the city have another night of innocence, let B. B. King and Etta James sing, let the free barbecue flow. Perhaps no one would notice that Gus Sterne was not there to preside over his happy kingdom.

The one good thing about Guzman was that he had instantly grasped what really happened from the moment he arrived at the hospital. "Pilar Rodriguez was Steve Villanueve's grandmother," Tess had said, and he had nodded sadly, with no need to have anything else explained to him. Then again, he didn't bother to admit she had been right about Gus Sterne, either.

He came back from the phones and settled next to her in one of the hard plastic chairs.

"Whose butt is shaped like these chairs, anyway? Not mine."

"It's not like you'd relax here under any circumstances. A comfortable chair would be a waste."

"Good point," Guzman said. "I never thought about it that way."

Oh shut up, Tess thought. Just shut up. And she heard Steve's voice in her head, saying the same thing.

"You know, Steve was a good cop," Guzman said, although he couldn't possibly know what she had been thinking. "Or so it seemed. Now I find myself wondering when he crossed that line. Did he become a cop to avenge his grandmother's death? Or did the opportunity present itself once he was on the force and began to hear about the information we had developed on Darden and Weeks? I guess we'll never know. But these things usually happen in degrees. A young man starts off trying to catch his grandmother's killer. Who could argue with that? Then one day, he's cutting a man's fingers off in a deserted restaurant, and setting up a deranged young woman to take the fall for everything he's done."

Tess thought Guzman might apologize now, but his voice trailed off and he stared at the beige walls.

"Why can't you admit I was right?" she asked fiercely. "I may have gotten parts of it wrong, but I handed you the solution. Gus Sterne hired Darden and Weeks. To kill Frank, not Lollie and Pilar. But I was close enough."

"You think if I had listened to you that night, this wouldn't have happened? Maybe you're right."

No maybe about it.

"So let's say I had. Only think back. You fingered Gus Sterne, but for the wrong reasons and for crimes he didn't commit. Remember, you thought he had killed Darden and Weeks, too."

"Still—"

"Bear with me. This is your wonderful life, Tess Monaghan. Just like the movie. If you're not here, we got an even sadder ending than we have right now. Let's say I arrest Gus Sterne—you think I was going to keep him overnight? No way. So the parade goes on, and everyone shows up to play their part. Except you're not there, because you didn't go search for Crow. Because you're not there, Clay's not there. Crow still gets stabbed, because Steve can't leave any witnesses. Emmie jumps, and Clay Sterne is shot, and Steve Villanueve gets promoted for responding so calmly in a crisis. Is that how you wanted this to end?"

Tess uncrooked her elbow, let the cotton gauze drop to the floor, put on the Band-Aid the nurse had given her. Donating blood usually made her queasy, but watching the syrupy blood slide into the tube had seemed fairly anticlimactic today.

"Still, you might have listened to me."

Guzman nodded, but he wasn't listening, not even now. His attention was focused on the automatic doors at the emergency room's entrance. Marianna Barrett Conyers stood on the threshold, not moving, the doors opening and closing, opening and closing, so she was revealed to them again and again. The effect was of a child playing peekaboo. Dolores stood at her side, still in her gray uniform, trying to urge her employer forward. Finally, Marianna crossed the threshold, but alone.

"Don't look now," Guzman said, "but the last piece of the puzzle just walked in."

Marianna's manner was stiff, her pallor ghostly. Tess couldn't help thinking of Boo Radley, lured out of his house to save the lives of the two children he had come to love.

Except Boo wasn't as creepy as Marianna.

"You wanted to see me, Sergeant Guzman?"

"What I really wanted was for you to come down here and thank someone."

"For saving Emmie's life? Yes, I am grateful—"

Guzman held up a hand. "No more bullshit. After twenty-one years, could we just stop with all your bullshit? I mean, sure, you can thank Tess for keeping your goddaughter from going airborne if you like. But I think you owe her a bigger debt for finally closing the case in which you were the number one suspect."

It was Tess who looked at Guzman in surprise, not Marianna. She merely sniffed the air and made a face, as if she had detected something distasteful.

"All those times I asked you over the years, and you always said you didn't know anything. Always said there was nothing going on, that it was just cheap gossip. You sat on the motive for your own husband's death for two decades. Why?"

"I had my . . . suspicions," Marianna said stiffly. "I am not one to repeat innuendoes and malicious stories."

"Well, here's my suspicion. You went to Espejo Verde that night. You were going to have it out with your husband and your best friend, for cheating on you. But they were beyond hearing anything when you got there, right?"

Marianna had refused to sit down, so she was still standing above them, hands folded primly over the purse she carried, her face determinedly blank.

"I went to see if something could be worked out. Lollie tired of men easily. She would have tired of Frank, too. There was no reason to take him, if she was going to end up throwing him over. If it was money she wanted, a chance to start a restaurant somewhere else, away from Gus, I could give her that. I just didn't want to give her my husband. But Lollie was already . . . gone when I arrived."

"She was fucking dead," Guzman said. "Could you, just once in your life, use the real words for things?"

Marianna didn't try to disguise her contempt for this man. She might speak in euphemisms, Tess thought, but deep down she was a mean and contemptuous bigot. For her, class distinctions were more important than racial ones. She hated the fact that a cop was speaking to her this way.

"It was dark, and I tripped over Lollie's body when I came through the door. Hers or Pilar's, I was never sure. I know I came up with blood on me—on my hands and knees, my suit. I went into the kitchen, and that's when I saw Frank."

Tears had started down her face, eroding the top layer of makeup. She didn't seem to notice she was crying. "Someone hurts you and you say to yourself, 'I wish they were dead,' and then you see what dead is. And you feel guilty, as if your wishes made it so. I don't know how long I stood there before I realized Emmie was crying, in the little room off the kitchen. She was wet. I changed her diaper. That must have been when the blood got on her. She was scared and nervous—she clung to me, she was just a little girl, left alone in the dark, and no one had come as she cried and cried. I got her back to sleep and then I left. An hour later, after I had changed and was on my way to Gus's house for the party, I called the police from a pay phone and told them I could hear a baby crying at the restaurant."

Tess sat there, trying to absorb all this, *Marianna* had found the bodies, *Marianna* had left the blood on Emmie. The little girl had not seen anything, she had no hidden memories to recover. Everything Emmie thought she knew about blood and death had come straight from her own imagination.

"I could have used that information," Guzman said. "Twenty-one years ago, ten years ago, even last week—I could have done something with that."

"But I didn't really know anything. It never occurred to me Gus was behind the killings, I honestly thought it was a robbery. And if it had gotten out about Frank and Lollie . . . well."

"What?" Guzman asked.

"People would have talked."

Tess rubbed her eyes, wishing Marianna would be gone when she opened them again. She knew pride could make people do stupid things—it had kept her, for example, from doing anything when Crow's postcard had first arrived. A week had gone by from the day of that first veiled plea for help and her decision to pick up the phone and call his mother. If she had started looking for him sooner, would things have turned out any differently? Where would she be? Where would he be?

A doctor was walking toward them down the hall, still in surgical scrubs. Did Tess only imagine it, or was he shaking his head ever so slightly from side to side?

"Miss Monaghan?"

"Yeah," Guzman answered for her.

"He's conscious, but he's very weak. You can see him"—a warning look for Guzman—"but the officers aren't to speak to him, or try to get him to speak."

Tess jumped to her feet, then wished she hadn't. What with giving blood and boycotting Guzman's cookies, the sudden movement made her woozy. She was going to black out, and she was furious. Her next-to-last conscious thought was that Crow was conscious, and now she wasn't, and wasn't there some weird symmetry in that? She reeled backward, into Guzman's arms, just like that stupid touchy-feely trust exercise. She fell, insisting to herself that she wasn't so foolish as to trust anyone ever again. Except, perhaps, Crow. It was just gravity, she told herself. Just goddamn gravity, up to its usual tricks. She was falling, helpless, incapable of doing anything about it.

That was her last conscious thought.

EPILOGUE

I always loved him,

I was just waiting for him to figure that he loved
me. It finally happened the night of the Coronation,
when I was presented as a Princess of the Court of
Shattered Illusions. Well, maybe that wasn't the
name, I don't remember everything. But I remem-
ber the important things. I said to him, just before
my turn: "I'm not going to take your arm." He
didn't understand at first. "What?" "I'm not going
to take your arm. When I do the curtsey. I'm going
to get up by myself. They applaud louder if you do it
by yourself." You see, the curtsey we do is really more
of a bow, extending one leg all the way out behind,
while practically touching one's forehead to the floor.
And the dresses are so heavy it's hard to stand. Most
of the girls need their escort's arm to get back up.
But I didn't, did I? I got the loudest applause of all,
and when I stood up, I saw in Clay's eyes that I was a
princess to him at last.

There was a party after. It was at the Maguires'
house in Monte Vista, a place we knew, we had

grown up playing with their kids. The yard was huge, and it was full of secret places, places where women in high heels and men in pumps weren't likely to go. It had rained all week, and the ground was soft. I slipped off my shoes and took his hand and led him into one of those secret corners, a place where the Maguire kids liked to build forts, screened by the pecans and the poplars and the cottonwoods. I kissed him. He was scared at first, and then he didn't want to stop. The old folks band was playing some song. "I Concentrate on You." It would have been enough, just to kiss him. But I took off my dress—not my princess dress now, just an ordinary dress from Neiman Marcus—and hung it on the tree. "What are you doing?" he asked. "If we don't take our clothes off, they'll get dirty," I told him. He had been with only one girl—this stupid, bookish grind. She didn't count. I had been with other boys, but they didn't count. Now I had him, I knew he wouldn't want anyone but me. All I had to do was wait, and see if he would come to me, on his own. Two nights later, he did. He came to my room in the middle of the night, but he didn't dare make love to me there, in the house, where Gus might hear us. We went to the garage and climbed into the old Lincoln, like two teenagers who didn't have anywhere else to go. If you think about it, we were two teenagers who didn't have anywhere else to go.

The sun was coming up by the time we finished, my necklace had broken, and we were picking the beads out of the upholstery, laughing, wondering what Gus would think if he found one. That's when Clay asked me: "Have you ever had breakfast at the Alamo?"

And that was the happiest moment of my life.

People say that all the time, but they don't mean it. They can't know it. I do. I am twenty-three years old, and the world seems intent on keeping me alive, even though the happiest moment of my life came six years ago, when Clay took me to breakfast.

I'm sorry for the pain I caused, the damage I did—not to Darden and Weeks, who only got the punishment they deserved, and only after I had laid beneath them, letting them inside me, wearing them out so they would sleep and then Steve could take them away, and do what he had to do. But I am sorry I almost took from you the person you love. That was never my intent. I sent you the postcard, thinking you could save him. I didn't know it would take so long, that Steve would try so hard to get rid of him, that Crow would prove so determined to take care of me.

I hope the happiest moments of both your lives are still to come.

Tess folded up the letter and tucked it under her water glass, so it wouldn't fly off in the strong breeze. Eating outside in mid-November—now this was a Texas concept she could embrace. It was seventy-five degrees with a bright blue sky. Larry McMurtry, whose work had been filling her time over the past two weeks, had written it was the sky that made Texas distinctive. Among other things, she thought. But you could almost fall in love with Texas on a day like today, in a restaurant like this one, La Calesa. It occurred to her that it was only now, when she had completely given into San Antonio and its charms, that she would be able to leave it. She had fought the city so hard, and it had fought her back.

She wondered if it would fight her for Crow as well.

"So who gets Emmie?" she asked Rick. "The courts or the hospital?"

"Her competency hearing won't be held for another few weeks. She seems determined to prove she's sane, which may be the best evidence that she's insane."

"And Gus?"

"He's been charged, and I'm sure he'll be indicted. I'm not so sure he'll be convicted. I hear that the city's most influential residents are lining up to be character witnesses. But Clay will testify against him. In the end, it's Gus's confession to his own son that will be the most damning evidence. With Darden, Weeks, and Steve Villanueve dead, everything else is hearsay, or strictly circumstantial. It's not a slam dunk by any means. Still, I'm glad I'm not Gus Sterne's lawyer."

"There was a time," Kristina put in gently, "when you would have salivated for a case like this."

"That was before I had to devote all my energies to getting my fiancé acquitted on charges of theft and criminal mischief. Not to mention assault."

"Assault?" asked Crow, who had been uncharacteristically quiet, picking at his food with no real appetite.

"Ketchup counts," Rick said, and kissed Kristina's hand, the left one, the one with the diamond ring on it, the one he never seemed to let go of. Crow started to laugh, then winced. Tess's heart went out to him. There was nothing worse than having laughter remind you of how fragile you were, how thin the membrane was between life and death. It had happened to her last spring, and her injury had been nothing more than a bruised rib. For Crow, the memories would last much longer.

"Are you coming back for our wedding?" Kristina asked.

"Are we both invited, or just Crow?"

"Both." She paused. "Although you'll probably be seated on the groom's side."

"We'll see," Tess said. "It's still a year off. A lot can happen in a year."

"Yes. I'm sure Kris and I will break up at least six or seven times before then," Rick said. Then very casually, too casually, he asked: "So what are you guys going to do?"

"First I have to break it to Mrs. Nguyen that Esskay is relinquishing her role as La Casita's mascot. That's going to be hard on both of them. But we've got to drive Crow back to Charlottesville, where he can reunite with his parents."

"Then what?"

"Yes, Tess?" Crow looked up. His face was so thin, his color so pale. How Felicia would love putting twenty pounds back on him. "Then what?"

"My business is in Baltimore, I have to go back there. My place is in Baltimore. But I thought you might want to come back, too. Eventually. Charm City could use some avant-garde polka music, too, you know."

"Give up all this"—he waved a hand at the beautiful day, at their food, at the slyly seductive city that surrounded them—"for *Baltimore*?"

"You'd also get me in the deal. If that's what you want."

"Is it what you want?"

"Yes."

"And we'll live together?"

"No." She couldn't help smiling at the shocked look on his face. "Life at Bond and Shakespeare streets is much too complicated these days, what with Tyner having a toothbrush on the premises—although not for long, I hope. Besides, living together, even unofficially, was what tripped us up the last time. We were playing house, which allowed me to play at our relationship. If I ever decide to live with you, I'll go whole hog. I'll get down on one knee and ask you to marry me."

Crow's mouth was a tight line. "I would like to point out that, traditionally, it's the man who gets down on one knee and does the asking. Even these days."

"I'd like to point out that, traditionally, it's the man who rides to the *damsel's* rescue," Tess said. "Even these days."

Kristina and Rick laughed, but Tess had never been more serious. Neither had Crow, it seemed. He sipped his iced tea—the others were drinking Tecates, but his antibiotics couldn't be mixed with alcohol—and cut his quesedilla into careful fourths, then eighths, still not eating any of it.

"Okay, your terms," he said. "But I have a condition, too. One day, I get to save you."

"Oh Crow—" She reached out and took his hand. The world was almost unbearably vivid. She was aware not only of the blue sky above them, but the coolness of his hand in hers, the peppers in the thin brown salsa, the lime in her beer, the prisms of light refracted by Kristina's diamond. It was enough. It was too much. Plentitude. She finally got it.

"Oh Crow," she repeated. "I think you just did."

About the author

About the book

Read on

Insights,
Interviews
& More ...

Meet Laura Lippman

© Jan Cobb

SINCE LAURA LIPPMAN'S DEBUT in 1997, she has been heralded for thoughtful, timely crime novels set in her beloved hometown of Baltimore. Now a perennial *New York Times* bestselling author, she lives in Baltimore and New Orleans with her family. ⌒

Baja Baltimore

I REMEMBER SO LITTLE from college, but the Shakespeare course I took with Professor Elizabeth Dipple is vivid in my mind. In particular, I remember her explanation of *Measure for Measure* as William Shakespeare's "problem play." (I also remember how the women in my dorm wing seized upon the line "Hail virgin, if thou be so." Ah well, we were sophomores; you must permit us our sophomoric wit.)

I'm not Shakespeare—I'm sure that clears up a lot of confusion in the literary world—but *In Big Trouble* is my problem book, the only one to date set outside Maryland. In it, Tess Monaghan heads to Texas to find her on-again, off-again boyfriend, who left her after intuiting that she was, briefly, attracted to someone else. So Tess goes to Texas, somewhat reluctantly, driving down the Interstate 35 corridor, stopping in Waco and Austin before landing in San Antonio.

The thing is—I love Texas, especially San Antonio, where I spent a big chunk of my twenties working at the *San Antonio Light*. I always bristle when I hear people slam the Lone Star State, falling back on clichés that were outdated when *Dallas* was showing in prime time. Texas is simply too big and too diverse to be pigeonholed that way. I didn't want to stay there, but that had more to do with my affection for my hometown of Baltimore than any antipathy toward Texas. So when I sent Tess there in her ▶

Baja Baltimore *(continued)*

ancient Toyota, her greyhound in the
backseat, I was excited to show people
what I knew about San Antonio.

And then I realized—Tess knew
nothing about San Antonio. She would
be prone to all the clichés I despised.
What to do?

I settled on writing a very conscious
homage to *The Wizard of Oz*, the film,
not the book. In the film, the three
farmhands have alter egos in Oz. So
Tess discovers alter egos for her usual
support system back in Baltimore.
I won't reveal the pairings, however.
I think it's more fun if readers suss
them out on their own, even if they
disagree. Especially if they disagree.

Through Tess, I tried to remember
all my Texas first times. Many of the
memories centered on food—my favorite
lunch at the Liberty Bar, my standing
order at Taco Cabana. The phrase
"Breakfast at the Alamo" was stolen
from a former colleague and friend,
David Hawkings. The plot itself was
inspired by a triple murder in Waco,
Texas, where I started my reporting
career. In 2014, *Texas Monthly* published
a lengthy article about that triple slaying
that called into question almost
everything I thought I knew about
it. That, in turn, provided the idea for
yet another book.

Whenever people ask me where
to start with my novels, I have lots of
advice. If you're anal-retentive, start
at the beginning, but please know that
Tess and I got better at our jobs. If you're

willing to dip into the middle, I often recommend *The Sugar House* or *In a Strange City*, because Tess is an accomplished private investigator. I always say, "But don't start with *In Big Trouble*." And yet people do. The book, published in one of the toughest years of my life, was nominated for multiple prizes and won two. But it is hard for me to reread it, in part because it brings back that annus horribilis.

And, in part, because it makes me yearn for a bean-and-cheese taco at the original Taco Cabana. And a chocolate milk shake from the Olmos Pharmacy. And that cheese dip from La Fogata and the so-called Jewish coffee cake at Twin Sisters Bakery, which sat opposite the Bookstop, where I spent many a Saturday morning buying armfuls of books. It was there that I discovered the work of James Crumley, someone who couldn't get out of South Texas fast enough. If San Antonio had given me only that, the discovery of Jim Crumley, whom I would later be able to call my friend, it would have been enough. But it gave me so much more. ∽

Laura Lippman
Baltimore, Maryland, 2015

Have You Read?
More by Laura Lippman

For more Tess Monaghan novels by
Laura Lippman check out . . .

BALTIMORE BLUES

In a city where someone is murdered
almost every day, attorney Michael
Abramowitz's death should be just
another statistic. But the slain lawyer's
notoriety—and his taste for illicit
midday trysts—make the case front-
page news in every local paper except
the *Star*, which crashed and burned
before Abramowitz did.

A former *Star* reporter who knows
every inch of this town—from historic
Fort McHenry to the crumbling projects
of Cherry Hill—now-unemployed
journalist Tess Monaghan also knows
the guy the cops like for the killing:
cuckolded fiancé Darryl "Rock" Paxton.
The time is ripe for a career move, so
Tess agrees when rowing buddy Rock
wants to hire her to do some unorthodox
snooping to help clear his name. But
there are lethal secrets hiding in the
Charm City shadows. And Tess's own
name could end up on that ever-
expanding list of Baltimore dead.

Reporter-turned-PI Tess Monaghan loves every inch of her native Baltimore—a quirky city where baseball reigns and homicide seems to be the second most popular sport. Local boy made good "Wink" Wynkowski wants to change all that by bringing pro basketball back to town—a laudable mission that's greeted with widespread cheers . . . and a muckraking front-page exposé of Wink's past in the *Baltimore Beacon-Light*.

The surprised editors at the "*Blight*" are sure they killed the piece. Instead, the piece kills Wynkowski, who's discovered asphyxiated in his garage with his car's engine running. Now the paper wants former newshound Tess to track down the rogue employee whose prank may have taken a human life. But there's more than cybercrime involved here—and Tess is about to discover firsthand that trying to stay alive in Charm City can be murder.

Have You Read? *(continued)*

BUTCHERS HILL

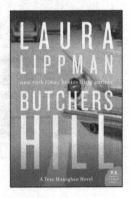

Tess Monaghan has finally set up shop as a PI-for-hire—but her first client is an odd one. Once notorious as the vigilante homeowner who shot a boy for vandalizing his car, Luther Beale has just gotten out of prison and says he wants to make amends to the kids who witnessed his crime. He needs to find them first, and that's where Tess comes in.

But as Tess starts to find the witnesses, they start dying. And now some ugly family business has reared its head, forcing her to confront the sins of her grandparents' past.

Baltimore local Tess Monaghan thought she knew the Sugar House—the long-standing factory that dominates the city's skyline—until a client named Ruthie asks the newspaperwoman-turned-PI to investigate a year-old "Jane Doe" murder and its grim aftermath. Ruthie's lowlife brother, Henry, confessed to killing a teenage runaway over a bottle of glue. A month into his prison term, he met the same fate as his victim, whose identity has never been established. If Ruthie knows whom her brother killed, maybe she'll also know why he died.

With only a few clues to guide her, Tess's hunt for the truth takes her from Baltimore's exclusive Inner Harbor to the city's seediest neighborhoods and into the halls of the Maryland State House. And when the supposedly solved murder case turns up newer, fresher corpses, Tess learns that there are all kinds of Sugar Houses.

IN A STRANGE CITY

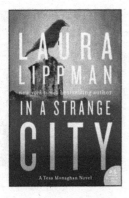

It is a Charm City tradition—on the birth date of Edgar Allan Poe, a cloaked figure visits the writer's grave and leaves behind three roses and a half bottle of cognac. This year, private investigator Tess Monaghan is among the witnesses of the cherished rite. And on this frigid January night, two caped visitors approach Poe's resting place. One leaves his tribute and escapes. The other dies, felled by an assassin's bullet. Why was the imitator there?

Common sense tells Tess to stay out of it. But someone wants Tess involved in the murder investigation in the worst way: an anonymous stranger who leaves roses and cognac and cryptic clues on her doorstep; someone who knows her habits, her haunts . . . and what she *knows*. And suddenly home is a safe haven no longer.

Five lives in Maryland have been
brutally destroyed over the past
six years—five unsolved homicides,
seemingly unconnected but for the
suspicion that each death was the result
of domestic violence. In hot water—and
court-ordered therapy—Tess Monaghan
accepts an assignment from a local
nonprofit organization, agreeing to
review police documents on each case
for inconsistencies and investigative
blunders.

But it turns out that a psychopath
can hide as easily in the fabric of a tiny
fishing community as in the alleys and
shadows of Charm City. Because another
common thread to five senseless murders
is beginning to emerge—and it's Tess
Monaghan herself.

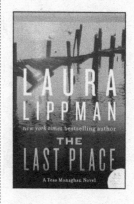

BY A SPIDER'S THREAD

Private investigator Tess Monaghan doesn't know quite what to make of her new client, Mark Rubin—a wealthy Orthodox Jew who refuses to shake her hand and doles out vitally important information in grudging dribs and drabs. The successful Baltimore furrier claims he and his beautiful wife had a flawless, happy marriage. Yet one day, without warning, Natalie gathered up their children and vanished—and the police can't do anything because all the evidence indicates she left willingly.

But the deeper Tess digs, the more she suspects that the motive behind Natalie's reckless flight lies somewhere in the gap between what Rubin will not say and what he refuses to believe. An intricate web of betrayal and vengeance is already beginning to unravel, as memory begets rage, and rage begets desperation . . . and murder. And suddenly the lives of three innocent children are dangling by the slenderest of threads.

No good deed goes unpunished . . .

Working as a consultant for the local newspaper, PI Tess Monaghan has no stake in the murder of a young federal prosecutor—until her well-meaning boyfriend, Crow, brings a street kid into their lives, a juvenile con artist who doesn't even realize he holds an important key to the sensational homicide. Tess's decision to protect the boy's identity no matter what could have dire consequences—especially when one of his friends is murdered in what appears to be a case of mistaken identity.

Crow and the kid go into hiding, but that doesn't ease Tess's woes. Federal agents threaten her with felony charges, even as a vicious killer draws closer. But to protect Crow and his ward, she'll have to find them first—and try not to bring the killer to them in the process.

ANOTHER THING TO FALL

When Tess Monaghan literally runs into the crew of the fledgling TV series *Mann of Steel* while sculling, she never expects to be hired on to serve as bodyguard/babysitter to the young female lead, Selene Waites. But the production has been plagued by a series of disturbing "mishaps." And the discovery of a corpse surrounded by photos of the beautiful, difficult superstar-in-the-making is causing *Mann*'s creator and Hollywood legend Flip Tumulty considerable distress.

Keeping a spoiled movie princess under wraps may be more than Tess can handle, since Selene is far more devious than she initially appears. But murder is an occurrence with which the fish-out-of-water PI is all too familiar—and a grisly on-set slaying suddenly threatens to destroy the careers and lives of everyone associated with this cursed show.

In the third trimester of her pregnancy, Baltimore private investigator Tess Monaghan is under doctor's orders to remain immobile. Bored and restless, reduced to watching the world go by outside her window, she takes small comfort in the mundane events she observes . . . like the young woman in a green raincoat who walks her dog at the same time every day. Then one day the dog is running free and its owner is nowhere to be seen.

Certain that something has happened to the woman, Tess is determined to get to the bottom of the dog walker's abrupt disappearance, even if she must do so from her own bedroom. But her inquisitiveness opens a Pandora's box of past crimes and troubling deaths . . . at a time when Tess has no place to run.

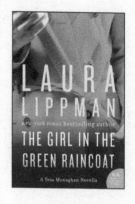